The Magdalene Creed

A Travers & Redmond Archaeological Action adventure

By

Desmond G. Palmer

This is a work of fiction. Similarities to real people, places, or events are entirely coincidental.

THE MAGDALENE CREED

First edition. July 3, 2024.

Copyright © 2024 D G Palmer and Desmond G. Palmer.

Written by D G Palmer and Desmond G. Palmer.

A TRAVERS AND REDMOND ARCHAEOLOGICAL THRILLER

THE MAGDALENE CREED

DESMOND G. PALMER

A Word From Desmond G. Palmer

Thank you for buying THE MAGDALENE CREED. The adventures continue in THE ACQUIRERS series, fast paced archaeological thrillers that take Natasha, Lucas and all of you around the world.

If you've enjoyed the book, I'd be very grateful if you could leave a REVIEW. It only needs to be a few lines. Not only does it keep me honest, so I don't stray from what makes these books a fun adventure romp for you, but it lets the algorithms know that people are reading them, and they'll push the books to likeminded readers.

To stay updated on my book releases, you should follow my AMAZON AUTHOR PAGE[1]. Alternatively, if you'd like to build a relationship with me, your next favourite author, and receive a FREE novella, PERIL in PERU, and experience Natasha and Lucas's honeymoon adventure, sign up to my NEWSLETTER.

• • • •

JOIN THE THRILL RIDE!
JUST VISIT THIS LINK[2]

---

1. https://geni.us/tAIp

2. https://www.subscribepage.com/q3q3d5

DESMOND G. PALMER
PERIL
IN PERU
SIGN UP TO MY NEWSLETTER AND GET A FREE,
DIGITAL COPY OF THE ARCHAEOLOGICAL,
ACTION/ADVENTURE NOVELLA, PERIL IN PERU!

Tony Braithwaite huffed as he violently thumbed his phone to end yet another unanswered call. 'Where the hell are you, Lucas?' he muttered and thrust the phone back into his pocket. Tony left King's Cross St Pancras station and groaned as he saw the grey clouds.

He hated Europe. Hated the hustle and bustle. Hated the smugness of the people, their arrogance. Hated the fact that they believed they had brought enlightenment to the world. He also hated the fact that most of his buyers were European. But most of all, he hated the goddamn weather. Especially the British weather.

Tony's every nerve was on edge, his senses heightened to a fever pitch. Each shadow was a threat, every stranger a potential assassin. He couldn't shake the feeling that his pursuer was always a step behind, ready to strike. Madrid, Vienna, Brugge, Amsterdam. He had seen the same face, on a street corner, in a crowd, at a cafe, in a mall. The same slim faced Frenchman who had broken into his hillside home in the Virgin Islands.

Tony made the short walk to the St. Pancras Renaissance hotel. As soon as he discovered the Frenchman had followed him from the Caribbean to Europe, Tony had been going to his safe houses and changing his aliases. He had used one name to come into the United Kingdom, and now he used another alias to check in to the hotel, informing the staff that he'd pay by cash.

In the time it took Tony to drop his light luggage and retrieve an item from it, he was on the move again, jumping into the back of the black cab he had the hotel staff call for him. '54 Bolsover Street,' Tony said to the driver.

• • • •

THE DOOR OF THE RED bricked building had barely closed behind Tony, as he rushed upstairs to the Acquirers office. He pushed the glass door wide open, a manic look in his eyes as he swept them left and right. 'Where's Lucas Redmond?'

Venice Jones stood up behind her front desk. The man's demeanour shook her, but she knew not to show her fear in situations like this, when she had to deal with a less than co-operative customer. 'Look, sir,' she said in a firm tone. 'I don't know how you got in here, but as I told you over the intercom, both Lucas and Natasha are unavailable.'

'Well, where are they?'

'They're on vacation. And they have given me strict instructions to only contact them in an emergency.'

'This is an emergency. Someone is following me. Probably wants to kill me. He's already killed my bodyguard.'

'Then perhaps you should report it to the police,' Venice suggested. 'We deal with recovering historical items here. Not security.'

'This is about a historical item. This Frenchman broke into my house in the Virgin Islands and tried to steal my map.'

'Virgin Islands? Map?' Venice repeated. 'What did you say your name was?'

'Tony Braithwaite. I'm an old mate of Lucas's,' Tony revealed. 'I showed him and his Mrs a map.'

'You mean Natasha?'

'Yeah.'

'They're divorced.'

'The fact of the matter is, shortly after I showed it to them, I made a new discovery on the map. And then some French bastard tried to steal it.'

Venice rubbed her chin as she listened. 'Tried to steal it? So you still have it?'

'He tore it from my grasp,' he said despondently.

Venice scrolled through her phone until she found Lucas's number and dialled it. She rotated her chair left, then right as she waited for the call to be answered. 'I don't know if this counts as an emergency, but I'll let them know what you've said. Where are you staying?'

Tony barely heard a thing the personal assistant said. He'd been walking around the reception area, finding it hard to believe that this was the place Lucas Redmond worked. The Lucas he knew in the past, the one that lived a double life, member of the SAS in one hand and a treasure hunter on the other, would never have settled for an office job. But there it was, a plaque with the name Lucas Redmond attached to an office door.

Suddenly, a shiver ran down Tony's spine. Glancing out the window below them and across the street, he saw the familiar figure of the Frenchman. 'How?' he mumbled as he stepped back.

'What do you mean how?' Venice asked with the phone to her ear.

'What?'

'Where are you staying?'

'At the renaissance hotel,' he replied. The moment Venice turned away, drawn by a report on TV about a planned papal visit to Notre Dame, Tony took an envelope from his inside pocket and slipped it in amongst the papers on her desk. Then he quietly left.

• • • •

SEVERAL MOMENTS PASSED before Venice turned around and realised that her unexpected guest was no longer there. Just as she thought that he might have gone to the toilet, a series of ominous sounds came from outside. An engine roared, tyres squealed. Then there was a crunch of metal and shattered glass. Finally, there was an ear-splitting scream.

Venice ran to the window overlooking Bolsover Street and saw Tony Braithwaite lying in the road behind a car. The driver, a well-dressed man, his mousy blonde hair tied in a bun and wearing round rimless glasses, climbed out, and bent down over the injured man. At first Venice thought he was checking on Tony, but she was wrong. 'What the hell?' she breathed, as she watched the man rifle through his pockets, roughly flipping him over, so she could see Tony's viciously twisted legs.

Her heart raced as she watched the man stand up and clench his fists. He threw his head back and after drawing in and letting out a few steady breaths, he disappeared into the growing crowd.

Chapter 1

Natasha Travers put her TaylorMade club across her shoulders and, whilst gripping either end of the driver, went through a series of warmup stretches. She took in the landscape of the Carden Park Spa Hotel. Set in a thousand acres of Cheshire forest, it is a beautiful part of the country, and from the golf course it's possible to see a huge amount of it, from the estates' vineyards to the Welsh mountains. It was all on view.

'Okay, Miss Travers,' Darren Watson, the golf services supervisor said, coming out of his office. 'I couldn't find another female golfer that could move up her tee, but I've found you a male golfer with a similar enough handicap. His sixteen is slightly below the male average compared to your twenty-five, which is slightly above the female average. Or we could always rearrange your booking, if you'd prefer.'

The plan had been to have Lucas play a round with her, but he predicted it would rain, and had decided to go swimming and hit the gym instead. However, the rain had held out, and the sun was peeping through the dispersing clouds. 'If he's okay with it, then so am I.'

'That's good, because that's him coming over now.'

Natasha turned around to see a dark-skinned black man with a bald head and a grey speckled goatee walking towards them. He wasn't much taller than her, but by the way he walked you'd think he was as big as the thick bearded olive-skinned man who walked behind him carrying his clubs.

'Henri Laval, this is Natasha Travers,' Darren said, introducing the two.

'A pleasure,' he said with a French accent, and held out his hand. 'Have we met before?'

Natasha shook it with a firm grip. 'No, I don't think so. What part of France are you from?'

'You're so sure I'm from France?'

'I'm not bad with languages,' she simpered, looking pleased with herself. 'It's definitely not Canadian. The former French colonies might have been a good shout, but I'm sticking with my first guess.'

'Trés bien,' he said with a broad smile. 'I am from Nice. My grandparents are originally from Chad. You have a very good ear. What is it you do?'

'I'm an archaeologist and anthropologist, and somewhat of a historian. And you?'

'I'm a collector of fine things. Seems we are in similar fields, with similar interests.'

Natasha nodded in agreement. 'I thought we were in the same boat regarding golfing partners too?'

'You mean Ali? He's my caddy. The person I was supposed to be playing with got held up in London.'

'Ah, I see. My partner decided that he'd rather play in the gym than do a round.'

'His loss is my gain,' Henri smiled.

Natasha picked up on the flirtatious tone, but completely ignored it. She was there to play golf. 'So, what are we playing? Match Play?'

Henri scrutinised her for a moment. 'You seem like the adventurous type. Why don't we make it more interesting?'

'What do you have in mind?' She queried.

'Skins,' he declared. 'Two-fifty for each of the first six holes. Five hundred for the next. Seven hundred for the six holes from thirteen to seventeen. Two-thousand for the 18th.'

'Pounds?'

'We can lower the price if it's too rich for your blood. I know that women—'

'Why don't we add a zero?' Natasha said firmly, cutting off the sexist remark that she knew was coming.

Henri whistled, then chuckled. 'Okay. If you're willing to risk the chance of paying out over one-hundred-thousand-pounds, then I'm game.'

Natasha swallowed. Her rising anger at Henri's manner had made her up the ante of the match without realising the full consequences. But she could hardly back out now. The challenge had been cast, and she had accepted. She nodded with tight lips, not about to give Henri the satisfaction of seeing the perceived fragile woman backtrack.

'You sure about this, Miss Travers?' Darren asked. 'If you are, I'll caddy for you.'

'Sure. I could do with a bit of extra cash.'

Henri let out a snort of derision. 'Shall we begin? I'll even let you tee-off first.'

Natasha placed her pink and yellow Titleist Pro V1 golf ball in the tee-box. She took a few practice swings, looking down the fairway, deciding on where she wanted to position the ball for the first hole. It was a par 4 hole with a fairly long 422 yard fairway. She stepped forward, eyed the ball, got herself in a comfortable stance. Natasha took a last look down the fairway. Then, in one smooth, swift motion, she struck the ball. Thwack!

The ball sailed out to around 200 yards, which brought an impressed whistle from Darren and a reluctant nod of approval from Henri. Natasha had just shown him she would not be a pushover, and eventually ended with a 1 under par.

Henri Laval's drive was equally good. His approach play, however, let him down, leaving him with a long putt which he sank, equalling Natasha's birdie.

'As there was no winner of the hole,' Darren stated, 'skins match play rules states that the pot rolls over to the next hole, meaning that the par 5 second hole is now worth five-thousand pounds.'

Natasha swallowed and hoped that the anxious feeling she was experiencing inside wasn't showing on her face. It didn't have to, because it showed in her play instead, as she lost the second hole. Natasha bounced back when Henri missed an easy putt, to end up with a one over par bogey, gifting her with the hole and her first money on the board. It wasn't the sign of a revival, however, as she narrowly lost the next hole. A few more wayward shots and she had lost holes five and six as well.

Henri bent down to retrieve his ball, throwing it high above as he stood up, snatching it out of the air. 'That's the first six down. These next six holes are worth five-thousand each. You already owe me £12,500. Are you sure you don't want to quit before things get out of hand?'

'For me or for you? And I think you'll find that it's ten thousand since I won the third hole.'

'So I assume you wish to continue, oui?'

'Bloody right, I do,' Natasha replied and stomped off to the next hole, with Darren trying to keep up, to a chorus of guffaws from Henri.

The seventh hole was a challenging par four with a narrow fairway and a well-protected green which caught Henri out. His approach shot landed plum centre of a sand trap, the lip of which was almost hanging from the bunker. He ended up being 3 over par compared to Natasha's 1 under. She had won the first five-thousand-pound hole.

The eighth hole could have been a nightmare with its water hazards and bunkers, but both competitors delivered accurate tee shots and the hole was drawn when they each got par, making hole nine, a ten-thousand-pound hole.

They amped the hazards up with the par 5 ninth hole. It had a fairway that sloped uphill with a sand bunker at the back. If you were too strong with your approach stroke, you could overshoot the hole and end up in the sand trap. Which is exactly what happened to Natasha.

'Bollocks!' she berated herself as she performed several practices of the stroke she should have played.

'Unlucky,' Henri grinned.

'Asshole,' Natasha said under her breath in response to his false pity. She picked up her wedge and waited for her opponent to take his shot. Henri avoided making the same mistake she had and ended up in an excellent position to make a birdie putt.

Despite her less than favourable position, being in the bunker provided Natasha with the perfect opportunity to attempt a shot she'd practicing, putting controlled backspin on the ball. It was a difficult shot which needed the golfer to combine swing speed, impact position on the ball, hand action and acceleration with a smooth swing. She was frustrated by how little she had actually progressed mastering the stroke. But Lucas had belief in her. Natasha smiled as she recalled the moment.

'You've almost got it,' he'd said. 'And I know you will get it, because you're the most competitive woman I know. So, don't beat yourself up about it, baby.'

Natasha's mind came back to the present as she swung and chopped the ball. It looped up and fell behind the pin. But didn't roll back toward the hole. Instead, it carried on forward off the green and back down the other side.

Henri won the hole, adding ten-thousand pounds to his winnings. 'Are you sure you don't want to quit?' Henri asked again after also winning the 10th and 11th holes.

'You should have learned by now that I don't quit.'

'Well, your bank manager might by the end of this match, going by the way you're racking up a debt. I must admit, I did not know that archaeology paid so well.'

'I own a business which specialises in finding lost treasure and returning it to the rightful owners,' she said with pride as she looked to avoid letting Henri rile her up again.

'And how do you know if the person who approaches you is the rightful owner?'

'They usually provide provenance, documentation, bill of sales things like that.'

'What about mythical and legendary items, then? Do you keep those? Sell them on the black market?'

'What? No, of course not,' she replied, shocked that he would even ask.

'That is very strange,' Henri said, confused. 'Because I'm sure I saw you at a black market bazaar in Teddington.'

'Teddington?' Natasha murmured, recalling the event.

'You bought an orrery, if I'm not mistaken.'

'Yes, I was there, but I was working undercover.'

'To obtain the Eye of Nineveh, I assume. That's the reason *I* was there.'

'What?'

'Of course! I told you I was a collector.'

'But the Eye is a country's heirloom.'

'And they did not know it was there until you found it.'

'For someone who I've only just met, and who claimed not to know what I did for a living, you certainly seem to know quite a bit about me.'

'You got me.' Henri cleared his throat as he tried to laugh it off. 'The truth of the matter is, I've been hoping to make your acquaintance once I knew you were here.'

Natasha was dubious. 'Really? What for?'

'Because I want to hire you to retrieve something for me.'

Chapter 2

The group were making their way to the 12th hole when Natasha heard the request, and she stopped dead in her tracks. 'This is a bit of a surprise, coming on the back of all your flirty and chauvinistic comments. All day I'd been getting the sense that you disliked me.'

'No, not at all. It's who I am.'

'Hardly an excuse,' she replied. 'Anyway, most people would make an appointment with the office if they wanted to hire us.'

'I would, but there are some people I don't wish to know my business dealings.'

'Anything we should be concerned about if we were to take the job?'

'Not at all.'

'You're sure? Are they're following you?'

'They could be.'

'This isn't the time to be vague, Mr Laval,' Natasha said as she turned to continue to the next hole. 'You came to me, remember?'

'I honestly don't know. For argument's sake, let's say yes.'

'Are they after the artefact for themself or do they just want to stop *you* getting it?'

'They are the same, are they not?'

'No, it could be a rival, or you could be under police investigation.'

'Ah, I see. Definitely a rival situation then.'

'And you're sure you have the provenance to prove that you're the rightful owner?'

'All the documents are at my chateau in Nice, passed down from my father, who got it from his father.'

'Of course, we'd have to see these documents before we could start anything.'

'I have no doubt that you will take the job, Miss Travers.'

'And how can you be so sure about that?'

'You have not asked what the artefact is yet.'

'Okay. So what is it?'

'I don't know for sure, but whatever it is, links between a group called the Cathars, another one called the Livonian brotherhood, and the Nazis.'

'What? That's quite a heady mix,' Natasha said, then fell silent as she gave more thought to the names he'd mentioned. The Nazis were well known to be treasure hunters. They even had a division of the Schutzstaffel, the SS, called Ahnenerbe, who were an elite team of archaeologists, scientists and historians tasked with searching sacred archaeological sites around the globe for evidence that the Aryans were from Atlantis. And thanks to Himmler's desire to replace Christianity with a modern pagan religion, they would also hunt for religious artefacts, the ark of the covenant, as well as...

Natasha's eyes opened wide, and her head spun to face Henri. 'You're not talking about the holy grail, are you?'

'Why do you say that?'

'The headquarters of the SS was Wewelsburg Castle. It had a room called the grail room, ready for them to display artefact when they found it.'

The Frenchman rubbed his chin. 'I have letters from various Nazi members, including one from Heinrich Himmler himself, which elude to a Cathar treasure. But they never mention what it is. There's a map too.'

'A map?'

'Yes,' Henri replied. 'It has no landmarks, so it is all but impossible to know where it is located. All it has is a "X" near the centre and in the corner is a white mantle with a black cross on the back of it.'

'Really?' It sounded remarkably like the map Natasha had seen at Tony Braithwaite's villa in the Virgin Islands.

'Have you seen something like that before?'

'No,' she lied.

'Do you think it could be a treasure map? Were these Cathars rich?'

'Nope. Quite the opposite. Catharism was a Christian dualist movement. They believed in two gods, the one in the Old Testament and the one in the New Testament. Earth was hell and that we would reincarnate until we've achieved enlightenment and go to the spirit world, heaven. They also lived a spartan, sexless life.'

'They didn't have sex?'

'Well, not all of them. There were two levels among the Cathars, the Perfecti who lived lives of extreme poverty as well as abstinence from sexual contact and were pescatarian. And there were the Credentes, who didn't have to adopt the austere lifestyle of the Perfecti, if they chose not to. So no, they weren't rich. However, they assigned significant importance to the role of Mary Magdalene in the spread of early Christianity. Far more than the church ever did. The Cathars saw her as perhaps even more important than Saint Peter, the founder of the catholic church. And coincidently, some scholars believe Mary fled to France after the murder of Jesus. The Cathar movement emerged in southern France. But there are many stories about her fate. Just as there are about her life.'

Henri smiled at Natasha. 'I can see that you're interested, so does that mean that you'll do it? You'll come to my chateau and see the documents?'

Natasha almost said yes straight away. She was desperate to see the map in particular. To see if it really is the same as Tony's. And if it was, what did it mean? 'I can't give you a decision right now. I need to think about it and also discuss it with my partner.'

'You are joking, surely. You should be jumping at this opportunity.'

'It isn't as simple as that, Mr Laval. If this artefact turned out to be the holy grail, then there would be more than one religious organisation claiming that it belonged to them. And depending where it was found, the country could stake a claim too. So yeah, I need to think about it.'

Henri sighed heavily. 'Fine. I'll give you until tonight, and the rest of this game, to decide.'

'Oh, yes. The game,' she exclaimed, suddenly remembering that they were playing a round of golf. 'Shall we continue?'

'I don't see why not. Unless, of course, you want to accept this job offer now and we can wipe out the thirty-two and half thousand pounds you owe me?'

'That's twenty-five-thousand, actually, and this round of golf is far from over.'

The 12th hole was a par-5 and was also the last of the five-thousand-pound holes. With the previous discussion of lost holy relics still in their minds, both golfers could only draw the hole.

'That's the end of the second six holes,' Darren announced. 'As you both hit par, the five-thousand prize fund rolls over to the next hole. Meaning the 13th, unlucky for some, is now worth twelve-thousand-five-hundred pounds.'

Natasha was the quicker of the two players to literally get back into the swing of things, winning the 13th and 14th holes, bagging twenty-thousand pounds in the process. That brought her up to twenty-seven-thousand-five-hundred pounds and a less painful five-thousand pounds down.

Henri Laval rallied, and the next three holes were tied, including the short 15th par-3 where Natasha managed a hole in one and Henri, incredibly, matched the feat.

'Okay, golfers,' Darren said as he adjusted his sun visor. 'This is the 18th hole. It would have been worth twenty thousand, but since neither of you could win any of the last three holes, it's now worth forty-seven-thousand-five-hundred. More than my yearly salary. If it's tied, we'll go to sudden death. Someone's going home happy.'

The 18th hole was a par-4 dog-leg left, which led to a green protected by two large bunkers. They flipped a coin to see who would tackle the hole first. Henri won, grinning like he had already taken the hole and its huge prize money. His drive was good, leaving him in the perfect position to go around the bend of the dog-leg.

Natasha stood back from her tee and looked down the fairway. She thought about taking the same route Henri had, but this wasn't the time to play it safe. If she was going to win, she'd have to be brave. Even if the line between bravery and stupidity was a thin one.

She glanced at the thick forest of trees that the fairway bent around to create the dog-leg.

'You're not seriously thinking of going over the trees, are you?' Darren asked Natasha in a whisper.

'Nope, I'm not thinking about it. That's exactly what I'm going to do.'

Natasha could hear Henri discussing her decision with Ali, but as she focused on the ball, and what she had to do, she shut it out and the surrounding noise. She stood over her ball, waiting for the right moment, waiting for the wind. The moment she felt it shift, blow her hair forward, she swung her club, striking the ball low and hard with all her strength, hoping that the wind would catch it and give it that little extra it would need to clear the trees.

Darren whistled as the ball rocketed away, flying high into the sky, almost disappearing from view, until it dipped towards the trees.

'Unlucky,' Henri said, with relief in his voice.

Natasha said nothing, just stared at the flight the ball had taken.

The four of them travelled down the fairway to Henri's ball, where he took his second shot to traverse the dog-leg. It was an excellent shot, which left him with an outside chance of a birdie. They then went in search of Natasha's wayward ball.

'We should look in among the trees,' Henri suggested.

As they approached the tree line, Darren held up a hand, then pointed further down the fairway on the right. 'I think I can see it,' he said with excitement, almost bouncing.

Not only was it Natasha's ball, it was also closer to the green than Henri's was, much to his chagrin. He took his third shot, which was looking like it might drop in the hole, but it circled the rim and came back out again, prompting Henri to curse in French.

Natasha approached her ball, knowing that a good shot here would leave her in the prime position to sink her third shot and win the hole with a birdie. But given the distance, Natasha only had one actual club of choice to play, which would give her the best chance.

She struck the ball with all the instructions on how to pull off the difficult shot ringing in her ears. The ball soared. Then, as it landed, Natasha groaned when she saw it bounce and carry on forward. It bounced again, shallower than the first. As it landed again, the ball intrinsically crept backwards, fast at first, gradually slowing as it turned away from the hole. That was until it kissed against Henri's golf ball, changing its direction. The ball trickled towards the hole, stopping at its edge. Gravity did the rest, and it plopped into the hole.

Chapter 3

Natasha squealed in delight, throwing her club into the air. Two under par, an eagle. She won the hole, along with the forty-seven-thousand-five-hundred.

'And that's the match,' Darren said with glee. 'That was one hell of a shot, Miss Travers. We don't get many eagles on that hole. You deserved to win it with that one. And after deductions, your total winnings come to forty-two-thousand-five-hundred pounds. Congratulations, Miss Travers.'

'Thank you, Darren,' Natasha replied, stifling an excited giggle.

'Well played,' Henri yielded.

'I trust I won't have to chase you for payment?'

'Of course not. I shall make the bank transfer as soon as we get back to the clubhouse.'

• • • •

TRUE TO HIS WORD, HENRI Laval paid what he owed, then bought Natasha a drink. 'Are you sure I can't convince you to decide to take the job offer immediately?' He sipped on his cognac and eyed her, waiting for an answer.

'As I said before,' Natasha replied, taking the wine offered, 'this could be a delicate undertaking, and one that I need to talk over with my partner. After this drink I will find him, and you will have our decision by the evening.'

Henri looked at his Rolex. It was just after 2 p.m. 'Fine. I am sure I can take advantage of a few spa treatments from now until six.'

'That should be enough time,' she said. He was giving her four hours to get back to him with an answer.

'Good,' Henri said, finishing the rest of his drink and standing up. 'I am in room 101. I look forward to hearing your response. But you should know that there are other treasure hunters out there that would be less moralistic than you, should the result go the wrong way.' With his words left hanging in the air, Henri turned and left, with Ali following behind.

'Do you think she will go through with it?' Ali asked in French.

'Without a doubt,' smiled Henri.

• • • •

AFTER A FEW LAPS IN one of the heated pools, followed by deep tissue massage and a round in the sauna, Henry Laval had all but forgotten about the money he had lost. There were ninety minutes left until Natasha Travers would confirm that she would go on his treasure quest. He thought he would enjoy some dinner before receiving the good news and sent Ali ahead to secure a table and make the order so that he wouldn't have to wait for it.

Henri entered his suite and immediately stopped. Something was wrong. The curtain was gently blowing in the evening breeze. But he had specifically told Ali to close the balcony door. The big Moroccan had been a loyal companion to Henri for several years and wouldn't make such a mistake. The Frenchman closed the door behind him and was about to flick on the lights when a spotlight from the desk shone on him.

'Take a seat,' a female voice said from the darkness.

'Who are you? What are you doing in here?'

'They have sent me here to find out why you're here.'

'Sent? By whom?'

'I'm sure you can guess who.'

Henri Laval visibly swallowed. 'It...it isn't what you think,' he stammered.

'What I think doesn't matter. It's what they think. And they think you are trying to mount a coup d'état.'

'What? No, that's not the case. I'm very happy with my role.'

'Then why are you going against protocol and starting an unsanctioned mission?'

'I am not. This has nothing to do with the group. But it is something that will benefit the entire organisation.'

'And what is it?'

'It could ultimately be the resting place of the holy grail. According to Natasha Travers, anyway.'

'Travers?'

'Yes. Instead of romancing her into doing my bidding, I found it much more beneficial to appeal to her sense of a mystery.'

'And what of Lucas Redmond? Have you killed him yet? If Travers is here, Redmond won't be far behind.'

'I have yet to see him.'

'Be as it may, all plans for religious relics are to be brought before the circle. As Madame De'ath failed to find the Mansa Musa gold and unite Africa in one religion, this has become even more paramount. But you have pursued an interest without the backing of the others.'

'And when the grail is brought to me, I will bring it to the circle.'

'It's too late for that. This isn't baseball. There's no three strike rule in the circle. You go against them, and they end you. You should know this.'

Henri could hear the woman moving in the darkness and could guess what was coming next. 'You should know that I wasn't working alone. They will kill anyone that shows the slightest bit of interest in my map unless I tell them to stop.'

'Then we had better make sure that Travers and Redmond find their way to your chateau then.'

'You don't have to do this.'

'Unfortunately, I do.'

Three pops from the woman's silenced pistol were the last things Henri Laval heard as three bullets thudded into his chest.

• • • •

'THIS COULD BE THE BIG one, Lucas,' Natasha said, after eventually finding him in a steam room.

'You might want to rethink your attire if you're planning on staying in here,' he smiled.

Natasha left and moments later returned in her underwear. 'Better?'

'Not exactly what I was thinking,' admitted Lucas, sitting up straight and eying Natasha. 'But it'll certainly do.'

She smacked his hand away as he reached out for her. 'This isn't the time for that. We've been offered a job.'

'Yeah, you said it could be the big one.'

'Is the holy grail big enough for you?'

'What?'

'I mean, it's pure speculation at the moment, but the signs are looking good. Nazis were looking for the same thing. Not only that, the person has a map that sounds suspiciously like the one Tony Braithwaite has.'

'Did you see it?'

'No, but he has invited us to his chateau to see it and the other documents.'

'Chateau? Who is this guy?'

'A rich collector. I told him I would run the job offer by you before accepting.'

'You know there's going to be some big decisions to make if it really is the holy grail.'

'I know. But I thought we'd cross that bridge when we find out once and for all if it really is the grail or not.'

'Okay. So, we're doing this then?'

'Yeah!' she squealed. 'We're going on a grail quest, baby.'

• • • •

AFTER DRESSING AS QUICKLY as humanly possible, Natasha and Lucas headed off to tell Henri Laval the good news. They were ready to get to work straight away, hoping that they wouldn't have to wait too long to see the map and letters Henri had.

'Ninety- nine, one-hundred,' Lucas read as he counted the doors they passed, 'and here we are at one-hundred and one.' Natasha was about to knock when Lucas stopped her. 'The door isn't closed properly,' he pointed out.

'Well, we can't just burst in, Lucas,' she replied, rolling her eyes, and knocked the door.

Both of them suddenly heard a chair crash to the floor.

'But on second thoughts...' Natasha knocked the door again, only this time she pushed it open. 'Henri? It's Natasha Travers. Are you okay?' She switched on the light as they stepped inside. The room looked like it had been ransacked. And Natasha made the startling discovery of the bloodied body of Henri Laval. 'He's still alive,' she exclaimed, as she dropped down beside him. His lips moved, and she held her head closer to hear the last words of his dying breath.

An agile figure suddenly darted out the balcony door, catching Lucas and Natasha by surprise. The curtains flapped behind the person as they made their escape, but Lucas wasn't about to let that happen and dashed after them. However, he pulled up short when Ali entered through the suite door.

The big Moroccan surveyed the scene, seeing Natasha beside his employer holding his hand, blood seeping from bullet holes, and yelled, 'What have you done?'

Natasha leapt back as the distraught bodyguard charged towards her. 'We haven't done anything, Ali. We found him like this.'

Lucas, unsure of the man's intent, met him head on, and the two men clashed like a pair of stags. 'Go after the other one, Nat,' he said through gritted teeth, 'while I try to make this one see sense.'

After a moment's hesitation, Natasha ran out into the immense grounds of the spa hotel, after the suspect.

• • • •

EVEN THOUGH EVENING was settling in, there were still people out enjoying a walk in the gardens, or a few laps on the outside pool. A huge contrast to the two people that came tearing by. Natasha slowly closed the gap on the would-be escapee, thanks to them occasionally being held up by innocent hotel guests enjoying an evening in the jacuzzi, or colliding with people stepping out of the spa hotel's outdoor pods.

With the assassin's chosen path blocked, they had to change direction. A hedge line divided the gardens from the pools. They passed it before suddenly coming to a stop and spinning around. Natasha's eyes opened wide as she spotted the pistol pointing at her.

Natasha dived to the side, hearing the soft sound of expelled gas, as four times the trigger of the suppressed gun was squeezed. She winced as she clattered over sun-loungers, but the little pain she endured was a far better choice than being hit by bullets. She'd been there, done that, and wasn't a big fan of it.

More bullets ripped through the hedge as the assassin shot blindly at her. But Natasha was already back on her feet, and using another of the rattan sun loungers as a ramp, she leapt over the hedge, diving straight at the shooter.

They fired wayward shots as the sudden appearance of the archaeologist caught them by surprise. Bullets whizzed past Natasha. She questioned her decision, having acted purely out of instinct, and thrown caution to the wind with her attempt to stop the assassin. But it paid off. Natasha was still alive. She hadn't been shot, and she crashed into the shooter.

The gun went flying as the two of them rolled across the neatly trimmed lawn, both finally settling into a crouched ready position, facing one another.

'Who are you?' Natasha demanded. 'Why did you kill Henri Laval?'

'He brought it on himself,' the assailant replied. 'And as for who I am, you can answer that yourself.' The woman pulled off her mask, and Natasha gasped, seeing the face of someone she had hoped she'd seen the last of. The woman Lucas had an affair with. The woman whose brother Natasha had killed.

'Chiara Harris?'

Chapter 4

The two women faced each other, locked in a tense stare, the hatred between them thick in the air.

'I would say it was good to see you again, Travers,' Chiara sneered, 'but I'd be lying.'

'Likewise. My life was going so well, knowing that I'd never see you again. But here you are, like a foul stink.'

'You didn't really think that I'd let you carry on with your nice, peaceful life? After what you did to Baron? He was my brother!'

'Baron was the leader of a terrorist group. He made his life choices. If you're a terrorist, expect to be on the wrong side of a bullet someday. In the end, it was him or Lucas. I made my choice, and I'd make the same one every time.'

'And now you'll have to pay the consequences for making it.'

'Is that why you're here? To kill me?'

'I had no idea you were here. You're a bonus. I was only here for Laval.'

'Laval? Why?'

'Do you think we're friends or something? I'm not telling you a bloody thing.'

'Fine. I'll just beat it out of you then.'

'I've waited a long time for this.'

'That's one thing we can both agree on.' Natasha's anger surged, fuelled by her vivid imagination of Chiara's involvement with Lucas. She remembered the day she found the other woman's hair in their bed. It made her seethe.

Chiara took this opportunity and lunged forward, launching a fierce attack. Her punches were driven by a mix of rage for the death of her brother and contempt she had toward the woman whose marriage she had ended. Natasha skilfully dodged the blows, her movements calculated and precise. The turf was being ripped up by their struggle as they grappled, each attempting to gain the upper hand.

It was a bitter clash of wills, a culmination of the resentment and animosity between them. Neither woman was willing to back down, their shared history feeling their relentless determination. The fight raged on, their movements becoming faster and more aggressive.

Natasha's mind raced, searching for weakness to exploit. She noticed a momentary lapse in Chiara's defence and seized the opportunity. With a swift manoeuvre, she landed a powerful blow to Chiara's abdomen, causing her to stagger backwards.

Breathing heavily, Natasha took the chance to press her advantage. She unleashed a flurry of strikes, delivering blow another blow. However, Chiara's resilience proved formidable. She retaliated with a ferocious counterattack, catching Natasha off guard.

The women fought with an intensity that bordered on savagery. Bruised and battered, they refused to back down. They met each blow with an equal measure of defiance. Fatigue weighed on both of them, their movements becoming slower and their attacks less precise. Their laboured breathing broke the evening air. But neither woman would concede defeat.

A blade suddenly flashed through the air, leaving a gash on Natasha's forearm.

'So you can't beat me with your own two hands? You have to resort to weapons?' Natasha goaded.

'All the better to kill you with,' spat Chiara.

Suddenly, sirens pierced the air, stopping them in their tracks.

Natasha smirked. 'It sounds like your transport has arrived.'

A loud engine roared above the screech of the police sirens. 'I think you could be right.' Chiara grinned.

Suddenly, a motorbike came screeching around the hedgerow. Natasha having to dive out of the way to avoid being run over. As she sat up, she saw Chiara climb onto the back of the bike.

'The next time we meet, Travers,' snarled Chiara, 'you won't get off so lightly.' Smoke shot out the rear of the motorbike as it tore off and disappeared into the evening, leaving Natasha tending to her bleeding arm. She headed back to the spa hotel and was immediately descended upon by armed police.

· · · ·

NATASHA SAT IN THE second interrogation room of the Wrexham Town police station. They had bandaged her arm, and she nonchalantly played with the dressing while she waited to be released. Although Natasha knew that she and Lucas had nothing to worry about – any evidence the police had against them was purely circumstantial – the waiting was still an annoyance. Especially when she and Lucas had things to do. Like find Henri Laval's flower. Whatever that meant.

'Find my flower,' Natasha murmured. 'That is the key.' Those had been Henri's last words before he died. And because of everything that had happened afterwards, the appearance of Ali in Laval's suite, followed by Chiara's escape, she hadn't had the chance to tell Lucas about it. Nor that it was his ex that had killed the collector. Although she was certain that the police would have told Lucas what she had said in her interview.

The door suddenly opened, and a blonde-haired man walked into the small grey room. He set his folders down on the table before taking off his jacket and hanging it over the back of his chair. Finally, he sat down and eyed Natasha sternly.

'I am Detective Inspector Collins,' he said eventually, lowering his chin so he was almost looking down at her.

'Where's Constable Devon? He was supposed to make a phone call and have this all cleared up.'

'The lead on a murder at a five-star spa hotel is above his pay grade, so I will be taking over this investigation.'

'Your investigation is out there, making good her escape,' Natasha sniped.

He opened his file and rifled through it until he came to Natasha's statement. 'Yes, you said a Chiara Harris was the shooter. Mr Redmond was more than a little surprised when he heard that. In fact, he had no idea.'

'Of course not. He wasn't there.'

'So you chased after this gun toting woman by yourself, did you?'

'Well, I didn't know she had a gun until she shot at me.'

'And what is your relationship with this Chiara Harris?'

'Relationship?'

'Yes, how do you know her?'

'She slept with my husband, not that it applies to this case.'

'I think it's not only relevant, but also a vital piece of evidence. It gives you motive.'

'Motive for what, exactly?'

'For setting up someone else to take the fall for your crime.'

'You have got to be kidding? Why would I kill the man that has just given me a job?'

'Why is there not a shred of evidence to suggest that there was anyone else in that room, just as Mr Ali says in his statement?'

'Because he came in after she'd gone out the back.'

'Convenient, wouldn't you say?'

'No, not really. What about all the people around the pool? They would have seen me chasing Chiara.'

'We spoke to them, showed them a picture of this Chiara, and not one of them could say for certain who you were chasing.'

'She was wearing a hood. What about the gun?'

'No prints of any kind.'

Natasha shook her head and let out a sigh. 'What about the motorbike she escaped on?'

'Kids are always riding dirt bikes where they shouldn't be around these parts.'

'Kids?'

'Yes, kids.'

Natasha rolled her eyes. 'You're joking, right?' She'd met people like Collins before. People that thought they were a big fish in a little pond and took every opportunity to prove it, even if they ended up being wrong. But she knew how to deal with people like that. You bring a bigger fish to the pond. 'Look, if you just get in touch with DCI Russell at—'

'This isn't a metropolitan police matter.'

'All I wanted to say is if you can't get hold of anyone on the other number, give the DCI a call, and he'll be able to clear things up.'

DI Collins gestured to the police documents on the table. 'All this can disappear, you know. All you have to do is answer my next question truthfully.'

'I've been truthful from the start.'

'Where is Henri Laval's ring?'

'His ring?' The question caught Natasha by surprise. Henri had pushed it off his finger into her hand before he'd died. But she'd thought of it and had slipped it into her pocket before chasing Chiara. Now she couldn't help wondering how Collins not only knew there was a missing ring, but why he was so interested in it. 'They processed all my possessions when they brought me here.'

'I know. I've checked them. And the ring's not there.' DI Collins gathered all the papers together in a neat pile before walking around to Natasha's side of the table and perched on the edge with his arms crossed. 'Which means you either still have it on you or you've hidden it.'

'You're joking? They searched me when I came in.' Natasha's chair screeched across the floor as she forcefully stood up. 'I've had enough of this.'

Quick as a flash, DI Collins' hand clamped around Natasha's throat and he slammed her back against the wall. 'Perhaps it's not on you at all,' he hissed into her ear. 'Perhaps it's in — '

Suddenly, the door opened and Constable Devon strolled in. 'Okay, so I've been trying the number you gave me and they finally transferred me to...what's going on here?'

'A difference of opinion,' Collins said as he released Natasha and quickly left, brushing past the constable.

She slid down the wall, gasping for breath. 'Is this how the Wrexham police treat innocent people?'

'Police? He said he was your appointed lawyer,' Constable Devon replied, before rushing out to find where the intruder went.

Natasha retook her seat, rubbing at her sore neck as she did so. Soon the Constable returned, the overweight policeman puffing slightly.

'Whoever that slippery bastard was, he's legged it. But I have put an APB out for him and circulated his description. He won't get far.'

'Whoever he is, he's got some balls to waltz into a police station like that.'

'What did he want?'

'I don't know,' she lied, unsure of whom to trust anymore, and changed the subject to avoid further interrogation. 'You said something about your call being transferred?'

'Oh, yes. So, I phoned the number you gave for...' He checked his notes. 'For a David Evans. I couldn't get through at first. Eventually, his personal assistant answered, apparently he is in meetings all day, but they transferred me to Mi5.'

'Mi5? Why?'

'I don't know. But you are to call a Julie Evans as soon as I release you and Redmond.'

Chapter 5

After a quick reunion and a tender hug, which left Natasha beaming, the intrepid couple were taken back to the Carden Park Spa Hotel to collect their things. For the entire car ride, Lucas could see that she was preoccupied, and gently squeezed her hand to bring her back to the present.

'Huh?'

'What's wrong?' Lucas asked, seeing the confusion on her face.

'The ring Henri Laval gave me,' she replied in a whisper, so Devon couldn't overhear them.

'The one the phoney policeman was asking about?'

She nodded. 'Why would someone risk walking into a police station just for a ring?'

Lucas shrugged. 'You tell me. He said nothing about it?'

'Nothing. All he said was, "Find my flower. That is the key," then he died.'

'Let me have a look at it.'

'It wasn't with the possessions the police confiscated. It must have dropped out when I was fighting your crazy ex.'

'Emphasis on crazy.'

'Still took her to bed though, didn't you?'

'And I'll be apologising for it for the rest of my life.'

'At least,' Natasha added.

'So, tell me, how did it feel punching her in the face?'

She smirked. 'I won't lie. Pretty damn good.'

As the luxury hotel was now the site of a murder investigation, police were everywhere and they cordoned parts of it off to the public. Thanks to Constable Devon, however, bypassing the cordon wasn't an issue for them, and Natasha was soon back in the hedgerows, reenacting her fight scene whilst Lucas searched the ground with a borrowed torch.

Eventually, he saw something glint under the beam of light. He crouched down and picked up the silver ring. 'H? For Henri?' Lucas questioned and held out the ring for Natasha to take.

'That's what I assumed too,' she said as she examined the ring under the light. 'But a capital H is also the Greek alphabet symbol for Eta,' Natasha explained as she checked the circumference of the ring, coming to a stop shortly after. 'I'm such a bloody idiot. I should have seen this from the beginning.'

Lucas took another look at the ring and saw the small engraving of three letters overlaid each other. BIC. 'Don't beat yourself up about it, baby,' he said, stroking Natasha's arm. 'The more pressing question now is why did they have him killed?'

'And why do they want the ring back so badly?'

They both fell silent as ideas were planned and subsequently dismissed from their minds. Lucas eventually suggested they head back to London, stating that whatever decision they would finally come to, flying out of the capital, was the most likely beginning.

· · · ·

AS THE COUPLE SET OFF south for London in Lucas's car, Natasha sat glaring at the screen of her phone, her mouth agape, looking like a Venus flytrap, according to Lucas.

'What do you expect? 102 missed calls from Venice!'

'I only got 74,' Lucas replied in an exaggerated whimper.

'Perhaps she knows that I'm the responsible one.'

'Were, darling. You *were* the responsible one. After this little fiasco, welcome to the slums of irresponsibility!'

'I'm not a fan of that postcode, thanks. Besides, it was your brilliant idea to switch off our phones to get the full spa effect, in a bubble away from everything, you said.'

'And I didn't hear you complain about it once. Not until you picked up your phone.'

'Well,' Natasha said, clearing her throat, 'I have to admit it was nice just to switch the world off and enjoy being in each other's presence.' She gazed wistfully out of the window as she recalled some of those moments before she shook herself back to reality. 'I'm going to call her back and see what the problem is.' As Natasha was about to press the recall button, the phone rang and she answered it.

'Hello?' The call had come from an unknown number.

'I'm sure I told that constable to have you call me as soon as you were out.'

'Julie Evans? Pleased to finally meet you. I've seen your photos on David's desk.'

'You mean Deputy Director General and Chief Evans,' Julie corrected.

'I...I guess I do,' replied Natasha slowly.

'Hi Julie,' greeted Lucas.

'What trouble are you causing now, Lucas?'

Natasha shot him a look and mouthed the words, what the f...

'It wasn't me this time.'

'You two are quite the duo, aren't you? One minute getting into firefights in the streets of London, the next stopping global conspiracies. Even saving a monarchy.'

'You could throw in saving religion as you know it, too,' Lucas added smugly.

'That's all well and good in international waters. But domestic issues are Mi5's jurisdiction. That's why David is in a bit of hot water. He overstepped his powers when he pulled you out of police investigations twice. And you being involved in this Cheshire murder wouldn't have helped matters much.'

'Like I said, it wasn't us.'

'But we know who committed it,' Natasha offered. 'Chiara Harris, at the bequest of the Bilderberg Inner Circle. They're a group of —.'

'I know who they are, Miss Travers.' There was a long silent pause from Julie, which she eventually broke. 'It's because of them, and in particular Peter Armitage, that there has been a departmental shakeup. Having someone with so much economic influence, worldwide and here in the UK, is a tremendous concern for the government. And because they seem hellbent on finding ancient artefacts to further their cause, and also the fact that the two of you have had the most dealings with this group, Section 7 is no longer the sole division of SIS. It now comes under both security services.'

'Which means?' Natasha asked.

'Your list of bosses just got longer,' Julie replied. 'David will still be in charge of overseas operations, but when it comes to domestic situations, you'll be answerable to Mi5 and me.'

'And ultimately the foreign office and home office,' Lucas grumbled.

'Exactly. You two are accumulating powerful friends, but with that comes powerful enemies. So be on your best behaviour and kiss the political ring, like David is doing now.'

Natasha's brow creased. 'What are you talking about?'

'You have to come into Thames House, have a debrief and be introduced to the Home Secretary with the other Section 7 agents.'

'We can't. We're on a case.'

They both heard rustling over the phone line. 'I see nothing about that here. Who is it for?'

'Henri Laval.'

'The man that was murdered?'

'Yes. Before he was shot, Laval claimed to have Nazi documents saying they were searching for an item. There was even a map.'

'A map? What were they searching for?'

'The holy grail.'

'*The* holy grail?'

'It *could* be the holy grail,' Lucas corrected. 'We won't know until we see everything for ourselves.'

'And BIC are on to it as well. We have the lead right now. We have Laval's Bilderberg ring, something which they want back. If we waste time playing nice with politicians we'll give the advantage to them.'

'Wait, Laval was Bilderberg? But you said they were the ones that killed him.'

'He wasn't just the inner circle, he was at the table.'

'A decision maker? One of the vowels?'

'Yes. He was code named Eta.'

'This is very interesting,' Julie mused.

'What is?' Lucas asked.

'The BIC killing one of their own. One of their higher ups, no less. This could be something.'

'Like?'

'I don't know. It could be nothing, or it could be everything. It could be a power struggle within the group. I mean, I doubt the two of you are very high on the Bilderberg list of friends after the amount of times you've stopped them, and yet Henri approached you. It could be what got him killed.'

'Well, Deputy Director General?' Natasha questioned, putting emphasis on each word of her title. 'Do we come in and play nice with the politicians, or do you let us do what we're best at and find this lost artefact?'

It didn't take Julie Evans long to decide. 'Alright, David and I will take care of Westminster. We'll get Ellen to represent you.'

'She'll love that,' sniggered Lucas.

'You just make sure you get this bloody thing, whatever it is, before they do.'

'Yes, ma'am,' Natasha replied, brightening up. There was a new adventure brewing, and she wasn't about to be locked up in a stuffy office listening to small talk with politicians when she could be on the greatest hunt of all, a grail quest.

'Keep me informed,' Julie insisted. 'And the next time you two go on vacation, make sure you're reachable.'

As soon as the call was ended, Natasha rounded on Lucas. 'You two were a bit familiar. How do you know the deputy director of Mi5?'

'It was a while back when I was in the SAS still. She was an agent working on exposing a terror cell in London who was buying arms from a certain dealer you might recall.'

'Who?' Natasha asked.

'La Peregrine.'

'Wait, the one that almost ruined our honeymoon?' Then she remembered another fact. 'The one you saw naked.'

'Briefly,' Lucas pointed out. 'We stopped the shipment being made, but because, at the time, we didn't know that La Peregrine was a woman, she slipped through our fingers. I know the Home Secretary too. He's a bit of a dick, though.'

'Why? What did he do?' Before Lucas had the chance to answer, Natasha's phone rang. She immediately answered it when she saw who it was. 'Venice, I was about to call you.'

'You two have to start realising that you can't just drop off the grid anymore. You have responsibilities.'

'Alright, Venice. Consider us duly chastised. So, why were you so desperate to get hold of us?'

'The other day a friend of Lucas's came in.'

'Friend?' Lucas repeated. 'That's a short list. Does this friend have a name?'

'Tony Braithwaite.'

'Tony? In London?'

Natasha could feel the car speeding up. 'What's wrong?' she asked Lucas.

'Tony hates Europe. He wouldn't be here unless it was serious.'

'He did say he was being followed,' Venice revealed. 'By a Frenchman who tried to steal the map he apparently showed you.'

'Frenchman? You don't think he's connected to Henri Laval, do you?'

'Who knows?' Lucas shrugged. 'But if the map he described to you is the same as Tony's, there's a possibility. Venice, did he leave an address of where he's staying?'

'The thing is, he left while my back was turned. He was in an accident outside the building, struck by a car.'

Lucas applied more pressure to the accelerator pedal.

Chapter 6

Lucas and Natasha returned to the hospital Tony was in the following morning. When they had arrived the previous night, visiting hours were already over. But today Lucas was able to learn the full extent of Braithwaite's substantial injuries: two broken legs, one with three breaks, the other with two. A broken wrist, forearm, and multiple cuts and bruises. He had also suffered a concussion and was unconscious when they brought him in. It had taken a full twenty-four hours to regain consciousness, and once he had, there didn't seem to be any adverse effect.

'You're a lucky guy, Tony,' Lucas said. He sat beside his friend, looking down at his hands, trying to avoid looking at Tony connected to all the medical equipment. 'The doctor says if you didn't have a thick head, you might not have made it.'

'If it makes them feel any better,' Tony replied weakly, 'I don't feel like I made it.'

'Now I understand your phobia of Europe,' said Natasha.

'Nothing good happens to me here. As soon as I'm cleared, I'm off back to the Caribbean.'

'Our PA said someone was trying to kill you?'

'Do you need any more proof?' Tony said, raising his cast. 'This was no accident.'

'She mentioned something about a Frenchman. Do you think it was him?'

'I really wish I knew. The car literally came out of nowhere. I couldn't see the driver. But I'm almost positive it was him. He came and sat down unannounced, whilst I was eating lunch on the beach,' Tony snapped. 'Then he came out with his nonsense offer for the map, thinking because he has a French accent, I'd give it to him for a pittance. And when I refused, the bastard threatened me. Bloody pisstaker said he was doing me a courtesy by offering me anything. The wanker.'

'Calm down, Tony. Remember where you are,' said a concerned Lucas.

'Alright, alright,' the patient replied and took a breath before continuing his tale. 'When me and Dean returned home from the rum distillery, we noticed the door was ajar. You've seen the security system I have on my treasure study? Well, what you didn't know is that there're motion detection cameras in there.'

'And who did you put it in there to catch?' Lucas wondered.

'That masseuse. She's good with her hands in more ways than one.'

'Three ways probably,' chuckled Lucas, a comment which got him a slap on the arm from Natasha.

'So, the cams picked up movement in that room. And when we played the downloaded file and saw when me and Dean entered, I went back further to the previous activation of the motion detectors and played that.'

'And?'

'It was that mousy-blonde-haired Frenchman, the son of a bitch, with his round rimless glasses, strutting around my study. Then we noticed something. The Frenchman entered the secure study, and then moments later we could hear the distinctive engine of my Stingray in the recording's background, and the intruder slipped into a cupboard behind my desk.'

'Cupboard?' Lucas asked. 'So it didn't record him leaving?'

Tony shook his head. 'Dean aimed his gun at the door and fired three times. The bullets penetrated the wood at three different areas in the centre of the door. Then he opened it, expecting to see the dead body, but the son of a bitch was lying on the floor. The bullets were nowhere near him. That's when I grabbed my go-bag, and he grabbed me. The map tore in half as he tried to rip it from my grasp. Dean recovered and jumped on him. Then I came looking for you guys.'

'So, what is it you needed to show us?' Natasha asked.

'I found something else on the back of the map I showed you. Another cross of some sort.'

'Go on,' she said, leaning forward in her seat.

'I was sitting there, studying the map, trying to figure out that passage while eating some fish and chips. I may not like London these days, but I still enjoy my fish and chips. So, I was there eating, and as you know Lucas, I like it with lots of salt and lots of vinegar. Anyway, a drop of vinegar landed on the map.'

'What?' Natasha squealed.

'I know! I grabbed some tissue and started dabbing at it. That's when I saw something coming through.'

'Well?' Natasha urged. 'What did it look like? Can you describe it?'

Tony thought for a bit. 'It looked like four pairs of parallel lines going across the map.'

'Grid lines?' Lucas asked. 'Or longitude and latitude?'

'Some were angled, so I wouldn't have thought so.'

Lucas saw Natasha's eyes narrow as her mind processed the information. 'You know what it is?'

'Maybe,' Natasha stated, her eyes locked on the wall ahead. 'I need to see it, to be sure.'

'Well, I stashed the piece I had in your office,' Tony replied. 'I thought it was the best place for it. Seems I was right. The nurses said my stuff was scattered all over the street, probably because of the impact, they said. Bollocks! That French bastard rifled through my pockets.'

'Looking for what?' Natasha asked. 'The rest of the map?'

'Or more likely, the pocket watch. I was about to check the newly revealed cross through the lens when I was called to the distillery. I haven't had a chance to check since, obviously.'

'Do you still have it?'

'I stashed that away, too. Back in the day, before I left for paradise, I had a little hiding spot in central London.'

'I remember it,' Lucas said. 'It's still there?'

'I know! I was shocked too when I saw it myself. Some things change and others stay the same.'

The pair reminisced about some of the times they'd used the drop off in the past. All the while Natasha sat silently thinking about the moral dilemma that she knew would come at some point. That was the moment she heard the tail end of Tony's question. 'Sorry, what was that?'

'Lucas said you cracked the passage. What is it?'

'Oh,' Natasha said, getting up to speed. 'Well, if you take all of those capitalised letters from the text, rearrange them, you end up with VALENCIA.'

'The city?' Tony tried to sit up, but soon found out it was impossible and sunk back into his pillow. 'The first marker is in Spain?'

'It could be, but there's—'

'No other place it could be,' interrupted Natasha. 'You know, I think we should actually make tracks now,' she said, standing up. 'Make a start trying to find this artefact and pick up the map and the watch.'

• • • •

THE COUPLE LEFT THE hospital in silence, with Lucas giving Natasha a look of curiosity. It continued several minutes into the drive to the Acquirers' office until Lucas decided he'd waited enough.

'Are you going to tell me what that was all about or not?'

'You were going to tell him about Henri Laval's map,' Natasha replied.

'Yes, and?'

'You probably would have mentioned the Nazi letters and the possibility that it was the holy grail that the map led to.'

'Yeah, probably. So what?'

'I can't give it to Tony. If it truly is the holy grail, then it shouldn't belong to one man. So I thought it best that he didn't know everything.'

'So you're planning on giving it to the church?'

'Maybe.'

'Which one exactly? If I'm not mistaken, Jesus is revered in all three major religions; Christianity, Judaism and Islam. So whose claim for it is stronger? The ones that killed him, the ones that betrayed him or the ones that ultimately follow a different prophet?'

'I don't know,' she admitted. 'I hadn't thought that far ahead. To be honest, I was only concentrating on who shouldn't have it rather than who should.'

'Well, maybe it's time to do that. You know where I stand on religion, but even I know what kind of affect a religious relic like this would have on those institutions and their followers.'

Natasha knew he was right. 'At the Church of the Holy Sepulchre in Jerusalem, where Jesus is said to have been buried, the Edicule over the burial site is controlled by three different Christian branches. They are so passionate about their own beliefs that minor disagreements often escalate into monks brawling with the others.'

'So much for loving thy neighbour. So, we give it to Section 7 then?'

'Many legends attribute miraculous properties to the grail, such as the ability to heal, grant eternal youth, or provide unlimited sustenance. True or not, it *is* a sacred relic of immense spiritual power and importance to religion. Right now, the only thing I'm sure of is that we can't let BIC find it before we do.'

'That I can definitely agree on. They say religion was created to control the masses, and it's obvious to see Armitage and his cronies are looking to use that fact to their advantage.'

'Praying on the poor, the destitute. Testing people's faith, those with hope. Trying to control and manipulate people through their beliefs, for his New Enlightened Order. It's despicable. I don't know what I saw in him.' Natasha saw Lucas was about to comment. 'And don't you say anything. You're in no position to throw stones.'

'True, but I wasn't going to say anything about Armitage. I just remembered that it's post day. The courier will come...'

'And Venice will hand over the packages without question, including the one Tony slipped in there. I'd better call her.'

. . . .

VENICE JONES TROTTED down the steps of the office building. She looked up and down Bolsover Street until she spotted the courier's van slowly driving away. 'Damn it,' she breathed, looking down at her Louboutin shoes, before slipping them off and running after the vehicle, shouting for the driver to stop.

However, he was oblivious to the fashionable blonde chasing after him because his music was so loud. He did see the man jump out in front of his van, waving his hands over his head, and slammed his foot on the brakes. 'Hey, man!' the courier shouted out his window. 'Are you crazy? I could have run you over.'

'Oh my god,' Venice huffed. 'I thought you couldn't hear me, Tim.'

'What? Oh, Venice. I didn't hear you. This madman jumped out in front of me.'

She looked towards the front of the van and saw a well-dressed man, his mousy blonde hair tied in a bun. He pushed his round rimless glasses up the bridge of his nose. 'Thank you very much.'

'Don't mention it,' he said in an Italian accent. 'A pleasure to help a beautiful lady in need.'

Although obviously not her type, Venice still enjoyed receiving compliments from all quarters. 'Grazie,' she replied with a blush and a smile as she slipped her shoes back on.

The man beamed. 'Ah, you speak Italian?' he asked in his native tongue.

'A little,' she replied, continuing the conversation in the foreign language.

'Nonsense. Your accent is no different from someone born in Italy.'

Venice giggled bashfully. 'That's kind of you to say.'

'Look,' Tim said, interrupting. 'I've got other pickups to make, so if you'd care to step aside, I'd like to be on my way.'

'Just a moment, Tim. It seems I've given you something by mistake.'

'You have got to be kidding me, Venice?'

'I'm really sorry, Tim. I'll be as quick as I can.'

'Fine. Let me park over there out of the way.'

Tim pulled the van over and got out. He quietly grumbled to himself as he walked down the length of the vehicle, cursing his lot. He opened the back doors of the van and was about to jump in. Venice, feeling bad for holding him up and delaying his next collection, stopped him.

'You've done more than enough, Tim. Just show me where the Acquirers' stuff is, and I'll quickly search it for this envelope and be out of your hair in no time.'

'Fine by me. It's in that first grey sack on the left.'

Venice dithered for a moment as she looked at the height of the van's clearance to enter the back and wondered how she'd be able to do whilst keeping her dignity and poise.

'Allow me,' the Italian stranger said, and before Venice could utter a word, his hands were around her slender waist, and he effortlessly lifted her into the vehicle.

'Thank you, again,' she smiled before turning towards the sack. As theirs was the last collection made, all the Acquirers packages were laying on top, which Venice immediately recognised.

'Do you need any help in there?' the Italian asked, as he watched her going through the sack.

'No,' she grunted in reply, and yanked out a manila envelope. 'I got it,' Venice said triumphantly. She opened it, sliding out the piece of map briefly, to make sure it fit the description Natasha had given her, then she walked towards the two men who were intently watching her.

'Allow me,' the Italian said as he helped Venice back down to the ground once more.

'Is that it?' Tim asked. 'Can I go now?'

'Yes, this is it. Thanks again, Tim.'

'Don't worry about it,' the courier said as he locked up the back of the van before climbing back into the driver's seat. 'I'll see you soon, Venice. Take care.'

'Well, now that all the excitement is over, perhaps you'll allow me to buy you a coffee?'

'Look, thank you for all your help, but you should know I'm not into guys.'

'Così è la vita,' he smiled. 'But I would still like to buy you that coffee. You can tell me how you came to be named after an Italian city, and speak the language fluently.'

Venice smiled. 'Okay. Let me just put this upstairs and then...wait, I think that's my boss's car.' When she was certain the Alfa Romeo in question belonged to Lucas, she waved the envelope above her head to catch their attention, and let them know she'd successfully retrieved the map piece.

Suddenly, the Italian snatched the envelope from her hand, and made a swift escape, running down the street, ignoring Venice's shouts of stop. The engine of the Alfa Romeo roared as Lucas accelerated past Venice after the thief, only to come to a screeching halt as a car pulled out in front of him.

The talented PA watched as Natasha jumped out of the passenger side and chased after the thief, disappearing around the corner, leaving Lucas to put the car into reverse and slot it into one of their reserved parking spots.

'Hey, Venice,' Lucas greeted the PA with a gently hug. 'You okay?'

'Yeah, I'm fine,' she replied. 'Sorry about the envelope. I can't believe I let a guy distract me.'

'Who was he?'

'A passer-by that was helping. Or so I thought.'

'Could you describe him?' Lucas asked after a moment.

'He was well dressed, actually. Pretty stylish. What you'd expect from a young Italian man, I suppose.'

'Rimless glasses?'

Venice nodded.

'Hair in a messy bun thing?'

'Yeah.'

'Bollocks! Sounds a lot like Tony's Frenchman.'

'Wait…the one he said was trying to kill him?' Venice swallowed as the realisation hit her.

'Yeah. And that hothead had gone off after him.'

• • • •

NATASHA COULD FEEL her ponytail rapidly bobbing left and right as she chased after the man who had robbed Venice. She didn't feel like she was closing the space between them, but neither was she falling further behind.

That was until the man swept left onto Great Portland Street and jumped onto the back of a passing 453 route master bus. Natasha hadn't given up hope, and continued to pump her arms, knowing that an opportunity would soon present itself.

It looked obvious to Natasha that this had been nothing more than an opportunistic snatch. The thief didn't seem to have an escape route planned. If he did, he wouldn't have chosen a bus with a stop just around the corner.

The big red bus slowed as it prepared to take its wide, left-hand turn, which Natasha had been expecting. The public transport vehicle pulled away again as it navigated the manoeuvre. With her focus completely on the pole of the bus's rear entrance, the moment she felt certain she was in range, her heart thumping in her chest, Natasha leapt.

Her fingers curled around the cold metal, but before she could plant her feet on the platform, the bus sped up. Her legs flailed about as she swung on the pole. Natasha could feel her grip slipping, perspiration in her palm making it impossible to hold on much longer. She reached out with her other hand, just as the driver applied the brakes for a bus stop, causing Natasha to be thrown into the back of the bus.

'Man, you must be desperate for this bus,' a passenger said, watching Natasha get to her feet.

'More than you know,' she replied and scampered up the stairs to the top deck.

Natasha had not yet reached the top when a foot landed on her chest, knocking the wind out of her and sending her tumbling back down several steps. She grimaced and ran back upstairs. This time she was ready for the attack, leaning back to avoid the range limit of the kick, before she rushed forward, pushing him back away from the stairwell.

Passengers rushed to the front staircase. They didn't know what was happening, but neither did they want to hang around to find out. Except for the youngster who tried to film the encounter for his social media. He soon found out what a mistake it was when the stylish man wrenched the phone from his grasp before crushing it under his foot.

'That wasn't very nice,' Natasha said. 'But then you don't seem to be a nice person.'

'Looks can be deceiving,' he responded with an Italian accent.

'It looks like you stole something from a friend of mine,' she said as he pushed the envelope into an inside pocket of his jacket.

'How can I steal something that was never hers to begin with?' This time, he spoke with a French accent.

Hearing the accent, Natasha took another look at the man, and realised that he fit the description of Tony Braithwaite's Frenchman. 'Who are you?'

'That doesn't matter. Just know that I am on the righteous course. The path you follow leads to nothing but damnation. Your arrogance will see to that. You are not worthy.'

Natasha looked at him with narrow eyes. 'Not worthy of what?' The man didn't answer. 'You know what this map leads to, don't you? Or the people you work for certainly do. Do you work for Peter Armitage? Is he your boss?' She was getting nowhere with her questioning. Against her better judgement, Natasha revealed more than she should have. 'Is this a map to the holy grail? The cup of Christ?'

The man suddenly charged towards her. Natasha had been wanting to get a response from him, but this wasn't the kind she had been expecting. The tight confines of the bus's upper deck made it difficult to deliver a swung punch. On more than one occasion, his arm hooked around a pole protruding from the chairs, leaving him open for her straight jab.

After a few of them rocked his head back, he switched tactics, resorting to unleashing forward thrust kicks. This change brought him instant success. With the speed and strength of the strikes, even blocking the hits, Natasha was still feeling them.

The onslaught of powerful blows forced her backwards until she collapsed onto the rear seat of the bus. He fell upon her, his forearm pressed against her throat. Natasha wriggled beneath him in desperation, fortunately stopping the man from getting his full weight on her neck and pushing all the way down on her windpipe.

Her knees stuck him in ribs and her elbows were driven into his trapezius muscles, a cumulative numbing sensation built in his arms. His hold on her weakened, and at the first opportunity, she got her knees under his chest and thrust with all her strength.

He roared in frustration as he staggered back against a handrail, which made Natasha smirk. 'You still think I'm not worthy?'

'What I think is inconsequential. It isn't me that will judge your actions, weigh your soul. Only the king can do that. I am but an instrument.'

'In that case, you won't need the map,' Natasha said and lunged at the Italian.

She grabbed hold of his jacket's lapel, and he clutched her wrists. As they tussled for dominance, edging ever closer to the staircase, Natasha noticed an ornate crucifix pinned on his lapel.

There was something about it. Natasha knew it. But before recognition could fully form in her mind, sunlight glinted off the metal, blinding her. She missed the top step of the staircase, and they were both sent tumbling.

Natasha almost rolled all the way out of the moving bus. A final desperate action stopped her momentum, bracing herself on either side of the open entrance. But it left her unable to defend herself as the Italian closed in on her, a big grin on his face.

'They only ordered me to get the map, that's why I went easy on you,' the Italian said. 'But once I report my findings, tell them what you know, and if you persist on following this path, you will not have that luxury the next time we meet. I *will* kill you.'

Without another word, he stamped on one of Natasha's hands. The hardcore people who had remained on the bus, despite the noise they'd heard from the upper deck, gasped, as in a last ditch effort to stop herself, Natasha grabbed a handful of his shirt.

He hammered her arms to break her grip and free himself, but it wasn't until he kicked the feet from under her that Natasha was sent tumbling from the bus.

She stood up, wincing at the stinging grazes on her knees, and watched the bus driving away, the Italian waving farewell with the envelope in hand.

Natasha turned away, heading back to Lucas and Venice, disappointed that she wasn't able to retrieve the map piece. She'd lost the chance to see the new markings Tony Braithwaite had discovered. There was a shining light, however. She opened her right hand. Sitting in her palm was the Italian man's crucifix. And now that she could examine it up close, she knew exactly what it was.

Chapter 8

When Natasha arrived back at the Acquirers office, Lucas fussed over her whilst also berating her for what he deemed was reckless behaviour. Natasha looked at him with a raised eyebrow as she unbuttoned her cargo pants and pulled them down.

'Reckless? I know for a fact that if I'd been the one driving, it would have been you jumping out after him. Don't even try to deny it,' she added, cutting him off.

'That's different.'

'What do you mean, *different?* Is it one rule for you and another rule for me? Is that it?'

'No, of course not.'

'Good! Because I signed up to this fully aware of the potential dangers involved. Just like you did, Lucas. Ow! Easy,' she said when Lucas applied antiseptic lotion to her abrasions.

'I know that, Nat. I also know you can handle yourself. But it's easier on my blood pressure when we do them together.'

Natasha smiled over her shoulder at him. 'You're just a big softy, really, aren't you?'

The door of Natasha's office opened, and Venice stood there, mouth agape. 'Am I...interrupting something?'

'What? No...' Natasha began, before she realised the compromising position she was in, bent over her desk, cargo pants around her ankles and Lucas's hand on her buttock.

'Oh! No, it's not what you think. He's just cleaning my scrapes.'

'Well, it could have led to what you were thinking.'

'Do you want me to come back?'

'Yes.'

'No!' Natasha said, pulling up her pants. 'Come in, we're finished.'

'You just lost your Christmas bonus,' Lucas whispered as Venice passed him.

'Don't listen to him,' Natasha replied as she tentatively took her seat. 'Whoever that guy was, French, Italian or whatever, one thing for sure is that he's not working for BIC. His affiliation is with another organisation.' She fished out the object she'd taken off the man's lapel and placed it on the table.

Venice picked it up for a closer look. 'What a strange little thing. Is it a crucifix or a sword?' She pricked her finger on the point of the long arm as a demonstration.

'Exactly,' said Natasha. 'It's both. *With the Cross and the Sword*. That's the motto of the Entity, or the Holy Alliance, as it was originally called.'

'Holy what?' Venice questioned.

'The Vatican's spy network. Allegedly.'

'There's no allegedly about it. They've been at the pope's beck and call for five hundred years. The Entity has killed monarchs, poisoned diplomats, financed South American dictators, protected war criminals, laundered Mafia money, manipulated financial markets, started bank failures, and financed arms sales to combatants of condemned wars, all in the name of God.'

'You can't be serious,' Venice said, shaking her head.

'Very,' Natasha replied.

'But it makes the Catholic Church sound like an institute of organised crime.'

'And there are those that believe it is just that. And that's without the full knowledge of the Entity's dealings. Their involvement in this makes perfect sense. I mean, they wiped the Cathars out at the behest of Pope Innocent III. And if that religious group truly did have the holy grail, there's no way that the Vatican would let anyone else get their hands on but them.'

'That's alright then,' Lucas shrugged. 'You were thinking about giving it to them, anyway. Or are you changing your mind?'

'Hold on,' Venice interrupted. 'Did you say the holy grail? The cup that Jesus Christ drank from at the last supper?'

'And that Mary Magdalene used it to clean his wounds,' Natasha finished. 'Supposedly.'

Venice was intrigued. 'What do you mean?'

'That idea just never sat right with me. If she wasn't at the last supper, as those people say, how would she know which cup he drank from?'

Venice was about to say something before she stopped herself. 'That's actually a good point.'

'Now, if you think of Jesus and Mary being a married couple, living in the house he had, which was close to the place he was crucified, inviting his friends into his home for the last supper. Wouldn't it make more sense for Mary, stricken with grief by what was happening to the man she loved, to return to her home, familiar surroundings, to get a chalice to clean the wounds of her husband?'

'Actually, that does,' admitted Venice. 'But were they really married? It says nothing about it in the Bible.'

'That's because the Council of Nicaea rejected anything that made Jesus seem remotely human. If Rome was going to be Christian, they were going to control the narrative. And in typical Roman fashion, to make the transfer more palatable for the masses, they blended Christianity with already established pagan beliefs. Mithras, for instance, was born in a Devine manner on the 25th of December. Not only that, historic Christian churches in Rome were built on top of temples to Mithras,' Natasha happily revealed.

'Seriously?' Venice exclaimed.

'Seriously,' Natasha replied.

'Okay. But you said that Jesus and Mary were married. Wasn't she a prostitute?'

'Just as the gospels say nothing about their marriage, it also says nothing about her being a prostitute. She was known as Mary the Magdalene, meaning she was Mary from Magdala, which was a city on the southwest coast of the Sea of Galilee, and known to be a bit of a haven for prostitution. But she and her family were rich.'

'How do you know?'

'Lazarus, her brother, invited Jesus to the home they lived in with their sister, Sophia. It was here that she anointed the head of Jesus with fragrant oils and washed his feet, then dried them with her hair. A rather intimate act, wouldn't you say? Considering that at that time, they deemed it improper for a woman to let her hair down in public. But here she was, drying the prophet's feet with it. Just as Jesus was elevated, Mary's importance was downplayed.'

'What do you mean?'

'You said yourself that you thought she was a prostitute when it couldn't be further from the truth. Mary Magdalene witnessed the most significant events surrounding the crucifixion. She was present at the mock trial of Jesus; she heard Pontius Pilate pronounce the death sentence; and she saw Jesus beaten and humiliated by the crowd. She was one of the women who stood near Jesus during the crucifixion to comfort Him. The first witness to the resurrection of Jesus, she was sent by Jesus to tell the others. If you read the Gospel of Mary, it almost sounds as if Jesus was tutoring her to be a leader in his ministry, something that would change the church as we know it. And that the Vatican saw fit to activate an agent to retrieve Tony's map makes me think the grail is at the end of this.'

'So,' Lucas began. He'd listened to everything Natasha had said. Now he had to burst the excited mood and remind them what this actually meant. 'Not only will BIC be trying to find this artefact, but now so is the Vatican? And they have the complete map, so you won't be able to see the new markings Tony found.'

'I don't think I need to,' she replied honestly. 'With the Entity's involvement, what Tony saw can only be the Cather cross. And don't forget, Lucas, the Italian may have taken the map, but we have the watch, or we know where it is, to be exact.'

'And without it, they won't be able to read the hidden messages,' realised Lucas. 'They won't know where to start.'

Venice looked at Lucas, then at Natasha. 'And I suppose you both do?'

'Valencia,' the couple said simultaneously.

* * * *

CARDINAL ELIAS WAGNER, a grey-haired, middle-aged man, heard his phone ring and glanced at the name displayed. He'd been waiting patiently for this call, but he was willing to wait a few seconds more. He finished buttoning his cassock and answered it. 'Is it done, my son?'

'Yes, Your Eminence. I have the other piece of the Braithwaite map.'

'That is excellent news, Gianpaolo,' replied Cardinal Wagner. 'You never fail to do god's work.'

'There is something you should know, however,' Gianpaolo said hesitantly.

'Go on.'

'The Travers woman, she knows more than we expected. She asked me directly if the map led to the chalice.'

Cardinal Wagner tutted. 'That is a shame. Henri Laval must have told her about his map before his untimely death.'

'And hearing its similarities to Braithwaite's one would surely pique her interests. Judging from my brief encounter with her, she will no doubt want to see it for herself.'

'Something which cannot be allowed.'

'What do you want me to do?'

Cardinal Wagner fell momentarily silent on the other end of the line. 'You know what needs to be done.'

'I need you to say it, Your Eminence,' Gianpaolo said.

'My boy, you have nothing to worry about. The pope himself absolves the work you do for the church. The safety of your soul is assured.'

'I still need you to say it.'

'Very well. Gianpaolo, the Holy See charges you with the task, under the duties of the cross and sword, to eliminate Natasha Travers and all those that have borne witness to the maps. For devotion alone, not to gain honour or money, the Church of God substitutes this undertaking for all penance. God be with you.'

'And also with you.'

The cardinal's phone buzzed as another call tried to come through. He looked at the name. This was an unexpected call. 'Keep me updated, Gianpaolo,' the priest said before he ended the call and answered the second one. 'This is Omega. I wasn't expecting this call, Alpha. Is there a problem?'

Chapter 9

This was the sixth time Natasha and Lucas had travelled to Valencia. There was something about Spain's third largest city that they both loved. The Bioparc in the city's west where the animals roam free and it's the people that are the ones enclosed, to the futuristic-looking City of Sciences in the east, the backdrop in many sci-fi tv dramas and movies. From the huge beach in the southeast, where they never struggled to find a spot to sunbathe, even at the height of summer, to the historic Old Town in the city centre, Valencia was a marvel. All bisected by the green swathe of parkland that was once the river Turia, but after a devastating flood, was dammed it up and is now the Turia garden.

There was a lot to love in the city, something they felt was missing from Barcelona and Madrid. They still liked those cities, but something continuously brought the pair back here.

What brought them to Valencia this time was the purported holy chalice, believed by many to be the true holy grail. But that information, coupled with what the pair had recently learned, threw up questions they didn't yet know the answer to. Natasha never really believed it was the actual famous relic. It was undeniably from the correct era and location. It just didn't look like something a simple carpenter would use.

Natasha and Lucas walked up the busy, tourist filled Plaça de la Reina towards the 13th century cathedral with its octagonal bell tower. The religious building was a mix of

Valencian Gothic, which was the predominant architectural style of the cathedral, but it also contained Romanesque, French Gothic, Renaissance, Baroque and Neoclassical elements.

She stopped at the top of the stairs, admiring the structure and thinking of its history. Lucas had walked on until he realised Natasha was no longer beside him. He turned back and could immediately tell that something was on her mind.

'Are you okay?'

'Did you know they built it over the site of a former Visigothic cathedral, which under the Moors had been turned into a mosque?'

'Actually, I did. You told me. What's the matter?'

'What we're doing, it just kind of hit me.' She looked around to make sure no one was in earshot, then continued in a whisper. 'We're going up against the church.'

'Or the church is going up against us.' Lucas smirked.

'Do you think we're doing the right thing?'

'Without a doubt,' he replied. 'The way I see it, we are stopping a valuable item from falling into the wrong hands, like we always do.'

'But this is the Vicar of God. The earthly representative of Christ.'

'Who, at the end of the day, is still a man and prone to make mistakes in judgement like any human being. Don't forget it was the church that threatened Tony and put him in hospital. And it's not just them we need to worry about; it's Armitage and his cronies. But we could just sit this one out and let them go at it.'

Natasha looked at him with a raised eyebrow. 'That's the last thing we should do. What if he successfully found the grail? God knows what he'd do with it.'

'Exactly.'

'But it's been hidden for centuries. Maybe we should have faith and let it stay hidden.'

'And what if we are God's plan to make sure it does?'

Natasha considered those words for a bit and a smile slowly crept across her face. She suddenly walked off with a determined stride. 'Come on, Lucas. We've got a grail to find. And this is as good as any place to start looking.'

● ● ● ●

THERE WAS ONE THING that always confused Lucas about the Valencian grail. If it really was the cup Jesus supposedly used during the last supper, why wasn't there more hubbub about it? Even an endorsement from the pope wasn't enough to obtain the visitor numbers that the British Museum gets for the Rosetta Stone or the Cairo Museum gets for Tutankhamun's treasure.

Maybe it was because there was no definitive proof it was what it claimed to be. There were those that didn't even believe the holy grail itself existed, mostly because the first mention of it was during the Middle Ages in the Courtly Love sagas.

The couple walked into the cathedral and immediately took a right and along a passage into the area known as the Chapel of the Holy Chalice. It was relatively small, but that didn't diminish its historical importance. Religious artwork, including frescoes, paintings, and sculptures depicting various biblical scenes, adorned the walls. The overall ambiance of the chapel was one of serenity and reverence. Its lighting was subdued, creating a tranquil atmosphere for prayer and reflection.

But the principal focus of that chapel was the holy chalice itself. It was displayed behind the altar, within a hexagonal protective glass and gold case on a raised platform. The chalice may once have been a simple, unassuming vessel, but during the Middle Ages, the 9cm diameter cup was mounted with a knobbed stem and two curved handles, all gold, and attached to a base made from an inverted cup of chalcedony. Whatever was in the case, the spotlight inside it certainly made it look impressive.

'I knew it,' Lucas said. 'Not a single person in here.'

'What are you on about?' Natasha asked.

'We've been here what, three times? And the most people we've ever seen in here was that old lady, that one time.'

'Yeah. But don't forget, we never came here during any religious festivals.'

'Even so, as far as everybody knows, this is the real deal. Didn't you say it was carbon dated too?'

'Yeah, the dark red agate which they made the cup from suggests it was produced in Palestine or Egypt between the 2nd century BC and the 1st century AD.'

'So, it is the right period?'

'Yeah. But agate was an expensive material. Roman emperors had cups made of agate, not supposed inn owners.'

'More proof that this isn't the real thing.'

'Exactly.'

Lucas smirked. 'Even though you thought it was when we first came here.'

'More out of hope than anything. The evidence at the time was very compelling. And I believed at the time, and still believe, that Mary Magdalene came from a rich family and wasn't the prostitute they made her out to be. And if she was rich, then having an agate cup at the home she shared with Jesus would make more sense than this being used in an inn.'

'Hmm,' Lucas said, looking more closely at the cup. 'But considering the austere life he supposedly led, would he have had something like this in his home?'

'No, he wouldn't. Practice what you preach, springs to mind. Come on, we should look around. See if anything looks out of place. One good thing about this place not being busy, Lucas, is that we won't look suspicious.'

'Except to whoever is watching those cameras,' he said, thumbing the two security cams in opposite corners pointing towards the chalice. 'And the way things are in this chapel, it'll probably be a couple of old fogeys.'

Natasha sniggered as she checked her side of the chapel. They checked everything they could. The walls, the pews, behind the drapes. But they found nothing untoward. That only left the altar and the shrine of the chalice itself to investigate, which were cordoned off behind a rope.

'Now what?' Natasha said deflated.

'We're not giving up yet, hon,' grinned Lucas. 'You go take a seat at the back, and I'll check it out. Then you can continue on from where I get to.'

'Continue on...what are you talking about?' Her question went unanswered as he turned her around and patted her on the backside to send her off to the rear pews.

Lucas waited until she had sat down before he vaulted over the barrier. Natasha immediately jumped back up, about to admonish him, but instead directed his search. 'There's nothing on or under the altar,' he said.

'What about the fresco? Perhaps there's something in one of the Bible scenes.'

'There's a lot of them.'

'It's a cathedral. They have them.'

'Less of the sarcasm, please. Uh oh.'

'What is it?'

Natasha's answer came in the guise of three burly Italians charging into the chapel. She immediately sat back down, watching the scene in front of her unfold, whilst trying to stifle a snigger. As soon as the guards had appeared, Lucas began speaking in tongues, acting as if he were being overcome by the Holy Spirit, like a TV evangelist.

It took all of Natasha's will not to burst out laughing at Lucas's overacting. But it did provide enough of a distraction. As he was strong armed out, he gave her a wink, and as long as there weren't more guards waiting in the wings, she might have just enough time to find whatever was here.

Natasha still had to work quickly and leapt into action. As Lucas had instructed, she continued from where he had left off, checking the frescoes for anything unusual. There were scenes from the passion of Christ, Jesus carrying the cross, the crown of thorns, the crucifixion, the resurrection, the trial before Pontius Pilate. There were earlier scenes too, the feeding of the five-thousand, his cleansing of the temple.

Natasha paused and frowned.

'Wait a minute,' she breathed, and went back along the fresco, stopping at the scene of Christ's resurrection. Natasha squinted as she studied the stone cut image. In the scene's background was a little tower.

'Now what the h...' she stopped herself, remembering where she was and cleared her throat. 'A tower. A tower,' Natasha repeated as she fell into deep thought, pacing back and forth, whilst twisting a strand of her hair. She knew the guards could return at any moment, but she had to figure out what this meant.

Then suddenly she stopped and opened her eyes wide.

'I've bloody got it,' she said excitedly, then slapped a hand over her mouth. She looked up at the rafters. 'Sorry,' she said.

Chapter 10

Natasha continued to berate herself as she checked some of the other fresco scenes to confirm they fit the theory. 'Okay. So now what?' she wondered, looking at the wall once more. Natasha found her gaze inexplicably being drawn to the image of the Last Supper and slowly reached her hand out. Natasha's finger came closer and closer, edging towards the little tower in the background, over the shoulder of Jesus Christ.

When her finger rested on it, she took a breath, and pressed it.

Click!

Natasha sighed with joyful relief, and headed to where the sound had come from, the reverse side of the Valencian chalice's podium. When she rounded the glass display, she saw that a hidden door had been unlocked. Opening it, Natasha reached inside and was surprised to discover that the intricately decorated stand was almost hollow.

Her hand searched the cavity until it brushed against something, and her eyes opened wide when she brought out a cylindrical leather case. Natasha checked inside again, just to make sure there was nothing else there, then she gently closed the hidden door, marvelling at the craftsmanship. Even though she had just seen the door opened, with it closed, she couldn't spot the edge of the opening at all.

Suddenly Natasha heard footsteps echoing down the passage towards the chapel. *The guards!* They'd taken longer than she'd expected, luckily. *Lucas must have put on quite the show to delay them so much.*

Natasha quickly climbed over the barrier and sat down, placing the leather cylinder behind her back. She willed her thumping heartbeat to be still as a guard came and stood beside her. He crossed himself before he looked down at her.

'Perdon, senorita,' he whispered. 'The man that was here...'

'The one that was trying to touch the holy chalice?' Natasha replied, feigning distress.

'Yes, that is the one. Did you see him do or go anywhere else while he was here?'

She shook her head. 'No. One moment he was sitting quietly, then he seemed to be taken by the Holy Spirit and leapt over the barrier to hug the chalice.'

'Are you sure?'

'Yes, I was sitting in the back. I saw everything.'

'I thought I had seen you there.'

'Once you took him away, I felt safer to come closer to the cup to bask in its glory.'

The guard looked at the chalice in awe. 'It is remarkable, isn't it? Anyway, the man has been escorted away from the cathedral. You won't be interrupted again. You may worship in peace.'

Natasha bowed her head in gratitude and watched as the guard left. Once she could no longer hear his footsteps, she stood up and left the chapel and exited the cathedral. Looking left and right, she eventually spotted Lucas sitting under the shade of a tree in the Plaça de la Reina.

Lucas held out the partially melted cup of ice cream he'd bought for Natasha, dulce de leche, one of her favourite flavours. She took a spoonful, smiling with delight as the sweet caramel melted in her mouth, stimulating her taste-buds.

'Well?' Lucas asked expectantly. 'Are you going to tell me what happened, or do I have to wait until you've finished your ice cream?'

'I found it.' She grinned, putting the spoon back in her mouth.

'Found what?'

Natasha held up the leather tube. 'This.'

'What is it? Where was it?'

'I don't know what it is yet. But where it was, was inside the pedestal of the chalice.'

'Inside? How'd you'd find it?'

Natasha scraped out the last of her ice cream as they made a move to their hotel. Lucas took the empty tub and spoon, depositing them, along with his own, in a nearby bin.

'So,' she began. 'I found some anomalies in the fresco scenes; They had added small towers to them.'

'Okay,' Lucas said, needing more information to see the significance of that titbit of information.

'The towers represented Mary Magdalene.'

Lucas stopped walking momentarily. 'Really? But why a tower?' he asked as he caught up with Natasha.

'Magdalene wasn't Mary's surname, or most probably wasn't. We don't really know. But in the Bible, there are some occasions where she is called the Magdalene. It may have been a toponymic surname, meaning that she came from the town of Magdala, which was a fishing town on the western shore of the Sea of Galilee. In Aramaic, the language of the region, Magdala means tower.'

'Hence the towers. Did you just go along pressing them all until something happened? I did my best acting to give you as much time as possible.'

'Did you know that Mary Magdalene is mentioned by name in the New Testament more times than anyone except Jesus and his family? She was at many keys moment in the passion of Christ as well, the crucifixion, the trial. So once I realised the tower was Mary, and I saw they were placed in scenes that she appeared with Jesus in the Bible. Then I saw the one in the last supper. A scene that, according to the Bible, she wasn't at. So I pressed it.'

'And it opened a door in the Valencian cup's stand? So what's in the tube?'

'The quicker we get back to the hotel, the quicker we can have a closer look and find out.' Natasha noticed Lucas was on edge and only paying half attention to what she was saying. 'Is something wrong?'

'We're being followed,' he whispered.

'What? Who?'

'The BMW and the motorbike beside it,' he revealed. 'I saw them waiting around the side of the cathedral, just hanging out there until you came out.'

Natasha took a quick look over her shoulder and spotted the saloon car with blacked-out windows slowly following them. She was reminded of the similar car she'd seen at St Dunstan's in the East, after the Eye of Nineveh had been recovered and The Baron had been killed. Chiara Harris had driven that car.

'Come on,' Lucas urged. He took Natasha by the hand, and surreptitiously lengthened his stride, not enough to show those on his tail that he knew they were there, but enough to look like a tourist needing to get somewhere.

They turned right onto Plaça de Santa Caterina with its gelateries, horchaterías, sellers of the local sweet drink made from tiger nuts, and delicatessens. Further down the street was the Santa Caterina church. Beside it stood the Santa Catalina Tower, an iconic unfinished structure and a popular tourist attraction.

Lucas took a quick look over his shoulder and saw the black BMW come to a stop. A man jumped out of the rear door. He spoke to the biker as the car drove off, and the man left the biker at the end of the pedestrianised road.

Seeing their pursuer increasing the pace of his stride trying to catch up, Lucas guided Natasha into the church and then into the tower. Its ornate details characterised its architecture, including intricate stonework and decorative elements. A perfect example of gothic styling it is one of the most recognisable symbols of the city. But at 51 metres tall, and 207 steps, Natasha wasn't best pleased to be running up them. Even Lucas was breathing hard because of the exertions.

The builders originally planned for the tower to serve as the belfry of the cathedral, but they left it unfinished. Now the bell tower offered 360-degree views of the city to whoever could brave the spiral staircase to the bell chamber. Natasha took a moment to take in the view through the opening nearest her.

She could hear the pursuer making his way up the stairs, huffing and puffing, occasionally stopping on his ascent. The stocky man walked up the final few steps, and Natasha turned around when she heard his demand, through his laboured breaths.

'Give me the tube.'

Natasha didn't reply.

The man took a moment to catch his breath. Once he had, he asked her a second time, more forcefully. Again, she refused to respond. His face twisted in anger as he moved towards her. Then he stopped, realising his mistake. 'Where is the other one? Where is the man?'

Lucas answered the man himself. He jumped into the belfry, from outside where he'd been precariously hiding, through the opening behind him, and landed a boot to his face. The man staggered back against the railing of the stairwell. After a few moments, he launched himself at Lucas, driving his shoulder into his sternum, forcing him against the wall hard.

The man quickly followed up, intent on capitalising on his advantage. He landed punch after punch in Lucas's stomach until the former SAS captain slowed him down with several elbows driven to the back of his head.

The man may not have received military training, but Lucas could tell he fought dirty. The man caught Lucas under the chin as he raised his head sharply, causing the back of his head to crack against the wall.

Lucas saw stars. Then barely saw anything as the man pummelled him with punches, until Natasha flashed out a kick, striking him unhindered in the side of his head. She was on him before he had time to recover, raining blows all over his head and face.

He shoved Natasha away, desperate to create space between them. But in doing so, he left himself wide open for Lucas. Having recovered his senses, thanks to the intervention of Natasha, he renewed his attacked on the street fighter. Unleashing a relentless assault, which the stocky man struggled to defend against.

When he did try to retaliate, Lucas caught his arm, turned his hip into his attacker, and threw him with a textbook judo throw. The man stopped himself from going out one of the belfry's openings, using his arms to anchor himself. An action which gave both Lucas and Natasha a good view of a familiar symbol on the inside of the man's arm. A cross and a blade.

'The Entity,' Lucas snarled as he step kicked the man out the opening, launching the man through the air and crashing into the roofs of the neighbouring buildings twenty metres below.

'Jesus, Lucas,' Natasha said, as they ran back down the staircase. 'Did you have to kill him?'

'It was a reflex,' he explained. 'It was either him or us, and I know I have a lot of absolving to do before I'm ready to kick the bucket, babes.'

Natasha thought for a moment. 'Okay, I see your point. I can't believe the church would want us dead, though.'

'Why not? We've pissed off drug dealers, arms dealers, self-proclaimed warlords. It was only a matter of time,' smiled Lucas.

'It's not funny, Lucas. You know my mum's Catholic. She can never find out about this.'

It wasn't long before they were bursting out of the church and across the road to Calle dels Jofrens, all under the surprised eye of the motorcyclist, who revved up his vehicle and turned into the pedestrianised road, heading after his quarry.

Chapter 11

Lucas and Natasha hurried down the familiar street. They could hear the engine of the motorbike behind them. Halfway down the street, they reached a stall selling perfumes, scarves and fans, and turned right, entering the Plaza Redonda.

The circular shaped plaza had been a popular spot for locals and visitors alike since the 19th century. Known for its lively ambiance, small shops, and market stalls selling a variety of goods, such as textiles, crafts, traditional products and souvenirs, Natasha always thought it was a great place to shop for unique items. Now they hoped that the circular layout might aid them in escaping the Entity.

Many people were sitting outside the cafes and restaurants, with their red wooden shutters, which lined the outer ring of the round square, relaxing and soaking up the atmosphere, enjoying a glimpse into the traditional charm of Valencia's Old Town, and looking at the fountain at the centre of the plaza.

Lucas and Natasha moved around the inner circle of shop stalls, ducking behind one after another, as the biker entered the plaza and got a rapid fire of verbal abuse in Spanish for riding his bike into the pedestrianised zone.

The biker ignored it all. He pushed up the visor of his helmet and scanned the abusive crowd, looking for the man and woman, the enemies of the Vatican.

'We're going to split up, Nat,' Lucas said as they stopped behind a stall selling postcards, posters, and other tourist memorabilia of the city.

'What? Why?'

'Because it'll be easier for you to get away with this.' Lucas took the tube from her and popped it open. He gave it a couple hard shakes, and a tightly rolled parchment slipped out into his hand.

Natasha bent her head, trying to get a look. 'Is that...?'

'No, time to worry about it now, Nat,' Lucas replied as he took an "I love Valencia" T-shirt from a nearby stall. He wrapped it around the rolled and aged paper before handing it to Natasha. 'When we split up, don't go back to the hotel. Meet me in Port Saplaya. Okay?'

Natasha nodded. Suddenly, she was grabbed from behind and spun around. Confronting her was an angry Spanish woman, shouting and gesticulating, accusing Natasha of stealing. The commotion was attracting attention. Coffee drinkers craning their necks, turning away from the biker as another hotspot of action brewed.

Lucas calmed the woman, throwing several euros her way, three times what the shirt was worth. His attempt to hush her was too late. The motorcyclist's head turned in their direction. Lucas's eyes locked with his. The moment he saw the biker flick down his visor, Lucas broke into a sprint, with Natasha following his lead.

With the sound of the motorbike revving, the pair weaved in and out of the growing number of tourists. They could hear its tyres squealing on the tiles of the Redona as they rejoined Plaza de la Reina, heading back toward the cathedral.

Lucas glanced over his shoulder as the bike burst out of the pedestrian area, to the sounds of car horns. The rider was going against the traffic so as not to lose them, a desperate act which Lucas knew he would have to match. Servants of God or not, he would do what needed to be done so that he and Natasha could escape.

The moment they arrived back at the grand building of worship, Lucas led them onto the road immediately to the left; Carrer dels Brodadors. 'This is where we split, Nat,' Lucas said as they came up to the first junction. 'You carry on that way, and I'm going to go this way. Don't forget, Port Saplaya.'

'Watch your back, Lucas,' she said as they hugged.

'You too. I'll see you soon, hon.'

• • • •

AS THE PAIR RAN OFF in their designated directions, the biker came to a halt at the same spot Lucas and Natasha had been standing moments before. He watched Natasha running down the narrow street of the Old Town, then turned his head to see Lucas running down Carrer del Micalet.

'They've split up,' the biker said into his helmet comms. 'He's heading to de la Mare de Déu. He has the tube. Yes, Your Eminence. We will leave no one that has seen it alive.'

With the communication ended, the biker spun his rear wheel, leaving a black skid mark as he took off after Natasha.

• • • •

NATASHA COULDN'T BELIEVE it. She didn't particularly like Lucas's idea of separating, but he had convinced her that the biker would follow him and the case. 'So much for that idea,' she grumbled as she came to another junction. Natasha looked both ways, then headed to the right.

The roar of the bike's engine reverberated around her in the narrow streets. With fewer pedestrians blocking his way, the biker was gaining on her fast. He flew past her, forcing Natasha to jump clear, like a matador, to avoid being struck. The biker skidded around and came at her again. He steered closer to her. She barely got out of the way this time. His knee caught her, the force pushed her against a big green bin standing against the wall beside her.

He skidded around again, revved the engine, spinning the wheel. Then he set off, charging towards her like a raging bull. Without a second thought, Natasha leapt onto the bin's lid, avoiding the motorbike again, and after a cursory look over the wall, she climbed up and over.

She landed in the onetime, backyard of a demolished house. Unfortunately, it wasn't a unique situation. Natasha had passed several buildings dotted around Old Town that were in a dilapidated state, almost looking like a post-apocalyptic scene. The global recession, and other incidents, had hit the country hard. The upkeep was too much for some owners and everywhere you looked, you'd see at least one Se Vende or Se Alquila sign; for sale, for rent.

Natasha heard the motorbike come back and then the engine shutoff on the other side of the wall. She looked around the detritus for anything she might use as a makeshift weapon, finally finding something suitable. Clutching the rough, jagged section of wall in her hand, Natasha could feel the gritty texture of the bricks and the weight of the mortar. It was a crude weapon, but it would have to do. She shifted slightly, trying to find the most advantageous angle to strike from while keeping her movements minimal and silent. Her back pressed against the cold, hard surface of the wall, she waited.

The biker's head and gun wielding arm popped up above the wall and swept from right to left. Natasha held her breath. She could hear him talking.

'I am about to eliminate her now, Your Eminence. Ciudad de las Artes? I will be there shortly to assist them.'

When the exchange ended, and the gunman saw nothing untoward on the other side of the wall, he climbed over.

The moment he landed, Natasha swung her arm and smashed the bricks in his head, cracking the helmet and leaving a sizeable dent in it. As he staggered, she struck him again. He fell, writhing on the floor, trying to get to his feet again, but Natasha wasn't about to let that happen. She wrenched his helmet from his head, and was momentarily stunned by how young he was, before finishing what the brick assault had started and put him to sleep with a left cross to the jaw.

'About to eliminate me, huh? Really?' Looking down at the unconscious man, Natasha suddenly had an idea.

• • • •

PLAZA DE LA VIRGEN is always busy with tourists and those that liked to sit outside, have a hot beverage and enjoy watching people go by, all to the relaxing soundtrack of the Turia Fountain. But today the screeching tyres of a black BMW disrupted the tranquil sound and setting as it fought for grip on the marble tiles.

Lucas looked at the commotion in disbelief and smirked. 'And they call themselves spies? They must be graduates of the James Bond school of subtlety.' His pleasure at the remark was short-lived, as the car's all-wheel drive kicked in and the driver aimed towards him.

Lucas turned and ran, heading down one of the side streets which branched off from the plaza. There was a shower of chairs, as the car bulldozed through the outside seating arrangements of the restaurants, in pursuit of him.

Like most of the streets and alleyways of Old Town, it was a narrow single lane, meaning the car had to contend with parked cars and other traffic. But when the road was empty, it would quickly catch up. Then Lucas saw an opportunity to get his own wheels.

'Hey, my pizzas,' the delivery man yelled, as Lucas jumped onto his electric moped and accelerated away.

They charged up Carrer dels Serrans, with the Torres del Serrans, Serrans Towers, looming large. Lucas tore through the gothic gate of the wall that once surrounded the medieval city, cutting straight across the traffic, skidding as he turned right to head down the steps into the Turia Jardin. The car had to go around the historic monument, zigzagging through the traffic to keep up its pursuit.

Despite having fewer obstructions on his route, Lucas couldn't make a clean getaway. The electric moped used up the last of its juice and came to a stop at the Ciudad de las Artes y las Ciencias, the City of Arts and Sciences.

Lucas jumped off and ran into the state-of-the-art complex. So striking was its design that they had used it as the backdrop in many Hollywood blockbuster sci-fi movies. All Lucas was hoping for was an escape route. But the black BMW came bolting down the slope from the street level, taking to the air, and screeching to a stop. Moments later, Lucas also stopped as a volley of bullets peppered the ground around his feet.

'Give me the package,' the Spaniard said, pointing the gun squarely at Lucas.

'What package would that be, mate?'

'The one on your shoulder.'

'Oh, this?' Lucas said in mock surprise. 'This isn't what you're looking for.'

'I'll be the judge of that. Open it.'

Lucas did as he was told and showed him the empty tube. 'See? I told you.'

'Where is it?'

'Why does the Entity want it so much? What are they trying to keep hidden?'

'No more games, Mr Redmond.' The Entity agent thought for a moment, then a smile crept across his face. 'It's pretty obvious, really. If you don't have it, then that can only mean Miss Travers does.' A familiar motorbike suddenly turned off the main road to descend the slope leading to the

City of Arts. 'It would seem like we have everything we need, Mr Redmond. All that remains is to take care of you.'

The Vatican spy brought his second hand up to steady the pistol as he aimed at Lucas. Suddenly, the motorbike accelerated hard, slamming into the back of the gunman at speed. His shot was wild, firing high into the sky, whilst he himself flew through the air, leaving him in an unconscious heap as he cracked his head on the ground.

'Need a ride?' Natasha asked as she flipped up the visor of the dented helmet. Lucas climbed on and the pair rode off as the sound of the Guardia's sirens grew in the distance.

Chapter 12

Ellen Paige climbed out of bed yawning, scratching her head, and the small of her back, all at the same time, whilst cursing the name Lucas Redmond. She barely had three hours sleep before her ringing phone rudely awoke her. Sourcing weapons and equipment in the real world, before fragging other online gamers in Apex Legends in the virtual world, takes a lot out of a girl.

Her sleep was a valuable commodity.

Now she was up, hours before she was due. 'I swear, Lucas, ever since this adoption stuff, you've become even more domineering,' she complained to her phone, as she pulled on a pair of baggy pants and a random UV-reactive T-shirt.

'Come on, El,' Lucas pleaded on the other end of the call. 'It's not all bad.'

'Is it not? You bailed and left me going to Thames House to hobnob with politicians. Hours of my life I won't get back. Now you got me doing errands.'

'Yeah, we did do that,' he chuckled, 'but now you get an all fees included trip to the south of France.'

Ellen ruffled her green hair so that it was on the right side of stylish grunge, before she lit the joint she had prepared last night and headed out.

• • • •

'WAKING UP EARLY WAS bad enough,' Ellen grumbled under her breath as she stepped off the Elizabeth Line, the new swanky cross London public transport, at Paddington station. 'If there was one errand, I could have that done and be on my way back to sleep land on no time. But two bloody jobs to do is taking the piss.'

To be fair, the first job wasn't particularly difficult, since Lucas had given her step-by-step instructions. He'd told her to go to Brydges place, one of London's narrowest streets, barely one metre wide in places, and a stone's throw away from the London Colosseum. Ellen counted the bricks until halfway down the alley she had found a brick with an innocuous "T4B". Anyone would think that it was just another declaration of love, like all the other messages. But little did they know it was actually Tony's initials. 'Tony Ford Braithwaite,' Ellen sniggered as she pushed the fake brick and heard a click. She looked up and down the alley, to make sure no one was trying to squeeze their way in, before she removed the phoney brick and took the pocket watch from the cavity behind. Once she put the cover back, she headed to her second errand.

It wasn't long before Ellen was walking into St Mary's hospital. Apparently, Tony Braithwaite had been moved from intensive care and Lucas wanted her to check up on him. He had Natasha's mum doing that for him, but she was a surgeon and wouldn't always have the time to do it. Besides, it'll be nice to have a familiar face look in on him.

'Familiar? Pfft! I met the guy once, years ago.' Ellen sighed. There was no point in complaining. She was here now. She might as well get it over and done with.

As she walked through the ward, Ellen noticed it didn't have the same smell that people associated with hospitals. Perhaps because this was the hospital of so many royal births, they had to tickle the olfactory membranes of the elite positively.

In a bed at the back near the window, she eventually found Tony. She didn't realise how banged up he was. At least he seemed to be sleeping, Ellen thought. 'How is he?' she asked the spectacled doctor that was attending to his drips.

'He's fine,' he replied, 'but he shouldn't be disturbed.'

'Disturbed?' Ellen wasn't in the mood. 'Do you think I'm going to start a rave in here or something, huh? Just because I have green hair and party appropriate clothing, doesn't mean I'm here to make a disturbance. Stop making an ass out of yourself with your assumptions, okay?'

'Hey, calm down,' another doctor said with a distinctive Spanish lilt, as she approached the bed. 'Let's just calm down and turn it down a notch, shall we? There are other patients here.'

Ellen turned to the new arrival, a Hispanic woman with chestnut coloured, shoulder length hair and tanned skin. 'Your colleague here seemed to think I was about to have a party over here.' Ellen paused as she saw the name badge. 'You're Dr Travers? Dr Sofia-Valentina Travers?'

'Yes,' Sofia said suspiciously as she took another closer look, before she finally recognised the girl. 'You must be Ellen! We met briefly at Natasha and Lucas's wedding. You had quite...a different look back then.'

Ellen smiled and ran her hand through her recently dyed green hair. 'Yeah, I hadn't gone through shit, and find my own individuality back then.'

'I see,' Sofia said to Ellen's pronouncement. 'Well *you* I know, but,' Sofia turned to the other doctor, '*you*, I don't know. You're not a doctor here. Who are you, and what are you doing with my patient?'

Without saying a word, the suspicious doctor rushed away, pushing past Sofia.

The man's disrespectful actions shocked Ellen. 'Hey, man!' she demanded. 'What the hell's wrong with you?' But her protests fell on deaf ears as he quickly made for the emergency stairs.

The alarm on Tony's monitors suddenly went off as his vitals unexpectedly began to flatline. Sofia jumped into action and began CPR as other doctors and nurses rushed to answer the call of the alarm. Ellen was caught in two minds: should she go after the fake doctor, or should she stay? The decision was made up for her when Sofia ordered her to leave.

As Ellen made her way down to the ground floor, she came to her senses, realising that she wasn't Lucas, and approached the first security guard she saw and convinced him to radio in about the fake doctor.

She left the professionals to do their jobs and slowly left the hospital. Ellen had only taken a few steps when she discovered that the guard would not find the imposter doctor. As she took her phone out, intending to give Lucas an update on Tony and tell him she was on her way to France, she saw the discarded doctor's white jacket. The man had changed his appearance.

• • • •

GIANPAOLO WATCHED THE girl with the brightly coloured hair leave. He had heard everything she had said in her phone conversation and smiled. As he turned to walk in the opposite direction, his phone buzzed.

'Yes, Your Eminence?'

'Gianpaolo,' Cardinal Wagner said. 'I wanted you to know that Travers and Redmond have found something in Valencia.'

'Another map?'

'Perhaps,' the cardinal replied. 'They killed one of your colleagues, and two others were arrested as well.'

'I thought I was the only agent on this assignment?'

'You were in London. I was given information and had to act on it quickly. So, I activated those Black Monks. My mistake was underestimating Travers and Redmond. I should have known better, especially after their previous dealings with the Bilderberg Inner Circle. It is a mistake I won't make again. Now the trail has gone cold.'

'Not true. Travers and Redmond have already gone to Nice.'

'Of course,' said the jubilant cardinal. 'They are going after the Laval map.'

'Yes,' replied Gianpaolo. 'And I have arranged a flight to take me there.'

'That is excellent news, my son.'

'However, I... I hope I won't be tripping over any other Black Monks.'

'No. You have complete authority in the field. If there is anything you need, the Entity will provide it, of course. Just make sure Travers and Redmond's quest comes to a premature end. They cannot be allowed to discover the truth.'

••••

NATASHA SAW THE DISTRESSED look on Lucas's face as he ended the call on his mobile. 'Everything okay?' The flight from Valencia to Nice took less than two hours, and in no time at all, they were sitting in the back of a taxi on their way to their hotel when Lucas had received his phone call.

'Someone just tried to kill Tony,' Lucas explained. 'Your mum is at the scene trying to save him.'

'What?'

'Ell didn't get a good look at him, but from what she did see, it sounds like it could be our Italian friend come back to finish the job.'

'The Entity are stepping things up,' Natasha said, her brow creased in thought.

'Yeah. They're not being very godly.'

'And they're just going to keep on coming until they stop us.'

Lucas's face hardened. 'Then we'll have to stop them.'

Natasha reached out a hand to squeeze his. 'I know you're worried about Tony, but we can't go around dishing out vigilante justice to everyone that hurts our friends.'

'I'm being serious,' he replied as he turned to face her. 'Have you thought what the Entity would do if we found whatever is at the end of this quest? Do you think that we'll get invited to the Vatican by the pope to have lunch? They've tried to kill Tony, twice. This time, they might actually have done it. They've tried to kill us, too.'

'So what are you suggesting? That we give up? That we call it quits?'

'No. We need to start playing at their level, and we find this damn thing and shove it up the ass of whoever is running the Entity.'

'Finding out who that is won't be easy. They are a spy organisation, after all.'

'And we do amazing things every day, baby. Have a little faith,' Lucas said, giving her his winning smile. 'Now, where do we begin?'

Their taxi pulled outside the Hotel Royal-Riviera in Saint-Jean-Cap-Ferrat, and Natasha only knew that Henri Laval had a chateau in the area. But she didn't have a clue what it was called or even where it was. *Find my flower. That is the key.* The words Laval had said before his death rang through Natasha's mind.

She left Lucas to check them in, giving her some vital moments to remember if there was anything else that might help them, anything that she might have missed, or initially overlooked, as being inconsequential.

As she flopped down in the hotel lobby's plush seats, almost defeated, her gaze fell upon the arrangement of newspapers on the elegantly carved table. There was a funeral taking place today; for Henri Laval. A local philanthropist who had met his untimely death whilst on a business trip. His only child, a daughter named Marigold, survived him.

Chapter 13

After a quick change of clothing into something more appropriate for a wake, whilst in the back of the taxi taking them to the Laval villa, Natasha searched for all the information she could find on Marigold Laval, and that was quite a lot.

From what Natasha read, Marigold Laval was a fascinating character who embodied the perfect blend of sophistication, intelligence, and privilege. As a French socialite, she effortlessly navigated the upper echelons of society with elegance and charm. With a natural grace and poise, Marigold effortlessly captured attention wherever she went.

And Natasha could understand why. With her long black hair, green eyes and slightly upturned nose, Mari, as she liked to be called, was a striking beauty, and despite her status as a socialite, Mari was far from being merely superficial. She possessed a sharp intellect and a thirst for knowledge, owing to her exceptional education. According to one interviewer, she was well read, with a passion for literature, history, and the arts. Her curiosity drove her to constantly expand her horizons and engage in intellectual discussions.

"'Marigold comes from a wealthy family, with her father being a highly successful entrepreneur and philanthropist. This background has instilled in her a strong sense of responsibility and a desire to make a positive impact on the world. She actively involves herself in various charitable endeavours, leveraging her family's resources to contribute to causes that are important to her'", Natasha read aloud.

'I wondered if she knew everything her father was involved in?'

Natasha shrugged. 'Who knows? But we'd better not mention it, just in case.'

'Agreed.'

The Laval villa was a harmonious blend of architectural beauty, natural surroundings, and lavish comforts, creating a haven of refined luxury in one of the most sought-after locations on the French Riviera.

'I hope nobody saw us turn up in that taxi,' Natasha said as they walked through the landscaped gardens featuring vibrant bursts of colour from an array of blooming flowers, neatly trimmed hedges, and palm trees swaying in the sea breeze.

'Don't worry about it. The way you look, hon, you'll fit right in.'

'You don't look too shabby yourself, Lucas,' Natasha said, casting an admiring eye over him.

He bent down and kissed her. Then she heard a familiar French voice behind her.

'I'd recognise that cute derrière anywhere, Ms Anyabaek.'

Natasha turned around to see Alain Mercier – with his thin moustache on his smarmy face – the art dealer from the black-market bazaar in Teddington where the Eye of Nineveh was for sale.

'I knew there was something more than employer and employee going on between you two,' Mercier continued with a smirk.

'There's been some mistake,' Natasha replied. 'I think you're mixing me up with someone else, sir.'

'No, no, no, cherie,' he said, leaning around to check out her behind again. Natasha put his head straight before Lucas could. 'I saw what the two of you did at the bazaar, you in particular,' he said, looking at Lucas.

'I'm surprised you saw anything,' said Natasha. 'Weren't you hiding somewhere?'

'Well, I have a lot of clients that would miss my incredible ability to find art. And my nous at getting it for the best price. In fact, I've done many jobs for the late Henri Laval. And Mari too.'

'Of course you have,' Natasha responded. She knew there were those among the elite, the rich and powerful, that had a selfish driving desire to have the best and most exclusive item. Sometimes going beyond the law to achieve it. Henri Laval struck her as just that type.

'And what have you done for poor Henri?' He saw the confused looks on both Natasha's and Lucas's faces. 'This wake is not open to the public. They invited only those that have contributed to the Laval Foundation to attend. There is security around checking.'

Natasha glanced at Lucas, acknowledging the sudden obstacle.

'Oh, I see,' Mercier smiled. 'You are the gate crashers, non?'

'No,' Natasha snapped, then softened. 'Well, not exactly. I met with Henri before he died. He wanted me to find something for him.'

'Something like the Eye of Nineveh, perhaps?'

Natasha gave him a noncommittal look.

'Oh, don't look at me like that. I saw you in the news. Standing in the background behind that police officer, letting him take all the plaudits. I didn't see him anywhere near that bazaar until it was almost all over. It was about the map, wasn't it?'

'Wait, you've seen it?' Natasha asked, her face beaming.

'I had a cursory look. The parchment, by the thread count, was old. Probably fourteenth century. But map reading isn't my forte.'

'But it is the both of yours, isn't it Miss Travers, Mr Redmond?' a voice with a sultry French lilt said. The elegant form of Mari Laval sauntered towards them, the crowd in front of her seeming to part before her. Behind her was the familiar and imposing figure of Ali. 'I was hoping to see you and Mr Redmond.'

Ali snarled at Lucas, who simply winked back at the big, bearded Moroccan.

'You were expecting us?' Natasha questioned.

'Yes, at some point. I can see you don't understand. Let me lay it out for you. I was the one that convinced my father to approach you.' Without another word, Mari swivelled on her heel and with her long-legged stride headed through the garden towards the villa. 'I even had your names put on the guest list, just in case,' she said over her shoulder.

'And if we didn't show up?' Lucas asked.

'That thought didn't cross my mind,' Mari said as she ushered them into a study. Alain Mercier was about to follow when Ali blocked his entry with a big, burly, hairy arm and closed the door. 'We would have met one way or another,'

Mari continued inside. 'I know my father didn't take the documents he wanted to show you to England.'

'I don't suppose you have them?' Natasha fished.

'No,' came the reply. 'He was very secretive about them. I don't even know where he kept them.'

'When we spoke, he implied they were at his chateau.'

'Lake view? Of course.' Mari nodded and gave a wry smile. 'He always loved that place.'

'Have you seen the maps yourself?'

'Only briefly. Like I said, father kept them well hidden, even from me. But we discussed the letters. Why do you ask?'

'When I spoke to Henri, and he described the map, he asked me if I'd seen anything like it before. I wasn't entirely truthful to him.'

Mari leaned forward in her seat. 'Go on.'

'Lucas and I had seen one before, and since then, we've found another.'

'Identical?'

'Yes, from what we can tell.'

'So you are close to solving this puzzle?'

'I wouldn't say that.'

'I disagree. You're further along than father could have ever expected. I want you to finish it. Finish what my father wanted you to do. Find out what these maps lead to.'

'It's not as easy as that,' Natasha said.

'Of course I'll finance the entire operation, and honour whatever finder's fee you had agreed.'

'Well, actually,' Lucas cut with a smile on his face, 'we hadn't settled on a fee yet.'

'Then all you have to do is name it.'

'This isn't what I was talking about,' said Natasha.

'Oh?' Mari said with a quizzical look.

'I don't know if they're looking for it too, or if they're just trying to stop anyone else from finding it. But they've tried to kill anyone that's seen the maps.'

'Who?' Mari asked, more intrigued than ever.

'The Entity, the espionage network of the Vatican.'

Mari sat back in her chair. Natasha watched her, tried to get a read on their host, positive that Lucas was doing the same. Despite being a twenty-five-year-old socialite, Natasha found her decidedly level-headed. She seemed determined to continue to strengthen her family's legacy. Natasha was sure that if they were to tell Mari about her father's dealings with the Bilderberg Inner Circle, the girl wouldn't breakdown and lose her mind like some in her social circle, such was her strength in character. Natasha had to admit, her admiration for the woman was growing.

'Do you think they killed my father?'

Neither Natasha nor Lucas revealed the truth.

'It doesn't matter,' Mari continued eventually. 'I won't let the church scare me into stopping what my father started. I want the two of you to finish this. Find out what these maps lead to, and you can name your price.'

Lucas rubbed his hands. 'I like the sound of that. Natasha?'

Despite the obvious dangers involved, Natasha's curiosity was already too invested in the quest to turn back now. 'When can we go to the chateau?'

'How does first thing in the morning sound?'

'Perfect,' Natasha replied.

Mari patted the table excitedly. 'Excellent. I'll have the car pick you up at nine.'

Natasha noted it was a statement rather than a question. 'Okay. We're staying at Hotel Royal-Riviera.'

'Good choice. Now, if you don't mind, I have other guests to attend to,' she said, standing up. 'Although I'm sure most of them will just want to make sure that my father's financial contributions will continue to come in, despite his passing,' she said dismissively. 'Until tomorrow, Miss Travers, Mr Redmond.'

• • • •

'ABOUT TIME YOU TWO turned up,' Ellen said in a puff of smoke. There were three roll-up butts on the ground around her feet.

'Things went on longer than expected,' said Lucas. 'But we got back as soon as we could.'

'Any news about Tony?' Ellen asked Natasha.

She slowly shook her head. 'But no news could be good news.'

'Let's hope so,' Lucas said solemnly as Natasha stroked his arm. 'Come on, let's go look at this map.'

They quickly made their way up to their two-bedroom suite. Lucas took a precautionary look out of the balcony, whilst Natasha went to the safe to retrieve the map they got from Valencia, and Ellen emptied Tony's items from her overnight bag. The hotel room was paid with cash and overlooked the marina, for security Lucas said, but when an organisation like the Entity were on your tail, you could never be over cautious.

With a final glance left and right, he went back inside to find Natasha spreading out the parchment she had found in the cathedral. 'A map?' He sat beside her and inspected it. 'A familiar map, I might add.'

She nodded with a wide-eyed grin that lit up her face. 'From what I can tell, it's the same as Tony's one. Obviously I can't be one-hundred per cent sure until I check it with the pocket watch. But the landmass seems similar.' She turned over the map and in the same corner was a white mantle with a black cross on the back of it. 'Even the heraldic cross is in the same place.'

'Yeah,' agreed Lucas. 'Exactly the same landscape and cross by the looks of it.'

'Landscape of where?' Ellen frowned.

'That, we don't know yet,' replied Natasha. 'But maybe the hidden writing will tell us something.'

Ellen looked sideways at the map. 'What hidden writing?'

Natasha picked up the pocket watch. 'That writing will be revealed with this,' she smiled.

Chapter 14

Ellen looked from the pocket watch to Natasha, then Lucas and back to the watch. 'What?'

'She's serious, El,' assured Lucas. 'When you look through the glass on the watch's cover, you can see the writing. On Tony's map there was a journal and a riddle.'

'I'm expecting to see something similar here,' Natasha admitted, as she took a deep breath and slowly let it out. She brought the lens up to her eye and peered through the glass.

Natasha cast her gaze back and forth across the front of the map, then she turned it over and did the same again. Finally, she sat back in her seat. 'There's nothing on it.'

'What?' Lucas was stunned and picked up the watch to see for himself.

'It's blank,' reiterated Natasha.

'What the hell?' Lucas gasped after a few moments, looking through the glass. 'Was it erased or something?'

Natasha shrugged. 'Maybe being in that Dias all these years could have affected it.'

'What is it supposed to show?' Ellen asked.

'Here, take this,' Lucas said, handing her the pocket watch, 'and have a look at what's left of Tony's map.'

'Whoa,' exclaimed Ellen, removing the glass from her eye to verify that what she could see was indeed invisible to the naked eye. 'That's pretty cool. So what did the complete text say?' she asked, showing the partial texts.

Natasha took a moment to recall the passage from memory before she repeated it in entirety for Ellen. 'The vault was located deep in the heart of the mountain, and the only way to access it was through a narrow passageway that required an alert mind and a steady hand. Inside, the air was musty and damp, and the only light came from a few flickering torches hanging from the walls. The walls of the vault were lined with cloth, and the floor was covered with a thick layer of dust. The only thing that seemed out of place was a small table in the centre of the room, upon which sat a mysterious elixir. The liquid glimmered in the dim light, and it seemed to radiate an energy that was almost palpable. The dawn was just breaking as they entered the vault, and the light filtering through the narrow opening in the ceiling was just enough to see by. They approached the table cautiously, and as they drew closer, they could see that the elixir was contained in a small canvas bag. The bag was made of sturdy material and looked as if it had been crafted with care. The iron clasp was still secured, and the bag seemed to be in excellent condition. They opened the bag, and to their surprise, the elixir was still ample and had not evaporated.'

Ellen raised an eyebrow. 'All that was on the map?'

'Beautifully handwritten. But now we have this map with the same drawn landscape, but with nothing written on it.' Natasha let out a sigh of frustration. 'The text led us to Valencia. I was hoping this would lead us to the next clue.'

'Good thing we've already got a lead, then,' Lucas prompted.

The spark returned to Natasha's eyes. 'Exactly! Henri Laval's chateau.'

• • • •

NESTLED IN THE SUBURBS of the beautiful city of Nice, the 13th-century French Chateau known as Lakeview was undergoing a meticulous renovation. Work was paused momentarily after Henri Laval's death, but work was due to restart any day.

With its captivating medieval architecture, the chateau had a rich provenance, once owned by esteemed aristocratic families like the House of Grimaldi. Through the centuries, it had witnessed grand festivities and significant historical events. However, it had also experienced a dark period during World War II when it served as a Nazi post.

It was the hope of Henri Laval for the restoration to preserve its historical charm while integrating modern amenities, offering visitors a glimpse into its past, from noble opulence to the shadows of war, and ensuring its enduring legacy for generations to come.

Mari Laval didn't have nearly as much interest invested in the old building as her father did. He had intended to live in it. She, however, planned to open it as a museum, or more than likely a hotel.

'Wow,' Natasha said, drinking in the sight of the medieval castle. 'This could be a really impressive hotel, if done right and sympathetically.'

'That's exactly what I told my dad,' Mari said, glad that someone else could see her vision. 'I plan on getting a landscape gardener to completely redesign the gardens with the view of using it as a wedding venue.'

'That would be wonderful,' gushed Natasha, visualising the opulent marriage ceremonies that could be conducted there.

With Mari leading the way, and her driver bringing up the rear, the entourage entered the castle where it became apparent to Natasha and Lucas exactly how extensive the restoration work on the chateau actually was. The grand hallway with its high ceiling had scaffolding erected all around, some of it used to bolster the fragile and dilapidated staircase, a 16th century addition which showed hints of what it once looked like. A lone restorer worked tirelessly to return it to its former glory.

'That's good to see,' beamed Mari.

'What? The worker?' Lucas asked.

'Oui. The crew weren't due to return to work until tomorrow.'

'Tomorrow?' Lucas took another look at the worker. 'Do you leave the chateau unlocked?'

'The site manager has a set.'

'After what happened to your dad, I think it would be wise to take some precautions from now on.'

Mari gave Lucas a stern look, which quickly softened as she nodded in agreement and turned to her driver. 'Ask who sent him here today, Jean-Michael.'

'Oui, Madame,' the driver said. He approached the contractor, and after a momentary discussion, returned to his employer. 'He says Giles sent him. They'll be sanding tomorrow, so he wanted the painting done, so it's dry when they start.'

'Giles Lapidge is the site manager,' Mari explained to Lucas and Natasha.

'All the same, I still suggest you practise caution from now on. Just to be on the safe side.'

Mari was distraught. 'For the rest of my life?'

'No, I wouldn't have thought so,' Natasha assured her. 'They're trying to stop us from finding the artefact. We just have to complete our objective and find it before they can complete theirs.'

'We're literally in a race,' said Lucas, 'and the stakes couldn't be higher. If we lose, we're dead.'

'Then we had better not fail,' Mari said. Without another word, she walked off, leaving Natasha and Lucas to follow in her wake. 'One of the first areas that my father had renovated and modernised was his private study.'

'Sounds like as good a place as any to begin our search,' Natasha commented.

They walked along a wide, high-ceilinged hallway, the numerous discoloured spaces where many portraits once hung, now removed for safekeeping during the renovations, gave a glimpse of how impressive the space could be.

Soon they stopped before a set of double doors, detailed with intricate and delicate panelling. Natasha could immediately tell that this section of the chateau was a seventeenth century addition. Mari grasped the golden doorknobs and pulled them open.

Inside, the study was decidedly modern. Clean lines, glass and metallic, with a few paintings here and there and a packed bookshelf to add warmth to the space. You'd be forgiven for thinking that you were in a city office and not a chateau on the outskirts of Nice.

'That's quite a makeover,' admitted Natasha, doing her level best to keep her face neutral. She was sure a building such as this would be protected, Grade II listed, so that any work undertaken would be sympathetic to the existing building. But then, money can be quite persuasive.

'I assume he's got a safe in here?' Lucas asked as he glanced around.

'Oui, he does,' Mari replied. She walked over to a large oil painting of a girl walking through a field of marigolds. 'He always loved these flowers.'

Natasha could see the resemblance of the girl. 'Is that you?'

Mari nodded. 'It was painted from a photo he took during a family vacation to Mexico. It's regarded as the flower of the dead there. But how can something with such vibrant colours be just for the dead?'

After a moment remembering that day as a child, Mari lightly slid her a finger down the right-hand edge of the painting. There was a low hum as a mechanism came to life, and the piece of art slowly descended to reveal Henri Laval's safe. It was incredibly plain looking, gunmetal grey with nothing on it but an oblong slot half an inch wide. Natasha thought it was nothing more than a metal block until Lucas pointed something out.

'There's a square panel here,' he said, slowly running his fingers over the surface.

Natasha couldn't see it, but he was the one that used to be a thief, so she took his word for it. 'Is that a keyhole?'

Lucas was shining the light from his phone into the slot. 'I don't know,' he replied and turned to Mari. 'Is it?'

'To be honest, I never saw my father open it. I only discovered it recently after his—' She took a moment to compose herself. 'It reminded me so much of him I tried to take it down. That's when I found the hidden switch.'

Whilst Mari spoke, Lucas inspected the hole. He held his hand over the hole, furrowed his brow as he looked at his finger covered it. 'The ring?' he breathed.

'What was that?' Natasha asked.

'The ring Laval gave you,' he said. 'I think the ring goes in this slot.'

'It would explain why that phoney police detective was asking about it,' replied Natasha. She pulled Henri Laval's ring from a pocket of her cargo pants and handed it to Lucas, under the gaze of Mari. 'I kept hold of it to protect you. If the people are asking about the ring, it must mean that they know what it is.'

Mari smiled and nodded. 'I understand.'

Lucas placed the ring up to the slot. 'Here goes nothing,' he said and pushed the band inside.

Chapter 15

The ring slipped perfectly into the slot until it was halfway ensconced within the cavity. Streams of a bright light inside leaked out, and Lucas pulled his hand away as the ring began to rotate. When it stopped, the square panel Lucas had identified flipped down.

'It's a thumbprint reader,' Lucas revealed to the two women after closer inspection.

'Thumbprint? My father's? How will we get in now?'

Lucas shrugged.

'Find my flower. She is the key,' Natasha said softly, thinking out loud. 'It's you Mari. It's your thumbprint.'

'Why would it be when he had no interest in showing me anything?'

'Perhaps he did. Perhaps someone murdered him before he could.'

'There's only one way to be sure,' Lucas said, stepping aside to allow Mari access to the safe.

Mari looked at Lucas, then at Natasha, who urged her on. The young French socialite anxiously rubbed her thumb before she tentatively placed it on the reader. Her thumbprint was scanned. A moment later, there was a faint click as the safe was unlocked.

'You were right,' Mari said. 'He *did* want me to follow him.'

'Of course he did,' Natasha said. 'Now let's hope we can find out something from the documents he had. Something that will tell us where to go next.'

Lucas reached inside the safe and took out everything, placing them on the desk. All three of them looked down at the documents in their protective sleeves like swooping predators.

'Does anyone else feel like Christmas has come early, or is that just me?' Natasha asked, glancing at Lucas and Mari, neither one of whom responded. 'I guess it's just me then. Fine.'

'Look,' Lucas said. He'd picked up one of the sleeves, taken out its contents and unfolded it on the table.

'The map,' Natasha whispered. 'It's the same landscape, isn't it?' She fumbled in her bag and retrieved the parchment she'd found in Valencia, laying them side by side.

'Exactly the same,' breathed Mari.

'Let's hope not,' Lucas said and explained himself when he saw the confusion on the young French woman's face. 'The map we got from Spain doesn't have any writing on it, whereas the first map we saw did.'

'That's how we knew we had to go to Valencia,' Natasha said.

Mari looked at her father's map again. 'But this one doesn't have any writing on it, either. Nothing except that black cross on the back.'

Natasha took out the pocket watch from her bag and, after having a quick look herself, handed Mari the opened pocket watch and smiled. 'Take another look at it with this.'

Mari received the timepiece, giving it a sceptical look, before she brought it up to her eye. 'Mon Dieu!

"The vault was located deep in the heart of the mountain, and the only way to access it was through a narrow passageway that required an alert mind and a steady hand. Inside, the air was musty and damp, and the only light came from a few flickering torches hanging from the walls. The walls of the vault were lined with cloth, and the floor was covered with a thick layer of dust. The only thing that seemed out of place was a small table in the centre of the room, upon which sat a mysterious elixir. The liquid glimmered in the dim light, and it seemed to radiate an energy that was almost palpable. The dawn was just breaking as they entered the vault, and the light filtering through the narrow opening in the ceiling was just enough to see by. They approached the table cautiously, and as they drew closer, they could see that the elixir was contained in a small canvas bag. The bag was made of sturdy material and looked as if it had been crafted with care. The iron clasp was still secured, and the bag seemed to be in excellent condition. They opened the bag, and to their surprise, the elixir was still ample and had not evaporated."

What does it mean?'

'It's the same passage as the other map,' Lucas said.

'It is,' agreed Natasha as she took the lens back from Mari. 'But the capitalised letters are different. T, H, A, R, G, E, C, A.' She continued looking over the rest of the map and found more writing in the corner. 'It's another riddle, just like on Tony's.

"Amidst history's embrace, a voyage takes hold,
Through eras of might, where legends were bold.
Follow the clues, like stars in the night,
To a city of splendours, a beacon of light.
Amongst timeless ruins, whispers of fame,
Reveal a civilisation that earned its acclaim.
From maritime prowess to trade's vibrant chore,
Achievements aplenty, forever galore.
Ingenious minds and a warrior's art,
Their legacy etched, a masterpiece of heart.
Unlock the secrets, let curiosity guide,
To a place where greatness and echoes reside."

If it's like the other one, then this riddle is a clue to the anagram.'

'But that riddle could be describing anywhere in the world,' Mari said.

Lucas saw the familiar look of concentration on Natasha's face and reassured the French socialite. 'It could be, but give Nat enough time, and she'll figure it out. In the meantime, let's have a look at these.' He picked up the first letter. It was in German, but beneath it was a copy translated into French, which Henri Laval had commissioned.

Date: October 17, 1938

To: The Fuhrer

From: H. Himmler

Subject: Unearthed Artefacts and Discovery

I hope this report finds you well and in good health. I am writing to apprise you of a remarkable discovery made during our routine patrol near the Czechoslovakian border. As part of our duties, my unit and I came across an intriguing find that demands your attention.

While inspecting the woodland areas next to our camp, I stumbled upon an ancient wooden chest partially buried underground. Upon careful examination, the chest revealed an assortment of antiquities, including an aged map, a series of letters written in old French, and an enigmatic relic, securely wrapped in delicate fabric.

Intrigued by this unexpected discovery, I enlisted the help of a local villager who possesses some knowledge of ancient texts. Together, we unravelled the historical significance of these artefacts. We traced the letters back to the period of the Albigensian Crusade, a time marked by religious conflict and persecution in the Languedoc region of France.

These letters narrate the escape of a Cathar, a member of a religious group with distinct beliefs, who sought refuge from the Crusaders' persecution in the rugged Pyrenees. The relic in question appears to hold deep significance to their faith and was carried by the brave Cathar on his journey.

What sets this discovery apart is the connection between these ancient letters and the Livonian Order, the military order located far to the northeast of Europe. The exact nature of this link remains a mystery, and they warrant further investigation to comprehend its implications fully.

Considering the uncertain political climate and the potential value of these artefacts, I have taken it upon myself to safeguard them discreetly. My primary concern is to avoid attracting unnecessary attention and ensure the security of our soldiers and the items in question.

While I am eager to share this significant finding with you, I must exercise caution until the situation stabilises. I am aware of the sensitive nature of such discoveries, and I trust that my judgement aligns with our commitment to our mission and the procurement of historical assets.

I humbly request your guidance on the best course of action moving forward. If deemed appropriate, I shall make arrangements to transport these artefacts to a secure location until a proper evaluation can take place.

Your wisdom and expertise in such matters are invaluable, and I eagerly await your directive.

Respectfully,

Heinrich Himmler

SS-Obergruppenführer

'Bloody hell,' Lucas said, running his eyes over the page again. 'A letter from Himmler to Hitler. I guess Hitler himself must have been here at some point. And these other letters are the ones Himmler mentioned?' Lucas asked as he glanced at the other documents.

'Oui,' Mari replied with a nod. 'I know father had them all checked for authenticity and translated.'

'It's Carthage,' Natasha blurted out as Lucas reached for another letter. 'The anagram is Carthage.'

'You mean Tunisia,' Mari corrected. 'Even I know it stopped being called that centuries ago.'

'Yes, but there is still an area in Tunisia called Carthage, along with a tonne of archaeological sites. That's where it's telling us to go, I'm sure of it.'

Suddenly, a voice came from the doorway. A voice that was all too familiar to Natasha as that of the Italian.

'Tunisia is wonderful this time of year,' he said. 'Unfortunately, none of you will get to experience it.'

'How dare you come in here?' Mari said to the restoration worker. 'Get back to your duties immediately.'

'Remember we said that there would be other people looking for these maps?' Lucas asked. 'Well, this is one of them.'

'He's an agent of the Entity,' revealed Natasha, looking at him sternly. 'A spy of the Catholic Church.'

'Not only that.' The Italian saw Lucas edging towards him and took a handgun from the pocket of his overalls, and pointed it at them, stopping Lucas in his tracks, and prompting them all to put their hands up. 'I am God's chosen assassin, and it is my sworn duty to eliminate all and any who have seen these maps.'

'Tony.'

'He was never going to escape me. And when I am done with the three of you, I will take care of your green-haired friend at your hotel.'

'Don't you touch her,' growled Lucas as he took a step toward their assailant.

'Get back,' the Italian said and aimed the gun at Lucas's face. He had no other course of action but to comply. 'Good. Now step back and you,' he indicated Natasha, 'give me Laval's documents.'

Natasha deliberately reacted slowly. She had no intention of making this any easier for him, especially when she caught sight of movement behind the gunman. Unfortunately, Mari wasn't as discrete, and the Italian's eyes narrowed as he caught her glancing over his shoulder.

He turned just as the driver grabbed his wrist. The gun went off.

Chapter 16

Lucas pulled Natasha down to the floor as she grabbed Laval's documents. Mari dived clear of the wayward bullet. It slammed into the wall inches above where her head had been. They fired more shots as Mari's driver, Jean-Michael, wrestled with the Vatican agent.

'Come on,' Lucas said to his companions. 'Now's our chance to get out of here.'

As they rushed past the two men, the Italian saw them, and not wanting the trio to get away, he quickly despatched Jean-Michael with a knee, an elbow and a judo throw. Two bullets from his gun put the driver down permanently.

Mari had no time to mourn the loss of her employee. Another two bullets from the Italian's gun splintered the door frame at the same moment they were running out of the double doors.

The pursuit continued along the wide corridor, the three of them desperate to make their escape. Bullets were whizzing past them, the accuracy from their would-be assassin severely compromised by the motion of running.

They reached the front door of the chateau and Lucas wrenched them open, only to immediately slam them closed once more.

'Bollocks!'

'What is it?' Natasha asked.

'We need another way out of here, Mari.'

'Nearest one is through the kitchen, but why?'

'It appears the other people that want the map are here too,' Lucas revealed and hurriedly grabbed the two women.

'What other people?' Mari quizzed. 'You didn't mention that there were other people.'

'The Bilderberg Inner Circle?' Natasha speculated.

They had taken only a few steps away from the door, in the direction of the kitchen, when they heard the Italian accent of the Vatican agent behind them. 'Stop right there,' he said, his gun pointed steadily at them. 'Enough running. All you have done is prolong the inevitable.'

He aimed the pistol squarely at Lucas. Being the most dangerous of the three, eliminating him first made perfect sense. It was exactly what Lucas himself would have done if the shoe were on the other foot.

Lucas's glare at the Vatican assassin was unwavering in the face of imminent death. It was met by the Italian's own coldness, who smirked as his finger slowly squeezed the trigger of his handgun.

Suddenly, there was an explosion. Fragments of the door, along with plumes of smoke, blasted into the hallway. The unexpected detonation sent the occupants inside the chateau crashing to the ground. The Italian's handgun slid across the stone tiles as two masked men breached the destroyed doorway, each of them brandishing a Heckler and Koch MP5 sub-machine gun.

They trained their guns on them, making sure that none of their targets moved an inch, especially the Vatican agent who had been reaching for his gun. With everybody safely covered, one of the intruders made a gesture with his hand, and four more armed and masked men entered. Once in position, they stood aside to allow Chiara Harris to saunter through them to stand before her victims in a pose which conveyed her power, hands behind her back, feet slightly apart.

'Well, well, well,' Chiara said. 'Isn't this nice? The ex and the ex's ex all together again.'

'I wish I could say it was nice to see you again,' Lucas said. 'But we both know that'd be bollocks.'

'Say what you like, Lucas. We both know that you get a twinge of desire whenever you see me. I can see it in your eyes.'

'That's not desire. That's a longing to see you dead.'

'Or see me in your bed? You know that you and me together make so much more sense than you and her,' Chiara said, throwing a disdainful gesture at Natasha.

'Is that really what you think?' Natasha said, getting in Chiara's face. This prompted the terrorist leaders' men to focus their guns on the archaeologist, stopping their advance when their leader held up her hand as Natasha continued. 'You want to know what I think? The way you're willing to use your sexuality at the behest of a psychopath makes you nothing more than Angela Redmond's bitch. I can't even call you a prostitute, because at least they get paid for what they do. You do it for free.'

The corner of Chiara's left eye twitched and her top lip curled in anger as she took a step towards Natasha, her fists balled up, ready for the second round of their fight. 'You just can't keep your mouth shut, can you?' She grabbed Natasha's bag and roughly pulled it off her, handing it to one of the terrorists. 'I'm going to enjoy shutting it once and for all,' she snarled.

As Chiara drew back a fist, there was the sudden bang from a gun. The force of the bullet threw one of the J Organisation terrorists back. There was a momentary pause as time stood still, people looking around to figure out what was going on, then all hell broke loose.

Another terrorist was taken out by the Vatican agent, who had used the cover of Natasha and Chiara's confrontation to retrieve his gun. The remaining terrorists levelled their MP5's, and let loose a barrage of gunfire, but he was already on the move.

Natasha attempted to wrench her bag from the hands of the half-distracted Chiara, but the terrorist leader had just enough wherewithal to tighten her grip at the last second.

With machine gun fire ringing out around them, a tug of war ensued between the two women. Their continuing competition, fuelled by their hatred for one another, ensued once more.

'Keep your head down,' Lucas yelled at the hysterical Mari. The terrorists had scattered once the shooting had begun, taking up defensive positions, and leaving an opening as he hurriedly escorted the socialite clear of the chaos and out through the half destroyed front door.

Mari shuddered. 'Are there any other people after these maps that I should be made aware of?'

'Bilderberg...Vatican...nope I think that's it. But don't take that as gospel,' Lucas chuckled.

Mari frowned. 'This isn't the time for jokes. My life is in jeopardy.'

'Fine. Check those SUVs. See if any of them have the keys inside and get it started,' Lucas replied. 'I'm going to get Nat.'

'SUVs?' Mari pouted, looking over at the vehicles.

Lucas cautiously returned to the doorway. A couple of wayward shots prompted Lucas to duck as they further damaged the remaining door, showering him with chips of wood. The hallway of the Laval Chateau continued to be redecorated with bullet holes from the exchange of gunfire between the Vatican agent and the J Organisation. And in amongst it all, Lucas saw Natasha still wrestling with Chiara for the bag of maps and documents.

'Bloody hell,' he muttered, shaking his head. 'They're as bad as each other.' At the first opportunity, he grabbed Natasha and pulled her towards him. The extra pulling strength proved too much for Chiara to resist. But the bag gave out before she did. The strap ripped, scattering the contents across the floor.

Both women scrambled to recover the precious documents, eager to get one over the other, totally ignoring the dangerous arena their feud was playing out in. However, it was plainly obvious to Lucas as the firefight continued to rage on around them. The masonry became more pockmarked by bullets with each passing moment. Debris fell in clouds of dust, then a nearby terrorist of the J Organisation collapsed beside Lucas, with two bullet holes in his chest.

That was all the convincing the adventurer needed to let him know that they'd outstayed their welcome. 'Come on, Nat, we're getting out of here.'

'What? No! Not without the maps,' Natasha yelled.

Lucas ignored her protestations and pulled her towards the exit. A barrage of bullets peppered the wall where she had just been. But the lucky escape didn't deter her. She continued to struggle in Lucas's grip until she saw a gleeful Chiara pick up the scattered maps uncontested.

With Natasha's resistance diminished, and despite her obvious disappointment, she allowed Lucas to lead the way out of Chateau Laval. They ran out through the destroyed doors and into freedom. Or so Lucas had hoped, before he saw Mari Laval behind the wheel of a yellow sports car.

'What the hell is this? I told you to check the SUVs, Mari.'

'This is my Rimac Nevera,' she replied proudly. 'An electric hyper-car, because Mari Laval cannot be seen in a petrol car. Do you know anything about the brutality of cancel culture?'

'No. But I know about the brutality of bullets and permanently being cancelled. Now move over.'

'Do you know the streets of Nice? Yeah, I didn't think so. So get in.'

Natasha was already at the passenger side, opening the door, when Lucas joined her. His annoyance at the choice of car was compounded when he saw the seats.

'A bloody two seater? Of course it is!'

'Just get in,' Natasha urged. 'I'll sit in your lap. I'm sure that'll keep you quiet.' As soon as the car-door was closed, the vehicle leapt forward with a whirr.

Chapter 17

The streets of Nice hummed with the evening bustle as Mari, strapped into the electric embrace of a Rimac Nevera, surged through the serpentine roads. The sleek, aerodynamic car hugged the corners with a precision that seemed almost surreal amidst the city's maze of alleys.

Natasha and Lucas were both impressed with the socialite's driving prowess.

'Oh, this is nothing,' she admitted, her eyes fix on the road ahead. 'You should see me around Monaco.'

In the rearview mirror, three menacing SUVs roared to life, spewing gravel and determination in their wake. Each vehicle had tinted windows, but Mari could imagine each car bristled with armed antagonists, their faces twisted with determination not to fail Chiara's orders.

The Nevera's electric whirr intensified as the socialite deftly manoeuvred through the labyrinth of streets, the high-performance vehicle responding to every flick of the steering wheel. The sound of gunfire erupted, shattering the afternoon's calm as bullets pinged against the Nevera's carbon fibre panels, leaving spiderweb cracks but falling to breach its resilience.

Narrow escapes and adrenaline-pumping close calls became the norm as the chase escalated. Mari surprised her passengers with how skilfully she navigated tight turns and narrow passages, exploiting the Rimac's unparalleled acceleration to evade the pursuing behemoths.

Sparks flew as the SUVs scraped against ancient stone walls; their drivers relentless in their pursuit.

'How are we going to get away?' Natasha asked, looking over her shoulder at the black vehicles bearing down on them.

'I've been wondering the same thing,' Lucas replied as they thundered towards the shimmering lights of the harbour. Lucas's mind raced, searching for an escape route. 'Waitaminute. You have a yacht, don't you, Mari?' A daring plan formed – a gamble on the open waters.

'It's a Millennium 140 super yacht, actually, but yes, I do.'

'Good! Get the crew to it prep for Tunisia.'

Mari immediately used the Bluetooth connection in her car to call the captain and make the arrangements.

'You sure, Lucas?' Natasha asked. 'What about your thalassophobia?'

'I'll cope. I'll stay in the cabin and try to sleep through it.'

With the harbour in sight, Mari unleashed the full power of the Rimac, thrusting them back in their seats and hurtling towards the awaiting vessel.

The SUVs likewise sped up, their drivers determined to prevent their prey from reaching their salvation. But the Nevera surged ahead, weaving through traffic with a balletic grace, defying the limitations of traditional cars. The Rimac's electric propulsion roared, a symphony of speed and technology pushing it to its limits.

With a last burst of acceleration, they headed for the entrance of the quay. As Mari stepped on the brakes, Lucas wrench the steering wheel. The Nevera skidded to a halt, blocking the way to the pontoon.

'Everybody out!' yelled Lucas.

Without missing a beat, the three of them leaped from the car, through the driver's side, and sprinted across the quay. The yacht awaited out at sea like a beacon of hope amidst the chaos, its sleek lines lapped by the gentle waves.

The terrorists, now in a last-ditch effort, weren't about to give up just yet. Their SUVs screeched to a halt next to the abandoned electric car. They clambered over the vehicle, continuing their chase, shooting at the escapees.

Bullets whizzed through the air, splashing into the water as Natasha, Lucas and Mari, hearts racing with the exhilaration of their escape, jumped into the waiting speedboat. The engine roared to life at the first time of asking, and the vessel pulled away from the dock, speeding towards the yacht, leaving their frustrated pursuers behind.

• • • •

THE FOUR MEMBERS OF the J Organisation terrorist group made their way back to their SUVs. Deciding between them who would be the one to tell Chiara Harris that Travers and Redmond had escaped; she took unwelcome news exactly as her late brother, Baron Harris had...badly. None of them were willing to accept the task.

They needn't have worried.

Seconds after arriving at Mari Laval's Rimac Nevera, they saw the dead body of their comrade thrown from the passenger side of the third SUV. Before they had time to comprehend what was happening, Gianpaolo jumped out of the driver's side of the vehicle and swiftly despatched the four men with an equal amount of shots from his silenced pistol.

A quick scan of the area left Gianpaolo confident that his actions had not been witnessed. With a slight smile of satisfaction, he sat back in the stolen SUV and made a phone call.

'Your eminence, I have the maps.'

'Praise be to God,' enthused Cardinal Elias Wagner. 'We can always rely on you, my son. And what of Natasha Travers and Lucas Redmond?'

'Unfortunately, she deciphered the location of the last map before I got them. They are on their way to Tunisia as we speak, but I will be on a plane within the hour, waiting for them. They will be eliminated soon.'

The other end of the line went silent.

'Your eminence?'

'I am here, Gianpaolo.'

'Do not worry about Travers and Redmond, your eminence. By God's grace, I will eliminate them soon.'

'That's just it, my child. Things at the Vatican have taken a turn, and I have been thinking things over. I believe a change of plan is in order.'

• • • •

NATASHA ENTERED THE cabin she and Lucas had been given and found him doing press-ups on the floor. She watched him for a moment, taking in his form from head to toe. 'How are you feeling?' She asked eventually, breaking the spell.

'I'm fine,' Lucas replied as he finished his final set. He stood up to see that Natasha was holding a drink out to him, which he gratefully accepted. 'Keeping my mind distracted has been a big help. And covering up the portholes too, so I'm good, hon. How's our host?'

Natasha shrugged. 'Taking everything in her stride, surprisingly. Mari says there's little difference between being chased by gunmen and paparazzi. Nothing's fazed her. She's up on deck now, sunning herself.'

'I guess the life of a socialite is tougher than we think,' he commented. 'How much longer before we dock?'

'Not long. An hour or so.'

'And what's the plan when we get there? Where do we start?'

'I've been able to get hold of an archaeologist friend, Khalid. He lives in Tunisia and has been excavating ancient Carthage. He's been kind enough to offer us a roof over our heads too.'

'Do you trust him?'

'What's that supposed to mean?'

Lucas finished his drink and put the empty glass aside before he looked pointedly at Natasha. 'This isn't an ordinary quest we're on, Nat.'

'Is it ever?'

'Well, no,' he agreed. 'But this one could have far-reaching implications. Just look at the people after us.'

The Bilderberg Inner Circle, bent on world domination for the rich and influential. The lives of humanity were nothing but pawns in the grand plans. And then there was the Entity, the Vatican spy network. They seemed determined to stop anybody from finding the grail, to the point of killing anybody that came into contact with the maps.

After Natasha's reflection, she sat next to Lucas on the bed. 'Okay, I see what you're saying, but we can trust Khalid. Do you remember Anan?'

'From your Nineveh dig? Of course I do.'

'All three of us worked together sometimes. And they had a bit of an on and off again fling. What I'm saying is that he's one of us. He would have been at that Nineveh excavation if he wasn't already tied up with his work at Carthage.'

'I hope you're right. Because I doubt either of those groups has thrown in the towel just yet, and we'll be bringing a whole load of crap to dump on his doorstep. Does he know what he's getting himself involved in?'

'Well, not exactly,' she said evasively. 'I just told him we were going to be in town and that we needed to check out Carthage a bit.'

'It's probably for the best, really. We don't want him getting anymore involved than is necessary. For his own safety.'

Natasha's brow creased. Although she hadn't told Khalid exactly why they were coming to Tunisia, she had every intention of telling him once they had arrived. Trouble often seemed to find her and Lucas on these quests. They expected things to go awry from time to time. But it wasn't right to put her friend in jeopardy, especially without his knowledge.

'I'm going to tell him as soon as we arrive.'

'Yeah, like I didn't already know you were going to do that.'

Natasha smiled at him. 'You know me too well.'

'That's why I love you, baby.'

'And you have just enough time to show me how much,' she said, leaning towards him, a mischievous glint in her eye. Although the chase and shootout had been several hours ago, Natasha's blood was still raised. 'And it'll be a much better distraction from your thalassophobia than doing press-ups.'

Chapter 18

As the sun dipped below the horizon, casting hues of amber and lavender across the Tunisian sky, Mari Laval's super-yacht, The Violet Rose, glided gracefully to a stop, a beacon of opulence against the fading daylight. The gentle lapping of waves provided a rhythmic accompaniment to the vessel's arrival.

On the deck, Natasha Travers, bathed in the warm glow of the setting sun, stood pensively, her eyes fixed on the ancient city. The juxtaposition of the contemporary yacht against the historical backdrop seemed even more pronounced in the fading light.

Amidst the quiet of the evening, the archaeologist smiled, reflecting on Tunisia's ancient maritime legacy. It was easy for her to imagine the great Carthaginian warships which would have departed here to partake in the Punic wars, many never to return. Her thoughts mingled with the whispers of the sea breeze, creating a moment where past and present combined.

'You look like you're a million miles away,' Lucas whispered behind her.

Her smile broadened at the comment. 'More like two millennia ago,' she replied. 'Carthage was once a great maritime empire —'

'Until the Romans copied their ship designs and defeated them. I *do* listen to you, you know,' he smiled, wrapping his arms around her waist.

'I know you do,' she replied as she put her hands over his. 'You can just imagine the hustle and bustle of the port back then.'

Lucas looked at the marina in the distance. 'I'm sure it would have been no more than it is now.'

'Are you kidding me? Multiply this by a hundred and you might just be getting close. Sea routes were the great artery of the period and Carthage controlled vast amounts of it.'

Lucas could hear the giddy excitement in Natasha's voice. It was infectious. 'Do you miss it?'

'Miss what?'

'Being a traditional archaeologist. Going to exploratory digs in historical places like this. Not being shot at.'

'You seem to forget that I was a traditional archaeologist when I was being shot at by Baron and his terrorist group. And the answer is no, I don't miss it, because I still do it. It's just with a lot fewer committees to appease. I mean, if I was still working with the university, they would never have let me go on this grail quest. They would have called it a fool's errand.'

'It still could be, for all we know.'

'I don't think so. The Vatican wouldn't get so involved if it was all for nothing.'

'Then why didn't they search for the grail themselves? They obviously knew about the maps, possibly even about the letters Laval had.'

'I'm sure they knew about the letters. But they were hidden, remember? They weren't found until the Nazi invasion. And as for the maps, they probably didn't know where to look for them. If it wasn't for Tony, we'd be in the same boat as them.' She felt him stiffen at the mention of his friend. 'I'm sure he'll be fine, baby,' Natasha said in a way of comfort.

'Awww, look at the lovebirds,' Mari said, suddenly joining the pair. 'Are you two ready to go ashore, or do you want some more alone time in your cabin?'

Natasha blushed at the thought that someone might have heard her and Lucas earlier.

'We're good to go whenever you're ready,' Lucas said.

'Good. We'll be taking the speedboat into the marina. You sure your friend will be there, Natasha?'

'Of course he will. Don't worry about Khalid.'

• • • •

AS THE SPEEDBOAT FROM the Violet Rose pulled up to one of the pontoons of the Sidi Bou Said marina, its occupants could see an excited, bearded man, wearing a Kufi cap and waving his arms over his head, a beaming smile on his face.

'I assume that's our man,' Lucas said with a chuckle.

'Same old Khalid,' Natasha said jovially, shaking her head as she jumped out of the boat and ran to hug her old friend.

'Natasha Travers! It is so good to see you again after all these years, my friend.'

'And you as well. You look good.'

'Not nearly as well as you. Despite what Anan tells me.'

'And what does Anan tell you?' Natasha asked with a raised eyebrow.

'Not as much as I'd like, to be honest,' he shrugged. 'Just that you seem to dodge bullets more than actually digging for things.'

'That's about right,' Lucas said before adding, 'I can't actually remember the last time I saw you with one of those little brushes in your hand, hon.'

'And you must be Lucas,' Khalid said, extending his hand. 'Anan has had much to say about you, too. Enough to make me wonder if you two had a fling.'

'What?'

'Yes. She knew a lot of details about you. Things like —'

'And this is Mari Laval,' Natasha interrupted, steering her friend towards the French girl, ignoring the glare Lucas was giving her.

'Very pleased to meet you. Now, if you'd all follow me, my car is just over here. I'll take you to my home, where I have some food ready if you're hungry. And you can tell me what you're really here for.'

• • • •

IT WASN'T LONG BEFORE they arrived at the home of Khalid. The charming town of Sidi Bou Said reminded Natasha of some of the Greek island towns with its cobbled streets and distinctive blue-and-white houses. People greeted Khalid as they passed. The older community appreciated his efforts to bring a spotlight onto their history-rich city.

Khalid led them through to the kitchen, passing photographs of him on different digs holding various artefacts. There were also pictures from his university days where Lucas noticed a decidedly fresh-faced Natasha. In the dining room, a pot of chorba, a soup of chicken, parsley, celery and lemon juice, with the famous short pasta called "bird tongues", was warmed up on the stove. Meaty keftas and baklava for dessert were already on the table waiting to be devoured.

After allowing his guests to have a few mouthfuls of soup, Khalid asked the question that had been burning in his mind. 'So why have you come to Carthage?'

Natasha swallowed the tasty meatball in her mouth. 'We're looking for a map,' she revealed.

'A map? You must be joking. I've been excavating here for the last eighteen months and we have found nothing like that. Trinkets, pottery remains and some beautiful swords. But precious little written documents.'

'It would probably be well hidden.'

Khalid was still unconvinced. 'What is it a map to, anyway?'

She smiled at him with a glint in her eye. 'It's a map to the holy grail.'

The spoonful of soup Khalid had been bringing up to his mouth paused as he eyed Natasha. '*The* holy grail?'

'Possibly,' Lucas corrected.

Khalid put the spoon in his mouth, only to find that its contents had already spilled out. 'If it is the grail, it would be a huge find. Probably the biggest of all time. What makes you think it's here, though?'

'We found one which sent us to Valencia. Then we found one in Nice which sent us here, to Carthage. Are you sure you haven't found any scrolls at all?' Natasha implored.

'None. I have found nothing that would even suggest...' Khalid stopped short as he made a recollection. 'There is something, actually.'

'What is it?' Natasha asked excitedly.

'That bit of graffiti, near Bursa Hill. I thought nothing of it until now, that is.'

'Of course!' Natasha said, almost jumping out of her seat. 'It was discovered in 197 C.E. around the same time as some of canonical gospels,' she explained, seeing Lucas's confused look.

'Graffiti? That's not exactly what we're looking for,' Lucas said.

'No, no. But it could be a marker,' explained Natasha. 'It shows a figure with donkey ears and a hoof carrying a book and wrapped in a toga.'

'Sounds like an entrance to a confused shop selling donkeys.' Mari yawned, swiftly losing interest.

Khalid took up the baton and continued the explanation. 'The accompanying inscription reads "the god of the Christians is a donkey who beds with his worshippers."'

'You might be on to something, Khalid,' said Natasha.

'You cannot be serious,' said the shocked French woman.

'I'm actually with Mari on this one, baby,' admitted Lucas.

'That's because you've both been duped by the great Pauline con,' Khalid said with a roll of his eyes.

Natasha smirked and shook her head. She knew exactly what sermon was about to be delivered.

'Don't worry, Natasha. I'll keep it short,' he assured her.

'Please do. I'd like to get to Bursa Hill early in the morning, so we could all do with a good night's sleep.'

'Relax, Natasha. Once they hear the facts, they will have no recourse but to believe.'

'I doubt that,' Mari replied.

'Would I be right in saying you are Catholic?' Khalid asked Mari.

'Yes. What of it?'

'Because they are the biggest perpetrators of the Joshua lie.'

'Joshua?' Lucas queried. 'I thought we were talking about Jesus?'

'We are. Joshua was his real name, or Yeshua, if you want his proper Hebrew name. Paul the apostle popularised Christianity. We can all agree with that, yes?'

Mari nodded. Lucas shrugged.

'A man who was not one of the twelve chosen disciples. A man who never met Jesus during his lifetime. A man who actually helped the Romans persecute followers of Yeshua's early ministry. Surely, if you're going to listen to someone preaching the word of the messiah, it would be better to come from someone that had firsthand knowledge of his teachings.'

'Mary Magdalene?' Lucas offered.

'I'll get to that,' smiled Khalid.

'A vision of the risen Jesus came to him while he was travelling the road to Damascus,' recounted Mari. 'How is it any different to angels teaching the illiterate Mohammed to pen the Quran?'

'Because, as you said, illiterate or not, the prophet Mohammed penned it. Not a bystander.'

Mari scoffed. 'Despite what you say, Paul's teachings resonated with people, or his Christianity wouldn't have become the dominant religion.'

'Because he sold it that way to the gentiles. In Leviticus there are six hundred and thirteen commandments. But if you were told that you only needed to follow ten specific ones, wouldn't you be more interested? And even more so as an adult man when you are told that you don't need to be circumcised to be part of this new movement?'

'An easier way to worship God,' Lucas thought out loud.

'Exactly. And to make it even easier for many of the gentiles, the Pauline Jesus shared many characteristics with the Greek, Helios, the Roman, Sol Invictus, and the Iranian, Mithras traditions. To compound it all, the historical Yeshua has all but been erased by the Pauline version, to the point we gloss over what we read with our own eyes.'

'What do you mean?' Mari asked.

'Christians would have you believe Yeshua was unmarried. In that age, such a thing was unlikely for a Torah following Hebrew man, as it would bring shame to the family. Not only that, but the Bible itself depicts his wedding.'

Chapter 19

The rays of the morning sun filled the streets of Sidi Bou Said with its golden glow. Just as Natasha had wanted, the party was setting off for Byrsa Hill at the crack of dawn. Last night she had stopped Khalid before he could really get into the swing of his diatribe against Christianity and their cover up of the historical Jesus. To her, getting to the site was far more important than him sharing his views on the religion.

The maps were gone. They were in the hands of their rivals now. Whose hands? She didn't know, but in this situation, the Entity was just as bad as the J Organisation. The hope that they didn't have the means or know how to read the hidden text on the maps was the only saving grace Natasha could cling on to. It was an advantage which she aimed to make the most of.

They climbed into Khalid's Mercedes and headed off. The drive from Sidi Bou Said to Byrsa Hill was a journey which took them through just a small portion of the captivating landscapes and historical surroundings Tunisia offered. Departing from the charming blue-and-white adorned streets of the town, their route along the coastline, offered glimpses of the azure Mediterranean Sea. Eventually, they joined a road which took them through Carthage, where the remnants of the ancient civilisation echoed in the form of ruins and archaeological sites.

'Are you going to finish your explanation from last night?' Mari asked from the back seat.

'About the wedding in Cana? You're familiar with the story, yes?'

'It's where Jesus turned water into wine,' answered Mari.

'Correct. After his mother told him that the wine had run out. Now, I assume you've been to a wedding as a guest?'

She nodded.

'And tell me, as a guest at that wedding, was it your responsibility to replenish the wine? Wouldn't that be the duty of the bridegroom? And look at the size of the wedding. It was no ordinary get together.'

'The size? It doesn't mention that in the gospel.'

'But we archaeologists can figure it out. Isn't that right, Natasha? Tell them about the vassals.'

She smiled thinly and nodded, not really wanting to get involved with Khalid's games.

'Come on,' Khalid urged. 'I promise to stop after this.'

'Fine,' Natasha sighed. 'The stone vassals of that period held between four-hundred and fifty and five-hundred and fifty litres of wine.'

Lucas's eyebrows shot up. 'That's a lot of booze.'

'Enough to get at least twenty-thousand people inebriated. That's the kind of numbers you would expect at the wedding of a king, right? The King of the Jews, perhaps.'

Mari was about to make a comment, but thought better of it, glancing out of the window instead.

'And another one sees the light,' Khalid said.

They soon arrived at their destination. After parking the dusty classic Mercedes, the group ascended on foot up the hill, and were greeted by an awe-inspiring panoramic view, revealing the sprawling city below and the majestic sea stretching into the horizon.

Natasha shielded her eyes from the sun as she gazed at the natural beauty and historical richness Tunisia offered. 'I can see why you enjoy working here, Khalid. It's beautiful.'

'If you want to swap expeditions, I would be more than happy to oblige,' Khalid said with a bow. 'After all, is it not right that a religious person should discover a religious find of this import?'

'But who are we to question the divine plans of the Almighty?' Natasha retorted.

Khalid nodded slowly in agreement. 'Then I'd better show you the piece of graffiti.'

He guided them through the ancient ruins of the former walled citadel, with Lucas on more than one occasion pulling Natasha away from other cultural points of interest within the site.

'Here it is,' Khalid finally announced, presenting a section of wall to them.

Her eyes lit up with glee as a smile slowly broke across Natasha's face. She stepped forward, her gaze darting over the image before her, a figure with donkey ears and a hoof carrying a book and wrapped in a toga. She read the inscription, written in Phoenician, out loud. '"The god of the Christians is a donkey who beds with his worshippers." That's not entirely true, of course, it was just the one.'

'Are you sure about this one, Nat?' Lucas asked, as he scrutinised the image dubiously.

'How many gods of the Christians do you know?'

He shrugged. 'Okay, on that basis, I suppose it is him. Still hard to get my head around though, and *I* wasn't brought up in a religious household.'

'Well, it shouldn't be. All the biblical prophets before Jesus were married, and as we know, he was brought up following Torah law, and one of the most important mitzvah is, be fruitful and multiply. The idea he was happily married is as normal as any of us doing the same.'

Lucas nodded along, seeing the sense in Natasha's statement.

Mari, on the other hand, was aghast. 'A donkey? You must be joking.'

'Don't take offence, Mari. Didn't he ride into Jerusalem on the back of a donkey?'

'Yes, fulfilling Zechariah's prophecy.'

'This was obviously done by a satirist, the Hogarth of the day, if you will. Jesus was a well-known political figure, an activist. The same thing happens to similar people today.'

'If this really is a marker of some sort,' Lucas deliberated, bringing them back to the reason why they were there in the first place. 'What do we do now?'

'Let's start by going over the riddle again,' she replied.

Lucas took out his phone and played the recording he'd made of Natasha.

"Amidst history's embrace, a voyage takes hold,
Through eras of might, where legends were bold.
Follow the clues, like stars in the night,
To a city of splendours, a beacon of light.
Amongst timeless ruins, whispers of fame,
Reveal a civilisation that earned its acclaim.

From maritime prowess to trade's vibrant chore,
Achievements aplenty, forever galore.
Ingenious minds and a warrior's art,
Their legacy etched, a masterpiece of heart.
Unlock the secrets, let curiosity guide,
To a place where greatness and echoes reside."

'Follow the clues, like stars in the night,' Khalid softly repeated.

'Does that mean something to you?' Lucas asked.

'Over here,' the archaeologist answered. He hurried further along the wall, scanning along its length until he found what he was looking for. A cluster of seven small cavities, one inch in diameter. 'We believe that, once upon a time, these may have held precious stones of some kind. Even without the gems, you should still be able to recognise it, Nat.'

Lucas answered before Natasha could. 'It's the Pleiades star cluster.' He continued when he saw the astonished looks on the other's faces. 'The Tuareg have a saying. When the Pleiades fall, I wake looking for my goatskin bag to drink. When the Pleiades rise, I wake looking for clothes to wear.'

'Cute,' Mari said, trying to find some shade. 'But what does that mean?'

'When the Pleiades go down with the sunset on the west, it means the hot, dry summer is coming. When they rise from the east with sunrise, the cold and rainy season is coming.'

'And it's not just the Tuareg nomads that use the constellation like that,' Natasha added. 'For the Mediterranean's, the rising of Pleiades heralded the start of the sailing season.'

'We have found other stars too,' Khalid revealed.

'That's all well and good, but how does that help us? Stay out here any longer and I will need another coat of sunscreen.'

Natasha rolled her eyes at Mari's comment. She had to admit, the girl had a point, though. This find on its own didn't help them. But there must be a connection. 'Pleiades. Pleiades.' She said the name over and over, twisting a loose curl of her hair, hoping that the answer would show itself to her. She paused and her eyes widened.

'You figured it out, haven't you?' Lucas smiled, recognising the signs.

'These other star constellations, was Orion among them?' Natasha asked Khalid.

'Yes, it was,' he replied. 'It's over by the remains of the amphitheatre.'

'Good! Then let's follow the stars,' Natasha grinned with excitement. The sense of achievement Natasha got from solving a clue, pushing her one step further along a quest, proving her problem-solving abilities, was just as thrilling to her as finding the artefact itself.

'Are you going to share some of your wisdom with us, hon?' asked Lucas as they quickly made their way to the Carthage amphitheatre.

'In mythology, the Pleiades were seven nymphs, companions of Artemis, and daughters of Atlas. Orion was a giant and also a hunting partner of Artemis. He had vowed to hunt down every living creature on earth. That included the Pleiades. He chased them for seven years until Zeus intervened and put them among the stars. Now remember what Khalid said about certain pagan deities being a substitute for

Jesus? The same was done to Mary the Magdalene. The goddess Artemis was associated with her,' explained Natasha.

Lucas let out a scoff of disbelief.

'You have to know that Magdala, the town Mary was from, was a region in Galilee which had a significant population of gentiles, or non-Jews,' explained Khalid. 'Her being linked with Artemis would not have been a stretch for them.'

'But to my knowledge, there isn't a constellation of Artemis,' said Lucas.

'Correct,' Natasha agreed. 'But the constellation of Orion was created when Artemis made a plea to Zeus. The Pleiades lead to Orion. Orion leads to Artemis.'

'And Artemis leads to Mary,' Lucas finished.

'Exactly. All the hidden messages were known by the early Christians.'

The Carthage amphitheatre was well-preserved with visible remnants of its original design. As the party came to a halt, they gazed in awe at the elliptical layout, typical of Roman amphitheatres. Before them lay a partially restored Roman structure, with sections of the outer walls and seating still standing. It was even possible to explore the tiers of seating surrounding the central arena. And, as Khalid pointed out, they could all see that each section of seating had a constellation at the front of them.

'Impressive,' breathed Natasha, as they slowly walked around the archaeological site.

'And there's Orion,' Mari squealed, pointing at the constellation a little further ahead of them. Before the others could question the socialite about her surprising astrological knowledge, she was already making her way towards the archway beneath the tier seating, only to find the way blocked by a gate.

'This area was explored over a century ago,' Khalid said. 'Nothing of importance was discovered here, so they gated and left it. We had not planned on reopening it.'

'Well,' smiled Natasha with her hands on her hips. 'I think it would be a good time to reopen it. They didn't know what to look for back then. But *we* do.'

Chapter 20

The rusty, sand-aged gate squeaked loudly, as it protested at being opened for the first time in almost one-hundred-and-fifty years. While Khalid had been attending to the entrance, Lucas had pulled out a couple of MAGlite MAG-TAC LED flashlights from his bag. After checking that they were both in working order, he handed one to Natasha.

'You ready?' Lucas asked, looking into Natasha's eyes.

'As ever,' she replied.

He smiled at her response. 'Of course you are. Okay, then I'll take the lead and—'

'Uh-uh. I think I should take the lead. You don't know what to look for.'

'Do you?'

'No, but I'm better equipped to notice anything poignant.'

'Yes, you are,' Lucas said with a slow, appreciative nod.

'Lucas. Focus.'

'I am.'

'On the mission, I meant.'

'If you two are quite finished,' interrupted Mari. 'This adventure isn't fun anymore. Just looking in there gives me the shivers.'

'Then perhaps you should stay here,' Natasha said.

Lucas rubbed his chin. 'That's actually not a bad idea. Fewer the people, fewer the risks.'

'If you remember the way, you could wait for us in my car,' Khalid said, handing Mari his car keys.

'At least someone knows how to look after me,' she pouted. 'The two of you should take note.'

'I don't even remember inviting her along,' commented Lucas as they watched the socialite disappearing into the distance.

'Me neither,' Natasha agreed. She shrugged and continued. 'Maybe things would be easier if we stopped picking up strays on these things.'

'We'll have to test that theory out one day, hon,' Lucas replied. He straightened the strap of his bag, then spun the flashlight in his hand as if he were a gunslinger. 'But first, let's find this map.'

• • • •

NATASHA SLOWLY SWEPT her MAGLite from left to right. Several times, to clear the way, she had to run her hand through layers of cobwebs, built up over the decades of no human contact. Occasionally, she'd catch a glimpse of something scurrying away to escape the light. It kept her on edge, especially as Khalid's warnings about the possibility of vipers, cobras and scorpions taking shelter in the tunnel rang in her ears. She was doubly glad that Mari had stayed behind; she could just imagine the screams if the socialite tagged along.

Their LED lights cast long shadows along the passageway, and they frequently cleared their throats in the musty air as their footsteps kicked up dust. Despite the likelihood of the fungus Aspergillus being low, she still had to be vigilant.

All the same, Natasha hard a tough time keeping her thoughts on the task at hand. Her mind kept circling back to what Khalid had said. Should someone with little faith in religious institutes really be the discoverer of such an important religious relic?

'I can understand where he's coming from,' Natasha mumbled to herself, 'but archaeology isn't like that. If it *was*, Egyptians would have rediscovered Tutankhamun and Machu Picchu, by Peruvians.'

'What was that?' Lucas questioned.

'Nothing. Just thinking out loud,' she replied, before returning to her thoughts. 'If I wasn't meant to find it, I wouldn't be here or something would have stopped me.'

'Is everything alright?' Asked Lucas when Natasha came to a sudden stop, causing him to bump into her.

'There's a stone wall up ahead,' she responded in confusion. The light from her torch shone down the passage to prove her point.

Khalid stepped forward, shaking his head. 'I guess they were right to gate off this section. There's nothing here. What now? We try another one?'

She shook her head. 'Not unless there's another tunnel with the Orion constellation. This has to be it.'

Khalid, unconvinced, shrugged and stood to the side.

'Then there must be a clue here,' Lucas declared. He passed his MAGLite over the wall and could discern scrapings in it. 'Look, more graffiti.'

'There's quite a bit, isn't there?' Natasha noticed. 'They read like the curses we saw in Bath. Here's one asking the goddess Artemis to make a gladiator named Marius, not be able to kill any bear he encounters. And here's an interesting one. "May the rod of he that carried my Libia away from me become as liquid, and..."'

'And what?' Lucas pressed when Natasha's voice trailed off to silence.

Natasha quickly flicked her torch to the side. Out of the corner of her eye, she had glimpsed something written nearby, and illuminated the worn scratches on the wall. She smiled. 'Aramaic.'

'The language spoken at the time of Jesus,' Lucas stated.

'Yes, exactly.'

Khalid, his eyes wide in wonderment at the find, took a step closer. 'What does it say?'

'Not a lot, really,' answered Natasha. She put her hand to her chin and pondered. 'All it says is "left".' After a moment, she swivelled around to face the left-hand brick wall, blinding Khalid in the torchlight in the process. 'Could it be that simple?'

Khalid moved aside as Lucas turned and brought his own torch up to bear on the brick wall. He meticulously examined each of the Roman bricks, slowly working his way further and further back along the passage. 'I don't think there's anything here,' he eventually said.

'Nothing?'

'Nope. A few scratchings in Latin. Something which looks like the zodiac sign for Pisces, but nothing in Aramaic.'

'The fishes,' Natasha and Khalid said in unison.

'Okay. The fishes. What about them?' Lucas asked.

'The fishes were a sign of Yeshua's ministry. One to represent the wisdom of Yeshua and one to represent the wisdom of Solomon.'

'Or more than likely, to represent Mary the Magdalene,' Natasha added.

'But why fish?' Lucas asked.

'Well, Yeshua fed five-thousand people with fish, and a fish swallowed Solomon's ring of power when God punished him,' explained Khalid.

'And,' Natasha took up the explanation, 'we know Mary came from a rich family in Galilee. They produced salted fish.'

'Considering what we've learned about Jesus and Mary, the latter makes more logical sense,' replied Lucas. He made his way back to the brick he had seen with the fish symbols, and with the MAGLite held between his teeth, gave it a more vigorous inspection.

With the sensitive, nimble fingers of a man who was once a renowned master thief, Lucas deftly ran his fingers over the brick. He slowed his search when it came to the edge of the hardened block of clay. Natasha and Khalid watched on tentatively, both edging forward when they heard Lucas let out a thoughtful sound as he pondered over something.

'What is it?' Khalid asked, exhaling deeply, only now realising he'd been holding his breath.

Lucas removed the MAGLite from his mouth. 'This brick isn't a brick.'

Natasha flicked a glance from the brick to Lucas. 'What do you mean?'

Instead of replying, Lucas fished his hand inside his bag and rummaged around until he found what he was looking for, his pouch of lock picks. He took out a tool suitable for the job at hand, one that resembled a dentist's scaler. Lucas had discovered that there was a slight gap between the brick and the wall. He scrapped it along the underside of the brick.

He slowly smiled as he felt the tip of the instrument sink into an ever so slight recess. With a determined expression, and by applying a little pressure, Lucas heard the barely audible click of the hidden catch release. 'I got it,' he said triumphantly, as he felt a faint tremor of excitement. After packing away his lock picks and returning them to his bag, he lifted the front of the ancient stone.

'Incredible,' breathed Khalid, acknowledging that the air hung heavy with the weight of centuries-old secrets.

Natasha watched with bated breath, her eyes wide, heart pounding in anticipation.

Lucas peered into the cavities' darkness, before bringing up his MAGLite. A shiver ran down Lucas's spine as he stumbled backward, his torchlight flickering wildly as it cast erratic shadows around them.

'What is it?' Natasha whispered, her voice barely audible over the pounding of her heart. She rushed to his side, her expression a mix of concern and curiosity as she scanned the darkness for any sign of danger.

Lucas's eyes widened in horror as he pointed his torch towards the recently opened space. 'Scorpions,' he gasped, his voice tinged with fear.

With growing dread, Natasha and Khalid followed Lucas's gaze, the torchlight revealing a cluster of fat-tailed scorpions emerging from the shadows. Their glistening exoskeletons glinted in the flickering light as they skittered out of the hole and across the stone floor, their venomous stingers poised to strike.

Adrenaline surged through the adventurers as they frantically searched for a means of escape. With nowhere to run and the scorpions closing in, they knew they had only moments to act.

'Back to the entrance!' Khalid shouted, his voice echoing through the chamber as he grabbed Natasha's hand, pulling her towards the passage.

Lucas followed close behind, his heart pounding in his chest as he fought to keep the swarm of scorpions at bay with his bag. With every step, the creatures grew bolder, their venomous stingers lashing out in a deadly dance.

Just as they reached the entrance, a scorpion lunged forward, its stinger inches from Natasha's exposed ankle. With lightning-fast reflexes, Lucas swung his bag, swatting the deadly creature away.

With a final push, the adventurers burst into the open air, their hearts racing as they stumbled into the blinding sunlight. Behind them, the scorpions rushed out of the shadows, like a blanket leaving the depths of the ancient cavern.

Suddenly, the scorpions exploded in gunfire. The intrepid adventurers instinctively ducked to avoid being shot.

Once the shooting had stopped and as they caught their breath, Lucas, Natasha, and Khalid exchanged weary smiles.

Though they had narrowly escaped the clutches of the ancient trap, something just as nefarious faced them.

Before them stood the Italian, his left hand gripped around Mari Laval's neck. With his right hand, he pointed his Glock at them. 'No more running,' he said in his accented voice. 'Give me the map, or I give you Laval's corpse.'

Chapter 21

Natasha and Lucas looked at Gianpaolo with a steely glare as they raised their hands. She had hoped they'd seen the last of the Vatican spy, but that truly had been wishful thinking. 'How did he find us?' she whispered to Lucas. 'They didn't have the lens. How could they read the invisible text on the map?'

'I don't think he did,' Lucas replied in a hushed tone. 'I think he was probably outside the door when you read it out.'

'You know this man?' Khalid asked.

'He's with the Entity,' explained Natasha.

'You are kidding me?' He looked over at the well dressed, spectacled man with awe and a significant amount of trepidation.

'Are you going to give me what I want, or do I have to prove that I do not bluff?'

Mari struggled when she heard him, but he tightened his grip on her throat. 'Now let's all just calm down, shall we? They'll give you the map. Won't you, Natasha?'

'I wouldn't make promises if I were you, Mari,' the adventurer said cautiously.

Gianpaolo pushed the gun barrel against the socialite's head.

Mari swallowed hard, her pulse quickening. 'What do you mean? Just give him the damn map.'

'We don't have the map,' Lucas said, his eyes firmly set on the Italian.

'Wait!' Natasha shouted, as Gianpaolo moved the gun to the back of Mari's head. 'We don't have it, because we haven't looked properly. You saw those scorpions.'

'Then I guess we all go and get it together,' Gianpaolo responded.

'Well, I don't see why I have to go,' whinged Mari. 'I was sitting in the car, minding my own business, because I didn't want to go into that dusty hole in the first place.'

'Now we *all* go in together,' he reiterated, and waved them on with his gun hand.

The captured adventurers slowly headed back across the amphitheatre towards the Orion marked tunnel. 'Can we at least put our hands down?' Natasha asked.

'Of course. You'll need them to hand over the map when you find it.'

Natasha gave him a wry smile. If it were just her and Lucas, they might have devised an escape plan of some sort, but they had Khalid and Mari to think about. She could see the worry on her friend's face, and knew it would ten times worse on that of the socialite. It wouldn't be fair to put their lives at risk in a foolhardy plan. Natasha just hoped Lucas was of the same mind. She glanced over at him, to see if there was any glimmer of what he was thinking, but before she could gather info, Khalid bent close to her.

'If this is how things are like being you, Natasha, I think I will stick with the more conventional side of archaeology. I don't think my heart could cope with this kind of adrenaline rush.'

'You get used to it,' shrugged Natasha.

'I'd rather not, in all fairness.'

In a short while, they'd returned to the scorpion trap. Lucas held the others back whilst he cautiously shone his flashlight inside, checking it was clear. 'It's empty,' he said over his shoulder and continued his inspection. 'There seems to be some sort of handle in here.'

Before Natasha could offer any words of warning, Lucas had already reached an arm into the cavity. It was a tight fit for his thick, muscular arm, but his fingers soon felt the object he had seen. 'It feels like wood,' he reported back. 'But it's not a handle. It's more like a lever.'

'A wooden lever?' Khalid clarified. 'Untouched after all these years? It is probably rotten, and the mechanism it once operated, useless.'

Suddenly, they all heard a heavy clunk and the sound of gears moving as Lucas pulled the lever. 'Sounds alright to me,' he grinned, getting to his feet.

'Look,' Natasha exclaimed. She shone her torch ahead as she walked towards the wall at the end of the passage. It was sliding aside. Her heartbeat quickened with every inch that was revealed. 'This walkway continues on further,' she gasped.

Eager to see exactly what was beyond, Natasha squeezed past the moving wall. The two sides of the portal were a far cry from each other. One side displayed the typical impressive work of Roman engineers, the side where Natasha now stood was the complete opposite. She slowly passed her hand over the rough-hewn walls. It was older than the entrance walls, she surmised. How much older she couldn't tell, but further down the passage, there was something that gave Natasha a hint.

'Khalid,' she called. 'Come here and have a look at this.'

The Tunisian archaeologist glanced quickly at their captor, almost as if asking for permission, before he tentatively passed the now fully open doorway to join Natasha. 'What is it? What have you found?'

'This,' she said, shining her torch on a particular area of the wall.

He bent his head closer to the crude engraving, adjusting his glasses as he did so. 'Is that supposed to be the Minoan snake goddess?'

'That's what I'm thinking,' Natasha agreed.

'But the Minoans died out hundreds of years before Carthage was established.'

'Yes, but who's to say that some had not settled here among the Phoenicians?'

'Trust you to get excited about finding a historical piece of erotic art, Nat,' Lucas said, looking at the image of a bare-breasted woman holding a snake in each hand.

'It's not erotic art, Lucas,' she replied with a sigh. 'This goddess is often identified with Astarte, the Phoenician goddess of fertility and sexuality. But more importantly for us, she was also associated with Athena.'

'Ah ha,' Lucas said. 'And Athena was associated with Mary the Magdalene. Therefore, we're in the right place.'

'Exactly,' Natasha said, dusting her hands off on her pants. 'We're in the right place?'

'Good. That means I can expect to have the map in my hands soon. Doesn't it?' The Italian said.

Natasha, in the excitement, had all but forgotten he was there and looked at him with scorn. 'You'll get what's coming to you. Don't you worry about that.'

'Empty threats won't find the map,' he replied and waved them on with his gun.

Reluctantly, the adventurers continued on. They knew they had to bide their time, hoping that an opportunity would present itself. And when it did, they'd have to be ready to take advantage of it.

The group continued onwards, following the passage as it meandered left and right. They passed hints of pre-Phoenician use of the tunnel, pieces of Minoan pottery, bits of a brazier, others of an oil burner. Khalid made frequent comments, wishing that he was able to properly document the finds they were having to leave behind on the archaeological site instead of having to rush ever forward.

That sentiment of displeasure soon vanished when they came upon a foreboding chamber adorned with statues of serpents. There were a vast number of intact Minoan artefacts. Various decorative elements, reliefs, frescoes, and painted decorations adorned the walls, depicting scenes from mythology, religious rituals, or the lives of the gods.

'It's a temple,' Khalid said with glee. 'A Minoan temple in the country that would become Carthage. This is a wonderful discovery.'

Lucas glanced over at Natasha. He knew her well enough to know that ordinarily she would be jumping up and down by now, but she was still examining the items around the room. 'What is it?' Lucas asked. 'Isn't this a temple?'

'This is some sort of storeroom,' said Natasha, voicing her thoughts. 'Probably part of a temple complex, yes. These offerings of precious metals, jewellery, textiles, and other valuable items would suggest they're dedicated to the gods and used to adorn the sacred space or support the maintenance of the temple.'

'I feel a "but" coming,' said Lucas.

'But I think this temple was repurposed. Sure, some of these artefacts are definitely Minoan, but some of them are from a much later date.'

'What are you talking about?' Khalid scoffed.

Natasha flipped two coins over to her former classmate. 'I found these. They no doubt spilled out of a larger tribute collection that was hurriedly spirited away.'

'Is that...?'

'Yes. Herod Antipas,' Natasha stated.

'And the other...?'

'Pontius Pilate.'

'What a minute,' Lucas jumped in. 'The Jewish ruler of Galilee and the governor of Roman Judea. That can't be a coincidence. But they're historical figures from the Common Era, hundreds of years after the collapse of the Minoans, and ancient Carthage, for that matter. So how did the coins end up here?'

'Like I said, it's probably a repurposed temple.'

'To become what? A Christian church?'

'Well, no,' she shook her head. 'Paul the apostle wouldn't begin those until the fifties, and both Pilate and Antipas were out of power by 39CE. Coins depicting their faces would have been uncirculated by then. So the coins would have been brought here when they were still in office. I would presume between 33 and 39CE.'

'That is the period directly after the death of Jesus.' Khalid scratched his beard as he finally caught up with Natasha's thinking. 'Are you suggesting that this is a temple to Mary?'

'Not to Mary herself, but to her ministry. A direct continuation of the ministry of her husband, Jesus. We already know from the Bible itself that the other disciples would often turn to Mary for an explanation of his teachings, so it makes perfect sense she would be the one to spread his doctrine.' Natasha lost herself in her explanation and unravelled her entire sphere of thought, almost as if talking out loud to herself. It was the reason why Lucas said she should steer clear of public speaking, because she tended to go off on a tangent, especially when it was a subject she was passionate about.

'We know Mary was on the run from the Roman authorities, just as the disciples were. But she was wanted even more so because of their children. So she ran, heading west with Joseph of Arimathea and the aunts of Jesus. The reach of the Roman Empire was long, hence all the cloak and dagger, clandestine activity i.e. the symbols, and hidden messages, the association with certain gods and goddesses. It had to be done in secret, literally underground. She likely preached the word of God here. Sharing the teachings of Jesus just as he had taught her.'

A reverent silence prevailed as everyone took in the significance of where they stood. Almost everyone. Gianpaolo, unlike the rest, was enraged.

'Enough of this blasphemous talk. Have you forgotten why we are here? Find me the map or you'll all become a permanent feature here. Do you understand, Natasha Travers? In fact,' he continued, 'I think you need some incentive, so you know I am not to be toyed with. And I only need one archaeologist.'

In one motion, without so much as a flinch, the Vatican spy raised his gun and fired. The bullet struck Khalid square in the stomach.

Chapter 22

A searing pain erupted in Khalid's abdomen as he dropped to the ground. The shock of the impact sent a jolt of agonising sensation coursing through his body, overwhelming Khalid's senses with an intensity that was impossible to ignore. Natasha rushed to the side of her friend, and immediately pressed her hands hard on the wound, desperate to stem the flow of blood. Khalid groaned in agony at the action, his pain-filled eyes falling on Natasha's.

'Don't worry, Khalid,' Natasha said with a forced smile. 'You'll be fine. You'll make it out of this.'

'When did you become so good at lying?' he replied through laboured breaths. 'I can feel the blood seeping down my side.'

'Don't worry about it,' she said, desperately trying to blink back her tears as she pressed harder against the bullet hole.

'Do you remember,' he said slowly, 'the fun-times we had back at Cambridge?'

Natasha chuckled. 'Of course I do. How could I forget your on-off romance with Anan?'

Khalid tried to laugh, but it was cut short by a wave of excruciating agony which rippled through his body from his wounded abdomen. Every breath became a struggle for Khalid. A profound sense of vulnerability suddenly came over him. 'Is this the end? It's getting cold. I don't want to go, Natasha.'

She gazed up at Lucas with pleading eyes. He gently shook his head in answer to her unasked question. There was nothing he could do. To punctuate the point, Lucas tried to pull Natasha away, but she refused to move. With surprising strength, Khalid suddenly grabbed her arm and pulled her towards him.

'You cannot give them the grail,' he whispered. 'It belongs to the world.' He let her go and sank back to the ground, his last bit of energy ebbing away as he gasped. 'At least I am to die in a revered place. Tell Anan I'll always love her.'

'You can tell her yourself,' Natasha said desperately. 'We'll get you out of here. Just hold on, Khalid. Khalid?' There was no answer. With her eyes red and tears streaming down her face, Natasha shot around to glare at their captor. 'You bastard. You didn't have to do that.'

'I beg to differ,' the Italian replied. 'You needed to be reminded of who exactly is in charge of this situation.'

'You'll pay for this,' she said through gritted teeth. She took a step towards the Vatican spy, her bloody fists clenched.

'Uh-uh,' he said, pointing his gun at her.

'You won't shoot me. You need me to find the map.'

He moved his arm over and aimed the gun at Lucas's face. 'But I don't need him. And now you know I don't make empty threats, I think you should get on with your task, signorina Travers.'

Veins stood up in her arms as her clenched fists shook. It was only Lucas's calming touch that stopped the distraught adventurer from doing something rash.

Lucas kissed her tenderly on the cheek before whispering words of encouragement to her. 'Be patient, baby. He's made a mistake, and he doesn't even know it yet. We just need to play the game and bide our time.'

It took a few moments for his words to penetrate through the rage Natasha was harbouring. But eventually they did. Her arms relaxed, tension released from her shoulders, and her fists unclenched. 'Fine,' she grimaced. 'I'll do it. I'll find the map.'

'Of course you will,' the Italian said with a smile. 'Your sense of the unknown wouldn't allow you to do anything else. Now, shall we continue?'

Natasha swallowed down her resurfacing anger and turned away from the Italian. The more space between herself and him, the better. With a heavy heart, and through trembling lips, she offered a final sorrow filled prayer for Khalid before turning her attention back to the chamber.

It took Natasha several moments for the vacant look on her face to recede and to get her mind back into gear after the murder of her friend. Slowly, she recollected exactly where they were, beneath the Carthage amphitheatre in a chamber which Mary the Magdalene might have stood in herself. 'So,' she said, taking a deep breath before examining her surroundings once more, 'if this is in fact the storage room of a temple, then there must be some way through to the temple itself. It's just a matter of finding where it is.'

'What are you looking for?' Lucas asked when he saw Natasha's head turn this way and that.

'I'm looking for some sort of clue that might indicate where I should concentrate my efforts, and where a hidden door might be.'

'Okay, cool,' he replied as he joined her search.

With the two of them searching, it wasn't long before Natasha noticed something. There were a lot of items stacked up, lining the walls around the chamber. All except one section. There were a cursory number of hemp baskets in front of it. Easily movable, Natasha thought. And they were. She slid them aside to get better access to the wall.

Natasha's assumptions had been correct. After passing her hands over the wall, she finally found that the wall could be pushed. Lucas joined her, seeing her struggling, and with his added strength, managed to push through the revolving wall.

'This probably hasn't been opened for centuries,' Natasha said as they both panted with the effort. After clearing her throat and waving away the plumes of dust and debris from her face, she shone her flashlight into the newly revealed room.

Natasha felt goosebumps on the back of her neck. Her mouth fell open slightly as she processed what she was seeing; a melancholy but hauntingly beautiful sight. The once vibrant frescoes that adorned the walls were faded, and barely discernible, with only faint traces of colour remaining. 'Amazing,' she breathed. She took a few steps closer and carefully dusted off the layers of grime and decay. 'These would have been brightly coloured,' she said. 'They'd depict scenes of Minoan mythology, probably religious rituals too.'

Lucas was a couple of steps behind Natasha, listening to what she was saying whilst scanning the rest of the newly opened area. Magnificent columns and pillars that supported the temple's interior were a shell of their former selves, having crumbled or collapsed over time, leaving behind scattered fragments of stone and rubble. In between the columns were snake statues similar to the ones they had seen before. On closer inspection, Lucas saw something of interest. The snake's head seemed to have what looked like a hinged jaw.

'Hey Nat, you should check this out. I think the snake statue's mouth opens.' He reached out a hand to test his theory, just as she was finishing up inspecting one of the pillars.

Small bits of stone suddenly came trickling down, bouncing off the statue and Lucas. He shone his torch upward to see what was causing it and saw a large stone block topple from the peak of the column. 'Natasha, move!'

She turned to Lucas, the look of a startled deer on her face. Then she felt his powerful hands shove her backwards, through the doorway and out of the path of the enormous block as it crashed to the ground. The force of its landing not only shook the terrain beneath their feet, but shook a column opposite enough to cause it to shed its top two blocks. Lucas dived clear as the several tonnes of rock smashed down, blocking his way out, and separating him from the others.

He cleared his throat of the dust the collapse had brought up, then he could hear Natasha calling him. 'I'm alright,' Lucas shouted back. 'What about you?'

'I'm fine,' she replied, then scowled at the Italian. 'I'd rather be on your side of this rubble if I'm being honest, though. You don't see any way back through, do you?'

'No, not without explosives,' he coughed. 'It's stacked pretty tight here.'

'Yeah, same here,' she responded, tapping the stone obstruction.

'Let me see if anything has opened higher up...uh oh.'

'Uh oh? What do you mean, uh oh?'

'Well, I was taking a step back to get a better view. Turns out the tiles between the statues are pressure-sensitive plates. Oh, and the snake head statues on the perimeter of this row of tiles? Their mouths opened and some sort of gas is being released from them.'

'Lucas!' Natasha said, with her fists on her hips. 'That's an important bit of information you should lead with. It could be poison gas for all we know.'

'I don't think so,' he replied.

'How do you know?'

'I took it flush in the face. The mouths closed as soon as I stepped off.'

'Damn it, Lucas.' Her concern for the ex-special forces soldier escalated when she didn't hear him respond. 'Lucas?'

'I'm here, I'm here,' he said to reassure her. 'I was just checking the tile that I stood on. It has an image of some sort.'

'An image? Of what?'

'Of this snake goddess, and it's not the only one. There are different ones too.'

'Hmm,' Natasha said, suddenly intrigued. 'Do all the tiles have them?'

'Actually, no. Just the ones flanked by the snake statues.'

'Interesting. Then we have to assume that these are the ones that set off the vapour release.'

'So I just have to hop over those then.'

'I wouldn't do that.' The words had barely left Natasha's lips when she heard Lucas's grunt of exertion.

'Bollocks!' Lucas shouted as he jumped back, and in so doing reset the serpent statues.

'What's going on in there?'

'It seems like the rows without the statues set off all snakes. As soon as I landed, the jaws of all the snake statues opened. They're releasing wispy vapours into the air.'

'It must be getting quite misty in there.' Natasha said, doing her best to hide her concern. 'How are you feeling?'

'Pretty good, actually.'

'Can you still see what's at the end of the parade of snakes and columns?'

'Nothing. It's just a blank wall, a dead end.'

'I thought so, but I don't think it is just a dead end. I think it's the way to the temple proper and the altar where the map should be.'

The Entity spy had remained silent, listening to the exchange, until he heard what he was waiting for. 'You are sure that is where the map is hidden, signorina Travers?'

'No. You can always speculate, follow the clues, read the signs, decipher the ancient codes, but in all fairness, there could be just another clue inside. We won't know until we get in. Or until Lucas does, I mean.'

'I hope it *is* in there,' Mari added. 'I'm not as comfortable with this dusty, tunnel rat look as you are, Natasha.'

She rolled her eyes and turned back to the doorway, wishing with all her heart that she was on the other side of it. 'Okay, Lucas. We're going to get through this together. All I need you to do is describe to me what you see on the tiles.'

'No problem,' he replied. Just as Lucas was preparing to tell Natasha, something caught his attention. 'Whoa!'

'What is it?'

'Everything is so vivid here,' he said, his voice decidedly slower than it had been moments ago. 'Wow! Look at that. I can see the stars, the Milky Way, contained in my body. I am the universe.'

'Bollocks,' Natasha breathed under her breath.

'Problem?' the Italian asked.

'Those vapours sound like they're some sort of hallucinogen.'

'I've had plenty of good times on hallucinogens,' Mari chimed in.

'I'm sure you have, but the more he's exposed to these gases, the more chance he has of developing serotonin syndrome, excessive serotonin levels in the brain. We need to get him out of there fast.'

It took Natasha several attempts to get to Lucas to concentrate on the description of the tiles, but eventually she had the information. 'Each step on a plate triggers a corresponding serpent statue to release the gas,' she said, thinking out loud. She continued as she twiddled a loose strand of her curly hair around her finger. 'The challenge is to avoid stepping on the wrong plates while unlocking the safe path through the gauntlet. The symbols on the tiles seem to correspond to the ones I saw on the wall. They tell a story of the serpent deity and its journey through trials, providing cryptic clues about the sequence of plates that are safe to tread. It must be like the Bayeux Tapestry; we just need to follow the scenes. This should be easy,' she concluded.

'So what now?' Lucas asked.

'You said there was an image of her moving a tree? That's was on the wall too. That must be the first tile.'

Natasha imagined Lucas confidently taking a step forward. And waited anxiously for the result.

'It didn't work,' Lucas yelled.

'What do you mean?'

'I mean, as soon as my weight was on the plate, there was a click and the snake's jaws dropped and hissed more vapours into the chamber.'

'Damn it! I don't under...wait a minute,' realisation suddenly striking her in mid thought. 'Since this is a repurposed temple, then it stands to reason that these tiles would be repurposed as well. The illustrations should be a visual narrative of Mary Magdalene's transformative journey from a woman plagued by demons to a devoted disciple, wife and messenger of the resurrection. The first tile is the one with the seven snakes coming from her body.'

Lucas followed her instruction. 'That's it! It worked. You cracked the code. What's the next one?'

The smiles on the faces of the three people on the other side of the wall each told their own distinct story. Natasha's was one of triumph, having conquered yet another puzzle. She saw the Italian smile too, no doubt thinking that he would soon have another map in his grasp, making the secret of the holy grail remain just that, a secret. Natasha noticed that Mari's smile came with a sigh of relief.

Once Natasha knew what to look for, the sequence of the path to spiritual enlightenment was straightforward. She just had to find the ones which captured the essence of Mary's story and the themes of her redemption and faith.

After the first tile, an illustration of Mary receiving healing from Jesus and depicting the moment she was freed from the possession of seven demons. The next was as The Follower: an image of Mary following Jesus, symbolising her devotion and commitment to his teachings, as well as her role as one of his closest disciples.

Next was Mary as the Witness: an illustration of Mary witnessing the crucifixion of Jesus, highlighting her unwavering presence during his darkest hour and her role as a witness to his sacrifice. Then came the Empty Tomb, depicting Mary Magdalene discovering the empty tomb of Jesus, symbolising her pivotal role as the first witness to the resurrection and bearer of the good news. Which was followed by the Messenger tile, illustrating Mary Magdalene proclaiming the resurrection to the disciples, symbolising her role as the apostle to the apostles and her pivotal role in spreading the message of Jesus' resurrection.

'I can't go on anymore,' Lucas suddenly shouted.

'Why not? There's only a few more to go, you said.'

'It's the snakes. They told me not to go any further.'

'The snakes?' Mari asked.

'It's the hallucinogen,' Natasha reassured her, and turned her attention back to Lucas, raising her voice so that he could hear her at the back of the chamber. 'Don't listen to them.'

'They say a woman of no faith will never find what you seek.'

'He is on to something there,' sneered the Italian.

'Yet here I am doing what you don't have the ability to do yourself,' she stated firmly. 'Look, Lucas baby, concentrate for me. What's on the next row of tiles?'

The following three rows depicted the stages of Mary, which resonated with the followers of her creed. The Penitent, showing Mary the Magdalene kneeling in penitence, representing her story as a repentant sinner who found forgiveness and redemption through her encounter with Jesus. The second tile was as the Teacher, illustrating Mary teaching and sharing her insights with others, symbolising her role as a teacher and spiritual leader of Christ's ministry. The Mystical Vision was the third one and depicted the Magdalene's mystical experiences and visions, highlighting her deep spirituality and mystical connection to the divine.

With each new revelation signifying the importance of Mary the Magdalene, Natasha could see the Italian bristle. 'What's wrong with you? Is it a tough pill to swallow knowing that your religious leaders marginalised a woman who was a significant player in the early church?'

'The church is never wrong.'

'Oh? Is that why they backtracked about her being a prostitute?'

'A decision to appease people such as you. It doesn't change the sanctity of the book or the message it spreads. We are not stuck in medieval times, as in other religions. We are progressive.'

'And you believe that bull?'

'I do not have to. My job is to protect the church, not its numbers.'

'Even if it means hiding the truth?'

Before an answer came, Lucas hollered, bringing Natasha's attention back to the last row of tiles to be traversed. 'I think this mist is getting to me. I'm feeling nauseous and lightheaded.'

Natasha listened intently. He was beginning to display symptoms of serotonin syndrome. She still had time, but it was fast running out. 'We'll get you out of there, baby. I promise. Don't worry about it. Describe the last row of tile images to me and I'll have you out of there in no time.'

'We're beings of light, Natasha,' Lucas replied. 'I'm not worried at all. I feel a connection to something greater than us, a profound sense of unity with the universe, and I know that I'll always be there to protect you.'

'It's my turn to protect you now, Lucas, so concentrate and tell me what you see on the ground.'

Lucas took a few moments to gather himself. He tried to will the vivid visual hallucinations, the patterns, colours, and shapes that were dancing before his eyes out of existence. 'The first tile is blank,' he finally declared.

Natasha concentrated, barely able to hear him through the enormous stone blocks. 'Blank?' She repeated, confused.

'The next one has the snake goddess on a pathway. Another has her crossing a bridge and the final one has her kneeling at a castle or it could be a palace.'

Natasha's look of confusion deepened. 'None of these stand out as representing the story or themes of Mary's life.' The archaeologist walked back and forth as she tried to figure out what the final set of images meant, so she could get Lucas out of the hallucinogenic vapours.

She wracked her brain for anything that she might have read which would lead her to one tile or the other. But nothing was forthcoming. 'What about the castle?' she murmured. 'She was known as the Magdalene, someone of Magdala. There was a place in Galilee called Magdala. Magdala also means tower. Could the castle actually be representing a tower? No, they would have just put a tower. They always have a tower somewhere when talking about Mary. Okay. What if it was a palace, then?' She paused and then was struck by a thought. 'Wait! Not a palace, but a temple. Solomon's temple! That would make sense.'

'Mary kneeling at Solomon's temple?' The Italian asked.

'No, not Mary. The Queen of Sheba, someone else associated with Mary the Magdalene.'

'What?' Mari squealed. 'How?'

'Let's get Lucas out of there, then I'll tell you.'

Natasha shouted her instruction to Lucas, and he dutifully followed it, stepping onto the tile of the kneeling woman by a temple. It clicked as it slightly sunk into the ground, and the wall ahead of Lucas moved, scraping as it slowly opened outwards.

'It worked!' Lucas shouted back.

Natasha punched the air, grinning broadly. 'Get in there, baby. Get out of the vapours.'

'It's just like the previous chamber,' he explained. 'There's structural decay. Pillars that supported the temple's interior, have crumbled and collapsed, and scattered fragments of stone and rubble all over the place. The roof has caved in too, understandable after all these centuries of life being built on top of it.'

Natasha could picture it clearly in her head. She had seen similar things in other sites. In the absence of human maintenance, the interior of the temple would have become overgrown with vegetation, vines and weeds creeping through cracks in the walls and floor as nature reclaimed the space. The temple would be littered with debris and detritus, fallen stones, broken pottery, and other remnants of past human activity, providing glimpses into the temple's former use and significance. Niches, and alcoves dedicated to the snake goddess, had deteriorated, leaving behind empty recesses in the walls where idols once would have stood.

Time out of the vapour was already having a positive effect on Lucas. Even if the air was musty, he could feel his head clearing of the psychedelic mists. 'I can feel the brain fog clearing,' he shouted. Lucas examined his surroundings, his attention eventually being drawn to an interesting object. 'There's a fragmented altar at the centre of the temple hall. It has sacred symbols and decorations on it, but they're too weathered to make out properly.'

'That's great,' Natasha shouted through the wall. 'That must be what we're looking for.' She waited to hear any further news from Lucas, and with every passing second, the anxious feeling within her grew and grew. She could hear things being smashed, and growing frustration from Lucas. 'What's going on, Lucas?'

'All we've been through was for nothing. The map isn't here.'

The Italian took a step toward Natasha, his grip on Mari still tight. 'What did he say?'

'Can you repeat that, baby?' Natasha shouted. 'I didn't quite hear you.'

'The map!' Lucas repeated. 'It's not here. The altar is empty.'

'It must be. Are you sure?'

'I've checked everywhere, Nat,' he replied. 'If it was here, it isn't now. I'm sorry, hon.'

'So am I,' the Italian said, hearing the news. 'It seems you cannot deliver on your end of the bargain, signorina Travers,' he said as he levelled his gun at her, before aiming it at the head of Mari.

'It's here,' she pleaded. 'I know it is.'

'Then where is it?' the Italian asked. He then shouted at the blocked doorway so Lucas could hear. 'Perhaps he has it in his hand.'

'What's going on out there?' Lucas yelled back.

'Perhaps you need another incentive to do as I ask,' the Italian hissed.

Natasha thought for a moment, her mind searched through the information she had, tossing aside things she deemed useless. Until she came to a hypothesis. 'We followed the breadcrumbs out of order!'

'What?'

'Tony found his map in a Portuguese galleon which sank in the Caribbean.'

'So what?'

'The Cathar map sent us here. The map that was here would have sent us to wherever Tony's map was originally. That map sent us to Valencia. And the map in Valencia was the blank one, with nothing on it but the landmass. We've been following the breadcrumbs out of sequence.'

'So we have all we need to find the grail?' Mari asked.

'I believe so. Yes.'

'His Eminence will be thrilled to hear that. Unfortunately, you are no longer needed here, signorina Laval.'

Natasha lunged at the Italian. The unexpected assault winded him, releasing Mari in the process. Natasha had him around the waist and delivered several good punches to his body. The Italian recovered from the initial attack and brought his gun up to Natasha's head. Before he could pull the trigger, Mari Laval grabbed his wrist and slammed it against the wall. The gun went off, echoing loudly around the chamber.

'What's going on in there?' Lucas demanded.

Mari continued to slam the Italian's hand against the wall until he dropped his gun. At which point he struck her with the back of his fist and sent her crumpled to the ground. Then he drove his knee up into Natasha once, loosening her grip. He tried it a second time, but Natasha caught it and whipped underneath, flipping the Italian over onto his back. Keeping hold of his leg under her arm, she was about to apply a leg lock to it, but he was on to her plan. With his free leg, he kicked her in the side of the head. Natasha saw stars and fell back as she fought to stay conscious. It was a battle she lost. The last thing she saw was Mari unconscious on the ground as the Italian carried her away. Then everything went black.

• • • •

LUCAS HAD NEVER FELT more hopeless in all his life. The gunshot still rang in his ears. He knew Natasha was in trouble in the other chamber, but there was no way he could get to her. He needed to get out, and fast.

Beginning to explore the ancient temple again, this time not looking for the map, but for a way out, his footsteps echoed throughout the temple, as his flashlight cast long shadows on the walls. Then he noticed a peculiar crack in one of them, barely discernible amidst the weathered stone.

'Hello. What do we have here?' Intrigued by the anomaly, Lucas approached and ran his fingers along its rough surface. To his astonishment, he discovered that the fracture in the wall was not a natural fissure, but a carefully concealed entrance. To what, Lucas didn't know. Neither was he in a position not to venture on.

Pulling away at the lichen and roots that had grown over the centuries, with brute strength, Lucas pushed his shoulder against the ancient stone. He felt it give way as it swung open with a soft creak to reveal the hidden passage within the temple's depths.

Stepping cautiously into the darkness beyond, Lucas found himself engulfed in a world of shadows, the air thick with the musty scent of ancient dust and decay. He forged further into the hidden passage, his keen eyes catching glimpses of long-forgotten artefacts and relics, their surfaces gleaming faintly in the dim light.

With each step, Lucas felt the weight of history pressing down upon him, the echoes of ancient footsteps whispering tales of forgotten gods and lost civilisations. Yet, despite the eerie atmosphere and sense of foreboding that surrounded him, Lucas was undeterred in his in his quest to find an exit, and line his pockets in the meantime. There were bound to be some fascinating pieces, he thought, eyeing up an impressive jewel laden necklace, which he knew wouldn't take much to bring it back to its former glory.

As Lucas looked among the discarded artefacts, he briefly flashed back to his days playing the role of Sebastian Jericho, master thief and criminal mastermind. Clearing out a haul such as this would have been par for the course for Lucas back then, but being with Natasha had toned down that side of him. She made him a better person. It was just one of the many reasons he had to escape and find her.

The passageway twisted and turned until Lucas encountered a shaft with a spiral staircase hewn from the rock itself. He could feel air filtering down. Not a significant amount of breeze, but it was enough to galvanise his determination.

Lucas started up the stairwell. The thought of freedom and seeing the sky again grew within his mind with each step he took, unaware that they were crumbling away behind him. The entire spiral stairway was collapsing in a chain reaction of destruction, and Lucas raced to reach the top, where he'd spotted a small opening that he hoped to be the exit.

He ran, taking two steps at a time, not looking back to see where the crevasse was. That would only slow him down, and he knew time was against him. Lucas knew the crack had overtaken him when the steps beneath his feet fell away. But he kept going, using his built up speed and momentum to jump from falling rock to the next falling rock and finally tossing his flashlight aside and making a desperate leap for the ledge of the opening.

With his legs dangling, plumes of dust wafted up to surround Lucas as the staircase crashed down into a pile of rubble. He pulled himself up, coughing as he did so. When he was safely in the opening, he took a few moments to clear his throat, and let his adrenaline normalise before moving on.

Finally, he navigated his way through the ancient temple's hidden passageway. Slivers of light streamed in, giving Lucas grateful illumination in the absence of his MAGLite. He could taste freedom. All he had to do was force his way past whatever was blocking the exit.

When he got closer, he could see that it was not an enormous capstone of a pillar, but collapsed statues, denying his exit this time. Sitting down, Lucas could use his powerful legs to push them, making just enough space to squeeze through and free himself.

Lucas breathed heavily after his exertions, but it was worth it to feel the sun on his face again. He smiled and dusted himself off. His next course of action was to figure out where he was, and get back to the amphitheatre. He had to find out what had happened. Find out if the Italian had really shot Natasha.

Suddenly, Lucas felt a hand grip his shoulder. Without a second thought, he instinctively threw the person to the ground and was about to follow-up on his attack when he heard guns behind him being cocked.

'Hold it right there,' a voice said.

Lucas could hear the voice was French accented and judging by the amount of guns he heard being chambered, the speaker wasn't alone. Lucas slowly raised his hands in the air.

In short order, two men grabbed him and forcefully led him through another one of the many historical sites that seemed to be scattered around Tunisia. It was one he remembered passing with Khalid, who had called it the Basilique de Saint Cyperien. He noticed that the sea was closer than it was at the amphitheatre and figured he was about a kilometre and a half north of the site.

It wasn't long before Lucas was being thrown to the ground in a secluded, untouched section. Collapsed pillars and bits of wall scattered about offered little for archaeologists or tourists to see, but provided the perfect setting for clandestine meetings. Lucas found himself on his knees in front of two people, a short stocky man, the remains of his hair pulled back into a ponytail. All he could see of the other person was their back, but from the way they filled the white suit they wore, he could guess it was a woman.

'We found this man sneaking around inside the cordon,' the gunman said.

'What is this?' The stocky man spat. 'Is this how the Peregrine does business? Do you know him?'

'La Peregrine?' Lucas mouthed, and took a second look at the woman. 'Leila?' The last time Lucas had seen the elegant Moroccan woman was on his honeymoon in Peru. She acted as the mediator for the arms dealer known as La Peregrine. What most people didn't know, however, was the fact that Leila herself was La Peregrine. She thought clients would be less likely to do business with a woman than a mysterious, unseen figure with a notorious reputation.

She looked over her shoulder and met Lucas's gaze. 'Yes, I know him. He wants to be one of my lovers. But he has nothing to do with this transaction. The Peregrine runs an impeccable business, Farhad,' replied Leila with her familiar French heavy accent. 'You know this. You know his resume. You know that his equipment is second to none.'

'Yes, I know all this,' Farhad said. 'But I don't enjoy working with an intermediary. And I don't like surprises. This man is a surprise. So I think I will end our business. *And* this man. I don't like the way he looks at me.'

Lucas got to his feet, holding his hands up. 'Don't mind me. I'm just a simple tomb raider who knows how to keep his mouth shut. I've just been doing a bit of looting. Look in my bag if you don't believe me.'

The gunman tossed Lucas's bag over to Farhad, who immediately looked inside and took out the necklace. His suspicious glare still didn't soften towards Lucas, however.

Leila, with her long stride, moved towards Lucas. She came to a stop in front of him. Her flower scented perfume wafting around him, her hot breath on his lips as she whispered. 'Well, well, well, if it isn't Lucas Redmond. How long has it been since Peru? Six, seven years since you almost ruined another of my transactions?'

'Yeah, something like that,' Lucas answered, staring into the arms dealer's brown, almond-shaped eyes.

'And where is that wife of yours? Should I expect her to come dancing her way in again?'

'I wouldn't bet on it.'

'Good. That means I get to play with you this time.' Leila then leaned forward and clamped her lips on Lucas's before exploring his mouth with her tongue. 'As good as I always thought it would be,' she smirked, reapplying her lip-gloss. Once she had finished, she looked over her shoulder to address her business partner. 'So, Farhad, you will not take my word for it?'

'Bah! The word of the Peregrine's woman means nothing. Unless, of course, you wish to...convince me of otherwise?'

'I thought you would never ask,' Leila replied with a smile, and stepped over to the gunman. 'Get rid of the extra. Then we will see if I cannot convince you to continue our trade to a mutually beneficial outcome.'

'Hmm, I like the sound of this. I agree,' grinned Farhad. 'Take care of it, Syed.'

The man lifted his gun, prepared to follow the command without hesitation. With Lucas's head in his sights, he held his breath and began to squeeze the trigger. Leila flashed into action and grabbed his wrist, changing the gunman's target from Lucas to Farhad. She put her finger over his and fired twice, then she dragged the gun out of his hand and, turning on Syed, shot him one to the chest, one to the head.

'I guess the deal's off,' quipped Lucas.

'I wouldn't be so smug if I were you. You've lost me another client. I expect to be compensated.'

'I'm sure we can arrange something.'

'We can talk after we deal with his men,' she said as she walked over to a metallic crate with a blue screen on its side. As she put her hand on the screen, it flashed green, and Lucas heard a series of locks being undone. She threw open the lid.

Lucas couldn't help but smile as he feasted his eyes on its contents. 'All the fun of the fair.' His hands reached in and picked up two SIG Sauer P226's, a familiar model of handgun. He displayed his prowess with them by despatching one of Farhad's men. Three more closed in, this time coming in behind the spray of bullets being spat from their sub-machine guns. Two of them ducked behind a toppled column, whilst the third shielded himself behind a statue.

While the bullets pinged around, Leila had been on her mobile phone. 'Pickup has been arranged. We just need to clear the hostiles.' The Moroccan looked into her crate of weapons and pulled out two Genesis Arms Gen-12 semi-automatic shotguns, handing one to Lucas. 'And these will do the job perfectly.'

A barrage of gunfire slammed into the crate. As soon as there was a moment of respite when their attackers loaded their machine guns, both Lucas and Leila stood and let loose with shotguns. The barrage from the unlikely partnership sent chunks of masonry flying, as they worked through the ten 12-gauge rounds held by the magazine clip. One of the men hiding lost his nerve and tried to make a run for it, but got nothing but a round from Leila's gun for the effort.

Dust was suddenly kicked up by the downdraft from the aircraft Leila had called in for her evacuation. It was a tilt-rotor, a type of aircraft with the ability to use the lifting rotors as propellers in forward flight by tilting them 90 degrees, thus combing the vertical take-off and landing capabilities of a helicopter with the speed, range, and comfort of a turbo-prop airplane. Lucas had seen them before, but not one like this. Leila's aircraft had four propellers, making it look like a life-sized drone.

The aircraft's arrival had startled Farhad's remaining guards, giving Leila the opportunity to load a fresh clip into her Gen-12 and terminate them with extreme prejudice. While she was doing that, a rope and harness descended to retrieve the cache of weapons. Once she had secured it, she strapped herself into the harness. 'Well?' Leila said to Lucas. 'Are you coming or not?'

Lucas could hear the sirens of police cars getting louder as they got closer. 'I need to go back to the amphitheatre and find Natasha.'

'If you stay here, chéri, the only thing you will find is how unsanitary Tunisian prisons are.'

He knew she was right, but that still didn't lessen the feeling of abandoning Natasha he was having. Lucas embraced Leila, and she held him tightly as they were being lifted into the air and eventually into the aircraft.

'Good work, Ashton,' she said to the man who had helped them aboard. 'What of the merchandise?'

'Secured to the magnalift,' he replied.

'Good. Then you can get us out of here.'

'Yes, ma'am.' He turned and left, heading for the cockpit.

Lucas studied his surroundings, seeing that they were in the hold of the tilt-rotor aircraft. It looked sparse, reminding him of the interiors he'd seen in many military planes he and his troopers had parachuted out of. Function over comfort. They reserved the comfort part for the next area. Lucas followed Leila through a door, up a short, narrow ladder, and along a gangway. They came to the well-equipped galley and then into a luxurious cabin on par with any private jet. Movement outside the window caught Lucas's attention, and he watched as the propellers tilted into position before the aircraft flew off.

'Ah,' Leila expelled as she sat heavily in her cream and black leather. 'Would you like a drink? Cognac okay?' She asked as she poured herself a drink.

Lucas accepted the alcohol and finished it in one go. She poured him another. He took his time with this one. 'You have to go back,' he said. 'You can stop and I'll repel down so I can find Natasha.'

His host crossed her long legs as she sipped at her drink, eyeing Lucas. 'That, I'm afraid, will not happen, chéri. This is a nonstop flight.'

'Then I guess I have to make you do it.'

'Oh, come, come Lucas. Do not be silly. Must we revisit this scene again? You try to choke me, I laugh in your face, and you discover I enjoy the pain and suffering, and your attempt to intimidate me comes to nothing. See? I have saved you the bother. Now sit down and enjoy the flight.'

Lucas reluctantly did as he was told. He glanced out of the window and saw that they were travelling over the water. 'Is that the Med?'

'Yes it is.'

'Where the hell are we going?'

'To my compound, of course. Since you ruined my transaction, I need to contact my next buyer and let him know that his shipment has arrived early.'

It wasn't what he was asking, but it wasn't long before he found out the answer for himself when they flew over familiar landmarks. 'You know, that looks suspiciously like Muammar Gaddafi's Bab al-Azizia palace complex down there.'

'That's because it is.' Leila smiled.

'Bollocks,' Lucas whispered.

'I would have loved to have taken it as my own,' she commented. 'But being in Tripoli is a bit too in the spotlight for my liking. Besides, it's too big, and it suffered damaged in the civil war.' She came over to Lucas, and leaning onto him, pointed out into the desert. 'That is my compound.'

He could feel her breath on his ear, smell her scent in his nose, as she pressed her breasts against him. 'Why are you bringing me here? You know my history in the SAS. What makes you think I won't give them the coordinates of this place the moment I get a chance?'

'Because I see something in your eyes, chéri. A spark of something that was once there. Something that wasn't on the side of the righteous, I think. I saw a glimpse of it in Peru, but it is even more clear now.' She held up his left hand. 'And you no longer have your wedding ring to keep it in check.'

'Just because I'm divorced doesn't mean I'm going to join you.'

'Not yet, anyway,' she said as she took her lithe body back to her seat, much to the relief of Lucas.

He continued to look at the Peregrine's desert complex and had to admit it was a pretty ideal location for her activities. Political instability and conflict had plagued Libya since the overthrow of Muammar Gaddafi in 2011. The country's vast desert expanses and porous borders made it a perfect transit point for arms smuggling.

At a rough estimate, Lucas judged the sprawling compound to cover at least a square kilometre. As they came made to land, Lucas easily saw that the compound reflected a design focused on security, secrecy, and functionality. High walls and sturdy fencing fortified the exterior of the compound to deter unauthorised access.

As they disembarked the plane at the hangar, Lucas observed a multitude of surveillance cameras and motion sensors. A two-man security patrol, one of whom was a dog handler, walked the perimeter to identify and neutralise potential intruders.

Lucas could see that any plans of making an escape were going to be all but impossible.

Chapter 26

Natasha initially didn't know where she was. The Vatican spy had taken her unconscious body from the hidden temple beneath the Carthage amphitheatre. When she had regained consciousness, she thought she was on a plane. He had injected her, and she'd passed out again. Now she'd taken off the hood, which was placed on her head, and looked at her surroundings.

She was alone in an office which blended reverence for tradition and spirituality with a modern administrative functional workspace. Natasha took in the renaissance-style architecture of the office, the ornate facades, arched doorways. 'The door,' she blurted, and crossed the marble floor, only to find it locked. She groaned at the half-expected disappointment.

Going back to her chair, Natasha admired the vaulted ceilings and intricate artwork. The frescoes depicted religious themes, and with all the other religious symbols and imagery, such as crucifixes, statues of saints, and bookshelves of religious texts, it wasn't a hard task for Natasha to deduce that she was in the Vatican. A glance outside the window confirmed she was in the Papal Palace itself, looking down at St. Peter's Square.

She was in Rome, and she did not know if Lucas had escaped the temple or if he was even still alive. She had no idea if the Italian had killed him like Khalid. Her hands trembled as she remembered the plight of her friend. Natasha clutched them together to stop them, as she sobbed gently. She regretted getting him involved in this quest. It was one thing for her and Lucas to put themselves in danger, but it was difficult to take when it was the surrounding people that suffered. All she could do now was make sure that his death wasn't in vain.

Just then, Natasha heard a key in the lock, and she quickly wiped her eyes. Whoever was about to enter, she didn't want them thinking they caused her distress.

A grey-haired middle-aged man opened the door, pausing a moment to look at Natasha, as if weighing her up. Then he slowly broke into a broad smile and walked into the room, closing the door behind him. He strode directly towards her with his hand out. 'My name is Cardinal Elias Wagner,' he said with his German accent. 'I am pleased to meet you finally, Miss Travers.'

Natasha was momentarily hesitant, but firmly shook the offered hand. 'Your Eminence.' Although she wasn't Catholic, Natasha had no problem showing respect when due.

'Come, have a seat,' he said, directing her to the plush upholstered seating area. 'We have so much to discuss.'

'The only thing I want to discuss right now is what has happened to Lucas and Mari?'

'It has reported to me that the young French girl has made her way back to her yacht.'

'And Lucas?'

'Unfortunately, he has vanished.'

'What does that mean?'

'My agents returned to the hidden temple and, with a controlled blast, made their way into the chambers. They found what looked like a collapsed stairwell, but they could not tell if he made it out before the collapse or if he...perished in it.'

Natasha looked down, searching her feelings. She couldn't explain it, but she knew in her heart that he had escaped. And if that was the case, it was only a matter of time before he came knocking. 'Find him, or you'll find me a very uncooperative prisoner.'

'Prisoner? My dear, you're my guest.'

'Lock up all your guests, do you?'

'That was just precautionary until I had a chance to talk to you.'

'So, what did you want to discuss? Because actually, I'm very interested in finding out why I'm here. One minute, your man is trying to kill us, and the next I'm chilling out here in Vatican City.'

Elias smiled. 'I'm not surprised that would cause some confusion. Rest assured, your deaths are no longer on the agenda. My objective has changed.'

'Changed? To what?'

'I want you to find the holy grail.'

'Excuse me?' She sat up, sceptical of what she'd just heard. 'Your agent killed my friend, and now you want me to work for you?'

'That was an unfortunate event,' Cardinal Wagner said solemnly. 'Gianpaolo is very devoted to the work he does for the church, and he will do anything to protect it.'

'Including murdering an innocent archaeologist? Very godly of him.'

'Everything we do here is for the glory of God. Sometimes these things are not pleasant, but necessary.'

'I can't believe I'm hearing this, from a man of the cloth, no less.'

'Yes, but a man none the less. I have to make tough decisions every day. But charging you with finding the grail is not one of them.'

'Why the change of heart? What if there's additional evidence with it, hidden documents or testimonies, suggesting Mary had a relationship with Jesus?'

'More and more people are coming to believe that fact as it is.'

'And they will realise that she plays a more significant role in the church than they were led to believe.'

'And that is the main point, what they are led to believe. The masses have no problem believing the grail in Valencia is the genuine article. Why? Because the pope himself, head of their church, endorses it.'

'And if I find the real grail? What then?'

'The pope will make an announcement proclaiming the mistake of his predecessors.'

'And what of Mary? Will they give Mary the accolades she deserves? Will the pope publicly acknowledge the falsehoods on which this religion is built? That the people have been misled for centuries?'

Cardinal Wagner sighed. 'What is your agenda, Miss Travers? To bring down the church?'

'I just want the truth out there. I want people to know that Mary was married to Jesus, and that she was the one that was supposed to continue the Ministry of Jesus.'

'That's all?' Without another word, he stood up and walked over to the nearest window and opened it. Cardinal Wagner looked over to Natasha briefly, to make sure she was watching, then shouted out the window. 'Mary was married to Jesus, and she was the one that was supposed to continue the Ministry of Jesus.' Once he'd finished, he closed the window and returned to his seat. 'There. Are you happy now? As you can see, the church hasn't come crumbling down.'

'Don't be facetious. That's not what I meant. Besides, you said it would need to be endorsed by the pope, and that's not you.'

'But I could be.'

'What?'

'With your help.'

'You want to be the pope?'

'Just because I wear a cassock, am I not allowed to have ambition? In Matthew 25, Jesus himself teaches that ambition is a good thing when we use God's gifts for His glory. Which is exactly what I would be doing. And so could you, as the pope's archaeologist.'

'Yeah, I don't think that's going to work,' she scoffed.

'Because you have no faith, you're a nonbeliever.'

'I have plenty of faith,' she corrected. 'I just don't have belief in all of this,' she said, flourishing her hand around.

'Hmm, I see,' he nodded. 'So you would allow your prejudices to hold you back? You could have unrestricted access to the Vatican vaults, but you choose not to.'

Natasha surreptitiously leaned forward. 'The entire vaults?'

'Whenever you pleased, Miss Travers.'

She gazed past Cardinal Wagner and out of the window, unsure of what to do. She had intended to have the grail placed in a museum, if she did actually find it. But this offer was unprecedented for an archaeologist not associated with the Catholic Church, and even then, there were some areas off limits to them. 'What will you do with the grail?'

'It will become the holy relic of all holy relics. It will be a beacon for the Catholic Church. No, not just for Catholics, but for all who believe in Jesus. It will usher in a new religious era.'

Natasha scrutinised the elderly man. 'A new religious era?'

'Yes, Miss Travers, we live in a period where science can achieve truly miraculous things.'

'I thought science and religion were at odds with each other?'

'There are those that believe science proves that there is no God. They believe that if all the holy books were destroyed, the books would reappear in a different form after a thousand years. However, science would come back the same if someone performed the same action, as scientific fact remains constant. They don't mention the fact that books are books. God is the one true constant. I believe God is the greatest of all scientists. Things in the universe just didn't happen by chance.'

'You seem to be a supporter of science.'

'I am. As I mentioned, technology has made astounding advances. Especially in the realms of DNA.'

Natasha's eyebrow creased. 'DNA? I don't see the connection.'

'Why is the grail holy? Because it held the blood of Christ.'

'Wait, you're expecting to find his blood still in it?'

'Yes. Dried traces probably, but still there none the less. And no less useful to my plans.'

'What could you possibly be planning?'

'Why drink wine and say it is the blood of Christ, if you could actually drink the blood of Christ? Why do you think all these stories of the grail claim it to have healing properties? The cup was just a cup until it held the blood of Jesus.'

'You're planning on synthesising any traces of blood in the grail? Is that even possible?'

'As I said, we live in an age of wonders, Miss Travers.'

Natasha struggled to digest everything she was being told. Part of her believed it couldn't be done. But she would be lying if she said that she wasn't the least bit intrigued by what Cardinal Wagner was proposing. What if what he was claiming was true? What if it was possible to use the grail to heal people? To synthesise the blood into some sort of drug. The world could be free of disease. 'But what if Jesus was just a man? There was no virgin birth. No miracles. No healing.'

'Then he will continue to be a beacon for the church. It may even be possible to discover if the bloodline of Jesus and Mary exists to this day. They did have children, after all. And over time, once I assume the role of pope, I will gradually reveal pieces of this information to the masses as the esteemed archaeologist, Natasha Travers, uncovers more discoveries.'

'I am sure the Vatican has plenty of people more suited to the task,' Natasha said.

'Perhaps,' he replied with a shrug. 'But none have come as far as you have.'

That's because they never had the lens, she thought to herself. 'So they have seen the map?'

'We found a copy in the vaults. An eighteenth-century Portuguese merchant obtained it in Positano before he joined a galleon destined for the Caribbean. There's so little information, no coast, no landmarks or anything of use, that they could not identify the landmass.'

'Positano? The Amalfi Coast? Hmmm,' she mused, twisting a strand of hair around her finger. 'Nice sent us to Carthage. Carthage sent us to Positano. And Positano sent us to Valencia. So where is Valencia sending us?'

'I've looked at them and can't tell what's missing.'

'Wait. That means maps are here!'

'Yes, of course they are,' he replied, making his way to his wooden desk, which exuded grandeur. He returned and handed the three complete maps, along with the torn piece of the fourth, to Natasha.

She flipped through them, one by one, a smile on her face growing ever larger. Eventually, she snatched up the blank map she'd found in Valencia, and started walking towards the door. 'I need to go to the Gallery of Maps.'

The smile on Natasha's face broadened as she headed for the door. 'We're going to need a pen too,' she called over her shoulder to Cardinal Wagner. He quickly made for his desk to retrieve the appropriate item.

Natasha wrenched open the doors, half expecting them to be locked, but much to her surprise, they weren't. There was no need to lock the doors when you have two Swiss guards standing there with their spears crossed, blocking the way out. She turned to the Cardinal. 'Do you mind?'

'It's okay, she will be coming with me,' he said to the guards. They stood to attention, clearing the way for them.

'We'll need those too,' Natasha said, eyeing the spears, before leaving with a determined step, forcing the confused Cardinal Wagner and the guards to jog in order to catch up and take the lead.

As they passed through the palace complex, making their way down the corridors and halls towards the northern wing, where a private entrance would provide direct access to the Vatican museums, Natasha's mind was going several steps ahead of the game. She knew she had cracked the mystery of the maps. She knew where they led. Just not the exact spot where they needed to look. But she was about to find that out. She still didn't know what she was going to do if the holy grail was there. Would she hand it over to Cardinal Wagner in the end? Revealing the facts is what's at the heart of everything an archaeologist does. But in this case, the ramifications of a revelation like this could potentially bring down Christianity itself. Which begged the question, who would she be doing it for?

Her internal debate continued as they entered the museums through the entrance reserved for papal use, still with the Swiss guards in tow. Natasha recognised where they were now, having taken the public tour years ago, and with a determined stride followed the designated route that led through the museums towards the Gallery of Maps.

As they progressed through the Vatican museums, visitors enjoying the rich cultural and artistic heritage of Vatican City were startled when they saw the Cardinal and a pair of guards hastily accompanying a woman, leaving them wondering what was going on.

They eventually arrived at the Gallery and Natasha steamed straight in, taking little time to admire the stunning frescoes depicting detailed maps of Italy and its regions. She had always appreciated the historical significance of the artworks. Painted by Ignazio Danti to allow Pope Gregory XIII, the same pope who commissioned the Gregorian calendar, to see the expanse of the Papacy, the Gallery of Maps was an astounding piece of geographical art. The frescoes featured different sections of the map of Italy and adorned the walls of the 120-metre-long corridor. But the one Natasha remembered seeing showed the Mediterranean.

'This is it,' she said, as Cardinal Wagner join her after having the museum security clear the gallery.

'Would you mind telling me what it is you expect to find here? What did you discover from the maps?'

'Each of the maps had a line drawn on them, on the left side, on the right side or top to bottom. I didn't understand them, couldn't figure out what they were. Until you told me that Tony's map had originated from Positano.'

'Okay,' he replied, still not understanding.

'Cities surrounding the Mediterranean contained each of the maps,' she said, pointing to the Amalfi Coast and then each corresponding city. 'Nice, Valencia, and Carthage. Actually, the Nice one was originally found in Eze.'

'North, south, east, west,' he said.

Natasha nodded, explaining, 'This next bit only works because of the era these maps were created in.'

'What do you mean?'

'It was the time they thought the world was flat,' she answered.

She pointed to the nearest Swiss Guard. 'You, give me your spear.' The guard looked at Cardinal Wagner, who gave his ascent, and then he followed the order. 'Now the two of you hold the other spear against the fresco, from Valencia to Positano.' Even though each of them was over six feet tall, they still had to stretch to reach the target.

Once she'd made sure that they held the shaft of the weapon in perfect alignment, Natasha put the map in her pocket and taking the other spear, placed it on top of the one held by the guards, so that it aligned with Eze and Carthage. 'Sardinia,' she smiled. 'Come here and hold this,' she ordered Cardinal Wagner.

'Astonishing,' he said in awe as he complied.

Natasha took the Valencian map from her pocket and held it up, trying to measure it with the fresco of the Mediterranean. The map in her hand had no landmarks or coastline. And the cross, which she knew was there, was only visible through the watch lens, which she wished she had with her now. She recalled her memory from the hotel with Lucas and Ellen, estimating where the cross she had seen was. Northwest on the blank map. It wasn't enough information. She needed to see Sardinia. Then Natasha remembered where she was, the Gallery of Maps. 'You can all relax now,' she said, walking off to find the fresco in question.

It wasn't long before they were standing in front of the colourful, beautifully painted map. Even though it was painted in the sixteenth century, Natasha didn't need the map to be a perfect rendition of the island. It hadn't changed much. She knew the island had a variety of ecosystems, mountains, woods, plains, sandy beaches, streams and stretches of largely uninhabited territory. Many travellers and writers had waxed lyrical about the beauty of its long-untouched landscapes. Natasha herself had always planned to visit the vestiges of the Nuragic civilisation, the Bronze Age people who lived there before the invasion and partial conquest by the Romans.

Natasha held up her map so that she could look at both that and the fresco at the same time. Her eyes darted from one to the other and back again. They didn't stop until she was sure she had it. 'There! That's where the cross is.'

'You're sure?' Cardinal Wagner asked eagerly.

'Pen,' she demanded, holding out her hand. As she received it from Cardinal Wagner, she shrugged. 'I'm as sure as I'm going to be. It's not exact, but it gives me a location to explore.' She sketched out some of the terrain that was visible on Ignazio Danti painting, onto the Valencia map, finishing it by marking the cross.

'That northern area,' Cardinal Wagner circled with his finger. 'That's the Province of Sassari. At a guess, I'd say that cross is over Bonorva.'

'Bonorva?'

'Yes. It's a small village of about three and a half thousand people.'

'I know that name,' Natasha said, then it came to her. 'Isn't that where the Neolithic Necropolis of Sant'Andrea Priu is?'

'It is. One of the most important sites on the entire island.'

'Even more so if we find the holy grail there.'

The pair, with the two Swiss guards in tow, made their way back to the office of Cardinal Wagner, passing the crowd of people eager to continue their tour of the Vatican museums and the staff desperate to let them, so they didn't have to field anymore of their questions.

'You haven't told me your decision yet,' Cardinal Wagner said once they reached the private entrance back to the Papal Palace.

Natasha had done so deliberately at first. Wanting to take as much time as she could, hoping that there would be further news of Lucas. But now she had no choice but to agree, realising too late that in the excitement, she had told Wagner exactly where to search. The only way to control the discovery of the holy grail was to be a part of the expedition.

'I've made my decision,' she replied. 'I'll find the grail, but I have some conditions.'

Cardinal Wagner's pleasure at hearing her news was clear for Natasha to see. He opened the door to his office and ushered her inside. 'Anything you need, Miss Travers, you will have.'

'I want one of your Entity agents to find out what happened to Lucas. I want to contact my friend Ellen and let her know what's happened, because I might need her help. I'm also going to need some gear. I'll make a list.'

'Is that all?'

'Actually, that freedom of the Vatican vaults, you mentioned? I'm going to need that in writing. On Vatican headed paper. A seal would be nice, too.'

'Is that all?' he repeated in a less pleased tone.

'Yes, that's all. For now.'

'Good, because I have a condition of my own,' he smiled. 'Gianpaolo will go with you.'

'Oh, what joy,' Natasha replied with a fake smile.

'You will find him to be an able stand-in for your missing Lucas.'

'I don't need a stand-in. I just need Lucas found.'

Picking up the phone and dialling, he said, 'I will get on that right now.' It only took a few seconds for the other end to answer. 'I want an update from Roberto. Just now? Perfect. Hmm, I see. Yes, I want him to continue.' He hung up the phone.

'Well? What's going on?'

'It turns out Mr Redmond did indeed make it out before the collapse of the stairwell.'

'Yes!' Natasha punched the air.

'Unfortunately, he stumbled into some sort of altercation. A gunfight.'

'What?'

'There were several men from a local Tunisian gang killed.'

'What about Lucas?'

'The reports say he flew away with a woman.'

'A woman? What woman?' Then Natasha thought that maybe J Organisation had caught up with him. 'Was it a woman named Chiara Harris?'

'I don't know. All he's said is that it was a tall, olive-toned woman.'

'That could be her. They'll be trying to get information out of him.'

'He doesn't know about Sardinia, so he has nothing to tell them.'

'True. But how far will they be willing to go until they believe him?'

Chapter 28

Lucas gave just the right amount of validation to appear impressed as he pretended to enjoy his tour of Leila's compound. The truth of the matter was, he was studying his surroundings, looking for a way out of it. Unfortunately, he was having a tough time finding any such thing. The two armed guards who accompanied them didn't help matters, either.

But he wasn't about to throw in the towel. He could wait.

'These are the maintenance and supply workshops for the vehicle depots we just passed,' Leila explained. She had insisted on locking arms as she took him around her facility, almost as if it were a simple walk in the park and not through a huge state-of-the art, illegal, arms distribution complex.

They approached the next utilitarian and unassuming building. Like all the others, there was an armed guard standing to attention, and like all the others, he gave Lucas a look that let him know he wasn't wanted there. Unfortunately for them, the person who paid their wages did. Lucas smirked at the idea, the sight of which made the guard bristle.

Leila caught the exchange between the men. 'You are enjoying this, eh?'

'Enjoying what? Being a captive?'

'How many times must I tell you, Lucas? You are not my prisoner. You are my guest. We're old friends, after all. Look at all the fun we had on your honeymoon.'

'In that case, perhaps you wouldn't mind opening the door so that I can get back to my wife.'

'Ex-wife,' Leila corrected. 'And I can't do that right now. You owe me, remember?'

'What is it you want? Payment for this shipment?'

'And Peru. I told you, you've cost me two very good customers, Lucas.'

'So how much are we talking?'

'More than you can afford.'

'I can afford quite a bit.'

'On your government salary?' Leila asked as she went through the door Lucas held open for her. 'Or perhaps you mean the extra cash you make from the sides jobs you do for the Acquirers?'

Lucas stopped in his tracks. 'You know quite a bit about me.'

Leila laughed. 'I've been watching you, Lucas, ever since we first met. You intrigued me. I wanted to know more about you.'

'You know, people go to prison for that kind of thing.'

'And what happens to men who break into women's bedrooms while they're in the shower?'

'Touché,' Lucas said, remembering their first encounter, when he thought she was the girlfriend of Le Peregrine, and not the arms dealer herself. He should have known there was something about her when she stood there as she stepped out of the shower, glistening with droplets of water, and she never lost her confidence or poise when confronted by a stranger, despite being naked.

'But this is all water under the bridge. Isn't it, Lucas?'

'If you say so,' he said as the tour continued. 'What else have you learned about me?' Before Leila answered, a slender, blonde-haired woman came up to her. Lucas could see the look of awe on the young woman's face as she handed Leila a note.

'This is Debra,' Leila said as she cast her eyes over the piece of paper. 'She is the head of research and development, which is this wing. She also ensures that the weapons and equipment remain in optimal condition for sale. Isn't that right, Debra?'

'It is Leila,' the technician said gleefully, in her American accent.

'It would seem that the second buyer is more than happy to take delivery of the shipment, and wishes to meet tomorrow. Is it ready to go, Debra?'

'Almost. His configuration called for less shotgun power and more assault rifles, and we're just making sure everything is up to our standard.'

'Ever reliable,' Leila stated and caressed the woman's cheek, causing her to blush profusely.

It was becoming clear for Lucas to see exactly how Le Peregrine commanded loyalty from her people. 'What do you expect me to do while you're gone?'

'Gone? You'll be coming with me.' After sending Debra back to work, Leila and Lucas left the R & D building and started towards the main building, which housed Leila's office and living quarters. 'This is a new contact. Sometimes, they try to be stupid, rarely, but some try to be. Thinking that they will steal the merchandise from Le Peregrine's girlfriend. I usually have a couple of extra hands when I meet new buyers, Diouf and Babou. Do you remember them?'

'Hard to forget those Senegalese assassins.'

'Well, today you will be playing their role.'

'Nice. Where are we meeting them?'

'South. Near the Libya-Sudan border.'

In contrast to what Lucas had seen of the compound, the primary residence was different. Upon entering the building, it exuded opulence and extravagance, yet with a distinct French flair. Leila mentioned that the interior, including luxurious furnishings, plush carpets, ornate rugs, and richly upholstered furniture, was all shipped from Paris. Gilded accents, intricate woodwork, and elaborate chandeliers adorned the hallway and rooms. A diverse collection of artwork and artefacts from around the world was also on display. Paintings, sculptures, and other decorative objects prominently displayed throughout the private quarters drew Lucas's attention. Before he knew it, Leila's bedroom confronted Lucas.

She opened the door and strolled right in. The palatial decor continued inside with its comfortable looking living space. As she crossed the plush carpet, Leila stripped off each item of clothing she wore and tossed it aside. Then she noticed Lucas was still outside.

She looked at him with a confused look on her face. 'What are you doing out there?'

'Thought you might want privacy,' he shrugged.

'Putain! You have seen all I have already. No? Close the door behind you.' Leila said and carried on disrobing and sauntered into the bedroom. Moments later, Leila turned on the shower.

Lucas scanned the room, thinking there might be something that could aid his escape. Then he stopped. He saw a miniature camera in the ceiling's corner blinking at him. Then another. He wouldn't be searching anything in there. Surely her bedroom wouldn't be under surveillance, too.

He entered the bedroom and raised an eyebrow at the king-sized four-poster bed. The whole residence seemed like someone had plucked it from Versailles, and this statement bed capped it all off. Lucas went to the window and glanced down. It may have been possible to climb down, even without equipment, but there was no chance he'd be able to use it. The windows had sensors and were probably alarmed. The more Lucas thought about things, the more he realised that the only way he would get out of Le Peregrine's compound would be through the front door.

Just then, the shower stopped. Lucas leaned against the window, looking as casual as he could. Even as Leila stepped out, wearing nothing but a smile.

'Having a bout of déjà vu, Lucas? Or are you just trying to find a way out?'

'I don't know what you mean,' he replied innocently. 'What else could I be doing here?'

Leila scrutinised him closely, weighing up what he said, trying to find any clues of deception on his part. She couldn't see any and walked towards him with a leisurely gait, her hips swaying hypnotically.

She draped her arms around Lucas with a gentle moan and kissed him, exploring his mouth, her lustful desire clear to see. With Leila's lithe body pressed against his, Lucas found his resolve diminishing fast, and he sunk into the kiss, his hands gripping her tight form.

Then he pulled away.

'What about having a bite to eat?' Lucas gasped.

'Quoi? You think about this now? While I am naked in your arms? A bed within touching distance?'

'Well, something tells me I'm going to need all the energy I can get to satisfy you, Leila.'

She laughed. 'You are right, Lucas.' Leila turned towards the door, which turned out to be a large walk-in wardrobe. She returned and slipped into a thong before dressing, putting on a purple tracksuit. 'Bon! We will eat, but I will expect to continue this tête et tête when we return, chéri.'

Lucas barely escaped her first salvo. But he wasn't sure how he'd be able to dodge another assault after dinner.

He didn't.

• • • •

DURING HIS TIME IN the SAS, on occasions, Lucas and his troopers had to do things in a morally grey area that others couldn't. Sometimes they had to do things to maintain their cover, other times they had to eliminate someone close to their intended target to force their hand into doing something. For these assignments, he had to compartmentalise his emotions. Put them in a box, intending to return to them later. Sometimes he worried he might enjoy being untethered by emotions so much that he might lose the key to that box.

Under the cloak of nightfall, Lucas dressed and looked down at Leila. She slept peacefully despite the red marks on her back and bruises on her buttocks. Lucas turned away, unmoved. His mission wasn't complete yet, and he entered her walk-in wardrobe.

Lucas silently searched her products. He knew Leila was a handful of years older than he was and he hoped to use the surgical gloves found in boxes of dye. But there were none. Given Leila's lifestyle, Lucas thought she would have had plenty of grey hairs by now. It turned out she wasn't dyeing her hair at all. 'Bollocks,' he said under his breath. He thought that he might have to go down to the kitchen to get a pair of marigolds to do the job. Then he spotted something he'd seen Natasha use.

He reached over and picked up the tub and smiled. 'This will do perfectly.'

As quietly as he had before, Lucas returned to Leila's side. He took her left hand, which was still bound with a leather strap to the nearest bedpost and, using the applicator, gently covered her thumb with a thick coating of Elizabeth Arden's Visible Difference Peel & Reveal Revitalising Mask. Lucas turned the tub over and read the instructions to find out how long he had to leave it. 'Bollocks! Twenty bloody minutes,' he whispered.

Just then, Leila stirred. 'Let me rest, mon chéri,' she said, still half asleep.

'Don't worry, love. I'm just going to the gents.'

'You mean the ladies,' she corrected, before her deep, rhythmic breathing persisted once more.

He looked down at his Patek Philippe watch and let out a sigh. 'Twenty bloody minutes.'

Chapter 29

The twenty minutes flew by as Lucas tried to stop Leila from disturbing the gel on her thumb. She rolled over a few times, but he made sure there was a clear space between her digits and the strap around her wrist.

Lucas watched the last seconds tick by, then gently peeled the dried gel from Leila's thumb. He studied it under the moonlight streaming through the window. He could see the lines of her thumbprint, but still did not know if this plan was going to work or not. Unfortunately, the only way to test it was out in the field in a live test.

He placed the print in a tissue taken from Leila's beauty table before heading to the bedroom door. He paused, stopped by the two cameras he'd seen there yesterday. There was nothing for it. He would just have to take a chance. Sprint across the room and hope the surveillance team wasn't up to scratch.

It would have been a tough enough job if it was just a case of getting out whilst the cameras were on, but Lucas had to make sure he did it without waking up Leila. Gratefully, he had the moon's light to help him see the layout of the unfamiliar room and plan his route to the door. He glanced over his shoulder at the sleeping Moroccan arms dealer one last time before he set off.

Within seconds, Lucas was out the door, softly closing it behind him. He waited a few seconds, just in case anyone was roused by his actions. Nothing. No alarms sounding and Leila wasn't at the door. Just as he thought he had eluded the grasp of Peregrine's security forces, Lucas looked down from the balcony and saw an obstacle, a lone guard coming from the direction of the dining room, a sandwich on a plate in his left hand and another sandwich in his other hand which he brought up to his mouth, taking a big bite out of it. He sat in the armchair near his assault rifle and carried on eating his food.

Lucas slithered along the balcony and down the stairs without making a sound or being seen. He reached the bottom, still unnoticed, and paused until the perfect moment. With quick reflexes honed by years of training, he sprang into action, swiftly incapacitating the guard with a well-placed blow to the temple.

Undeterred, Lucas pressed onward, his determination fuelling his every step. He scoured the dimly lit corridors, searching for any means of escape from the desert complex. With keen hearing, he listened at doors, and with sharp eyes scanned each room he determined was unoccupied. His fingers brushing against the cold steel of locked doors and barred windows. The way in was looking more and more like it would have to be his way out. There had been two guards flanking it when he had arrived. He assumed there would be no less security at night.

Lucas went to the front door and, as he had expected, he could hear a guard outside mumbling. He was cursing the other guard. The extra sandwich had been meant for him. Lucas couldn't help grin to himself as a thought crossed his mind. 'You're going to get a sandwich alright, mate. And the filling's going to be knuckles.'

He slowly opened the door. Before the guard could react, Lucas pounced like a tiger on prey and unleashed punches just as ferocious as the wildcat. Lucas looked to see if there was anyone nearby that might have heard the scuffle. There was no one, so Lucas propped up the guard the best he could in the likely event that when the patrol came around, they could see someone in position.

With the cover of darkness, Lucas moved with the agility of a shadow, navigating through the labyrinthine passages of Peregrine's Libyan compound. During dinner, she explained it had once belonged to Muammar Gaddafi, one of many such places he had dotted around the Sahara Desert. She had taken it and improved it to suit her needs. Now Lucas was attempting to break out of it.

The desert air whispered secrets on its gentle breeze, smoke from a strong cigarette. He stealthily bypassed the watchful eyes of the sentries, his senses heightened to the slightest sound or movement, and crept along the perimeter. Lucas spotted another pair of guards patrolling the perimeter fence. With silent precision, he ducked behind a stack of crates, waiting for the opportune moment to slip past undetected. The guards passed by, oblivious to his presence, their attention focused on the vast expanse ahead of them.

With the guards out of sight, Lucas seized the moment, darting across the open space with silent strides. His heart pounded in his chest as he reached the edge of the logistics and support area, the cool desert breeze offering fleeting relief from the oppressive heat.

Attempting to cross the Sahara with no equipment, let alone water, would be suicidal. He'd seen a couple of modified dirt bikes in the vehicle depot when Le Peregrine had given him the tour yesterday. They'd be perfect! He could push the motorbike to the front gate, and far into the desert, away from the compound, before revving it up and riding off to Egypt.

This plan relied entirely on the makeshift thumb print he had made with Leila's beauty product. There was no Plan B if it didn't work. He'd have to bide his time, hoping and praying for another opportunity.

He carefully took the delicate dried gel from the tissue he'd placed in his cargo pants and fitted it over his right thumb. Lucas took a deep breath and put his thumb on the digital reader. Nothing happened. He pressed it firmer. Still nothing. To make matters worse, when he pulled his thumb away, the gel had stuck to the screen. 'Bollocks,' he cursed, then looked around. He really didn't have time for this. A patrol could pass any minute. But as he tried to peel it off, scraping at the gel, inadvertently making it smaller, the screen went green. And the warehouse door whirred open, rising into its housing.

Lucas ducked inside, the moonlight illuminating more of the depot as it became fully opened to the night air. He made straight for the KTM 450 XCF motorbikes and checked they were roadworthy with full tanks. They were. In another stroke of luck, Lucas spotted a small table tucked away in the warehouse's corner. It wasn't the dusty desk which caught his attention, but the item that was resting on top of it. A satellite phone, its screen illuminated by a faint glow.

With hands trembling from excitement, Lucas picked it up and dialled a familiar number, Natasha's. There was no answer. Then he remembered she'd used Mari's phone on her yacht to call Ellen. She probably left her phone at Chateau Laval. The next number he called was Ellen herself.

'Come on, Ellen,' he urged. 'Pick up the phone.' Just as he was about to give up, she answered.

Her voice was sleepy, but it still portrayed her anger perfectly. 'Hello? Whoever you are, this had better be good waking me up out of my sleep.'

'Ellen?' he whispered urgently into the receiver. 'It's me, Lucas.'

'What the hell do you think you're doing just dumping me here and pissing off? You can expect a nice and hefty credit card bill coming, because I've been having the time of my life here.'

'Ellen, I need you to find Natasha. We got separated in Tunisia, and I'm currently in Libya.'

'Libya? What the hell are you doing in Libya?'

'La Peregrine took me here.'

'The arms dealer? And somewhat of a competitor. Wait, how do you know her?'

'We go way back. But that doesn't matter. Find out where Natasha is. I'm going to find a way out of here and head to Egypt.'

'I already know where Natasha is. She's at the Vatican.'

'What? Where?'

'She phoned me last night asking me to find you. I thought she was bullshitting about the chase and jumping on a yacht to Tunisia. Then you two being separated. She said she's made a deal with the guy in charge of the Entity. Apparently, we're no longer on their hit list. She just has to find the holy grail for them.'

'Did she say where she was going to look?'

'No, I got the impression that she was being watched. But she whispered something.'

'She did? What was it?'

'They are all points of a compass. Look at them flat. Then she said Positano was the missing one.'

'That's it?'

'Yeah, to the letter.'

'Points of a compass?' Lucas repeated it over and over. 'And what is they and them?'

'What's Positano?'

'It's a cliff side village on the Amalfi Coast. Beautiful views there. Wait a minute. She said Positano was the missing one?'

'Yeah, exactly that. You know what it means?'

'Each map sent us to a different location: Nice, Valencia, Tunisia. And now Positano. They're the points of the compass. Where they cross must be where she's gone.'

Without even being asked, Ellen booted up her laptop and opened a 3D image of the Earth. 'Okay, I'm plotting a line from Nice to Tunisia and another from Valencia to Positano.'

'Flat. She said look at them flat. Probably a flat map, not a globe.'

'Okay, losing the 3D switching to 2D.'

'Well?' He was getting impatient. The more time he hung around here, the chance he had of being discovered.

'Hold your horses,' she replied. 'It's coming now. It's Sardinia. A place called Cascata di Rebeccu.'

'Sardinia? Excellent! Thanks, Ellen. You're the best little sis a guy could have.'

'Maybe you should show it, once in a while.'

'You're right. Let Natasha know I'm coming. Call David. Tell him I'll need transport from Egypt to Sardinia. Pack the essentials, Ellen, and meet me there. Natasha's going to need our help.'

'When I said that you should show that I'm the best sis, this wasn't what I had in mind.'

'I thought you wanted to get out in the field more?'

As the words left his lips, Lucas sensed, all too late, a presence behind him looming shadows in the depot entrance. Before he could react, firm hands seized him from behind, wrenched the phone from his grasp before throwing him over the motorbikes to the floor. After several kicks to the ribs, they dragged him up, pinning him against a nearby Humvee.

'You shouldn't have come here, Lucas,' Le Peregrine murmured from the shadows. It laced with a hint of amusement. 'But it was to be expected.'

'Can't fault the hospitality, I will write you an excellent review on trip adviser. Unfortunately, I've got places to be.'

She strolled towards Lucas in a leisurely manner until she was beside his ear, whispering. 'Well, mon chéri, you are about to taste the other end of the hospitality scale. You could have continued to enjoy my company in the comfort of my bed, Lucas.' She sucked his ear and gently nibbled his earlobe. Then, without warning, she bit it hard, delighting in his grimace. 'But now you will have the company of my men to look forward to.'

The forearm in his throat pushed a little harder to emphasise the point. Lucas braced himself for the rough night ahead. His daring escape had only led him deeper into the heart of danger. One saving grace was that he knew Natasha was alive, and it galvanised him.

Chapter 30

The morning came, bringing with it the promise of adventure. Natasha felt refreshed after a good night's sleep, wondering if it was her current surroundings which had anything to do with it. The bed embraced her with a soothing warmth, easing her tired body.

Someone brought her a simple but nutritious breakfast. As was everything she had asked to be delivered: a change of clothes, a postal bag, grapple hook with rope, MAGLite's and glow-sticks, and various other items she and Lucas would always carry out into the field. The letter allowing her access to the Vatican vaults wasn't there, not that it entirely surprised her. Cardinal Wagner seemed to be a very shrewd character, and more ambitious than she had ever believed a clergyman to be. Natasha noted how certain he was of becoming pope, but there were two blinding obstacles in his way. Deciding who becomes the next pope is down to the cardinals who nominate during the conclave ceremony. However, the bigger obstacle Natasha saw blocking the way of Cardinal Wagner's ascension was the fact that the current pope was alive and well.

'Come in,' Natasha said in response to the sudden knock on the door.

'Good morning, Miss Travers,' Cardinal Wagner said, entering the room. 'I trust you slept well?'

'Very well, actually. And thank you for the clothes and other things. They'll do perfectly.'

'Good! We have to keep God's archaeologist happy.'

'Quite. I couldn't help but notice that the freedom of the vault letter wasn't there.'

'I have it right here,' he said, pulling out an envelope from his pocket and handing it to Natasha.

As she absorbed the shocking content, all she could say was 'This seems all in order.'

'As you can see, I have fulfilled my side of this transaction.' He held out his hand for the letter. 'When you have fulfilled yours, I shall return this to you. In the meantime, I will keep it locked away in my safe.'

'Fair enough. I suppose I should get a move on then.'

'Yes, you should. Gianpaolo and his men are waiting.'

'Men? I thought it was just going to be him?'

'This is such a delicate stage in proceedings. I want nothing to jeopardise matters when we are so close to rewriting history.'

'Last-minute changes jeopardise things.'

'I'm sure you will cope. I have the utmost faith in your abilities.'

She looked at him with a sidewards glance. 'I'd like to call my friend to find out if she's had any better luck with finding Lucas. Since you have said nothing about him, I'm assuming your man is still drawing a blank.'

'You're correct. Roberto has been in contact with the Tunisian police, and they have no further information.' He handed her a phone from his pocket.

'I see,' Natasha responded as she dialled Ellen's number. 'Ellen? It's me.'

'I've been waiting for you to call. I've spoken to Lucas.'

'You have? You found him? Is he okay?'

'He was, but I'm not sure for how much longer.'

'What do you mean?'

'Lucas was speaking to me on a satellite phone he'd found in Le Peregrine's Libyan compound. He was planning to escape and cross into Egypt. But the line went dead.'

'Peregrine? It was her that took Lucas? Not Chiara?'

'Strange you two should know an arms dealer. He said she was in Peru on your honeymoon.'

'Our paths crossed, that's all,' she said defensively, and changed the subject. 'You said the line went dead? Was it cut off?'

'Could be the battery went dead. Or perhaps someone discovered him,' Ellen said slowly, her voice tinged with dread. 'I won't know until I get to the rendezvous in Sardinia.'

Natasha smiled inwardly. 'That's great news. Make sure you take every precaution to be safe out there. Do you understand?' She saw Cardinal Wagner tap his wrist. 'Okay, I have to go Ellen. All going well, I hope to see you soon.' Natasha ended the call and handed the phone back.

'So you have found your Lucas? God be praised. If you do as we agreed, you will see him in no time at all, Miss Travers. Now, if you will excuse me. When you are ready, there is a guard outside who will take you to Gianpaolo. May God be with you.'

Cardinal Elias Wagner closed the door behind him as he left. He had only taken a few steps before he was taking another phone from a different pocket. He called a number on speed dial, and someone answered it immediately. 'Alpha? Travers is about to leave, and she has agreed to the terms you suggested. I also have news regarding Redmond. Apparently, he is in the hands of someone called Peregrine. You have heard the name? Then he is all but eliminated then. Yes, Gianpaolo will ensure that no tricks are played and the holy grail is handed over. Then we will move onto the next phase.'

• • • •

IT WAS A SHORT FLIGHT, a little over one hour, from Rome to Sardinia's Alghero airport. The drive from there to the picturesque village of Bonorva took a similar length of time. Nestled in the rolling hills of northern Sardinia, breathtaking natural beauty of lush green valleys, rugged mountains, and olive groves dotting the landscape, surrounded it. The village provided a tranquil and idyllic setting for residents and visitors to the island.

Natasha wished she was in more amiable company, someone who would share her appreciation of the village's historic centre with its charming cobblestone streets and medieval alleyways. Her eyes would light up when they passed ancient churches, or palaces. Whenever she tried to enter one, someone pulled her away.

The people of Bonorva greeted them with open arms several times and invited them to sample the village's unique charm and culinary delights, showcasing their warm hospitality. Natasha smiled back at the people, interested in trying some foods whilst taking in the history and traditions.

'We are not here for sightseeing, signorina Travers. The only cultural heritage of this region that should be on your mind is the Necropolis of Sant'Andrea Priu and where the grail is hidden.'

'Don't worry. Unlike you and your goons, I'm able to process multiple things at once. But as for finding the grail, I won't know anything until we get there and see the place with my own eyes.'

A fifteen-minute drive into the rolling hills was all it took to reach the Necropolis of Sant'Andrea Priu. The setting added to the allure, Natasha thought as she stepped out of the car and looked around, shielding her eyes from the afternoon sun. She picked up her bag, slung it over her shoulder with the strap across her chest, and set off with the five Entity agents in tow.

As they followed the path up to the necropolis, they saw visitors, part of guided tours, exploring the site's ancient tombs and rock-cut chambers, marvelling at the craftsmanship and symbolism preserved within. The guide impressed Natasha. He knew his stuff, interpreting signs and offering insights into the history and significance of the site, allowing visitors to immerse themselves in the rich past of the region.

'Where do we begin our search?' Gianpaolo asked as they meandered around the site.

Natasha shrugged. 'I don't know. It might be best to go along with him for now. He knows the place better than I ever could. And we might just spot something that tie into Mary Magdalene and the grail.' She realised something and scoffed. 'Why did I say "we"? You lot aren't going to be any help finding anything. It's not your forte, is it? Killing innocent people is what you're good at.'

Gianpaolo gave her a cold, hard stare. 'I do God's bidding.'

'A collection of ancient tombs dating back to the Nuragic civilisation characterised the necropolis,' they heard the guide say. 'These people thrived on the island of Sardinia during the Bronze Age 18th to 15th centuries BCE. 'These tombs, known as domus de janas or fairy houses in Sardinian, were carved by the people of the Nuragic civilisation into the natural limestone rock formations of the area,' the guide explained.

Natasha noticed the Necropolis of Sant'Andrea Priu featured a diverse array of burial structures, including single-chambered tombs, multi-chambered complexes, and even a few monumental tombs with elaborately decorated facades. 'Question,' she said, interrupting the guide. 'Would I be right in assuming the tombs were hierarchical? These huge tombs were for the leaders and wise folk of the tribe?'

'Yes, that is correct. Some tombs exhibit intricate carvings and engravings depicting geometric patterns, symbols, animal motifs, and other insights into the spiritual beliefs of the Nuragic people. It is likely that they were used for funerary rituals and ancestor worship.'

'Thank you very much,' she said, letting the guide continue on his way with the tour group. She held back with her unwelcome shadows. 'These larger tombs might be what we're looking for.'

'What makes you say that?' Gianpaolo asked.

'One thing I have noticed so far is appropriating other sacred sites and symbols was normal back then. The Mary movement had taken to using a Phoenician temple, which was a Minoan temple, before that in Tunisia. Even the Catholic Church has built places of worship on top of temples to Mithras. They all do it. Why should this be any different?'

'That's all you have to go on?' Said one of the other Entity agents. 'This sounds more like guess work to me than anything else.'

'It's faith in human nature, more than anything,' replied Natasha. 'There are several reasons it was done. Usually to help transition a conquered people to the victor's religion, showing their gods are weak.'

'There is only one God,' the same agent stated.

'Then there are other religions created to control the masses,' Natasha smiled. 'This is the one.'

He sneered. 'More guesswork?'

'Not at all.' Natasha pointed at a crude carving of an ample, fecund woman. 'That is the Earth goddess. Her curves symbolise the fertile land and nurturing qualities of the Earth. In some early religious circles, people often regarded Mary the Magdalene as the Earth-mother. Her journey from a woman troubled with demons to a devoted disciple reflects themes of redemption and spiritual renewal, echoing the cycles of growth and transformation found in nature. In this interpretation, Magdalene serves as a bridge between Christian spirituality and the ancient reverence for the Earth as a sacred entity. She embodies the Christian virtues of love, compassion, and redemption while also symbolising the interconnectedness between humanity and the natural world.' Before stepping into the tomb, she patted the agent on the cheek. 'When you know, you know.'

Lucas, his torso bare, hung from the ceiling of what he could only describe as being akin to a bunker. It was figuratively and literally cold. All he had to look at were the four bare uncovered brick walls and the purpose-built hook from the centre of the ceiling. That, and the strategically placed table with various implements designed to inflict maximum physical and mental pain.

One of the three men punched Lucas in the stomach. He let out a sharp expulsion of air, then smiled. 'That the best you got?' The man, who had struck him, was only 5'6", and wasn't a trained fighter. He hadn't put his weight behind the blow. Lucas believed him to be nothing more than a street thug and made a mental note to make sure he would show him how punching was properly done.

Of course, that depended on him escaping. And right now he couldn't see how he could exact such a trick.

The short man sneered. 'You like the funny, huh?' he stomped over to their table of deadly toys, and returned wearing brass knuckledusters. He unleashed a vicious, two-hook combo on their prisoner's ribs, which left Lucas swinging. 'You still like the laughing, funny man?'

As he swung back, Lucas coughed up some phlegm and spat it straight into the little man's face. It was more blood than anything else. The man literally saw red and roared as he punched Lucas over and over.

The former special forces captain was almost certain those had cracked a rib, maybe two. But he couldn't think about that right now, as he swung his legs back, then forward and with all the force he could muster, connecting with a kick under the henchman's chin, sending him to the ground, barely conscious.

Lucas felt a heavy blow in his kidneys for that one. Then he saw it came from the same big guard who had held him up against the Humvee. Another one he owed. 'Isn't it customary to ask questions during an interrogation?'

The big man grinned. 'Who said anything about an interrogation?'

'Bollocks,' Lucas said under his breath. There were no questions asked because this was going to be a torture session, simple as that.

Suddenly, Lucas felt a sharp pain in his side. The third and final guard, a slim faced, bucktoothed man, had introduced himself, presenting the knife he'd just used on Lucas, now covered in the prisoner's own blood. So this was the sick, crazy one, Lucas said in his head.

As if to prove the point, the man slapped salt in the open wound. The excruciatingly painful sting was immediate and intense, causing Lucas a burning sensation that can seem to penetrate deeply into the stabbed area. Lucas was familiar with the technique, both in performing it and being on the receiving end. He knew the salt crystals exacerbated the pain by irritating the exposed nerve endings and tissues, causing a throbbing or searing discomfort. He could resist it, somewhat. Of course, the things they did hurt Lucas, but he showed them very little of it. His defiance hurt them more mentally than anything they physically did to him, and he knew it.

Blood pooled beneath his feet, dripping from the cut above his eye and the various new wounds on his naked torso. His mind drifted, detaching from the pain. Natasha and the mission consumed his thoughts. Lucas had to survive this. He had to get out. He couldn't let them win. He wouldn't.

Each time they struck, he clung to a memory, a fragment of hope. He recalled his training, the drills that had prepared him for moments like these. Endure. Resist. Escape. The words echoed in his mind, a mantra that kept him grounded, kept him sane.

They didn't know the stories behind the many scars Lucas had over his body. Didn't know that he had been to some of the most dangerous hellholes on the planet. They didn't know that he had been at the end of some of the most vicious acts of torture.

Hours blended into an unending nightmare, yet Lucas remained unbroken. His tormentors, once so eager, now showed signs of frustration, their cruel laughter fading into angry curses. They were losing their grip, their control. And Lucas was biding his time, waiting for the right moment to turn the tables.

So by the time the morning came, Le Peregrine's men had lost some of the enthusiasm. Where was the fun in torturing someone if they didn't beg, and didn't show fear?

'Le Peregrine told us he would not break easy,' the little man said.

'Then we go on until he does,' said the twisted, buck-toothed one. He picked up a pouch from the table and brought it back, opening it in front of Lucas. Inside was a small bottle of a clear liquid and a syringe. 'Do you know what this is?'

Lucas read the label. Amytal-Scopolomine. He knew exactly what it was. It was a neural-inflammatory, a synthetic version of salt in an open wound. But whereas the salt only impacted the applied area, the synthetic drug caused every nerve ending in your body to feel like it was on fire. Just seven cc's was enough to cause indescribable pain. Whilst administering anything above risked inducing a lethal heart attack.

'I can see in your eyes that you do. So, we might as well skip the building up part and go straight to eight cc's.' Keys suddenly jangled outside the door to the chamber. 'Next time you won't be so lucky.'

The door to the torture chamber opened, and Le Peregrine sashayed in wearing a purple version of the suit she wore yesterday. 'Well, you've looked better, Lucas,' she said, examining the work her men had done to him. 'I bet you wished you hadn't been so foolish now, eh?'

'I don't know. The anguish I went through with your guys was pretty much on par with how it felt having sex with you, to be honest.'

Le Peregrine was stunned for a moment by the comment. Then she burst out into laughter. 'You can speak all the falsehoods you want, mon chéri. But I know the truth.' She leaned closer, gripped his jaw, and looked him straight in his eyes. 'You have a darkness in you. I saw it in your eyes last night, mon chéri. It is desperate to be free. And I gave it a taste of that freedom. Of what it could be like to be unshackled, unleashed. And it enjoyed it. You enjoyed it. You've been playing the role of hero. Now it's time to come home. Be who you're meant to be.' She clamped her mouth to his in a hungry kiss, savouring the slight metallic taste of his blood as she licked her lips when she pulled away. 'Clean him up and get him ready,' she ordered her men.

• • • •

LUCAS WAS GIVEN A GUARDS outfit to wear: black cargo pants with black polo shirt, and was soon being man-handled by Le Peregrine's men to one of the two tilt-rotor aircrafts that were being prepped for take-off. One had a retinue of fifteen of the arms dealers men in the hold. The second, which would be taking the cargo, two crates of weapons, was also the one taking Le Peregrine herself.

'As you have earned my mistrust, Lucas, you can travel in the hold.'

A person forcefully pushed Lucas into a seated position, restraining his hands with zip ties. He wouldn't have minded the break from his deviant host, but with ten other men, most of whom scowled at him, plus the two metal crates, it was cramped, to say the least.

Fortunately, the journey to their destination was a short one. The landscape looked even more desolate. A perfect location for an illicit arms deal to go down. Soon, the aircraft swooped in for a landing, their propellers pointing straight up as the wings rotated ninety-degrees. The landing was a soft one, and as soon as the light in the hold turned green, Le Peregrine's men moved into action like a well-oiled unit.

As the hold door opened, the two guards flanking Lucas dragged him out. The sand hadn't settled from the landing yet. It still swirled around as the propellers slowed to a stop. He held up his hands to shield himself from it, and the beating rays of the sun. He was gripped and forced towards the cabin exit where Le Peregrine descended, with the guard who had roughed Lucas up in the depot close behind her.

'How did you enjoy the flight, Lucas?'

'I've had worse. It could have done with some inflight refreshments, though.'

'Those are reserved for my special guests, which you no longer are.'

'I'm confused as to why I'm here? Before, you said you wanted me as a personal bodyguard.'

'Well, now that position has been filled,' she pointed to the guard behind her. 'But there was no way I was going to leave you behind. No, no, no, mon chéri. I would worry about what I would return home to.'

'A smouldering pile of bricks probably,' smirked Lucas.

'*Exactement!* So I decided to keep an eye on you here.'

'And what a lovely place it is! You know how to make a guy feel special.'

'Enjoy it while you can. You'll be back at the compound soon enough.'

'Why? For what reason?'

'Because I can,' she snapped. 'That is all the reason you need to have.'

Lucas knew there was more to it. He'd seen a softness in her when they had been alone, and it scared him. The things she'd said hadn't been far from the mark. That's why he needed Natasha, to keep him on the right side of the line. But the draw was strong, especially with women like Anne Shepard,

Chiara Harris and now Leila pulling him in the opposite direction.

'Why are you looking at me like that?' She swallowed, nervous of his piercing gaze.

Lucas had been looking at her. He'd seen her eyes dilate. But then he noticed a plume of dust in the distance. 'We have company.'

She turned around, and saw what Lucas had seen, and smiled. 'The buyer is here.'

It was a convoy of various vehicles, a saloon, two SUVs, and a van. They pulled up, the van coming in reverse, and several armed men got out of the SUVs. The back door of the saloon opened and a middle-aged man with long greying hair which was tied back in a ponytail and sporting a goatee climbed out. He slipped on a pair of sunglasses and approached. 'I take it you're Leila,' he started, eyeing her up and down. 'Le Peregrine's go between?'

'I am. And you are Barry Sullivan. I have your order ready for you. Would you like to inspect it?'

'You can call me Baz, and yes, I would.' He rubbed his hands together in anticipation. Barry followed Leila, and she led the way to the cargo which was being unloaded from her aircraft. As they passed Lucas, Barry took a glance at him, then a second longer one, and creased his brow as he continued on.

Lucas had no idea why the man looked at him like that, and one of his guards shoved him in the back to follow the others. When he got there, she had already placed her hand on the palm reader and opened the first crate. Barry was examining one of the assault rifles, making sure the merchandise was what he was expecting and was in working order.

'And the ammo?'

'Right here in the second crate along with the Glocks.'

He came over and picked up a magazine. 'I'd like to test this gun.'

Leila's guard took a step towards him, but she stopped him with a hand and smiled at Barry. 'That is not how things are normally done. If you wanted to try before you buy, I would have arranged for this transaction to take place at Le Peregrine's compound, and you would have had the firing range at your disposal. But as you are a new client, and you don't know the quality of Le Peregrine's merchandise, I will allow it, this time.'

Barry loaded the machine gun. And took aim at Lucas. 'I know you,' he shouted. 'I know your face. What are you? Police? Is thins some undercover sting?' Seeing their boss agitated, Barry's men raised their weapons, prompting Leila's to do the same.

'You got the wrong guy,' Lucas replied, holding up his tied hands.

'Lucas may be several things, Barry, but he is no police officer,' Leila assured him, trying to calm the situation.

Barry picked up the name. 'Lucas? Lucas? Lucas Redmond? Yes! That's it, Lucas Redmond.'

'Perhaps you do know him then,' the Moroccan shrugged her slender shoulders.

'I knew I recognised you,' he said, lowering the gun. 'From way back. You used to work for Sebastian Jericho when you were a kid. I always wondered what happened to you. I heard rumours that Jericho was dead.'

'Dead? Nah, he's not dead. How can you kill a ghost?' Lucas said. 'I remember you now. You worked for Tully Byrd, right?'

'Until he kicked the bucket, and I took over the biz. And now I'm expanding it, I got a new partner. Man, it's funny seeing you two working together.'

'Why funny?' Leila asked.

'Well, just the fact that you both act as intermediaries for men that have rarely been seen, if at all.'

Leila looked at Lucas. 'That is quite the coincidence wouldn't you say? It puts a few pieces of the puzzle in place for me, too. You and I have some things to discuss when we return, Lucas. But first, Baz, I assume you are pleased with the products?'

'Oh yeah, for sure. Let's do this.'

Barry waved over an associate of his. He carried a laptop and, after placing it on top of one of the crates, booted up Barry's bank account. Once it was open, he faced Leila. 'Can I have the account number please?' He typed in the details and a few seconds later declared the transfer complete, which was corroborated by one of her own men.

'Now that the business has concluded, perhaps you would like a drink while we disable the crate's palm readers and hand them over to your men for loading?'

'Sounds like a great idea,' Barry replied. 'But I think we might have to hold off on that for a bit.'

'Pourqoui? What for?'

'For your boy here,' he thumbed at Lucas. 'It appears he's not only on your shit-list, but he's on my new business partners list too.'

'And who is your business partner?'

'Ah, here she comes now,' Barry said as a helicopter came over the horizon.

Chapter 32

Since the Necropolis of Sant'Andrea Priu was recognised as one of the most important archaeological sites in Sardinia and designated as a UNESCO World Heritage Site, Natasha wanted to ensure that they didn't cause any damage during their search. And to be sure of it, she told Gianpaolo and his men to stand aside and let her do what she does best. The chambers provided valuable evidence of Sardinia's prehistoric past and contributed to an understanding of ancient Mediterranean civilisations. She wasn't about to let these Entity thugs destroy anything.

But as time went on, after searching for several minutes with no results, they were getting antsy, especially the one that had been riding Natasha's back from the start.

'This is pointless, Gianpaolo,' he said in Italian. 'A waste of our time. Why would his eminence entertain this woman? Especially when she is a nonbeliever and has such disregard for the church?'

'Our duty is not to question, Alfonso,' came the reply. 'We have been given an assignment, and it is our duty to complete it.'

'Like a good little soldier,' Natasha added, also in Italian. She kept searching, not needing to see their faces to know that they were taken aback. But the thought made her smile. 'Assumption is a mother, isn't it? And you all are making another one, potentially a bigger one. Assuming that Cardinal Elias Wagner is doing all this, hunting for the holy grail, for the glory of God.'

'Of course he is,' Alfonso snapped, taking offence at the idea that he would do otherwise.

'Like I said, good little soldiers.'

'Just do what you were brought here to do, signorina Travers,' Gianpaolo said, concluding the discussion.

Natasha had been making her way around the chamber, scanning the walls, looking for any clues. Alfonso was leaning against a section of wall, bored. 'Move,' she ordered. He looked at her with a haughty glare, prompting Natasha to stand tall and erect. She'd spent enough time with Lucas to learn the signs when a challenge was being made. Alfonso snorted and skulked away.

She watched him walk away, noting that he was going to be troublesome if, as she hoped, Lucas ever got here to mount a rescue. She had been delaying things as much as she could, but her tactics were drawing the attention of the Entity's lead field agent.

'You still haven't found anything yet?' he asked her.

'These things take time.'

'Or perhaps you are stalling for time,' he countered, and showed the top of one of the doorjamb. 'Is that not the same image as the one you pointed to outside?'

'Yes, it is,' Natasha explained, on the defence, but luckily, she'd found something else of interest during her delayed search. 'But there are these marks too,' she said. 'They're dotted all around. They're not deep. I thought they were just random scratchings at first.'

'And they are not?'

'No, I don't think so.' She searched in her bag until she found what she was looking for, a small notepad and pen, and copied down the mark. 'It reminds me a lot like Aramaic. But it's not complete.' Natasha searched again, this time focussing on engravings that resembled parts of Aramaic words. By the end of her exploration, she had amassed a page full of the ancient text. 'It's an Aramaic anagram,' she revealed.

'I assume you can solve it?'

'Of course I can,' she replied. In truth, she already had, but it was another chance for her to delay matters. She sat with her back to a wall and would randomly write something, only to scribble it out moments later. While she was pretending to decipher the text, in her mind she was replaying her conversations with Cardinal Wagner. The more she thought about it, the more she was certain he was going to do something unthinkable. What if he was planning to eliminate the pope? That's crazy, she thought.

'Have you discovered something?' Gianpaolo asked, seeing Natasha staring straight ahead.

'Hmm? Oh yeah, the message. It reads "as above, so below".'

'Which means?'

'I don't know,' she shrugged. 'I guess we carry on looking.'

More of the Vatican spies were becoming frustrated with their current assignment, some of them even voicing their opinion with disgruntled sounds. Natasha's heart danced with delight at the slightest hint of dissent. She was willing the cavalry to come charging in as soon as possible.

They moved into another chamber of the elaborate ancient tomb. It was lit by spotlights standing in the corners.

Rows of hieroglyphic inscriptions adorned the walls, which Natasha believed depicted scenes from ancient mythology, historical events, or religious rituals. She noticed that each hieroglyph in the walls was meticulously carved into the stone, unlike the Aramaic scratchings in the previous area. 'This is amazing,' enthused Natasha. 'This is ancient man forming complex compositions. They could be telling stories or conveying symbolic messages.' Unfortunately, she was preaching to an uninterested audience.

'The grail, signorina Travers.'

In addition to the hieroglyphs, the chamber was adorned with carved reliefs, decorative motifs, and symbolic glyphs, which added to its mystique and historical richness. Natasha noticed strange engravings on the ground, lots of circled crosses of differing sizes. It baffled her at first, but when she looked up, she understood what the Aramaic message had meant. The ceiling displayed engraved crisscrosses, similar to the ones on the ground, some larger than others.

'Are you telling me that these mean something?' Gianpaolo asked, throwing up a hand dismissively.

'As above,' she said, looking up, then she looked at the ground, 'so below. They're stars. The constellations as these Neolithic people would have seen them. They are like ancient, engraved star charts, I suppose, depicting the positions of stars, planets, and celestial bodies.'

Gianpaolo looked up at them again with a more appreciative eye. 'I think you are right. I see the Big Dipper.'

'Of course I'm right,' proclaimed Natasha. 'It's just a matter of finding out what the connection to Mary and the holy grail is. Keep following the breadcrumbs until we find the loaf of bread.'

But at that moment, Natasha couldn't see what the connection might be. Until she thought more about the phrase from the previous chamber. 'It must mean something, or else why go through the trouble of engraving it at all?' she said, looking down, pacing back and forth, deep in thought. 'If this was the last resting place of the holy grail, maybe even Mary herself, it must be something that followers of the Magdalene Creed would know. Just as at the Carthage amphitheatre...wait a minute.'

She twisted her head around so that she could get a good look at the constellation at her feet. A moment later, she was looking up at the ceiling. Then she was searching the ground again. Natasha stopped when she found what she was looking for, and once more looked at the ceiling, moving around slowly. To the onlookers, it seemed aimless. But again, she pointed to the ceiling with mounting excitement.

'Are you going to explain what you've found?'

'In the riddle on the map that led us to Carthage, it said follow the clues, like stars in the night. At Carthage there were jewels set in the shape of constellations. In particular Sirius, the Pleiades and Orion. Mythology links all of them to Artemis, and the Gentiles link her to Mary the Magdalene. And look here,' she pointed out the Sirius constellation on the ground and then again on the ceiling. 'Here is the Pleiades, and also over here.'

'And what of Orion?' Gianpaolo asked.

'It's not on the ceiling,' she said with a wide grin. 'I can't find it, anyway.'

The Vatican agent had a look at the ceiling to make sure she wasn't stalling for time again.

'The only place I have found the constellation of Orion is over here.' Natasha led the way across the chamber to a corner in the back. 'You see, the three crisscrosses?'

'Yes,' he replied. 'Orion's Belt. And what now?'

Natasha got down onto her knees and gently blew the detritus from the engraving. For the first time, she noticed the three stars which made up the belt differed slightly from all the other stars she had seen. The surrounding circles seemed to be a bit more pronounced, just enough to catch the eye of someone that was looking for anything out of place. And in Natasha's mind, this constituted as something fitting that description.

She traced her finger around each star of Orion's Belt. The texture felt just like the rest of the stone ground, but the wider circle made Natasha think of something. Using her index finger, she applied a bit of pressure, pressing it like a button. The star depressed slightly, causing her to let out a chuckle.

'Nothing happened,' Alfonso said with a derisive sneer.

'Nothing yet,' she corrected. Natasha spread her fingers so that they covered the three stars of Orion's Belt, and pushed them all together. The wall in front of her lifted, while part of the ground in front of it dropped in staggered stages to create steps that joined to the descending staircase behind the wall.

The Vatican spies came closer to witness what was happening. Natasha got to her feet, dusting herself off with a grin of triumph on her face. She knew most of them, all of them except Gianpaolo, didn't think she would find anything. She got a kick out of proving them wrong.

Gianpaolo glanced into the darkness before turning to his agents. 'Alfonso, you will remain here. Guard the entrance to the tomb. Do not allow anybody to enter. The rest of us will accompany signorina Travers down the steps.' After his men had all acknowledged his orders, Gianpaolo turned to Natasha. 'After you, signorina.'

Natasha took the MAGLite from her bag and thumbed the flashlight on. Her eyes sparkled with a bright-eyed look as she gazed down the dark steps. Her skin tingled, and she took several deep breaths to quell the fluttering in her stomach. She wondered what she was about to find in the dark depths of the staircase, but there was only one way she would ever find out. Natasha took the first step on the staircase, the latest in this quest for the holy grail and another step closer to her destiny.

Lucas's eyebrows pinched together. 'She?' he repeated. It took him a matter of seconds to come up with a name. 'Please tell me you didn't hook up with Chiara Harris and J Organisation?'

'Okay. I won't tell you,' Barry sniggered. 'This has been a most lucrative deal for me.'

'What did they have you do?' Lucas asked.

'Wear this cam,' he pointed at the fake button on his jacket. 'They knew you were with Le Peregrine, but I don't think they knew he would send you with his woman. Just stay calm sweetheart, let them take Lucas and everything will be fine.'

'Bloody hell, Barry,' Lucas growled. 'Chiara's a terrorist. She will not let any of you survive this.'

'What are you talking about? We've made a deal.'

'But she takes orders from someone that wants me dead. So I think you're shit out of luck.'

Hearing all this, Leila made a signal to her bodyguard, who repeated it to the others.

Lucas noticed the movement but wasn't expecting what happened next. Leila's guards fired on Barry's men. The British gangster took out a knife and tried to attack Lucas, but he was on the attempted thrust in a flash, grabbing his wrist and bending it backwards which such force that his elbow gave out. Barry screamed, but two shots fired by Leila cut it short. Lucas let go and the lifeless body slumped to the floor.

'Another one you owe me, Lucas, or should I call you by another name,' she teased.

'I don't know what you're talking about,' he replied, shielding himself from the firefight.

'You and I playing the same game, is what I am talking about. Playing the advocate when we are actually the mastermind behind it all. Leila and Le Peregrine. Lucas and Sebastian Jericho. I knew you had a dark past, Lucas.'

'I'm not him anymore,' replied Lucas. When they had put the zip ties on him, Lucas had clenched his fist and tensed his forearms. Now they were relaxed. He had a bit of space to play with. It was enough to rotate them from their crossed position and from there, Lucas lifted his hands above his head, and in one fluid motion, brought them down with as much force as he could, snapping the plastic restraints.

The action brought an appreciative sound from Leila. 'Tell that to the bruises you left, mon chéri.'

Suddenly there was a thunderous rumble from a 50cal gun attached to the helicopter. The huge bullets peppered the sand and ripped through one of the SUVs, causing it to explode, flipping in the air before crashing down, a twisted wreckage.

Lucas dived for Leila, taking her to the ground as her bodyguard was blown away. The helicopter gunner had zeroed in on their primary target, and they weren't worried about collateral damage.

'I think I've paid one back. Don't you?' Lucas asked, looking down at Leila. Bullets slammed into the aircraft beside them, reminding them they were in a pitched battle. Before she could say anything, Lucas scrambled to his feet, taking the dead guard's machine gun, dragging her up and running for the second tilt-rotor aircraft.

Bodies were falling around them, Lucas adding a few of J Organisation's men to the tally. 'Go on,' he pushed Leila. 'Get on the plane, get out of here!'

'What about you?'

'It's me they're after.'

Suddenly, the ground shuddered as the tilt-rotor behind them blew up, thick plumes of smoke raising up in the air. Lucas turned and fired back at the helicopter, giving Leila the cover she needed to reach her aircraft.

The pilot had already begun preparing for take-off, whilst the co-pilot had been shooting from the cabin stairs. Leila reached them and looked over, expecting to see Lucas running to join her. However, he was running in the opposite direction. 'Come on,' she said to the co-pilot as she climbed the stairs. 'He is drawing the fire of the helicopter. Pick up the rest of our men. We must take this opportunity.'

'You're leaving him behind?' the co-pilot asked.

'It is his decision. Besides, I think he will not stay away for long,' Leila replied as she watched Lucas in action.

Lucas was glad to see Leila's tilt-rotor lifting off, even though it meant he was stranded with a helicopter gunner hellbent on trying to end him. 'I hope you know what you're doing, Lucas,' he said to himself, diving out of the way of another salvo from the gunner.

It circled around, and for the first time, he locked eyes with the gunner. It was indeed Chiara Harris. He sneered as he scrambled for cover, seeing the sheer delight on her face at his plight. 'You are not dying here today,' Lucas said. 'Especially not by that bitch's hand.'

With the rest of Leila's men retreating to her aircraft, the last remnants of Barry's J organisation contingent were looking to make a run for it, too. Some headed for the SUV, the wheels throwing up sand as the vehicle peeled away. Lucas jumped on their plan of escape, making a beeline for the saloon Barry had arrived in. But one terrorist beat him to it. Lucas's curses soon turned to words of relief as huge bullet holes peppered the car, several hitting the unfortunate terrorist. The only means of escape left was the van, and Lucas saw two men jumping into it.

He broke out into a sprint, running down the van before they could leave. The rear doors were still wide open, with only one crate being loaded before the chaos had ensued. Lucas could hear the engine turning over as he got closer.

The engine finally revved up and drove off just as Lucas made a desperate lunge for it. He clattered into the crate, adding more pain to his already damaged body.

The passenger turned around to see Lucas in the back. 'Son of a bitch! It's the guy.'

'Get rid of him, or they'll take us out too!'

The man didn't need to be told twice. He climbed into the back of the van and got a kick to the face for his troubles from the prone Lucas. The terrorist caught the second kick and with a cruel grin, he stomped on Lucas's raw, tortured wounds. Lucas's scream pierced the air, the pain visibly more intense than anticipated. The sadistic smile on the terrorist's face widened, and he stomped again, relishing the anguished cries.

'The chopper is coming around again. Throw him off!'

The man attempted to do just that, but Lucas put up too much resistance. They grappled as Chiara's bullets perforated the roof, missing them by inches. Neither one could get the upper hand as the van jumped up and down, trying to escape at high speed on uneven terrain. One particularly violent bounce separated the men, throwing them into opposite sides of the van. The terrorist charged at Lucas, who used his foot to shove him back. As he recoiled back off the side, Lucas hit him with an elbow under the chin. For good measure, he grabbed his head and slammed it into the metal crate, before tossing him out the back.

'About time,' the driver said, as he saw the body tumbling behind them in his side mirror.

'Tell me about it,' Lucas said.

Startled, the driver took a swing at him, which was easily blocked. Then Lucas put a gun in his face.

'Now you can either head east to Egypt, or I can drive there myself. Your choice.'

'I'll — I'll drive,' he stammered.

'Good,' Lucas nodded and slowly pulled the gun away. 'Now, let's see if there's anything in this crate for the damned chopper.'

Lucas lifted the lid of the weapons cache, his eyes darting over its contents. Handguns, machine guns and a long-case. His eyebrows creased as he reached down for it and placed it on top of the crate. 'Oh, this will do nicely,' he smiled. Inside the case was a dismantled UAR-10 sniper rifle.

Despite having a relationship with Chiara in the past, his feelings for her had long vanished. That happened when he discovered she was purposely sent to seduce him, break up his marriage, and isolate him from his friends. All so that his Machiavellian mother, who had just returned from her faked death, could resume her parental duties.

He often wondered how he would feel if he ever had the opportunity to put a bullet in her, if he could even pull the trigger? The truth was, he felt nothing.

Even though the ride wasn't smooth, putting the rifle together wasn't an arduous task for Lucas. In fairness, the rough ride aided them by making it difficult for Chiara to get a good hit during the helicopter's low strafing runs.

But as much as it aided, it also hindered.

Lucas braced himself against the rear of the van, using a foot to stop the door swinging back and forth. He put the stock into his shoulder and lifted the rifle. And waited. The chopper came swooping back down, hovering in the air as it turned to face its side to the van.

Chaira started to come around, and then froze when she saw Lucas aiming a sniper rifle at her. Lucas squeezed the hair-trigger, but then the van lurched in a ditch, sending his bullet high above his intended target to strike the rotor's engine. The rough bouncing caused Lucas to unintentionally shoot again, hitting the pilot in his leg this time.

Out of self-preservation, the pilot pulled away, but it was an action fuelled by panic. He hadn't regained height. As the helicopter tilted, its propellers caught on the sand dunes. The pilot lost all control. The aircraft dug into the sand and flipped over, slamming down and throwing up a sandstorm. It rocked because of the rotor blades still trying to do their job until the engine was cutoff.

The crashed helicopter was fast disappearing in the distance, but Lucas could still see two people climb out of the wreckage.

'Bollocks,' he whispered. He climbed back into the passenger seat.

'We did it,' the driver squealed. 'We're home free.'

'Well I am,' Lucas amended. 'You can hitch a ride with your boss.'

'What? But I thought...?'

'Yeah, you thought wrong.' In one fluid motion, Lucas both opened the door and shoved the terrorist out of it. 'Tell that bitch I'll get her next time.'

Chapter 34

As Natasha descended the narrow stone staircase, the four Entity agents behind her, she felt a sense of anticipation coursing through her veins. The air grew cooler with each step, the faint scent of damp and ancient stone in the air, but also something else. Paraffin? Beams from their flashlights lit up the rough-hewn walls, casting eerie shadows of the procession that danced like spectres in the dimness as they continued on their way.

She examined the walls as they went down. From the cursory looks she was having, they were enough to tell her it was tools used long after the Neolithic age, which were used to engineer the stairway and whatever was at the bottom. The discovery of the stairs behind the wall of the Neolithic tomb had filled Natasha with a mixture of excitement, knowing that she was delving deeper into the secrets of Mary and the grail, but also trepidation because she was going into the unknown and did not know what was at the bottom of the stairs.

The staircase had felt they went on for an eternity endlessly going downward, leading them deeper into the heart of the earth, but finally they reached the bottom and emerged into a cavernous chamber bathed in soft, ethereal light.

'Where's that light coming from?'

'The walls appear to be adorned with some sort of crystal fragments. It's refracting the light from the flashlights.'

The walls had intricate carvings and symbols, their meanings momentarily lost on Natasha. Then she saw what looked like a drum, and wondered, *Could these other symbols be instruments also?*

'Come and look at this,' Gianpaolo said.

In the centre of the chamber stood a pedestal. Natasha approached with a sense of reverence. She could feel the weight of history pressing down upon her, a tangible presence that seemed to whisper secrets of a bygone era, and she was its amplifier. Natasha looked down at the top of the pedestal and saw more Aramaic engraved on it, and around the stem of the pedestal.

'What does it say?'

She read it a few more times, walking around the structure as she did so, before answering. 'It's a riddle. "I am the first digit, small but mighty, a single digit standing tall and upright. Without me, there is no beginning, no start, no end. What am I? I am the middle digit, neither first nor last, caught in the rhythm between the beats. When you find me, you know you're halfway there, balanced on the precipice of possibility. What am I? I am the final digit, the last note in the symphony, bringing closure to the melody. With a flicker of my presence, the cycle completes, and a new beginning awaits. What am I? I am the sum of the digits when added together, a number with a resonance like no other. Vibrating in harmony, be penitent, for I hold a secret frequency. What am I?" It's nine, six, three,' Natasha revealed at the end.

'How can you know that?'

'The last clue gave it away. It's a frequency. A resonance like no other. Vibrating in harmony. You didn't get a bit of a heavenly vibe hearing that?'

'Heaven? No, I did not.'

'Not even the penitent part? Well, this frequency is associated with spiritual awakening, inner harmony, and alignment with the universe. Some people believe that listening to or meditating on tones at this frequency can promote feelings of deep relaxation, connection, and well-being. Nikola Tesla said, "If you want to find the secrets of the universe, think in terms of energy, frequency, and vibration." He specifically mentioned 369, 693 and 963. It's also called the God frequency.'

'What is it about people trying to scientifically define God? Trying to reduce the almighty to a sound.'

'Isn't there some phenomena about the voice of God? And isn't voice just a series of vibrational frequencies? If God has a frequency, then that surely means god is real. It's the proof that many people would need.'

'Faith is all they should need,' Gianpaolo replied. 'Faith can inspire compassion, kindness, generosity, and altruism, making a more compassionate and cohesive society. Believing in something greater than oneself can give life a deeper significance and help people navigate difficult times with resilience and hope. People can draw strength from their faith to overcome obstacles and persevere in the pursuit of their goals, even in the face of uncertainty and ambiguity.'

'And you're being narrow minded if you think all those qualities are exclusive to people of faith. I don't follow any religion, but I am kind and generous. I have faced plenty of obstacles and persevered. At the end of the day, I believe we are all looking at the same god, just through slightly different tinted glasses.'

Truth versus Faith. It was an intellectual battle which had continued to gain traction since the cultural and philosophical movement known as the Age of Enlightenment during the 17th and 18th centuries. Enlightenment thinkers sought to challenge traditional authority, superstition, and religious dogma, advocating for principles such as freedom of thought, separation of church and state, and the rights of individuals.

For a moment, Natasha wondered if people would have regarded her as one of those thinkers, if she had been around at that time. Sure, she supported freedom of thought and the rights of individuals, principles they advocated for. But she didn't challenge people's superstitions, or their religions, despite the things she'd said to Gianpaolo. She just wanted the historical Jesus to be acknowledged as the Pauline Jesus was. Natasha's brow creased. That was something that Cardinal Wagner seemed to want as well, judging by his change of heart regarding the holy grail, as well as his plans to release information about the union between Mary and Jesus. Which surely put him at odds with the Catholic Church. How could he possibly be its protector?

Natasha was just about to question Gianpaolo about him when an agent joined them at the pedestal.

'I found this metal rod in the corner of the chamber.' He handed it to Gianpaolo, who handed it to Natasha.

'What is it?'

She examined it and discovered that it was just a plain solid metal rod roughly 12 inches long and a half inch in diameter. There were no markings on it, she could see. 'It's just a metal rod,' she shrugged.

One of the other guards yelled that he'd found another one and brought it over. As he did, a low hum briefly filled the chamber, echoing off the stone walls with a haunting resonance.

'Did you hear that?' Gianpaolo asked.

'Yes. It appears we are in some sort of acoustic chamber. Oh!' she squealed, suddenly realising what the rods were for.

'What is?'

'The rods. When you strike two metal rods together, they vibrate at their natural resonant frequency. I bet that the frequency of these is 963hz.'

'Well, hit them and see what happens,' the agent said.

'I assume it's not as straightforward as that,' Gianpaolo commented.

'No. The force and technique used to strike the rods together can also affect the frequency they produce. But we've come this far. I suggest we push on.'

Gianpaolo nodded.

Natasha's heart quickened, and with trembling hands, holding the middle of each of them, she struck the rods together. The note resonated with the crystals, sending vibrations coursing through the very foundations of the chamber. Without warning, at irregular intervals, jets of fire suddenly shot out from hidden vents in the walls and floor, engulfing sections of the chamber in flames. The flames reached several feet in height and length. One agent was consumed by the first streams of fire. His terrible screams penetrated Natasha's entire body, but there was nothing she or his fellow agents could do. It wasn't long before he fell silent.

'Stay alert,' Gianpaolo ordered his remaining men. 'The flames move from the outside to the inside. It gives you a split second to get clear. You need to time your movements carefully, wait for lulls in the flame jets before making a dash to the next section.'

Natasha examined the ground even closer than before. She could see the tiny vents now, all but invisible in the darkness. 'There doesn't seem to be any of those vents around the pedestal.'

'It must be a safe haven, then. You two have to join us here.' They both nodded and waited for the next burst of flames to arrive.

Their eyes scanned the room for any signs of danger. With each passing moment, the tension in the air grew thicker, the anticipation of the next eruption of flames weighing heavily on their minds. Jets of fire erupted from hidden vents in the walls and floor, casting flickering shadows across the room. The flames danced and roared, filling the chamber with intense heat and light.

The agents pressed forward, their hearts pounding in their chests. They moved with precision and determination, navigating the chamber with practiced ease. As the flames subsided, before they had time to catch a breath, another jet of fire erupted from the wall right behind them. One agent reacted quickly, ducking out of harm's way just before the flames could engulf him. The other wasn't so fortunate. Tongues of flame soon swallowed him. The surviving agent dashed for the pedestal, arriving just as more streams of fire blasted from the ground.

Natasha had waited until he had joined them before she tried the rods again. She didn't want to risk him being caught in another death trap if the frequency struck was wrong again. Lowering her hands down the length of the metal rods, giving them more space to vibrate, she hit one against the other.

The tuning rods produced a distinct tone that spread outwards. A beautiful singular note re-echoed around the chamber. The crystals acting as both resonators and amplifiers. Each time the note reverberated around the acoustic chamber, the louder the note became, until they were covering their ears trying to shield against it.

Natasha dropped the rods. The ever-increasing sound of the God Frequency drowned out her screams of agony.

Chapter 35

Alfonso hated this assignment more and more with each passing moment. Being ordered to play security guard at the doorway was a waste of his talents. But he fancied following Travers down those stairs even less. Up here, at least, he didn't have to listen to her blasphemous talk. He didn't know how Gianpaolo tolerated it, but he had always focused on the end goal of his missions, though, and not allow anything to distract him from it.

'Let him play nice with the annoying woman,' he said, and carried on leaning against the entry to the tomb. That's when he saw a short girl, smoking a joint, her hair different shades of purple, walking toward the tomb. 'Hey, this tomb is closed to visitors today.'

'Why's that?' Ellen Paige asked, blowing smoke in his direction.

'Preservation work.'

'Really?' she asked, craning her head around him. 'I don't see anybody?'

'That's because they're further inside the structure,' he replied, slowly losing his patience with her.

'Well, if they're deep inside the tomb, I should be able to see what's in this first chamber quickly.'

'I already told you no. Now get out of here, kid. There're plenty of other tombs you can go nose around in.'

'But they don't have a guard. So this one must be pretty special to have a lookout.'

'Who are you?'

'First, I'm no "kid", I'm a grown ass woman. And second, who I am is none of your business.' With impressive speed, Ellen slammed the taser she had hidden behind her back into the gut of Alfonso, sending 150,000 shocking volts surging through his body. He crumpled to the floor, unconscious. 'That's what you get for being disrespectful, my guy.'

Ellen had a tough time dragging the body inside, but she somehow managed to, puffing hard when she'd finished. She put her earbuds in and made a call.

'Ellen?' Lucas asked. 'Is everything alright?'

'Yeah, apart from you being late, as always. Where are you?'

'I should be coming in to Alghero soon. David really came through for me, sent a helicopter to pick me up and organised a plane for me at Cairo. I'll have to owe him for this one.'

'Then you'll be glad to know that I found the tomb where Natasha's signal went dead. There was a guard at the entryway, but he's catching up on his sleep now,' Ellen said, looking down at the man she'd left in the foetal position.

'Good work, El. I'll make a field agent out of you yet. Any sign of Natasha?'

'Nothing yet,' she reported. 'Hold on. There is a staircase going under a wall in another chamber. That must be why the signal went dead. I'll leave a beacon for you to follow with your gps.'

'I don't like this plan, Ellen. Both you and Nat will be out of radio contact. And you have no clue what you'll find down there.'

'Don't remind me. I'm not a big fan of it either, but someone's got to scout ahead, and you're not here to do it.'

'Just be careful down there.'

'And you just hurry up and get here.'

• • • •

THE SOUND REVERBERATING around the chamber was unbearable. Natasha had dropped to her knees, sure that her head would explode at any moment. The other two men with her were in just as much agony, but their machismo wouldn't allow them to fold.

Natasha toppled over to her side, attempting to make herself as small as possible, hoping it might aid her somehow. Her mind became analytical as she tried to distract from the pain she was suffering. She thought about the chances of suffering acoustic trauma caused by the extreme sound waves. *Not only can the phenomena cause damage to the eardrum, it can also induce non-auditory effects on the body, such as damage to internal organs, disruption of bodily functions, and even death in severe cases. These effects may result from the rapid compression and decompression of air molecules caused by the sound waves, leading to changes in pressure that can affect various tissues and organs. This is a worse death than being burned alive. I was so certain I was right, but it must have been the wrong frequency again. Perhaps if I strike the rods one more time.*

She opened her eyes and saw one of the rods, but beyond it she saw something more intriguing. With her hands still covering her ears, Natasha crawled toward the far wall. Gianpaolo watched her. *He probably thinks I've lost my mind,* she thought to herself. *Truth is, I regained my mind. I should have picked up on it sooner. "Be penitent" and what does a penitent person do?*

Gianpaolo's gaze continued to follow Natasha until she disappeared into the wall. His jaw dropped, but he was soon rushing over to where the archaeologist had vanished. It wasn't until he got down into a prone position that he saw the gap to another chamber at the bottom of the wall. He turned to his men and waved them to follow before he crawled through the gap.

The two men followed. As the first of them was about to kneel, he turned as his compatriot reached out and touched his shoulder. He saw the man he had trained with and worked with on many assignments, frozen in an unheard scream, blood dribbling from his ears and nose, his eyes bloodshot. The Entity agent dropped to the ground, dead.

Natasha heard Gianpaolo's soft prayer as he learned of another of his agents falling on this treacherous quest for the grail. But those were the dangers that accompanied the way of life of an adventurer. You're always on the edge. You tread a fine line between success and failure. But it was what gave her the adrenaline rush high, and partly why she did what she did.

A soft ethereal glow bathed the chamber they had emerged into, with walls that were adorned with shimmering crystals of various shapes, sizes, and colours. Crystalline formations protruded from the floor and ceiling, refracting light and casting prismatic reflections across the room. Natasha looked up, searching for the light source, and saw a single hole, three inches in diameter.

The ringing in their ears took several moments to fade, their equilibrium a little longer before the three of them continued their exploration. At the centre of the chamber stood an altar, upon which rested a large crystal with intricate geometric patterns. Surrounding the central crystal were smaller crystals arranged in a circular pattern, each emitting a faint humming sound.

Gianpaolo's last remaining agent was panic-stricken. 'Oh no. It's that sound thing again.'

But Natasha wasn't so sure, shaking her head as she continued her exploration. 'I don't think is.'

'You're sure?'

'No, not one-hundred per cent. But we've all looked around and I haven't seen any rods, or any other tuning device. Have you?'

'No, I haven't. The only thing here is crystal and the altar.'

'So it would only make sense that they would have something to do with us getting out of here.'

'Agreed, but what?'

Natasha shrugged. 'Beats me. But I'll find out what soon enough.'

She went to inspect the altar, checking its structure to see if it was movable. It was firmly in place. As were the crystals on top, the big one and the seven smaller ones. It was at that moment Natasha made a connection. The seven crystals were all different colours. 'Red, orange, yellow, green, blue, indigo, and violet,' she said, as a smile crept across her face. 'Do you know what this means?'

'They're colours of a rainbow,' the agent said.

'Yes, they are. But they are also the colours of the seven chakras; Root Chakra: Muladhara - RED, Sacral Chakra, Svadhishthana - ORANGE Solar Plexus Chakra, Manipura - YELLOW Heart Chakra, Anahata - GREEN Throat Chakra, Vishuddha - BLUE Third Eye, Ajna - INDIGO Crown Chakra, Sahasrara - VIOLET. These are must chakra crystals.'

'But what is the significance? How does this help us?'

'It's suggested that during the missing years of Jesus's life, he travelled to India and Tibet, where he would have learned all about chakras, their healing prowess, and about healing your body with your mind.'

'India? Tibet? How do you suggest he would have travelled that far?'

'With merchants and traders, of course. The start of the Silk Road took place in 130 BCE Well before the birth of Jesus. And when he was older, if he was to make this journey, it makes perfect sense he would take his wife with him. Meaning that she would have had knowledge of the chakras too.' Natasha twisted a strand of hair as she continued to speculate further. 'It is possible that the other disciples questioned Mary about this "secret knowledge" after Jesus was killed.'

'Again,' Gianpaolo said, to bring her back to the here and now. 'How doesn't this help us?'

Natasha went to the crystal hit by the sunlight and scrutinised it. She put her hand out to cover it from the light, and the room went dark, as there was nothing being reflected. Tentatively, she touched the crystal and found that it was cool to the touch. Then she took hold of it and realised that she could twist it in place. The refracted light changed as different crystals were now being bathed in light, including one of the seven chakra crystals on the altar.

They all saw what happened. The yellow crystal was glowing and the humming emanating from it became more pronounced.

'You figured it out,' Gianpaolo said, almost in praise of the adventurer.

'I think so,' Natasha confirmed. 'We have to adjust the crystals around the chamber so that the beam of light hits all of those chakra crystals.'

'And what?'

'That I don't know.' She looked down at her watch. 'But what I do know is that we don't have all the time in the world. We're getting light through that hole because it's midday. The sun is overhead at the moment. But in about thirty minutes, it will have moved away. And no light means no solving of the puzzle.'

'Then I would suggest you begin, signorina Travers,' he said, pulling his gun out of its holster.

'What's that for?'

'In case you feel the need to stall again, and delay things until tomorrow.'

Natasha snorted. 'I'll do it, because I want the truth out in the open, and not because of your pathetic threats. If any of you had an inkling of how to find the holy grail, I wouldn't be here. Now stay out of my way.'

Ellen took a tentative few steps and heard an awful deaf-ening sound rise from the depths of the darkness. The further down she had gone, the louder it had become. She paused, wondering if she should carry on. She took the time to roll herself a joint. Then the sound stopped. 'Keep it to-gether, Ellen,' she said to herself. Even with her high-pow-ered headlamps on, she descended the steps slowly. 'You've played enough video games and watched enough horror movies to know that musty, dark staircases are a prime loca-tion for a scene to make you jump out of your skin. Usually where the sexy one of the group gets popped, and you're top of that list, hon. Don't become a statistic. You know you got that Bad Bitch Energy.'

Despite all of her worrying, there was no long-forgotten beast waiting for Ellen at the bottom of the steps. But when she saw the charred, smouldering remains of two bodies, she felt her heartbeat quicken. 'There's a goddamn dragon down here,' he head swivelling around looking for its lair. That's when she heard faint voices in the air. She held her taser tightly and edged toward the sounds, which seemed to come from the wall. As she neared, Ellen came across anoth-er body. How this one had died wasn't obvious to her, but judging by the blood trailing from his eyes, ears and nose, it hadn't been pleasant.

Ellen could clearly hear Natasha's voice now. She heard the mention of a gun. *'So, what do I do now?'* She wondered.

NATASHA STOOD IN THE dimly lit chamber, her heart pounding with urgency. Before her lay a daunting puzzle, unlike any she had encountered before. She glanced at the seven humming chakra crystals on the altar, their gentle hum filling the air with an almost palpable energy. She'd figured out the key to unlocking the chamber's secrets lay in refracting and reflecting the single beam of light to bathe the crystals in its glow.

With only thirty minutes until the sun shifted out of position, Natasha knew time was not on her side. She approached the master crystal, her mind racing as she studied its facets and angles. With a trembling hand, she made her first adjustment, hoping it would catch the faint beam of light and send it to a chakra crystal.

But as the minutes ticked by, Natasha's initial optimism waned. Each combination and placement she tried seemed to yield no results, wasting precious seconds with each failed attempt. It was becoming as annoying as the Rubik's cube. She would get three of the crystals lit, but when she rotated the master crystal, she would lose two to gain a different one. Beads of sweat formed on her brow as frustration and desperation threatened to consume her.

With each passing moment, the tension in the chamber grew thicker, the ticking of the mental clock echoing in Natasha's ears like a relentless drumbeat. She moved from crystal to crystal, adjusting and realigning with increasing desperation, each failed attempt weighing heavily on her spirit. Time seemed to slip away like grains of sand through her fingers, and Natasha's resolve faltered. The task before her felt more insurmountable, the fear of failure looming like a dark cloud over her. Gianpaolo's sceptical glare didn't help her, but how could she prove she wasn't stalling?

Amidst the chaos and uncertainty, Natasha refused to give up. Refused to lose. With grit and determination, she continued to experiment with different combinations and placements, moving faster and faster, each moment bringing her closer to the brink of exhaustion.

And then, just when all hope seemed lost, Natasha's efforts finally paid off. With a final change, the beam of light refracted and reflected, bouncing around the chamber, bathing the seven humming chakra crystals in its radiant glow. A sense of relief washed over Natasha as she beheld the scene before her, her heart soaring with triumph in the face of adversity.

Each crystal shone in a different colour, hummed a different note, but all together they were a harmonious choir, which intensified, filling the chamber with an ethereal resonance. Natasha watched in awe as the energy flowed through the crystals, converging on the larger crystal at the centre of the altar. With a low, reverberating hum, the larger crystal resonated in harmony with the chakra crystals, its surface pulsating with a soft, golden light.

Then it stopped. The midday sun had moved out of position. But not before there was the sound of something hitting the ground.

In the fading light of the chamber, Natasha stood, her spirit ablaze, knowing that she was on the verge of the greatest discovery of her life. With bated breath, and flashlight in hand, she stepped forward, her eyes widening in astonishment at the sight before her. The Entity agents came and stood beside her, adding two more beams of light to hers.

The side of the altar had opened. Inside the hidden chamber lay the skeletal remains of a person, their weathered bones draped in tattered robes that spoke of a bygone era. The Vatican agents crossed themselves.

'Is that her? Mary the Magdalene?'

'I don't know,' Natasha admitted as she crouched down to get a better look. 'But it is a woman, judging by the pelvic bone. The crooked fingers suggest possible arthritis, so it could be an elderly woman. But that's just an educated guess.' As she investigated the tomb, Natasha noticed an Aramaic message written above the head of the woman. '"She is now home, in peace".'

'Home in Italy,' the agent said proudly. 'Even her own followers knew that the Catholic Church was the true way to God.'

Natasha rubbed her brow and shook her head. 'You really believe that?'

'Tell me, what else could it mean?'

She had to admit, in that moment, she couldn't, and she wouldn't rule it out either. If archaeology was the search for fact, Natasha didn't have enough of them, either way, to make an informed decision about the meaning of the message. Perhaps there was a clue inside.

Beside the woman lay a collection of pages, yellowed with age and written in ancient script, which Natasha identified as Aramaic. 'These might be the writings of Mary, her gospel, her teachings for the followers of her ministry.'

But it was the object that lay beside the woman, partially wrapped in cloth, which drew Natasha's gaze like a magnet. There, nestled among the robes of antiquity, rested a cup made from agate, its smooth surface shimmering in the light of their torches.

The holy grail.

For centuries, it had been the object of myth and legend, sought after by kings, scholars, and adventurers alike. And now, here it lay before Natasha, a tangible link to the mysteries of the past.

Wiping the sweat from her hands, Natasha reached out and grasped the cup, feeling its cool weight in her palms. It was a moment she had dreamed of her entire life, culminating in years of searching and sacrifice.

But as she held the holy grail in her hands, Natasha knew her journey was far from over. For, if the stories were true, the cup held not only the power to heal but also the wisdom of generations past. And, according to Cardinal Wagner at least, the blood of Jesus himself.

Curiosity abound, Natasha looked into it the grail. There was no dried blood to be seen, just dust and cobwebs. Cardinal Wagner was wrong, after all.

Natasha's brow creased as she examined the grail in more depth.

'I'll take that, signorina Travers,' Gianpaolo said. He had a hand outstretched, his gun in the other. 'The church thanks you for your efforts.'

'What about the other artefacts?' Natasha asked, the aged pages in her hand. 'This scripture is very important.'

'The Vatican will send a team to reinter her. She is a most valuable relic.'

'So what? You're going to shoot me now?'

'Of course not. You made an arrangement with Cardinal Wagner, and you have fulfilled your part. The Holy See will not renege. This,' he said, showing the gun, 'is for the person hiding in the other chamber. Show yourself or I will shoot.'

'Let's not do something stupid,' said Ellen, and she crawled into the crystal chamber.

'Ellen Paige,' Gianpaolo said. 'Who else is out there? Lucas Redmond?'

She shook her head. 'I'm on my own.'

His eyes narrowed. 'And where is the agent I left?'

'Sleeping off 150,000 volts.'

'Incapacitated by a child?'

'What's with the heightism and you guys? Just because I'm short doesn't mean I'm in school. You lot need to get out of your little frat house and see the world.'

'Don't mind her, Gianpaolo,' said Natasha, coming to Ellen's side. 'As you said, I've done as Cardinal Wagner wanted. The question now is, will you do what he wants?'

'I don't know what you mean.'

'You know that he has designs on becoming the next pope, right?'

'He will have a long wait for that,' the other agent interjected. 'The current pope is in very good health.'

'But what if he doesn't intend on waiting? What if he plans on taking matters into his own hands? He wants the grail to strengthen his standing with the cardinals. He has to be stopped.'

Gianpaolo sighed. 'Cardinal Wagner had hoped the idea of having an ally in the pope might have been enough to keep you in line. But he was told that your morality might be an issue.'

'He was told? By who?'

'That doesn't matter now.' Gianpaolo levelled his gun at her.

'What are you doing? We were told not to harm any of them.'

'I was given further instructions should they prove a threat.'

'A threat to who?' Natasha pushed. 'The Vatican or Cardinal Wagner? I thought you served to protect the Catholic Church? Not one clergyman. You think it will survive a scandal of this magnitude? A pope murdered by one of its own?'

Felipe pulled out his own gun, pointing it at Gianpaolo.

Chapter 37

The two men, colleagues, friends, brother in arms, each looked at the other with a steely glare, neither one backing down, each believing that their cause was the right one. The tension crackled in the air like electricity as they circled each other, their weapons held with taut grips. Natasha, with one hand holding the scripture of the Magdalene Creed, her other hand holding Ellen's, backed away from the two men, surreptitiously manoeuvring towards the crawl space.

'Come on, Filipe. What are you doing? Put the gun down.'

'I am following orders.'

'As am I.'

'And what are those orders?'

'I cannot tell you.'

'Is what the signorina Travers said about Cardinal Wagner true? Is he going to assassinate the pope?'

'I cannot tell you, Filipe.'

The agent shook his head. 'No, I don't believe it. You were the best of us, the one we all aspired to be. And you're conspiring against the person we have all sworn to protect. For what?'

'A new world is coming. There will be terrible times ahead, an Armageddon. The people will need the church more than ever, and we need a new stronger leader to take us through the darkness and into the light. And once Cardinal

Wagner becomes pope, he will appoint me as head of the Entity.'

Natasha made Ellen go first through the hole. She scampered through, but before she could stand, Alfonso grabbed her.

'We meet again, little kid,' he said, but stopped when he heard Filipe's voice.

'What's happened to you, Gianpaolo? Murder the pope? You sound insane.'

'Or indoctrinated,' Natasha suggested. 'I never did fully understand Wagner's change of heart about the grail. One minute he has you trying to destroy all the maps and anyone who had come into contact with them. The next, he wants me to use them to find the grail. Despite doing so would reveal all the church believed and taught about Jesus to be wrong. It would shake the very foundations of the Catholic Church. And then, with Wagner as the head of it, he might just very well rebuild it into something different. Something for this new world you mentioned. Or did you mean a New Enlightened Order? I suppose it was Peter Armitage who told Wagner about me.'

'Hey, what's going on in here?' Just then, Alfonso came through the crawl space.

As Filipe turned to see another colleague join them, Gianpaolo seized the opportunity and squeezed the trigger of his gun. Filipe reeled back as the bullet slammed into his left shoulder. He fired in retaliation, but Gianpaolo had moved. The shot went wide. Then he took two more bullets. Alfonso looked on in shock. He couldn't believe his fellow agents were trying to kill each other.

The moment the bullets flew, Natasha ducked and made for the crawl space. She could hear Ellen urging her to hurry. However, Natasha's escape came to a halt as Filipe's lifeless body fell on top of her.

Alfonso knew there was no turning back now. Gianpaolo had crossed the line by killing their fellow agent. 'You betrayed us! You betrayed everything we stand for!' With a sudden surge of fury, knife in hand, he lunged at his former colleague, whose shots flew wide of the mark.

The combatants engaged in a brutal struggle, the piercing sound of knife against gun filling the air in the dimly lit chamber. Gianpaolo and Alfonso moved with lightning speed, each strike calculated and precise as they danced around each other in a deadly ballet of death, the former still with the grail in hand.

They grappled, each clutching the other's weapon hand. Alfonso's eyes burned with a fierce determination, the memory of Filipe's death driving him. With a swift and decisive move, he disarmed Gianpaolo, wounding his arm with the knife. His gun clattering to the ground, leaving him weaponless and vulnerable.

Ellen grunted as, with all her strength, she pulled Natasha by her arms. Inch by inch, the archaeologist was slowly making her way from beneath the deadweight on her back. With the sound of the battle ringing in their ears, they knew their window of escape was running out.

'You should have known better than to betray us, Gianpaolo. Now, you will pay the price,' Alfonso said as he advanced.

Gianpaolo backed away until he felt the altar at his back. The knife in his opponent's hand gleamed in the dim light. He may have lost his gun, but he was not defenceless for long. Without hesitation, he reached behind himself, took hold of the large crystal and, with incredible force, smashed it into Alfonso's head. Disorientated the agent staggered back, crystal shards embedded in the vicious wound, as blood gushed down the side of his face.

Gianpaolo bent down and retrieved the dropped knife and delivered the fatal blow, the blade sinking deep into Alfonso's chest. He watched the dying man's eyes widen in shock and pain as he collapsed to the ground, his blood staining the ground. Gianpaolo stood over his fallen adversary, his chest heaving with exertion as he surveyed the scene before him. He had the holy grail, now he had to deal with Natasha Travers. He turned to the crawl space, but she was nowhere to be seen.

• • • •

AS SOON AS NATASHA was free of the dead Entity agent, she and Ellen had both agreed they'd probably out-stayed their welcome. Going back up the long stone staircase was a much more arduous task than it had been coming down them. Walking up would have been bad enough. But running up them put both of their fitness levels to the test.

'Come on, Ellen,' Natasha encouraged the younger woman. 'We can't slow down now.'

'I have to,' she panted back, slowing to a walk. 'I feel like my heart is going to burst out of my chest.'

'That might well be the case if we let Gianpaolo catch up to us.'

'For all we know, that other guy might have stopped him. We could be running for nothing.'

'You mean the one that you got past?'

'Good point,' conceded Ellen after a moment of remembrance.

'There was a reason why Gianpaolo was given this extra assignment.'

'Yeah. You and your big mouth.'

'What?'

'From what I heard, if you hadn't let on to him you knew their plans for the pope, we might not be in this situation.'

'Well, you know me,' Natasha grinned sheepishly. 'I don't like people taking me for an idiot.'

Suddenly, there was a bang from below them.

'And now that trait is going to get us both killed, idiot!'

'I guess we know who won. Move it, Ellen!'

The two women pounded up the steps, reinvigorated by a surge of adrenaline. Ellen switched off the lights on her headband, trying to be less of a target for their pursuer. Neither of them needed the miniature flashlights now that they were so close to the exit. It loomed ahead of them like a beacon of freedom.

Natasha glanced over her shoulder and could just about make out Gianpaolo, the ambient light from the exit catching the metal of his gun as he pumped his arms. She knew he was gaining, fast, but not fast enough as they burst into the constellation room. And ran right into the necropolis guide Natasha had followed when she had first arrived.

He glowered at them. 'What are you doing here?' He grabbed both of them, Ellen twisting around, trying to free herself.

Natasha did the same at first, then stopped when she saw his necklace. 'You're a member of the Livonian Order,' she gasped.

'Who?' Ellen asked, still trying to free herself.

'They were a military order located far to the northeast of Europe. Think knights templar or knights hospitaller and you'll be on the right track.'

'Oh.' Ellen paused. 'That must mean you're the guardians of the grail, right?'

'You beat the traps? You've endangered the grail?'

'Now, let's not get hung up on who did what. Let's just say that at this present moment, it is in the hands of someone who intends to do dark things with it.'

'You should go,' the guide said. 'I will deal with this thief.'

Natasha had so many questions to ask him, but she had no time as Ellen shoved her out of the beehive-shaped tomb. And it was a good thing she did, as they had barely gone ten metres when they heard a shot, quickly followed by two more.

They ran past curious tourists who had heard the sounds of gunfire, rubbernecking until they saw the gun wielding man, then screams and panic ensued. But even through the chaos surrounding them, Natasha couldn't believe Gianpaolo had never lost sight of them. On two occasions, people fell around her and Ellen, taking bullets meant for them.

The crowd peeled off as they realised that this wasn't a random shooting. The gunman had his sights on two women in particular. A would-be hero amongst the dwindling crowd tried to tackle the shooter. But his heroics got him a bullet in the stomach.

Another man in the crowd charged Gianpaolo, smashing into his side, taking him out with a vicious rugby tackle, which sent the gun and the grail flying.

Hearing the groan as the body of the Vatican agent violently expelled air, Natasha glanced back and slowed to a stop. 'Lucas?'

'Hi darling,' Lucas said with a broad smile. 'Sorry I'm late.'

'About bloody time you got here,' Ellen berated.

'Yeah, missed you too, El.'

'Ah, Mr Redmond,' Gianpaolo said, getting to his feet. 'At least I won't need to hunt you down now. I'll finish you all here one by one, then present the holy grail to the Vatican as a hero.'

'Really? And how are you going to do that when I break your neck? Don't think I've forgotten what you did you did to Tony.'

'Don't worry about him. When I'm done with the three of you, I will go back and finish what I started with him.'

That last comment threw Lucas into a rage. They lunged at each other. Despite both men being bruised and battered, neither one of them held back during the ferocious encountered. The adrenaline pumping through their bodies dulled the pain and allowed them to fight on, passing the threshold which would have caused others to quit.

'Stop right there!' Two guides, this time armed, shouted as they came rushing towards the fighting men.

'Looks like we will have to continue this another day,' Gianpaolo said. He broke from combat with Lucas, sprinting for his gun. With a well-timed baseball slide, he retrieved the gun and, with cold efficiency, took out the two guides. He trained the gun on Lucas, but he was already moving for cover as Gianpaolo shot, missing his target. The Vatican agent tried again, but the gun was empty.

Lucas heard the clicks of the empty gun. A chance had opened up to him. He saw Gianpaolo scoop down to pick up a dark-coloured cup as he ran. Just as Lucas was about to give chase, Natasha stopped him. 'What do you mean let him go? If we don't stop him now, we'll be looking over our shoulder for ever.'

'Yeah, Nat?' Ellen added. 'What's up with that? We're letting him get away with the holy grail?'

'It doesn't matter,' Natasha shook her head. 'I don't think it's the real thing.'

It felt like such a long time since Travers and Redmond had been back in London. Crisscrossing the Mediterranean to Spain, France, Italy and North Africa, and for Lucas, an unscheduled trip to the Libyan desert, was all well and good, and in some respect par for the course when it came to adventuring. That's not to say they didn't enjoy it.

They both loved to travel and experience new cultures, but returning home was always a pleasant feeling. Even if it meant having to go into the office. Not that going to the SIS building in Vauxhall Cross was like going into an ordinary office.

Section 7, the branch of the secret intelligence service which, working in collaboration with local agencies, located and safeguarded historical items which might fund terrorism, was always a buzz with activity, even in the evening when most other office workers would go home. But terrorists never slept, and neither did the tomb raiders and unlicensed archaeologists, so neither did S7.

'This has got to stop,' said David Evans, the chief of this division of S7, as Natasha, Lucas and Ellen took a seat in his office. He had wanted them to come in as soon as they had landed in London from Sardinia, and a car had met them at the airport to make sure of it. 'You can't use Section 7 transport and equipment whenever you please, for your own personal dealings. It is for official government business. Not to bail you out of trouble.'

'I appreciate you coming through in Egypt, sir,' Lucas said.

'Yes, well, I couldn't just leave you in the hands of La Peregrine. Now what's all this business about? A shoot out in Sardinia? I had a tough time keeping your faces out of the Italian media.'

Before they could answer the question, someone knocked at the door, and Anita Khan, David's PA, opened it. 'Deputy Director General Evans, sir,' she announced and stepped aside to allow Julie Evans, David's wife, to enter.

Of the three S7 agents, Natasha was the only one who had not yet met Julie in person. The photographs on David's desk had failed to capture her elegance and striking features. She had a slender and graceful figure and carried herself with poise and confidence. Her long, flowing dark hair was styled in loose waves, framing facial features that expressed a classic beauty with high cheekbones, expressive eyes, and a warm smile that broadened when she saw Lucas.

'It's good to see you again, Lucas,' she said, as they embraced. 'You look exactly the same as you did the last time I saw you...battered, bruised and bloody.'

'You say the nicest things, Jules,' laughed Lucas.

'David, please tell me you're getting this man a doctor.'

'They're on their way up. You've already met Ellen, and this...'

'And this must be Natasha Travers,' Julia shook her hand firmly. 'It's nice to finally meet face to face.'

'I agree. I hear you are quite the force in Thames House, Julia.'

'As a woman, I feel that sometimes I have to go that extra mile to be heard, which is fine. I give one-hundred per cent every day, and I expect no less from the people that work with me and for me. If they love me or loathe me, I don't care, but they all respect me.'

'I love you and loathe you, Jules,' Lucas chuckled, then saw David Evan's raised eyebrow. 'Her intel saved my ass on more than one occasion when I was back in the SAS, sir. If it wasn't for her, I might have snuffed it ages ago.'

'You did the hard work, Lucas,' Julia said, shaking her head. 'I just told you where to go. Anyway, enough going down memory lane. What did I interrupt when I came in?'

'I was just about to tell David about the events which took place in Sardinia. Gianpaolo, an agent of the Vatican spy network, the Entity did the shooting.'

'The same man that tried to kill my friend, Tony Braithwaite, outside the Acquirers office, and again at the hospital. He might have succeeded if Ellen hadn't been there.'

'Okay. But why? Was he a rogue agent?'

'No. Cardinal Elias Wagner, the head of the Entity, wanted me to find the grail for him. But when I pieced things together, became certain of his true motives, Gianpaolo revealed he had a second set of orders. Kill us. Lucas turned up just in time. We found this as well.' Natasha carefully took the aged, yellowed pages from her bag and placed them on David's desk.

'What is this?' Julia asked.

'That is the scripture of Mary's ministry.'

David and Julia both looked up from the pages, their mouths agape.

'We also found the holy grail,' Ellen added. 'And Mary's remains.'

'Possibly Mary's remains.'

'You actually found her? And the grail? Where is it?' David asked excitedly.

'She let Gianpaolo leave with it,' Ellen revealed.

'Only because I'm certain it's not the real thing. It's made from agate, the same semi-precious stone as the Valencian cup. Roman centurions were drinking out of vessels made from this, not carpenters or rabbis. In the Bible Jesus tells a rich person to give away all their possessions and follow him. Wouldn't it have been hypocritical if Jesus were then to have a chalice that only the Roman elite could afford?'

'That is a fair point,' David admitted. 'Do you think Cardinal Wagner will know it's not the real thing?'

'Possibly. He was planning on taking a sample of the dried blood of Jesus and synthesising it. Extracting DNA to see if the bloodline of Jesus continues today. Or if there were any medicinal properties to it. But there's no blood in it.'

'That all sounds farfetched to be true,' Julia said. 'Is that even possible?'

'When you have billions backing you, who knows?'

'What do you mean?'

'I have a feeling that the Bilderberg Inner Circle is involved. Cardinal Wagner himself could be a member.'

'What makes you say that?' David pressed.

'Just some things Gianpaolo said about Wagner being informed that I would be interested in helping him if the Vatican vaults were offered as an incentive.'

'And you bit hard,' Ellen sniggered.

'No more than you would have done if they'd offered you unrestricted access to Area 51.'

'Point taken.'

'And the bastard sent J Organisation after me in Libya,' said Lucas.

'He was in the room when Ellen told me she'd found Lucas,' Natasha explained.

'So if the Vatican doesn't have it, where is the real holy grail?'

'That I don't know.' She shrugged. 'But there was a message inside the altar where we found the remains, the grail and the scripture. It said, "she is now home, in peace." One of the Vatican agents believed it meant there in Sardinia.'

'Surely, it meant Galilee,' Julia said. 'That was her home, right?'

'Yes, it was. I was thinking the same thing.'

'Right! So rest up. We're sending you off to Jerusalem in the morning.'

'Having the holy grail was only a part of Cardinal Wagner's plan. He intends to become pope. The grail was to curry favour with the cardinals. But for his full plan to come to fruition, he'd need to kill the pope.'

'You're not suggesting he's going to assassinate Pope Leo Alexander?'

'I am. With the grail, fake or not, and the remains of an elderly woman, if she is Mary or not, Wagner will spin whatever kind of story he wants. He can still influence the cardinals into supporting him for pope as the man who brought back the greatest holy relic to the Catholic Church. If he gets

BIC funding to falsify documents and tests, who will denounce him?'

'You will,' David stated. 'And it begins with stopping the assassination attempt.'

'In two days, on Friday,' Julia said, taking over, 'there is a papal visit to France. Pope Leo Alexander will perform mass at Notre Dame to celebrate the completion of the rebuilding of the cathedral after the fire of 2019.'

'So we just tell those Swiss Guard dudes and they'll keep Wagner under wraps.'

'If only it were that simple, Ellen. At the moment, with no hard evidence, it'll be a case of Natasha's word against Cardinal Wagner's. And you can imagine whose they are more likely to believe. All we can do is contact my opposite in the French security service and tell that we have wind of a credible threat to the pope. But we will have to do this. We must catch him red-handed.'

'That might be difficult,' said Lucas. 'He'll have his man Gianpaolo do the deed.'

'Then we take him. Perhaps he'll turn on Cardinal Wagner.'

'And if he doesn't?' Natasha queried.

'Taking the knight off the table might force the bishop to make the move instead. I'll go make that call to France, and Lucas, go get yourself bloody checked out.'

• • • •

HIDDEN WITHIN THE LABYRINTHINE corridors of Vauxhall Cross is the high-tech laboratory known as Haven, where creativity and ingenuity thrived. Natasha had taken the Magdalene scripture down to be examined while Lucas himself was likewise being examined.

When Natasha entered Haven, she was met with a sleek and minimalist interior design that showcased clean lines, metallic surfaces, and state-of-the-art technology. The atmosphere was often bustling with activity, as scientists, engineers, and technicians worked diligently on various projects. But late in the evening was a lot less hectic, so it was easy for Natasha to spot the person she was after, a petite woman, standing at around 5 feet 2 inches tall.

Despite her small stature, Destiny Poole possessed a lively and vibrant presence that commanded attention wherever she went. Her boundless energy and enthusiasm were infectious to those around her. One of Destiny's most endearing features was her cute, upturned nose, which sat perfectly in the centre of her heart-shaped face, adding a touch of youthful charm to her appearance. Her features were soft and delicate, framed by a cascade of blonde curls that tumbled down past her shoulders in playful waves.

Destiny heard her name called and turned in her swivel-chair, her almond-shaped eyes sparkled with intelligence and curiosity, their deep ocean blue reflecting her friendly and approachable nature. 'Natasha! Are you lost or something?'

'Funny, Dessy. I come down here to give you something that I know you'll love and what do I get for my efforts?'

'You brought me something?' Destiny squealed. 'Is it the holy grail? Please tell me it's the holy grail.'

'It's not the holy grail,' Natasha said, shaking her head. 'How did you hear about that, anyway?'

'People like to talk to me.'

Natasha gave her a sceptical look. 'Is that so?'

'So if it's not the grail, what is it?'

Natasha carefully fished out the old, yellowed pages from her bag.

'Oh, this is nice. This is very nice.' Destiny received the artefact and placed it down in front of her. 'This is high-quality stuff. Ancient, high-quality stuff.'

'If it really is Mary's written scripture, I'd expect it to be around two-thousand years old.'

Destiny looked closely at the front page. 'With nothing but this cursory look and feel, I would say that is a pretty accurate ballpark. I'll give it a thorough material analysis, spectroscopy, chromatography, radiocarbon dating, the lot.'

'Honestly, I was more interested in finding out where it was written. If you can do it.'

'Nothing too easy, then. It's challenging to determine the country of origin of a piece of parchment solely based on the ink used, as ink composition alone may not provide definitive information about where the parchment was produced.'

'So you can't?'

'Well, ink analysis can still offer valuable insights and clues that, when combined with other lines of evidence, may help infer the parchment's potential origin. Different regions and time periods have used various ink formulations, often reflecting local materials and production techniques. Chemical analysis of the ink can reveal its composition, including the types of pigments, binders, and additives used.'

'You're the best, Dessy. I knew I could count on you.'

'Yeah, I know. I'll have the results for you as soon as I can.'

As Natasha and Lucas made their way through the bustling streets of Paris, the imposing silhouette of Notre Dame Cathedral loomed on the horizon, its restored ancient spire reaching towards the heavens like a silent sentinel.

For Lucas, the sight of Notre Dame stirred memories of a recent time when he had almost died, poisoned by an assassin's blade, only to be saved by a childhood crush, Anne Sheppard, now a grown woman, their feelings rekindled. He remembered the warmth of Anne's hand on his body, the softness of her voice as she whispered words of comfort. As they approached the cathedral, Lucas felt a pang of nostalgia wash over him, a bittersweet reminder of the life he had once known before ever meeting Natasha, the life they had enjoyed together and the storm of the tumultuous end of their marriage. Anne had helped him, just as Natasha had on many occasions. They were so similar in so many ways, yet different in just as many. And it was only recently that he discovered they had been rivals in school.

But now, as Lucas stood before the cathedral once more, he found himself confronted with the ghosts of his past, memories of love and loss that he had long tried to bury. He glanced at Natasha, his heart heavy with guilt and regret for the pain he had caused her, for the mistakes he had made in his quest for redemption. Maybe her life would be better off without him in it.

Natasha sensed his turmoil, the unspoken words that hung heavy in the air between them. She reached out a hand for his, her touch a silent reassurance that she was there for him, that they were in this together. They both had skeletons, crosses to bear, but she knew they were stronger together. Natasha knew that whatever challenges lay ahead, they would face them as a team, united.

For Natasha, the sight of the majestic edifice stirred a different set of emotions, a surge of excitement and anticipation ringed with a hint of apprehension at what lay ahead. Their purpose was to prevent the attempted assassination of Pope Leo Alexander I. They didn't know how it would be done. They didn't know exactly when it would be done. The identity of the assassin was unknown to them. Although they could speculate who it would be, Cardinal Elias Wagner's top agent, Gianpaolo of the Entity.

When Julia Evans contacted the French police with the small amount of information she had, they almost laughed her off the phone. But if it was a credible threat, as the British had suggested, they had to act upon it. They permitted her to send two of her agents to assist and despatched additional police, many of whom were in plain clothes, concealed among the swelling crowd of onlookers taking every bit of space in the parvis.

'I never imagined that there would be so many people,' admitted Lucas, as he scanned the crowd. 'This really is like looking for a needle in the haystack. He could be anywhere.'

'I don't envy you that task,' Natasha patted Lucas on the back. 'At least I know Wagner will be somewhere near the pope. This is more than just a papal visit. This is an event.'

'Or a circus.'

'A who's who of political dignitaries and celebrities.'

'Like I said, a circus.'

'A terrorist could have a field day here.'

The notion struck Lucas. 'Bloody hell!'

'What's wrong?'

'We've been so focused on the Vatican connection. We've been so sure that it would be the Entity that attempted to kill the pope. The individuals behind Elias Wagner have been overlooked.'

'Bilderberg Inner Circle,' Natasha gasped.

'And who do they use to do their dirty work?'

'J Organisation.'

'I don't know,' he said to her, lowering his voice. 'Any number of these people could be a terrorist in disguise waiting for the pope to exit.'

'Or they could already be inside.'

'Good point. Head inside Nat. Keep eyes on the pope and see if you can find Wagner in there too.'

She nodded. 'What about you?'

'I'm going to have a sweep around here. It's a long shot, but someone might be antsy.'

'Be careful, baby.'

They kissed before going their separate ways through the crowd.

Lucas continued to watch Natasha until she passed security and entered the cathedral. He pushed his way through the throng of ardent worshippers, knowing that not all of them were here to listen to the word of God, many of them could be an assassin in waiting. BIC terrorist or Vatican spy, who could say. Suspicion hung in the air as Lucas's gaze fell upon each person, regardless of gender.

Then he spotted a man. A man who was doing his best to look as if he was watching the renovated cathedral, but was actually paying more attention to the crowd. Lucas noticed that whenever a police officer was approaching, he would move away, blend into another part of onlookers. Could this be the man he was looking for? It wasn't Gianpaolo. Perhaps a member of J Organisation? Who knew? But it was very possible that he had a rifle of some kind underneath his long coat.

Lucas edged towards the man, doing a good job of not drawing attention to himself. Skills he'd used in the SAS, originally learned as a youngster under the tutelage of his mother, Angela Redmond, thief, intelligence broker, master manipulator, and ranked number two in the Bilderberg Inner Circle ranks.

The former captain of the British special forces was almost breathing down the man's neck, as he stood close behind a raven-haired woman. The man, an opportunistic pickpocket, did not know the trouble he was in. Not until it was too late.

Before either he or Lucas could react, the woman had spun, slit both his wrists, and returned her hidden blade to its sheath. The action had revealed the familiar white streak in the woman's shoulder length jet black hair.

'Anne? What are you doing?'

'Hi, Luca,' she said with her Australian accent. 'Close your mouth, hon. You'll catch flies.'

Before he could reply, she had taken him by the hand and pulled him away from the dying pickpocket. Moments later there was a scream behind them as the thief collapsed, police rushing to the scene. Anne dragged Lucas down the steps to the Promenade Maurice Carême, named after the French poet. Once they were along the Seine, Anne pushed Lucas against the wall.

'I've missed you,' she breathed, her body pressed against his.

'We can't do this, Anne,' Lucas said as he pushed her arms down from around his neck. 'You know that.'

'Your mouth is saying one thing, but your body is saying the complete opposite, love.'

'Fortunately, it's the head on my shoulders that runs things around here.'

'When did you become so boring, Luca?' Anne pouted.

'When I'm trying to stop an assassination. Please tell me you're not involved in it, Anne.'

'Are you serious? You're acting like you don't know me at all. I'm a treasure hunter, not an assassin. You, of all people, should know that.'

'Okay. I'm sorry. It's just you working with Angela...'

'It was your mum who sent me to help you out. She doesn't want Armitage to succeed with his religious take over.'

'So you know who the assassin is?'

She took a picture from her pocket.

'Gianpaolo,' Lucas said, recognising the man. 'So it is him. He's a Vatican spy.'

'Who works directly for Elias Wagner. Who also just happens to be Omega of the BIC'

'We suspected as much, when J Organisation turned up and tried to kill me in Libya.'

'Oh, I heard about that. Shacked up with an arms dealer, right? You really do have a type, don't you...dangerous women,' she smirked.

'I was kidnapped, not shacked up. You think I gave myself these bruises?'

'What I think doesn't matter, sweetheart. It's what your darling, Natasha, thinks that counts. That's if you told her everything. Or is it a case of what happened in Libya stays in Libya?'

'You've been around my mother too long.'

'That's not a bad thing.'

'And that's a matter of opinion.'

'She cares about you, you know?'

'Of course she does. She cares about what I can do for her.'

'All she wants is the family back together.'

'Only for as long as it benefits her.'

'You'll come around, eventually. And you'll realise that's she's not the bad guy you think she is.'

'No, she's much worse.'

'At least she doesn't pretend to be what's she's not.'

'What? And I do?'

'I didn't say you in particular, Luca. But now that you mention it, maybe there is a part of you that longs to be free and unshackled. Why else would you be doing shady acquisition jobs on the side?'

Lucas huffed. 'I thought you were here to help? Not give me a psych evaluation.'

Anne opened her jacket, revealing a double holster sporting a pair of Glock 19s. 'This girl knows how to accessorise,' she grinned.

'What else can you tell me? How will he do it?'

'No idea. Armitage has been playing this one close to his chest. He shared very little about the plan, Angela said. He's paranoid...'

'Or he's on to her.'

'Exactly what I told her.'

'And?'

'She said it's too soon for her to make a power grab. That she has other contingencies, and keeping the pope alive is part of it.'

'And to that she's sent just you? I know you have skill, Anne, but I could have done with a few more bodies. It's a vast crowd to check.'

'Who said I was alone?'

'Who are you here with? Wait, do you hear that?'

Just then, they heard the distant sound of helicopters approaching.

Chapter 40

The soft glow of candlelight danced across the ancient stone walls of Notre Dame Cathedral, casting flickering shadows upon the polished marble floors. The air was thick with anticipation as the faithful gathered in pews, their murmurs and hushed voices mingling with the solemn strains of sacred music. At the altar, the priests made the final preparations before the pope was ready to deliver his sermon and bless the newly rebuilt sanctuary.

Natasha moved cautiously, her eyes darting around, ready to react to any potential threat lurking in the shadows. A hand reached out for her from an aisle, and a familiar voice greeted her.

'Mari!' she said as they hugged. 'I'm so glad you're okay. I felt awful leaving you there in that tunnel.'

'How do you think I felt waking up to find nobody around? I thought they might have killed you. But what are you doing here?'

'The pope is in danger,' whispered Natasha.

'What?'

'Possibly by the same man who took us.'

'But didn't you say he worked for the Vatican?'

'It's a complicated story.'

'What can I do to help?'

'If you see him, tell the police officers straightaway.'

'Okay, I can do that,' Mari said, then noticed Natasha's attention was elsewhere. 'Are you alright? You look like you've seen a ghost.'

'Yeah,' she said, still looking off. 'Yeah, I just thought I saw someone, that's all.'

'Was it him?'

'No. But it's something I should check out, anyway. We'll catch up later.'

Natasha didn't wait for a response from the socialite. She could feel her heart racing, and goosebumps along her arms, as she rushed down the side aisle on the opposite side of the cathedral. She had been mistaken. Natasha was certain of it. That it had been a trick of the eyes. That she had just seen a lookalike and nothing more.

The door leading to the upper parts of the cathedral closed softly. Natasha took a quick look around before opening it and walking through. She could hear someone making their way hurriedly up the steps, and after taking a breath, Natasha dashed up after them.

Four-hundred and two later Natasha was at the top of the Notre Dame towers, entering the upper room. She never caught up with whomever she was chasing, and she hadn't slowed down much. Cautiously, she entered. Standing by the windows looking out was a woman with glossy black hair.

'It can't be you,' Natasha said, disbelieving her own eyes. 'I saw you die.'

'Hello, again Natasha,' Aleksis Conastine said. 'This is quite the view. You should take a look. Don't worry, I won't throw you out.'

Natasha slowly made her way forward. The closer she got to the woman, the more she could see that it truly was the woman who had attempted to assassinate an entire royal family to claim the throne for herself as the king's illegitimate daughter.

'How are you alive, Aleksis?'

'By planning. I had concealed scuba gear in the Aruco River long before I would ever require them. The timely aid of a benefactor helped as well. I never planned on falling from a helicopter to be part of my escape plan. But it added some believability to my demise.'

'It's you, isn't it? You're BIC's assassin.'

Aleksis chuckled. 'Peter Armitage doesn't even know I exist.'

'I don't understand. If you're not here working for the Inner Circle, who are you working for?'

'I didn't say I wasn't working for them. Just not Peter Armitage.'

It took Natasha only a moment to realise who she it had to be. 'Angela Redmond saved you?'

'You know, I met her once at Sandhurst. She didn't introduce herself or say who her son was. But she said she was proud of him. She said she'd noticed me as well. Said I was a talent, and I had great things ahead of me.'

'Angela says a lot of things, but that doesn't make them true.'

'You only know a skewed version of Angela Redmond. If you spent more time to know the woman, then your view of her may very well change.'

'I know she abandoned Lucas, pretended to be dead. Heartless actions that affected him, and still do.'

'Do you know why she did that? Did you ever ask Anne? What she did was for Lucas. What she does now is still for Lucas. I wish I had parents that loved me that much.'

'You could have.'

'No, Natasha. We don't all get to have perfect upbringings, like you. My stepfather never told my mother I existed, had her committed, then killed her. I killed my birth father. And then there's Tomaz...' she trailed off, too pained by the memory.

'I'll admit it must have been difficult for you. But there were some choices made that were bad ones.'

'And what about your choices, Natasha? Choosing to be silent. Choosing to keep secrets.'

Natasha looked at her with narrowed eyes. 'I don't know what you're talking about.'

A knowing smile crossed Aleksis' mouth. 'The truth will be out eventually, Natasha. But not today. Today, a plan needs to be stopped, and a pope saved. Now, do you want my help or not?'

Natasha's mind was in turmoil, so many emotions running through her head. Could she really trust a woman who had tried to kill her? What if she really was here to kill the pope? She was a master liar, after all. But Natasha needed to stay focused. Keep her mind on the task at hand, stop Elias Wagner from usurping the position of Roman Pontiff. 'Okay. I accept your offer.'

'Good, because I think I can hear them coming.'

At the altar, Pope Leo Alexander I stood in regal splendour. He smiled at the people before him. The president of France sat in the front row. Beside him sat the archbishop of France, and next to him sat Cardinal Elias Wagner. Along with other dignitaries, world leaders, charity leaders, and celebrities, the French police lined the cathedral, and the camera crew from Vatican TV filmed the event.

The pope cleared his throat softly, and with his voice resonating with the weight of centuries as he delivered a sermon to bless the newly rebuilt sanctuary. 'As we gather in the hallowed halls of this magnificent cathedral, we stand witness to the resilience of the human spirit and the enduring power of faith. Today, we come together to celebrate not only the physical restoration of Notre Dame Cathedral but also the renewal of our collective spirit and the reaffirmation of our shared values.

'Just as this sacred edifice has risen from the ashes, so to have we emerged stronger and more united than ever before. Faced with adversity and uncertainty, we have found solace in our faith, drawing strength from the timeless teachings of love, compassion, and forgiveness.

'As God's representative on earth, I am reminded of the profound importance of this sacred space, not merely as a symbol of religious devotion, but as a beacon of hope and inspiration for people of all faiths and backgrounds. In its soaring arches and exquisite craftsmanship, we see the divine handiwork of human creativity and ingenuity, a testament to our capacity to transcend the ordinary and reach towards the divine.

'Let us remember that Notre Dame Cathedral is more than just a building; it is a living testament to the enduring power of faith, a sanctuary where the weary find rest, the lost find solace, and the broken find healing. May its walls echo with the prayers of the faithful and the songs of praise, serving as a constant reminder of God's infinite love and mercy.

'As we bless this newly rebuilt cathedral, let us rededicate ourselves to the values of compassion, generosity, and reconciliation. Let us strive to build a world where justice and peace reign supreme, where we treat all God's children with dignity and respect.

'And so, let us lift our hearts in gratitude for the blessings bestowed upon us, and let us go forth from this sacred place renewed in our faith, strengthened in our resolve, and inspired to live lives of purpose and meaning.

'May the grace of God be upon us all, now and forevermore. Amen.'

The congregation repeated the repeated the solemn agreement. But amidst the serenity of the cathedral, a shadow loomed on the horizon. Unbeknownst to most of the people in the edifice, sinister forces were converging on Notre Dame, drawn to their target within its hallowed walls.

The thunderous roar of helicopter blades broke the tranquillity of the sacred space. Four sleek, black helicopters descended from the sky, one hovering ominously above the cathedral itself. Gasps of disbelief rippled through the crowd as they watched in horror. From the helicopters emerged teams of armed terrorists, clad in black tactical gear and wielding high-powered rifles. With military precision, they rappelled down ropes, some descending upon Notre Dame, the rest in its courtyard, like dark angels of death. The peaceful atmosphere within the cathedral was dispelled by the sound of shattering glass as a group of terrorists burst through the windows, their dark silhouettes framed against the moonlit sky. With a shout, they surged forward, their weapons glinting ominously in the dim light. Natasha and Aleksis burst out the door and sprang into action, their movements fluid and precise as they met the attackers head-on.

Chapter 42

Pandemonium erupted as the J Organisation stormed the parvis, their weapons unleashing a barrage of gunfire that sent worshippers scrambling for cover. The police returned fire as they fell back, forming a perimeter at the cathedral entrance, but the J Organisation was relentless. The plainclothes officers who had been among the crowd were now left in the open and although they had used the element of surprise to their advantage, taking out two of the terrorists, they were cut down in a hail of bullets.

Amidst the chaos, Lucas and Anne dashed up the steps from the Seine, weapons in hand. 'Natasha,' he whispered, pausing at the top as he saw terrorists descending ropes and crashing through the windows of the cathedral. All he could do was hope she could handle things inside.

Anne pulled him aside as a spray of bullets riddled a nearby tree. They were moving against the tide of people who were surging away from the trouble. Members of the public were being shot, others tripped and trampled on, caught up in the terrorists charge toward the place of worship.

The two of them crouched behind a statue of Charlemagne, screams and shots ringing out, gunpowder smoke drifting on the air. It was a war zone in the 4th arrondissement of Paris.

'I wasn't expecting an assault of this magnitude,' admitted Lucas.

'Neither was I,' Anne grinned, adrenaline already coursing through her veins, expedited by her racing heartbeat. 'Like I said, Armitage has been pretty tight-lipped about this op. But isn't it more fun this way?' She popped around the corner of the statue's huge stone plinth, let off two shots, and ducked back around. 'Not knowing what to expect, I mean. Kinda keeps you on edge!'

'You are one crazy woman, Anne Sheppard,' Lucas replied, firing his gun, then smiled. 'But I think you're on to something. As long as they don't have any heavy metal.'

Suddenly, in a matter of seconds, two hundred 45mm bullets pounded the stone plinth they hid behind. Dust and chips of stone flew up around them until the gun ran dry.

'Sounds like you didn't get your wish.' Anne took a quick look around the corner. 'One of the heli's has a guy with an FN Minimi light machine gun in the cabin. He's loading up a new belt.'

'We'd better take him then.'

Lucas and Anne each stepped out, trained their guns on the helicopter, and unleashed a rapid barrage of bullets. The machine gunner had just finished reloading the weapon when he was hit several times. As was the cockpit. The pilot jerked right, then back left. The dead gunner fell from the cabin, his safety harness still attached. He swung beneath the chopper like a pendulum. Until he and the cable got tangled in a nearby tree. The pilot tried to pull free but was instead pitched into one of the other hovering choppers.

There was an ear-splitting screech as metal clashed with metal, then bodies were hit by the force as the helicopters exploded, raining fire and debris down below. The mangled wreckage fell to the ground, exploding again as the fuel tank of the second aircraft blew. Black smoke rose into the air, windows of the surrounding buildings were blown out.

'Well, that went better than expected,' Anne quipped as she reloaded her Glock's.

'No time to gloat, babes,' Lucas said, dragging her by the arm. 'I think we've garnered some unwanted attention.' They were soon darting down the side of the cathedral.

A J Organisation commander had spotted Lucas and Anne. 'It's Redmond! You four peel off from the group and take him out.'

Chapter 43

Bedlam engulfed the cathedral as screams, shouts, and gunshots reverberated through the ancient stone walls. With VIPs running around in disarray and their bodyguards trying to keep them safe, the police attempted to confront the gunmen, but it proved nearly impossible to shoot the perpetrators without causing collateral damage. Unburdened by hang ups, the J Organisation freely sprayed their bullets.

Amidst the chaos around, the pope stood resolute, his unwavering faith shining like a beacon of hope in the face of darkness. With a steely resolve, Natasha sprang into action, her every movement calculated and purposeful. Evading gunfire and dodging debris, she raced towards the altar, her heart pounding in her chest.

Just as the terrorists closed in on their target, Natasha intercepted them with a breathtaking display of skill and agility. Engaging them in a ferocious battle, Natasha's fists flew with deadly precision, striking assailants with blinding speed and ferocity. The air crackled with tension as she and the terrorists clashed in a whirlwind of violence, their struggle echoing through the hallowed halls of the basilica. She fought with the strength of a tiger and the grace of a prima ballerina, as she danced through the melee with grace and agility, her every movement a testament to her skill as a warrior. But then, with a decisive blow, Natasha incapacitated the mercenaries, sending them crashing to the ground in defeat.

'Your Holiness,' Natasha pulled the pope aside, all thought of protocol out the window. 'You must get out of here?'

'You saved me, child.'

'Don't waste my efforts by sticking around, Your Holiness.'

'Yes, of course. The sacristy. It has an emergency exit. I will get out through there.' Pope Leo Alexander I made his way to the annex, grabbing hold of the Archbishop as he went. Just as the pair arrived at the door of the preparation room, Natasha glimpsed Cardinal Elias Wagner join them.

'No, wait,' she shouted. Before she could make a move towards the endangered pope, someone slammed a rifle butt into the back of her head. The henchmen were no mere thugs. They were seasoned veterans of countless battles, their strength and cunning matched only by their ruthlessness. After a moment of lax concentration Natasha now stared at the barrel of an assault rifle.

'I guess this is the end of your interference in other people's business, Travers,' the terrorist sneered.

Two shots rang out. Then a third.

Natasha flinched.

The terrorist fell to the ground, dead.

Natasha turned around and saw Aleksis holding a smoking gun.

'You're welcome,' she said, before Natasha said a word. 'Pay attention. I may not be there to save you next time.'

Despite the efforts of the terrorists, more VIP's were making it to the emergency exits. They were never the target. That was the pope. With each passing moment, his fate hung in the balance, the outcome of the battle uncertain. But every time Natasha attempted to reach the sacristy, someone intercepted her, countering her every move with ruthless efficiency.

• • • •

THE SACRISTY OF NOTRE Dame Cathedral served as a crucial space for the preparation and storage of sacred items used in religious ceremonies. It was a place where priests and clergy members prepared for mass, donning their sacred vestments and retrieving the liturgical objects for worship. As a vital part of the cathedral's infrastructure, the sacristy played a central role in facilitating the rituals and ceremonies that took place within the hallowed halls of Notre Dame.

Now it was to play a new role as escape route for Pope Leo Alexander I. The attempt on his life rattled him. But that emotion paled compared to how he felt about the terrorist attack on the fabled cathedral.

'This is unbelievable,' he said solemnly, shaking his head. 'An unprecedented attack on the church. Elias, I thought your department was supposed to prevent things like this from happening? If it wasn't for that woman, I would be dead. I want her found. Do you hear me?'

'I think it would be prudent to get you safely away from here first, Your Holiness,' the archbishop said. 'The exit is this way. Follow me.'

Cardinal Elias Wagner gave a nod to the cameraman, who broke his equipment and retrieve a gun from within which he pointed at the pope. He tossed the hat of a Vatican

TV worker he'd been wearing and Gianpaolo smoothed his hair.

'What is this betrayal?'

'Betrayal?' Elias repeated, astounded by the accusation. 'This is the utmost devotion to the Holy See, to the position you currently occupy. But not any longer. Finish it.'

If there was any thought in Gianpaolo's mind that killing the pope wasn't the right thing to do, it only manifested itself for seconds before it was gone. With a steely look in his eye, he hardened his resolve and prepared to shoot the pope.

The door to the sacristy suddenly burst open and five men piled in. Four of them, guns drawn, surrounded the French president, and scanned the strange tableau before them.

'What is going on here?'

'A terrorist after the pope!' Elias yelled.

Gianpaolo was stunned by the actions of his mentor, as the first of the bullets from the secret service men's gun ripped his flesh. He staggered agonist the wall, firing his own shots, hitting one in the face and another in the neck.

Cardinal Wagner used the chaotic scene around them to force the pope towards the exit. When the archbishop tried to intervene, the head of the Entity shot him with a Heckler & Koch USP Compact handgun that Elias had hidden in his cassock.

Pope Leo Alexander I was in shock as a man he had trusted since his appointment as head of the Catholic Church dragged him out of the sacristy exit. His faith still unwavering, he prayed for God to forgive his wayward priest.

• • • •

AMIDST THE CHAOS OF battle, Natasha's mind raced, searching for a way to gain the upper hand. With a tremendous explosion rocking the cathedral, it sounded as though the fight was even more ferocious outside, and hoped Lucas was alright.

'We can't keep up this dance of death,' Aleksis said, pointing to the main entrance. 'We're the only ones left, and it looks like they're getting reinforcements.'

'You're right. Brute force alone won't be enough to overcome them. We need to outsmart them as well. Quickly, up these stairs.' With a nod to Aleksis, together they jumped up from behind the pew, each scooping up a Heckler & Koch G36C carbine lying beside dead terrorists, before breaking out into a sprint, drawing the terrorists deeper into corridors and upper echelons of the cathedral, as bullets riddled the surrounding walls.

The two women bolted up the steps, bursting out the door, which led to the world-famous flying buttresses of the apse of Notre Dame. They continued to follow the semi-circular termination of the main building. Natasha, by chance, caught sight of Lucas down below with a black-haired woman.

She slowed down. 'Isn't that Anne Sheppard?'

'Yes,' Aleksis said. 'You didn't think Angela would send me here on my own, did you? This was a precision operation on our part and needed the two of us to pull it off without a hitch.'

'Well, there's been a hitch. The person who wants the pope dead went into the sacristy with him, and who knows where he is now?'

Aleksis, daunted by the sudden sound of a machine gun at the door they had passed through moments ago, urged Natasha into action. 'Did you bring us up here to die with a view, or did you have some sort of plan?'

'I had a plan,' Natasha revealed, as she suddenly dashed along the walkway. 'But it seems to be flying away.'

The helicopter, with its rappel cables still down, was pulling away from the cathedral. It was being signalled down by a RAID chopper. But Natasha and Aleksis had other ideas. They watched the cable drag behind along the buttresses, giving them the slim hope they needed.

They arrived at the edge of the cathedral and made a leap of faith.

Aleksis kept hold of her carbine, and caught the cable in a firm grip, which was a good thing as the terrorists who'd followed them up there began shooting at the stowaways. Natasha had thrown her automatic carbine so she could grab the cable with both hands. Now she wished she hadn't, as the J Organisation terrorists took aim.

Chapter 44

Lucas and Anne, their hearts pounding with adrenaline, crouched behind one of the many trees of the park, Square John XXIII, behind Notre Dame Cathedral. The trimmed canopy of the tightly grown trees provided shade from the sun and, in this instance, somewhere to hide. They had thought to escape into the streets, but their hopes were dashed when they discovered a traffic accident had blocked the way.

'Do you see them?' Anne whispered, her voice barely audible over the continuing sound of the war zone on the other side of, and within, the cathedral. The sound of the helicopter hovering overhead added to the cacophony, along with the general panic of Parisians and tourists alike.

Lucas peered cautiously around the corner, scanning for any sign of the terrorists chasing them. 'Not yet,' he replied, his grip tightening on his SIG Sauer. 'But they'll be here soon. We need to stay hidden until we see an opportunity to strike.'

As if on cue, the four terrorists came to a skidding halt on the park's gravel, kicking up dust, their weapons ready and their intent clear. Lucas and Anne exchanged a glance, preparing themselves for the deadly confrontation that lay ahead.

With a silent nod, Lucas broke cover and darted across the courtyard. Suddenly, a burst of gunfire came from the terrorists, sending bits of bark and shards of stone from the statues flying. Lucas dived for cover. Bullets whizzed past his head, missing him by mere inches. He had drawn their fire. Now Anne stepped out, firing her dual handguns. Sudden retaliation surprised the terrorists. One of their number succumbed to the hail of bullets as the others took shelter, giving Anne the time to join Lucas.

In an urgent tone, Lucas said, 'We need to find a way out of here. We don't have the time to stay trapped in this courtyard forever. We need to get to the pope.'

Anne nodded grimly, her eyes darting around the park for any sign of escape. 'There's a narrow alleyway on the other side of the cathedral,' she said, her voice determined. 'If we can make it there, we might have a chance.'

On an agreed count, they broke cover and sprinted across the courtyard, dodging gunfire and leaping over benches. The alleyway loomed ahead, a narrow passage leading back to the main entrance of the cathedral. As they reached the mouth of the alleyway, a figure emerged to block their way, a menacing grin on his face. It was one of the terrorists, his weapon raised and his finger poised on the trigger. Lucas and Anne froze in their tracks, their hearts sinking with dread.

'Lucas Redmond,' he sneered. 'The Bilderberg Inner Circle has a nice fat bounty on your head. And I'm aiming to collect it.'

'I don't suppose there's anything I can say to change your mind?'

'Nope.'

'And what about you?' Lucas said, looking over the man's shoulder. 'I'm British intelligence.'

'I'm not going to fall for that childish trick,' the terrorist laughed.

'Mr Redmond,' the French voice said, 'I know who you are.' Before the terrorist had time to react, a shot rang out, and he crumpled to the ground, his weapon clattering on the cobblestones.

'Thanks for the save,' Lucas said to the man standing at the sacristy emergency exit.

'I'm French secret service,' he said. Your help would be greatly appreciated. The French president is in my company, but I am the last remaining member of the detail. Ensuring the president's safety is my top priority.

'And you need a hospital,' Lucas said, looking at the agent's blood drenched side.

'I'll be fine. There's a medical team at the safe house.'

'We need to keep moving,' Anne said, her voice urgent. 'The others won't be far behind.'

'Okay, let's do this,' Lucas said, taking the lead. 'Mr President, stay between these two and I'll take point. We'll commandeer a car and get you out of here.'

With Lucas leading the way, they raced down the down the length of the cathedral, their footsteps pounding the ancient stones as they fled. Behind them, the terrorists gave chase, their shouts and gunfire ricochetting around them. Anne, returning fire whenever she could, hitting one of their pursuers.

Two more to go.

As the procession reached the front of Notre Dame, Lucas had expected to see the J Organisation troops still in a pitched battle with the gendarmes. But the bodies of the police officers strewn across the steps of Notre Dame's entrance told the story. Lucas's blood boiled, a fire ignited in him. He knew who was to blame, and he made a promise that he would make them all pay, from Gianpaolo to Peter Armitage.

He prepared to storm the cathedral, when a chopper lowered in front of them, its blades whipping up a wind which buffeted them. In his rage at seeing the murdered officers, Lucas had overlooked the fourth terrorist helicopter. It was a mistake that would cost all of their lives. But if it was to be his time, Lucas had no intention of going out on his knees.

As the aircraft turned to give the gunner the perfect view of their targets, Lucas raised his handgun, his eyes blazed with determination, ready to empty his magazine at them, hoping that he'd get the kill shot before they did. He smiled at the prospect of facing death once more, knowing that one of them was going to be disappointed.

His finger hovered over the trigger. Then his eyes opened wide, and he shouted. 'Down!'

Lucas had spotted the logo on the chopper's side. It was RAID, the French national police tactical unit. The gunner in the back fired, and the terrorists behind Anne flew back several feet as the heavy calibre bullets tore through them.

When the shooting stopped, Lucas and the others got to their feet. The helicopter landed and officers disembarked, quickly fanning out and engaging any terrorists in sight, most of them advancing into the cathedral itself.

With the French president safely onboard, the secret service agent turned and shook both Lucas and Anne by the hand. 'Thank you for your help. You have done France a great service.'

'Don't mention it. The pope was their actual target.'

'Then you should be happy.'

'Why?'

'He's safe. I saw him leave Notre Dame with a priest.'

'Which way did they go?' Panic rising in Lucas's voice.

'They came out of the sacristy, but I lost sight of them in all the madness.'

Lucas and Anne ran back to where the sacristy was, in the vain hope of finding something, anything, that might point them toward where Wagner might have gone with the pope.

'This is hopeless, babe,' Anne said. 'We've next to no chance of finding the guy. I think you have to concede the fact that Armitage has won. He's going to have control of the next pope and his New Enlightened Order is going to make strides for power.'

'Bollocks to that! I don't enjoy killing in cold blood, but for him, I'll make an exception.'

'If you're serious, I can help with that. I can find out where he'll be so you can put a bullet right between his eyes.'

The idea was becoming clearer in his mind as Lucas formulated a plan. Would he use a sniper rifle? Or something up close and personal? Poison? A planned accident? The choices were endless and, considering all the pain and suffering Peter Armitage had caused, he deserved them all. 'He's put a target on my head? Then I'll have to take his first.'

Anne smiled. 'This is going to be fun.'

Suddenly, there was a rustle from a nearby bush, causing both Lucas and Anne to take up their guns once more. With silent hand gestures, they devised a strategy to flank the position the sound had come from. They stealthily made their way around the bushes. Lucas could see the arm and leg of someone leaning against a tree. Lucas could deduce from the significant amount of blood on the tree trunk and dripping onto the ground that the person leaning against the tree had suffered severe injuries, yet their determination to survive was keeping them alive, for the time being. As he got closer, he could hear their laboured breathing. They didn't have long.

'I hoped we might have been able to finish what we started in Sardinia,' Gianpaolo said, as Lucas crept around the tree to see the Entity spy in a bloody mess.

'To be honest,' Lucas said, still keeping his gun trained on the man, as did Anne, 'so did I. What happened to you?'

'Cardinal Wagner betrayed me. Used me. I don't know if he ever intended me to succeed him, or if he wanted to be a pope with direct control of the Entity.'

'Tell me where he's gone. I can make sure he doesn't make it to any conclave.'

Gianpaolo stared into Lucas's eyes. 'If the pope wasn't killed here, there was a secondary location.'

'Go on.'

'If I tell you, there is something which you must do for me.'

'I'm listening.'

'Finish me. I don't want a long, lingering death. If the police find me, they will try to save me. I'm done. Just end it.

You and I are alike. We deserve a warrior's death. To die in battle.'

'Fine. I'll do it. Now tell me where Wagner has taken him.'

'The Conciergerie,' Gianpaolo said with a sigh.

'Cute choice.' Anne nonchalantly leaned on a neighbouring tree. 'That place has seen centuries of political intrigue, judicial proceedings, and cultural significance. Once a royal palace in the Middle Ages, it also served as a prison during the years of the French Revolution. So it now being the location of a pope's murder fits perfectly.'

Lucas glared at the Vatican spy. 'Bollocks. I don't buy it. There's too much activity around there. It's right next to the supreme courts. Tell me the truth.' Lucas suddenly pushed his fist into one of the assassin's gunshots, causing him to howl in pain. 'Tell me the truth! Where is Elias taking the pope?'

'I'm telling you the truth. I owe him nothing.'

'How will he get him inside? Past the security?'

'There is work going on in the Conciergerie.'

Anne nodded, letting Lucas know it was the truth. 'They're doing renovation work in part of the museum.'

'There is a back entrance for the workers. I have a key-card, as does Cardinal Wagner. The basement is where it will happen.'

Lucas roughly searched Gianpaolo, eventually finding the card in an inside pocket. After showing it to Anne, he slipped it into his own pocket, turned and walked away.

'Hey,' growled the Vatican spy. 'We made a deal. I've given you what you wanted. Now it's your turn. Do it! Come back here, you bastard! If you don't do it, I swear to God almighty, I will stay alive just to kill everyone you hold dear. Starting with your darling Nata—'

With speed and cold-blooded accuracy, Lucas shot Gianpaolo twice in the chest and once in the head. The Entity spy was dead. Lucas knew there would be no one to mourn him. At that moment, he knew they were completely different. Often he had done bad to do good, but Lucas had still touched the lives of many. The only mourner that might have shown up for Gianpaolo was soon to go the same way. Cardinal Elias Wagner.

'I almost thought you weren't going to do it.'

'I almost didn't, but there are times in life when you come across someone that sets to destroy that life. If he survived, I have no doubt that he would have done exactly what he said he would do.'

'So you did it to save me, did you?' Anne asked in a sweet, mocking voice.

Lucas smiled, grateful for the brevity. 'Not just you, Anne.' Suddenly, a gun landed near Lucas and Anne, both of whom looked up to see what was going on. 'What the hell? Is that Aleksis Conastine? Wait, is that the help you talked about? It looks like you have some explaining to do, Anne.'

The G36C compact assault rifle in Aleksis Conastine's determined grip spewed a stream of bullets, her momentum swinging her back towards the apse of Notre Dame. She had beaten the J Organisation terrorists to the punch, getting her shots off before they could do the same. Two of them succumbed to her attack, slumping to the ground, dead.

Then her gun clicked empty.

She turned to Natasha, who already had a look of dread on her face. She knew what was coming. They were in point blank range of the terrorists. One of them had a wicked smirk across his face, behind the gun he held at eye level.

Unexpected shots struck him. Fired from below, he didn't have a chance to shoot back as he toppled headfirst from the top of Notre Dame's apse. The remaining two gunmen turned their weapons on the new target. They had just squeezed their triggers when RAID officers came charging through the door, ordering them to drop their weapons. They complied.

With the last helicopter ordered to land by a second RAID chopper, the attack on Notre Dame Cathedral was at an end.

Natasha and Aleksis jumped clear moments before the aircraft touched down, as officers rushed over to arrest the pilot. Lucas stormed over with a determined stride. Barely acknowledging Natasha's hug, he grabbed Aleksis and dragged her away. Natasha knew that look in Lucas's eyes and made to follow, but Anne blocked her path.

'Get out of my way, Anne,' growled Natasha.

The Australian shook her head. 'You must have known this was going to happen. If you didn't, I guess you're not as bright as you like everyone to think you are.'

'I knew. I just don't want him to do anything he'll regret.'

'Like choosing you over me?'

'I said regret. That choice was the best one he ever made.'

'Is it though? I've always been straight with Lucas. He knows what he's getting with me, no masks or falsehoods. You, on the other hand, are a different matter.'

'I've always been upfront with Lucas, even taking him back after the Chiara Harris business.'

'But was that done out of love or out of guilt?'

'What are you talking about?'

'Armitage found out about your little secret. You should have known that he was the kind of person who wants to know every little detail about anyone he's sleeping with. Once he knew, it was only a matter of time before Angela found out too. And now I know. The question is, should Lucas know?'

Natasha suddenly flew into a rage, grabbing Anne's arm. 'If you love Lucas, as you say, you won't breathe a word of it to him.'

Anne met her intense, confrontational glare. For a few seconds, it looked like the longtime rivalry was about to reignite into combat. But Anne's demeanour softened. She wrenched herself free of Natasha's grip and leaned in close. 'It's probably best he doesn't know. There's no telling what he'd do.' Anne walked away, putting some space between them as she lit up a cigarette. 'But he'll find out, eventually. Secrets have a way of coming out. But I think it'd be better coming from you. And I'm telling you that because I *do* love Lucas.'

Natasha felt melancholic as she watched Anne amble towards the Seine.

· · · ·

ALEKSIS COULD BARELY keep up with Lucas as they rounded the side of the cathedral. He threw her against the wall of the hallowed building and clamped his hand around her throat. For several long seconds, he squeezed. The atrocities she had committed flashed through his mind, the people she'd helped to kill, the fact that she'd brought two countries to the brink of war, that she had almost killed Natasha and him. Not to mention their mutual friend Tomaz. Aleksis should be dead. All Lucas was doing was rectifying that fact.

But he couldn't. For all the bad she'd done, he couldn't forget the years of friendship they had developed. His hand went limp, and she gasped for air, almost collapsing to the ground.

'Why are you here, Aleksis? How are you here?'

She scoffed. 'Come on, Lucas. You were at Sandhurst. Who got top marks for planning operations?'

'You always had an escape route planned out.'

She nodded.

'Now you work for Angela with Anne.' He slumped against the wall. 'You could have vanished. Stayed dead. Made a new life for yourself. However, what you've essentially done is substitute one person's doctrine with another person's.'

'But my father's,' she stopped and corrected herself. 'Jerald Larsgaard's doctrine involved brainwashing me, moulding me into a weapon, and utilising me for his revenge.'

'And Angela's isn't?'

'No. She didn't force me to come here. She gave me the option, and I came because of you, Lucas. Because I still think of you as a friend.'

'Even after you tried to kill me?'

'That wasn't me. That was all my half-brother, Karl's doing. After what you did to his twin, Marcus, he lost control a bit, became fixated on you. Wouldn't listen to reason. He truly was his father's son.'

Lucas looked over at her. 'So you didn't try to kill me?'

'Of course not. How could I, after all we'd been through?'

Lucas smiled, remembering those teenaged years. 'But the attempt on Natasha *was* you?'

'There might have been a tiny bit of jealousy involved there,' Aleksis admitted. 'Sometimes I wondered how life would have turned out if I had chosen you and not Tomaz.'

'God knows,' Lucas shrugged.

'I know. We would have done several tours. Been awarded honours by the SAS several times, and probably become instructors by now with two or three children.'

'Wow, that's a big development from just a bunk up.'

Aleksis looked solemn. 'I know that's what I called it, but it meant more to me than that. I did not know Larsgaard had someone watching me. They must have seen us together at some point and reported back to him.'

'You received a phone call from him days before you accepted Tomaz's offers,' Lucas remembered. 'He ordered you to start a relationship with Tomaz. that's why you became distant toward me.'

'My life wasn't my own. I was Larsgaard's puppet. But I grew to love Tomaz.'

Hearing the things he'd done, Lucas grew a deep loathing for the man. 'If I'd known any of this when I met him, he might not have made it to prison.'

'Luckily he wasn't there for long,' Aleksis said without further explanation. 'I suppose you will tell Tomaz that I am still alive?'

'I have to, Aleksis.'

'No you don't. You chose not to tell him what happened between us. You can choose not to tell him you've seen me. I'm no threat to him.'

'You know how fragile he was back then with girls. If he'd known anything about us, he never would have built up the courage to tell you he liked you. Besides, you never told him either.'

'Because he needed you. He looked up to you, Lucas. He still does.'

'And that's why I have to tell him, Aleksis. Come on, we should get back.'

'Hold on, Lucas.' Aleksis stood in front of him, went onto her tiptoes and kissed him hard. 'I wanted to see if it was just as good as it was back then,' she said when they separated. 'It was.'

. . . .

ANNE WAS JUST FINISHING a call on her mobile phone when Lucas and Aleksis returned. 'Well, it looks like we have finished our work here. It's time to go, Aleksis.'

'What? I thought you said you were going to help save the pope?'

'Nope. The target was Gianpaolo, remember? I was here to stop the assassin, not a priest. If you can't handle a single man of the cloth, Lucas, maybe you're getting too old for this.' Anne turned and began walking away, Aleksis following a few seconds later. 'Perhaps a change of scenery would do you good. You know how to find us.'

'Are you okay?' Natasha asked Lucas as they watched the two women disappear into the crowd of onlookers.

'Yeah, I'm fine,' replied Lucas. 'I'm ready to end this, though. Put a stop to Cardinal Wagner and Armitage's plans all in one go.'

'Amen to that. Come on, we have a police car waiting to take us wherever we need to go.'

'The Conciergerie. That's where Gianpaolo said he'd be.'

The officer looked at them quizzically when they told him their destination. 'But that is only a mile away. Look at the crowds, the traffic. I believe it would be quicker for us to go on foot.'

Lucas glanced at Natasha, who nodded back. 'Alright, let's do this.' After getting new fully loaded weapons, they were on their way.

In less than five minutes, they had arrived. The Conciergerie exuded an aura of medieval grandeur, with its sturdy stone walls, soaring towers, and intricate Gothic architecture. Its turrets and battlements rose defiantly against the Parisian skyline, casting long shadows that whispered tales of bygone eras.

'Okay,' Lucas addressed the RAID officers. 'I want the two of you to enter through the main entrance. And we'll come in through the back. We were told they'd be in the largest hall.'

'That could be the Hall of the Guards or the Hall of the Men-at-Arms,' one officer informed them.

'Perfect. You take the first one, we'll take the second one.'

The two French police continued their way to the front of the Conciergerie, while Lucas and Natasha turned off and headed for the builder's entrance. A makeshift blue hoarding had been erected around the ordinary exit, with a keycard entry panel to restrict its use to the contractors and security personnel.

Lucas swiped the card. The light went green, and they entered a place where history hung heavy in the air. A sense of reverence pervaded the space, as the very stones themselves bore witness to the trials and tribulations of those who once walked within these hallowed halls. They quickly became engulfed in a maze-like network of corridors and chambers, where the whispers of centuries past reverberated. Of all the spaces, the Great Hall stood out with its grand vaulted ceiling and majestic columns, evoking a sense of royal splendour and regal authority.

There was a tourist sign pointing to a stone spiral staircase which read, Salle des Gens d'Armes, Hall of the Men-at-Arms. Slowly, Lucas and Natasha descended.

The massive hall was divided into four naves by a row of massive pillars in the centre, flanked by two rows of cylindrical columns. It was part of the royal palace of the French monarchs, originally constructed in the 14th century. It served as a barracks for the men-at-arms, who were the royal guards tasked with maintaining order and security within the palace and the city of Paris. The hall featured impressive Gothic architecture, characterised by its high vaulted ceilings, towering columns, and grand archways. The space was vast and cavernous, and it was easy to imagine had enough room to accommodate a large number of soldiers and their equipment.

Throughout its history, the Hall of the Men-at-Arms had witnessed many important events and ceremonies, including royal banquets, assemblies, and military drills. It hosted various court proceedings and official functions during the reign of the French monarchy. Now it was to witness the murder of a sitting pope.

The dimly lit hall seemed to pulsate with the weight of history, its ancient medieval walls bearing witness to the clash of one man's faith and another man's fanatic delusion. Lucas and Natasha, their hearts racing with urgency, glad they weren't too late, quietly moved to the nearest pillar. They could hear the voices of the clergymen echoing around them.

'You have lost your way, Elias,' the pope said. 'But it's not too late to seek redemption.'

'No, Christophe,' Elias replied, using the pope's real name. 'My redemption can only come from God himself, and when the people see the truth and the Catholic Church is all that remains, I will not need redemption because I will have been elevated to sainthood.'

'Really?' Lucas mocked. 'Because I don't think you'll be getting anywhere near one of those, to be honest.'

Elias immediately pulled the pope to his feet, using him as a human shield, his gun held at his head.

'I agree,' added Natasha. 'Falsehoods maybe. But Saint Elias? That's not going to happen.'

'But Natasha, what about our deal? The freedom of the Vatican vaults can still be yours. Just help me become pope, then I sign the letter and make it official.'

'Whatever Peter Armitage told you was wrong. Yes, I love learning and soaking up knowledge. I live for it. But I will not trade that love for my soul, Wagner. I won't let you kill the pope on my watch. Besides, the holy grail is a fake.'

'You don't know that.'

'Maybe not a hundred per cent. But if you look at the historical facts about Mary and Jesus, then you conclude that it must be. We know that red agate was an expensive material then. Not everyone would have been able to afford to have a chalice made of it. We also know that Mary was from a rich family.'

'So it is likely that she would have had one then,' Cardinal Wagner said with triumph. 'You have debunked your own theory.'

'I haven't finished yet. Pope Leo Alexander, what did Jesus say to the rich man who wanted eternal life?'

'In Matthew 19, Jesus said, "If you want to be perfect, go, sell all your possessions and give to the poor, and you will have treasure in heaven. Then come, follow me."'

'So, if he is saying that to people, surely he would have to live by the same ethos, right? Practice what you preach. We know Mary followed Jesus as his wife. If that is the case, then it stands to reason that she would have done as he preached to the rich and gave up all her richly possessions. So a red garnet chalice could not have come from the household of Jesus and Mary and therefore cannot be the holy grail used to wash the wounds of Jesus.'

Cardinal Wagner bristled. 'It doesn't matter if the chalice is fake or not. With the funds of the Bilderberg Inner Circle behind me, convincing people of our truth will be a simple matter. The blood of Christ will be in the chalice. As long as the words come from the right person, people will believe anything.'

'And in this instance, the right person is the pope,' said Natasha.

'Precisely.'

'This is madness, Elias. Killing me will guarantee nothing. You will not become pope. I have no doubt that your tricks and lies will not sway the cardinals. Becoming pope is not a popularity contest. During a papal conclave, principles of prayer, discernment, and the guidance of the Holy Spirit as they deliberate guide the cardinals and cast their votes. It is a spiritual and solemn responsibility. You know this, Elias.'

'And I also know that they are all men just the same. Subject to the failings of men. They are just as easily deceived as the masses, and you're a fool if you can't see that.'

The Pope shook his head. 'To err is human; to forgive, divine.'

'You sanctimonious bastard,' Cardinal Elias spat. His grip tightened on the gun, as his hand trembled with anticipation, his gaze fixed upon his helpless prey.

'Don't do it, Wagner,' Lucas ordered, his SIG Sauer aimed at him. 'You pull that trigger and you'll be laying there next to him. No role of Pontiff for you, and no religious control for the N.E.O.'

'Killing me doesn't stop the inevitable. The New Enlightened Order will come into effect.'

'Not if I kill all your BIC buddies.'

Elias scoffed. 'Kill me and there will be another person to take my place and my ring. Business will continue as always.'

'Then I will take out the head, your Alpha, Peter Armitage. Then what?'

Elias laughed. 'You just don't get it, do you? There are eighteen members of the inner circle, seven who sit at the table making the decisions. You kill Alpha and one of those seven will take his place. Most probably Epsilon. She is a very capable woman, and somewhat dangerous. She would be my pick, but Upsilon would no doubt challenge her.'

'Epsilon must be Angela,' whispered Natasha.

'I was thinking the same thing,' Lucas whispered back. 'She's next in line.'

'You heard them, Elias. You are on a fool's errand. If you kill me, they will kill you, and the conclave will appoint a new pope. You are alone, Elias, you cannot win this.'

'I'm not alone,' Cardinal Wagner grinned.

'If you're expecting to see Gianpaolo, I'm afraid you're in for a big disappointment,' Lucas said, then he heard a click behind him.

'Your mistake was thinking Gianpaolo was the only Vatican spy loyal to me.'

Lucas glanced over to Natasha and saw one of Wagner's men behind her, too. 'It looks like it's going to be all yours, Nat.'

'No problem. Just say when,' she replied.

'Now!'

Lucas's voice rang out, slicing through the tense silence like a knife. They sprang into action, their movements fluid and precise. They both ducked, avoiding their respective guards, but Lucas also swivelled towards Natasha and shot the guard behind her twice in his side. Meanwhile, Natasha kept her aim firmly on Elias Wagner. She squeezed the trigger of her gun and with pinpoint accuracy, honed through her years as a youth modern pentathlete, and more recently, being put through her paces at Pontrilas Army Training Area, she struck her target.

Cardinal Wagner took the bullet in his shoulder before he could even react. His gun clattered across the stone floor, the metallic echo ringing out like a death knell to the clergyman's lofty plans. But his resolve remained unshaken, his fanaticism driving him ever closer to the brink of insanity. With a guttural cry, Cardinal Elias Wagner clamped his hands around the throat of the defenceless pope.

The second Vatican spy brought his gun down to bear on Lucas, who rolled backwards out of the way, kicking the man's hands up in the air as he did so, leaving him open for the double shot.

Natasha raced to aid the Pontiff, her heart pounding in her chest with the weight of the task at hand. His fate hung in the balance as his life teetered on the edge of oblivion.

In a blur of motion, Natasha lunged forward, her every muscle tensed as she collided with Cardinal Wagner, their bodies crashing to the ground in a tangle of limbs and fury. The pope fell to the ground, rubbing his throat and gasping as he crawled away.

With a primal roar, Elias turned his anger on Natasha as they grappled, their bodies locked in a deadly dance of strength and determination. Each blow she threw struck him with the force of thunder, reverberating through the chamber like a symphony of violence.

Lucas helped Pope Leo Alexander to his feet, the Pontiff's eyes locking with his in a silent exchange of gratitude.

Then a shot rang out, echoing around the ancient chamber.

Cardinal Elias Wagner collapsed face first to the ground beside Natasha. Lucas glimpsed someone dressed in black rushing up the spiral staircase. He darted after them. They were quick, agile, but Lucas was gaining. Until they took several shots at Lucas to slow him down. It worked. By the time he'd blasted out of the exit, the assassin was climbing into a waiting car and speeding off.

'Bollocks,' said Lucas.

Natasha and the pope soon emerged from the depths of the Conciergerie, their hearts heavy with the weight of what could have been but buoyed by their triumph of safeguarding the leader of the Catholic Church.

As they waited for the police to arrive to take the pope to safety, he turned to the adventurers. 'Thank you, my friends,' he whispered, his voice a prayer of gratitude amidst the darkness. 'You have saved not only my life, but the spirit of faith itself.'

'Your holiness,' they both replied.

'So,' he continued, 'would I be right in guessing that you've both been on a quest to find the holy grail?'

Epilogue

In the heart of the Lombardy region, nestled along the glistening shores of Lake Como, lies the enchanting town of Bellagio. Renowned as the "Pearl of the Lake," this idyllic sanctuary captivates with its timeless beauty and unparalleled charm.

At the water's edge, a picturesque promenade stretched along the lakefront, offering panoramic views of the azure expanse and the majestic peaks that rose dramatically on the horizon. Here, elegant villas and grand hotels stood as silent sentries, their graceful facades reflecting in the tranquil waters below. Among them, a waterfront villa reigned supreme, its stately presence commanding attention and admiration from all who passed by.

Within the villa's hallowed halls, a world of luxury and indulgence awaited, where every detail spoke of elegance and sophistication. From the ornate frescoes that adorned the ceilings to the exquisite furnishings that graced the rooms, no expense had been spared in creating an ambiance of unparalleled beauty and comfort, a haven of peace and serenity amidst the timeless allure of Lake Como.

And it was exactly how Angela Redmond liked it to be.

She had grown up in the urban streets in her younger days, but always knew there was a better life waiting for her. And as she became more proficient in her illicit business, garnering more and more high-powered clientele, she finally got to see it, taste it, now she lives it. And she has no intention of relinquishing it. Peter Armitage's plan for a New Enlightened Order and her own plans to extend her reach cannot coexist. By helping her son and, by association, S7, she has slowly been weakening his position as Alpha. If Lucas doesn't end up killing him, then a mutiny might be in order to relieve him of power.

Surrounded by manicured gardens and verdant lawns, the villa exuded an aura of opulence and refinement, its architectural splendour a testament to a bygone era of aristocratic grandeur. From its sun-drenched terraces and shaded verandas, she could behold the breathtaking beauty of Lake Como unfolding before her eyes. As could her two guests currently soaking up the sun.

'Personally, I think this is by far your best European sanctuary, Angela,' Anne said.

'I agree. I devise most of my best plans here. It must be the serenity of the lake.'

'It is peaceful here,' Aleksis added. 'A nice place to recharge.'

'And you are always welcome here, just like Anne. You have proved your value to this family already, Aleksis. As I knew you would.' Suddenly, there was a gentle beeping coming from a laptop. 'It's time to hear what Armitage has to say for himself. Excuse me, ladies.'

Angela logged into the encrypted server of BIC And watched as one by one Alpha, Upsilon, Omicron, and Iota joined. The spaces for Eta and Omega remained blank. But not for long.

Shortly, Alpha addressed the group. 'I know you are all busy, so I will keep this brief. You are all no doubt aware that Operation Hugo was stopped and our man in the Vatican was killed in action. As a result, we have two vacancies which I have now filled. I give you Eta and Omega, the newest members of the Bilderberg Inner Circle.'

A young blonde woman appeared in the space for Eta. Moments later, an Asian man filled the spot for Omega.

Angela sat back in her seat, rubbing her chin, her brow creased. 'Marigold Laval and Liu Chan. Bold moves Peter. What are you up to?'

••••

NATASHA SAT AT HER table on the terrace of her St Katherine's Dock apartment. It had been several days since the shooting at Notre Dame and, as she drank her morning tea, Natasha noted that there was no mention of her or Lucas in any of the national or international papers she had strewn across the table. Section 7 is still doing a good job of hiding their identities.

Lucas poured himself a cup of tea, went outside and, after kissing Natasha on the head, took a seat. 'Still reading that stuff? Don't worry. Evans has this it locked down. The French president gave us medals and there was still no coverage anywhere.'

'I know. Mine is at my parent's house because they didn't believe it. But that's not what I've been checking for. With all the shooting within the cathedral itself, with all the world leaders, dignitaries and VIPS, do you know how many casualties there were among them?'

'The way they spray, quite a few I'd imagine.'

'There was one. Just one man. A single bullet to the head.'

'Who was it?'

'A man named Karl Müller. Apparently he was the director general of the World Trade Organization. He was about to sign a groundbreaking trade pact aimed at levelling the playing field and promoting greater equity in the global economy. At its core was a series of bold reforms designed to curb monopolistic practices, combat tax evasion, and dismantle the opaque networks of offshore wealth that had long served as havens for the super-rich. By closing loopholes and tightening regulations, the agreement sought to ensure that corporations and individuals paid their fair share of taxes, contributing to the common good and fostering a more just and inclusive economic system.'

'Sounds like he could be a person worth killing to some people we know.'

'And I think it was Aleksis who did it.'

'What? You're joking, right?'

'Look at this photo,' she showed him a page in the Financial Times. 'This is Karl Müller, and this is a J terrorist. And I swear this is where I was standing when Aleksis saved me. She shot three times and when I backed away, I saw him on the ground.'

Lucas thought for a moment. 'One shot to the head did sound like an execution.'

Natasha's phone suddenly rang. She answered it, switching it on speaker. 'Hello, David. You're on with Lucas too.'

'Good!' David replied. 'I have Destiny here with some news.'

'Hey, guys,' came the chirpy voice of Haven's lead technician. 'I hope we aren't interrupting anything.'

'Your timing is perfect,' assured Lucas.

'Were you able to find anything, Dessy?' Natasha leaned forward expectantly.

'Well, it was difficult, like I said it would be. But luckily for you lot, difficult is a walk in the park for me. Although the writing style on the manuscript would suggest it is from Galilee, once I checked the chemical composition of the paper and ink, I discovered it is in fact from Africa.'

'Are you sure?'

'The data doesn't lie, Nat. The ink utilised had natural ingredients, plant extracts, minerals. It utilised natural ingredients, such as a binder derived from acacia trees, charcoal for black ink, and mineral-based pigments like ochre and iron oxide for the colours.'

'You know what region it's from, don't you? It's Ethiopia, isn't it?'

'Way to spoil the surprise, Nat. Haven't you ever heard of building up to the big reveal? Yes, it's Ethiopia. Although the chemical composition of the ink shared some similarities with inks used in other regions, such as other African countries, there are also distinct characteristics that set it apart as being an Ethiopian manuscript.'

'Which makes perfect sense when you think of Mary's historical association with the Queen of Sheba, who we know to have been from Ethiopia. Why compare Mary with someone from Ethiopia if she wasn't from Ethiopia? Unless there was a blood connection between them. According to legend, the Wolaita people of Ethiopia can trace their lineage all the way back to Menelik I, who was the son of King Solomon and the Queen of Sheba.'

'So she could have been Wolaita,' Lucas stated.

'Exactly. And with Jesus descended from the Davidic line, associating Solomon and Sheba with Jesus and Mary makes more sense.'

'That also makes them distant cousins,' Dessy added. 'But this is royalty, right?'

'She was also called the Magdalene, which is a toponymic name, meaning she was from a place called Magdala. Yes, there is a region in Galilee by that name, but there was also a place in Ethiopia that had the same name. And what about the message we found in Sardinia? "She is now home, in peace". Sardinia was never her home. Ethiopia, on the other hand, was at least where she was born, and possibly laid to rest.'

'So the holy grail is in Ethiopia?' David Evans asked.

'I didn't say that,' Natasha corrected. 'But it is a distinct possibility. The Magdalene Creed scripture was written there, and someone possibly took her there. If she took the grail with her, who knows?'

'Well, that's what you're going there to find out,' David declared. 'I'll have a plane ready for you.'

* * * *

NATASHA AND LUCAS HAD gone straight to Amba Miriam, the fortress and market town once known as Magdala. After speaking to an old lady, they hired a car and headed north, following her instructions to one of the many mountain churches found in Ethiopia.

As Lucas and Natasha approached the base of the towering cliff, the magnitude of their task loomed before them.

The church, perched high above, seemed to defy gravity itself, its ancient stone façade blending seamlessly into the sheer rock face. Dread filled Natasha as she faced the treacherous path, with jagged rocks threatening to trip her up and the terrifying abyss below haunting her thoughts.

'You're sure you want to do this?' Lucas asked. 'You could wait for me here.'

'I'm going up, Lucas. I have to.'

He smiled and gave a kiss. 'Okay, let's do this!'

With each step, the tension mounted, palpable in the air like a dense fog. Lucas's brow furrowed in concentration as he navigated the narrow ledge, his muscles tense with anticipation. Natasha, trailing close behind, felt her heart pounding in her chest, the adrenaline coursing through her veins. His presence offered a small measure of reassurance, but the sense of danger was ever-present, lurking in the shadows of the towering cliffs.

At last, they reached the last stretch of the ascent, a series of narrow handholds and precarious footholds that led to the entrance of the ancient church. With a silent prayer, Lucas gripped the rough-hewn rock with white-knuckled determination, his fingers finding purchase in the crevices of the cliff face. Natasha followed suit, her breath coming in shallow gasps as she fought to control the rising tide of fear within her.

Step by agonising step, they inched their way upwards, the tension mounting with each passing moment. One wrong move, one slip of the hand, and they knew they would plummet into the abyss below. But they pressed on, driven by a sense of purpose that transcended their fear. Their minds focused solely on reaching their destination.

Finally, after what felt like an eternity, they reached the entrance to the ancient church, a dark portal that seemed to swallow them whole as they stepped inside. The cool air of the interior enveloped them like a shroud, and for a moment, they stood in silence, their chests heaving with exertion and relief.

But their respite was short-lived, they knew their journey wasn't over yet. With a shared glance of determination, Lucas and Natasha wondered what awaited them within the hallowed halls.

It was an old grey-haired Ethiopian man.

'My name is Tesfaye,' he said. 'Your faith is strong, for few succeed in the ascent to witness the glory of our murals.'

'You only have murals here?' Natasha asked.

'Yes. We are not a grand cathedral,' he replied. 'But I think you will still find them to be very interesting. They are a testament to our cultural heritage.'

'What are you?' Lucas asked. 'Some sort of security guard?'

The grey-haired man chuckled. 'Do I look like I could stop anyone? If you are desperate enough to climb up here to rob this humble church then you surely are in dire need. Not that there is anything worth stealing here. But if there were, it would be by the will of God.'

Intrigued, Natasha moved further inside the remarkable church as she heard Lucas asking Tesfaye about his eating arrangements. The murals were indeed fascinating. The vibrant colours impressed Natasha, and she looked at them with awe. The story of King Solomon and Queen of Sheba was there on the walls to see.

Then, as Natasha was examining every inch of the images, something caught her eye. In the background of one of the Solomon and Sheba images was a tiny image of the snake goddess. Natasha's heart beat fast. She quickly searched all the murals, looking for other images she had seen on this quest for the holy grail. Orion's Belt was in one. Pleiades in another. Then she found a small image of a jar. Her brow creased. She couldn't remember seeing that as a clue, although she knew that an alabaster jar was another link to Mary. When she anointed him with oils, they were in an alabaster jar.

Natasha reached out and touched the image, and realised that it wasn't flush with the wall. She pushed it. A small section of the wall opened at her feet. She bent down and reached her hand inside and pulled out a small clay cup. She looked into it, and her heart raced. It had a dark line running around it, possibly from blood-stained water.

'Lucas!' Excitement rushed through Natasha's body. 'It's here. It's the real holy grail! Lucas?' She turned around but didn't see Lucas or Tesfaye. She saw a hazy vision of a middle-aged woman talking to a young child.

'Teacher,' the young girl said. 'I've heard you speak of existential bliss before, but I still struggle to understand what it truly means. Can you explain it to me again?'

The middle-aged woman sighed with a smile. 'Ah, my dear child, existential bliss is a state of profound contentment and fulfilment that arises from within, independent of external circumstances.'

'But how does one attain such a state? Is it through material wealth or worldly success?'

'No, young one, material possessions or external achievements do not hold the key to finding existential bliss.'

'So, it is about finding meaning and purpose in life?'

'Indeed. Existential bliss arises when one discovers their unique path and embraces it wholeheartedly, finding joy and fulfilment in the journey itself.'

'But what if life is filled with challenges and hardships? How can one experience bliss in the face of adversity?'

'Bliss is not the absence of challenges, but rather the ability to navigate them with grace and resilience. It is about embracing life's trials with equanimity and finding strength in the face of adversity.'

'I see. So, it is about finding peace within oneself, regardless of external circumstances.'

'Precisely what I said at the beginning,' the woman smiled. 'Existential bliss is not dependent on fleeting pleasures or external validations. It is a state of inner harmony and contentment that comes from living authentically and in alignment with your deepest values and aspirations.'

'Thank you, mother, for your wisdom. I will strive to cultivate existential bliss in my own life.'

'You are most welcome, my dear child. Remember, the journey to bliss begins within.'

Natasha had been watching the vision with wide-eyed curiosity. She could not act or do anything until then. 'Mary,' she breathed and walked towards the woman.

The middle-aged woman turned to look directly at Natasha with soft features. Then was gone.

'Natasha, are you alright?' Lucas asked with urgency.

Natasha blinked several times. 'Where is she? Did you see that?'

'See what?'

'Mary, talking to a child...her child. I walked towards her. I was standing right next to her.'

'No, you've been standing right here for the last few minutes. Like you were in a trance or something.'

Natasha looked down at the cup in her hands, reflecting on what she'd just witnessed. She walked over to Tesfaye. 'What was that? What did I see?'

'I don't know,' the old man shrugged. 'Only you know what you saw, Natasha. Many people have visions. Many don't.'

Her brow creased. 'The woman...that was Mary, wasn't it?'

'Is that the feeling you had?'

Natasha didn't know exactly what she felt. 'I believe so.'

'Have faith in your intuition, young one.'

She pondered on the words she'd heard in her vision. Was that what the Magdalene Creed was? The path to existential bliss? Is that what Christianity was supposed to have been? Her mind was a whirlpool of conflicting emotions. The significance of what she held was overwhelming. The holy grail, something that had been the subject of countless myths and legends, something that millions had sought, killed for, and died over. And now it was in her hands, its ancient weight pressing down on her soul.

'Is that really the holy grail?' Lucas's voice sounded distant in her mind.

'Yup,' Natasha nodded before she bent down and put it back where she had picked it up from.

'What are you doing?'

'Putting it back,' she replied, but the words felt hollow. Inside, a battle raged. She thought of the implications of her decision. What if this relic could truly change the course of history? Could it bring peace, or would it only spark more conflict? She thought of the church, of David and Section 7, of the pope. And then she thought of the vision she had just seen, Mary, serene and gentle, with her child. 'It's like you said,' she continued, her voice resolute. 'Whose claim for it is stronger? The ones that killed him, the ones that betrayed him or the ones that follow a different prophet? I'm not sure any of them deserve to have it, to be honest. And we don't need it, either.'

'But what are you going to tell David? And the pope, for that matter?'

'Well, Pope Leo Alexander will just have to make do with the scripture. I assume he will just have it filed away in the Vatican vaults. And David will be fine. We'll let him know it was here, but it got relocated and there are no clues. It's a dead end.'

'And you're okay with this?'

Natasha closed her eyes, taking a deep breath. 'I'm very okay with it, Lucas.' But even as she said the words, doubt gnawed at her. Was she making the right choice? Could she live with the repercussions? Her faith told her to trust in a higher plan, but her rational mind questioned the wisdom of leaving such a powerful artefact hidden.

'Your faith is strong,' Tesfaye said as they returned to the entrance. 'We climb mountains not so the world can see us, but so we can see the world. Now your wisdom is also strong.'

'I hope so,' Natasha said. 'Because I've been wondering how we're going to get down from here.'

'Ever heard of wingsuits?' Lucas asked with a broad grin on his face. He threw his backpack down and started unpacking.

As they prepared to leave, Natasha couldn't shake the feeling that she was at a crossroads. She hoped that, in the end, her decision would prove to be the right one, and that leaving the grail in peace was the true act of faith and wisdom. But the uncertainty lingered, a reminder of the immense responsibility she had just shouldered.

The End

A Word From Desmond G. Palmer

Thank you for reading THE MAGDALENE CREED.

The adventures continue in THE ACQUIRERS series, fast paced archaeological thrillers that take Natasha, Lucas and all of you around the world.

If you've enjoyed the book, I'd be very grateful if you could leave a REVIEW. It only needs to be a few lines. Not only does it keep me honest, so I don't stray from what makes these books a fun adventure romp for you, but it lets the algorithms know that people are reading them, and they'll push the books to likeminded readers. To stay updated on my book releases, you should follow my AMAZON AUTHOR PAGE[1]. Alternatively, if you'd like to build a relationship with me, your next favourite author, and receive a FREE novella, PERIL in PERU, and experience Natasha and Lucas's honeymoon adventure, sign up to my NEWSLETTER.

• • • •

JOIN THE THRILL RIDE!
JUST VISIT THIS LINK[2] OR SCAN THE QR CODE

---

1. https://geni.us/tAIp

2. https://www.subscribepage.com/q3q3d5

DESMOND J. PALMER
PERIL IN PERU
Sign up to my newsletter and get a free digital copy of the archaeological action/adventure novella, Peril in Peru

Also in The Acquirers series

Years ago they found an artefact, rumoured to be a gift from the gods. Now it has vanished from the British Museum…into the wrong hands.

London. Natasha Travers feels her world falling apart. Stuck working with her soon to be ex-husband, Lucas Redmond, the brilliant archaeologist is alarmed when a priceless gemstone they recovered six years before goes missing. And the stubborn treasure hunter suspects a setup when her estranged husband is accused of the crime.

Battling her confusing feelings for the unfaithful man she still loves, Natasha's heart sinks further at an ultimatum from a notorious terrorist: deliver the stone to him, or he'll murder her parents. But with only thirty-six hours to produce the goods, the determined duo of Travers and Redmond, struggle to decipher the cryptic clues that could save her loved ones from a horrible fate.

Can they prove Lucas's innocence, free Natasha's parents, and recover the jewel before their time runs out?

The Eye of Nineveh **is the high-octane first book in The Acquirers archaeological thriller series. If you like flawed heroes, fast-paced suspense, and fun escapism, then you'll love Desmond G. Palmer's action-adventure tale.**

They're tracking the truth across the world. But with shadowy figures pulling the strings, will calling on the gods of old lead them to their graves?

Natasha Travers lives for adrenaline hits. And after accidentally signing herself up to remain co-owner of a business with her ex-husband, former SAS captain Lucas Redmond, the skilled treasure hunter is looking for any excuse to spend some time abroad. So, when a friend and fellow archaeologist calls from Romania with tales of strange South American coins, she jumps on a plane... and straight into a global conspiracy.

Discovering that the artifacts portray Peruvian deities of creation and death, Natasha is mystified when the tests reveal they're forged from an unknown metal. But after she learns of her friend's ties to the local mafia, a spreading epidemic, and an ancient curse, she fears humanity could be battling a genocidal threat.

Will poking into the past launch a catastrophe or save the lives of billions?

The Cursed Treasure **is the page-turning second book in The Acquirers archaeological thriller series. If you like conflicted characters, breathtaking adventures, and heart-stopping twists, then you'll love Desmond G. Palmer's race against the clock.**

In a race against time, Natasha and Lucas must uncover the identity of Nemesis and prevent a devastating war.

When a series of assassinations rock the royal family of the alpine country of Bebiria, tensions between them and the neighbouring nation of Keguia escalate. As the clock ticks and the body count rises, archaeologist Natasha Travers, Lucas Redmond and the king's second son, Tomaz, are determined to uncover the true identity of the killer known as Nemesis. But what they find is a twisted web of secrets and lies that threatens to plunge the two countries into war. As they race to unravel the mystery of the Marques of Death, they must also confront their own pasts and the darker side of human nature.

Can Natasha and Lucas stop the killings and prevent a catastrophe before it's too late?

The Marques of Death, **the third book in The Acquirers archaeological thriller series, will keep you guessing until the very end.**

What is the secret of Mansa Musa's gold?
Natasha Travers and Lucas Redmond, agents of MI6's Section 7, are dispatched to Jamaica to investigate the disappearance of two fellow agents who were investigating the enigmatic voodoo priestess, Madame Aurora De'ath. However, they soon discover that Madame De'ath possesses a mysterious influence over Lucas, and she compels Natasha to embark on a quest for the hidden Mansa Musa gold if she wishes to free him from the spell.

Their journey takes them across the ancient lands of the Mali Empire, where they must navigate treacherous encounters with African warlords, rival treasure hunters and the New Enlightened Order (N.E.O.), a secretive society intent on using the gold for their own ends.

With danger lurking at every turn, Natasha and Lucas gradually unravel a far-reaching conspiracy that threatens the very fabric of the world. As they face unrelenting adversaries, Travers and Redmond find themselves in a race against time, driven by the urgency to uncover and thwart the malicious intentions of the N.E.O.

Can they summon every ounce of their courage and skills to put an end to the nefarious plan before it's too late?

The Musa Deception, **the fourth book in The Acquirers archaeological thriller series, immerses you in a gripping tale of action, adventure, and suspense, that will keep you on the edge of your seat from start to finish.**

FREE EBOOK FOR SUBSCRIBERS

Discover the Ultimate Honeymoon Adventure in 'Peril in Peru'

Dive into 'Peril in Peru', where love and danger intertwine in a honeymoon like no other. Newlyweds Natasha Travers and Lucas Redmond are thrust into a heart-pounding adventure in this explosive prologue to The Acquirers series. Their mission: infiltrate a drug lord's heavily guarded ranch and retrieve the legendary Slippers of Viracocha. But with deadly assassins lurking at every turn, their survival hinges on sheer skill and unbreakable bravery.

If you crave flawed heroes, relentless action, and thrilling escapism, 'Peril in Peru' by Desmond G. Palmer is a must-read. Don't miss the chance to embark on this electrifying journey!

Travers and Redmond Will Return In

The Silk Road Star Map

Embark on an electrifying journey along the ancient Silk Road, where hidden secrets and deadly betrayals lurk in the shadows.
In this heart-pounding archaeological thriller, renowned explorer Dr. Natasha Travers and her enigmatic partner, Lucas Redmond, are thrust into a perilous race against time amidst a celestial alignment of all the planets in the solar system.

When an legendary orrery surfaces in India, Natasha and Lucas find themselves ensnared in a web of intrigue that spans from the bustling bazaars of Istanbul, and the vibrant markets of Samarkand to the treacherous mountains of Bhutan. As they follow the celestial clues left by ancient cartographers, they unravel a conspiracy that could rewrite history itself and unlock the cosmic mysteries hidden within the alignment of the planets.

But with ruthless adversaries hot on their trail and the fate of nations hanging in the balance, Natasha and Lucas must navigate a labyrinth of ancient temples, shadowy alleyways, and perilous mountain passes under the watchful gaze of the celestial alignment. With each step, they draw closer to uncovering the truth behind the Silk Road star map—a truth that could illuminate the mysteries of the world or plunge it into darkness.

From the bustling streets of Kathmandu to the majestic palaces of Agra, "The Silk Road Star Map" is a pulse-pounding adventure that will leave readers breathless until the very last page. Prepare to be swept away on a whirlwind expedition filled with danger, discovery, and the timeless allure of the Silk Road amidst the backdrop of a cosmic event of unprecedented significance.

www.ingramcontent.com/pod-product-compliance
Lightning Source LLC
Chambersburg PA
CBHW051318190726
48290CB00001B/210